THE SUFFRAGETTE

Janet MacLeod Trotter

Published by MacLeod Trotter Books

New edition: 2011

ISBN 978-0-9566426-3-9

www.janetmacleodtrotter.com

Janet: "**Very often the suffragette movement in the UK is associated only with London but there were many brave women in the North who got involved in the fight for the vote and this novel is a tribute to them.** My own family has links with the women's emancipation movement. Three of my Scottish great aunts were suffragettes and my great grandmother (also called Janet) once brandished her umbrella at Winston Churchill in Edinburgh and shouted 'Votes for Women Mr Churchill!' My Great-aunt, Isobel Gorrie, was praised by the leadership as being the best seller of their radical newspaper in all of Scotland. My other inspiration was Emily Wilding Davison, who became a martyr to the cause when she was trampled to death by King George V's horse at the Epsom Derby while protesting. Emily is buried in a Northumberland churchyard close to where we live.

The photograph on the front cover is of my great grand aunt Elizabeth, sister of the redoubtable Janet."

Janet MacLeod Trotter was brought up in the North East of England with her four brothers, by Scottish parents. She is a best-selling author of 15 novels, including the hugely popular Jarrow Trilogy, and a childhood memoir, BEATLES & CHIEFS, which was featured on BBC Radio Four. Her novel, THE HUNGRY HILLS, gained her a place on the shortlist of The Sunday Times' Young Writers' Award, and the TEA PLANTER'S LASS was longlisted for the RNA Romantic Novel Award. She has been editor of the Clan MacLeod Magazine, a columnist on the Newcastle Journal and has had numerous short stories published in women's magazines. She lives in the North of England with her husband, daughter and son. Find out more about Janet and her other popular novels at: www.janetmacleodtrotter.com

Also by Janet MacLeod Trotter

Historical:

The Beltane Fires
The Hungry Hills
The Darkening Skies
Never Stand Alone
Chasing the Dream
For Love & Glory
The Jarrow Lass
Child of Jarrow
Return to Jarrow
A Crimson Dawn
A Handful of Stars
The Tea Planter's Lass

Mystery:

The Vanishing of Ruth

Teenage:

Love Games

Non Fiction:

Beatles & Chiefs

Chapter One

1903

Mabel Beaton stared numbly from behind the starched net curtains of the downstairs parlour, waiting. From the open door she could hear the murmur of the women's voices drifting in from the kitchen across the corridor, concerned and doleful, yet edged with the excitement of gossip. She was aware of the clink of china as her sister-in-law Violet prepared tea and the clang of a poker on the grate as someone stabbed the fire.

Never before had she felt so cut off from her neighbours and friends, cocooned in shock. Mabel could not go to them now or find any comfort in their chatter, so she continued her vigil by the window among the peppery-smelling houseplants and the slow tick of the marble clock.

'Here's a cuppa, hinny.' Mrs Liddle bustled into the unlit room, washed in sepia light from the late September sun. 'You must keep your strength up.'

'Ta, Mrs Liddle,' Mabel answered dully, 'just put it on the table—' She broke off, suddenly aware of what she had said. They both looked at the table in silent awe, then with a wary glance, the stout neighbour plonked the cup down on the mantelpiece with a nervous rattle.

'You get that down you before the bairns get home,' Mrs Liddle coaxed 'It won't do for them to see you pale as a ghost.'

Mabel turned her back swiftly to hide the tears that filled her dark blue eyes. 'I will be the first to break the news to them,' she said with a firmness she did not feel. 'I don't want Violet blurting it out, do you hear?'

'Aye, hinny,' Mrs Liddle agreed and retreated to the warmth of the kitchen.

From her lonely post by the window, Mabel could see down the wide terraced street with its neat bay windows and tiny borders of flowers bowing in the wind behind sturdy railings. A prosperous street of gleaming brass door knockers and blackened boot grates, it had been their home for ten happy years. Their house was built on the lip of the steep hill, with open fields and a tree-lined park at the back. She could see all the way down to the River Tyne and beyond to the hills of County Durham without interruption. From here the noise of the riverside yards and factories was muted and the smell of industry bearable. Here, her family were safe and well nurtured, their future assured - or had been until earlier in the day.

Mabel's thick small hands flew to her pale face to stifle a sob of panic. 'Oh, me poor bairns!' she gasped to herself and as she did so caught sight of her eldest daughter, Susan, toiling up the hill.

Either side of the plump twelve-year-old walked Mabel's youngest two, Helen and Jimmy, held in a protective grasp to frustrate escape among the other returning school children. Susan panted, pink-cheeked, her straight fair hair lifting in the breeze and covering her face, yet she would not let go of her siblings to brush the annoying strands away.

As they passed a game of skipping, Helen pulled mutinously at her elder sister's hold, her sandy-coloured curls tossing around her petulant face. Mabel could see Helen shouting and Susan placating and knew at any moment her pretty six-year-old daughter would resort to tears to get her way. For a moment she forgot her own torment and watched to see who would win. In less than a minute, Helen had wormed her way to the edge of the skipping game, her face a smile of triumph while Susan stood by resignedly, lifting the weakling Jimmy into her arms.

Mabel let the heavy velvet curtain drop back into place, roughly brushed away the tears from her face and took a deep breath.

'Susan's nearly home,' she told the assembled women as she entered the kitchen, her small body stiff and dark head erect as she steeled herself for the ordeal.

'Let me come with you.' Violet rose from her chair at the head of the table where she had been holding court. Alec's chair, Mabel thought to herself with a swell of resentment.

'No,' Mabel answered sharply, 'they'll hear the news from me.' Ignoring the offended look that her sister-in-law conveyed to the others, she forced herself to walk briskly across the well-swept floor and out of the door.

The street seemed comforting in its normality, filling up with children and the sound of their games. The clatter of horses' hooves on the cobbles and the sparks from a rolley's wheels announced the arrival of the rag and bone man at the top of the street. 'Candy rock for stocking legs!' he cried in a sing-song voice, drawing the children to his approaching cart like a magnet. Soon the buzzers from the shipyards would sound the end of the daily shift and the men would be swarming up the hill.

'Helen, stay here!' Susan called after her wilful sister. 'Don't get too near that horse.'

At that moment, Helen caught sight of her mother and dashed towards her. 'Mam, give me something for the ragman - he's got candy and windmills. Give us something, Mam!'

Mabel grabbed her youngest daughter to her velvet blue skirt and gave her a hug, her resolve to appear strong almost evaporating.

'Not today, pet. Come inside,' her mother answered hoarsely.

Helen drew away. 'No! I'm staying out to play.'

By now Susan was at her side, with the dark-eyed Jimmy flopped in exhaustion against her round shoulders after his walk up the hill from school where he had started only three weeks ago.

'Our Tich is all done in,' Susan smiled at her mother, kissing her brother on his sallow cheek.

The runt of the litter, Mabel could not help thinking as she reached over to take her small son from the panting Susan; he was so unlike her robust daughters. Alec had always defended Jimmy. 'The wain'll grow up to be bigger than me one day,' her husband had joked. 'Carry his dad to his grave single-handed!' Mabel shuddered at the memory of those chill words.

'Where's Maggie?' she asked, squinting into the low sun.

'Fighting with the lads,' Susan said crossly. 'She doesn't know when to leave well alone, Mam.'

Mabel gave a fleeting smile at her daughter's grown-up disapproval.

Just then, Maggie came running over the brow of the hill, pursued by two older hefty boys. One of them pulled at her dark ringlets while the other tried to grab the books she was clutching. Mabel could see that they were hurting her, her ten-year-old daughter's grey eyes were smarting with tears and she was kicking as hard as she could with her black scuffed boots.

'Get off us!' Maggie shouted.

'Teacher's pet!' the twin boys taunted, managing to wrench the books from her hold. They dropped them on the cobbles and pages of jotter scattered in the wind.

As Maggie took a swing at Billy who still held her hair, Mabel felt a protective anger ignite within her. Dumping Jimmy on the pavement, she went to her daughter's rescue. She waded in with surprising strength for such a small woman, slapping Maggie's tormentors about the ears and sending them sprawling into the gutter.

'Keep your grubby hands off me lass, you little wasters!' she yelled. 'She's got more brains in her little toe than all you Gordons put together. Now clear off!'

Billy and Joshua Gordon gawped at the angry woman with the tight bun of dark hair. They knew the wife of the riveter, Alec Beaton, had a temper, but they had never been on the receiving end before. Scrambling to their feet they sped off up the street in humiliation.

Mabel saw Susan had flushed with embarrassment at the outburst and Jimmy was clutching his sister in fright. But Maggie shook her black ringlets out of her slim face and fixed her with an unblinking look, the precious books forgotten for a moment.

'What's wrong, Mam?' she asked directly. 'Why are the curtains drawn and it's not even dark?'

Mabel flinched at the child's capacity to see what the others had failed to notice. Of all her children, Maggie had the ability to sense what her mother felt without having to be told. Alec often said that Maggie had the gift of second sight like his Highland mother, but Mabel scoffed at such notions. 'She's just sharp, is our Maggie,' she would reply. 'Nothing gets past that one.'

Mabel licked dry lips, suddenly unable to tell her children what they had to know, hating the vulnerable, perplexed looks on their faces. She bent down to salvage Maggie's schoolbooks, gulping back the misery that choked her. Helen had come sidling up to listen and Mabel was aware of neighbours hovering in their doorways watching the drama unfold, relieved that the ordeal was not theirs.

'Come into the house, hinnies.' Mabel gathered them to her side nervously, the fight having left her drained and lightheaded.

They followed obediently; even Helen was subdued by their mother's strange behaviour. But Maggie grabbed her arm as she shut the door on the prying outside world.

'It's Da, isn't it?' she said simply. 'He's had an accident at the yard.'

'Who told you?' Mabel asked sharply, but from the look on her daughter's face she could tell it was just intuition.

'What's happened?' Susan blurted out, tears already in her eyes.

Mabel threw her arms about her girls. 'Your dad fell from some scaffolding this morning. He - he's got away.'

'Got away where?' Helen demanded, confused.

'He's dead,' Maggie explained in a tight voice. Susan let out a loud howl. Helen and Jimmy began to sob too, infected by their eldest sister's shock. 'Where is he?' Maggie asked, dry-eyed.

Mabel felt herself begin to shake, she wanted to cry like Susan and the younger children, but Maggie's stoical acceptance helped her keep a grip on her emotions.

'Mrs Liddle has laid him out in the parlour,' she whispered. 'You don't have to see him yet. Aunt Violet has your tea ready, there's plenty of time—'

'No!' Susan cried. I can't go in. Oh, poor Da! I want me da!' She clung to her mother in distress and Helen started screaming, which brought Aunt Violet and

3

Mrs Liddle rushing out of the kitchen to take charge.

But Maggie strode to the closed parlour door and threw it open. She stared into the gloom, her eyes adjusting to the murky ochre half-light. There, resting on the table in his best suit, was her father. She crept towards him, half expecting him suddenly to sit up and tell her it was just a game. But no smile came to his colourless lips under the sandy moustache and she shuddered to see a patch of matted hair around a gash to his head that Mrs Liddle's administrations could not hide.

Maggie opened her mouth to scream, but nothing came out. She felt her chest heave in the tomb-like room with its smell of polish and death and geraniums and thought she would suffocate. This waxen figure was not her cheerful father, he would be coming home any minute now with the wave of workers flooding out of Pearson's shipyard.

At that moment the harsh sound of the factory claxons and the riverside buzzers drowned the mournful sobbing from the hallway. Maggie turned and ran, pushing past her mother and sisters and evading Aunt Violet's grasp until she was out in the fresh air of the chilly September afternoon. Then she tore down the hill and did not stop until she reached the slick steel ribbon of the River Tyne.

Sitting on the landing steps of a local rowing club, Maggie stared out on the glinting oily expanse of river, trying to rid her mind of the image of her father slipping from the wooden scaffolding and falling to his death. What terrified her most was that she had seen it in her mind's eye earlier that day as they played with hoops in the school yard - a man falling from a great height like a rag doll. She rubbed her eyes savagely and told herself she must have made it up. Never again would she allow her mind to wander in its fanciful way and play tricks in her head. Then someone shouted at her to clear off and at last Maggie was able to cry - the huge sobbing tears of a ten-year-old - which sent her running for home and the safety of her mother's arms.

The day before her father's funeral, Maggie came home from school to find Granny Beaton had arrived from Glasgow. She sat in the parlour beside the open coffin, bound in black taffeta and a severe look, like a picture of the late Queen Victoria. Helen and Jimmy cowered away from her and Susan busied herself helping her mother in the kitchen, but Maggie stared in fascination at the craggy-faced woman who looked as old as the hills and spoke in a strange soft voice, beckoning her to come closer.

Scared as she was, Maggie stepped into the sombre room, keeping her look from straying to the corpse ready to be nailed up for its final journey to the cemetery.

'And you must be Margaret,' the old woman said in a slow lisping voice.

'Maggie,' she answered stubbornly, her heart hammering.

'Come, let me look at you,' Granny Beaton commanded and held out a bony hand. Maggie did not take it, but she stepped nearer, amazed to see faded red hair where there should have been white poking out from underneath the ancient woman's black cap and ribbons.

'You're like your mother right enough,' Granny Beaton nodded, with a catch of her breath.

'How long are you staying?' Maggie asked bluntly.

Her grandmother's watery brown eyes widened in surprise and then her lined face broke into a delightful smile.

'As long as your mother needs me, Margaret,' she replied.

'Maggie,' Maggie insisted. They regarded one another for a moment 'Why have you never been to see us before?'

Granny Beaton let out a soft sigh. 'I'm not a great one for the travelling - Maggie,' she explained. 'I've had to move about more than God intended. But I came for your christening - I came for all your christenings, so I did.'

'Tell me about your travelling, Granny.' Maggie edged closer, until she brushed the rustling material of her grandmother's black gown.

Granny Beaton placed a hand about her slim shoulders and pulled her into the crook of her arm. She smelt musty as mothballs and Maggie felt a moment of fear, but the soft voice was speaking to her again in its hypnotic lilt, as if Granny Beaton was trying out a new language that did not come easily.

That afternoon, Maggie heard for the first time the stories she was to demand constantly from her Highland grandmother in the days to come, of a childhood in the shadow of vast mountains, of legends and timeless songs, of a time when Granny and her people were moved down to the seashore to pick a living from the sea.

When Mabel entered the darkened parlour she was amazed to see Maggie sitting on Alec's mother's knee, enthralled by the tale of the family's eviction from their thatched home on the crowded shoreline by the men of power and money who owned the land and the long trek which took them finally to Glasgow.

'And they threw earth on the fire,' Granny Beaton's voice was almost a chant, 'and the heart went out of the place. And the wailing of the women could be heard on the hilltops that day from Sgurr Beag to Druim nan Sgarbh. And they put our things into an open cart in the rain and charged us money for the hire of it.' Granny trembled

Mabel shuddered at the stark words, wondering what was to become of her own family and possessions now there was no wage coming into the household. She had been able to pay the rentman this week as usual, but next week, where would she find the seven shillings to keep them in the house of which she was so proud? She was suddenly angry with her mother-in-law for filling the child's head full of gloomy tales that had such a prophetic ring about them.

'There's no need to go frightening Maggie with such stories, Mrs Beaton,' Mabel broke in abruptly, 'especially at a time like this.

But the look on Maggie's face told her it was too late. The girl's grey eyes were a mixture of wonder at the story and indignation at the treatment of Granny and her people.

'And Da was only a bairn and they still threw him out the house?' she asked furiously.

'Aye, barely weaned,' Granny sighed.

'Then they were bad, wicked men!' Maggie shouted, almost in tears.

'That's enough,' Mabel commanded, grabbing hold of Maggie and pulling her from her grandmother's knee. 'There's no point dwelling on the past. Come and get your tea.' She almost dragged the girl from the room, leaving Granny Beaton sitting alone with her dead son and her ghostly memories.

Maggie remembered little of the funeral day, except the moment when they were all bidden to kiss their cold, dead father goodbye. She recalled the chill waxen feel of his cheek and was thankful when the undertaker covered him up with the polished oak lid and carried him from the parlour.

The children watched from the front door as the coffin was heaved into the horse-drawn hearse which Aunt Violet had enviously told Mrs Liddle was costing twenty shillings to hire. 'Sparing no expense, is Mabel,' Aunt Violet had said disapprovingly in Maggie's presence. 'Would have thought she'd be better spending it on the bairns. She'll find out now what it's like having to scrimp and save.'

'She'll likely have money put by,' Mrs Liddle had answered briskly and given Violet a warning look.

The horse snorted and stamped to be off, nodding its black-plumed head as the undertaker climbed onto the carriage in his black top hat and took the reins. Then they were clattering off down the street and Aunt Violet was ushering the children indoors.

Maggie and her sisters sat around fidgeting in their Sunday dresses, while their mother and aunt and several neighbours busied themselves in the kitchen preparing the funeral tea. Later, their father's workmates and friends would return from the burial and eat the dainty sandwiches and wedges of homemade sponge cake and express their sorrow at losing a fine colleague. Uncle Barny, Aunt Violet's invalid husband, was the only male relation that the family could muster for the funeral and he was a Dodds not a Beaton. But Maggie liked her mother's amiable brother with his large red nose and false cork leg that often stood propped in his kitchen next to the poss stick. He was full of colourful stories of soldiering in the Boer War that Aunt Violet could not bear to hear; far from seeing him as a hero at the siege of Lichtenburg, she blamed him for his carelessness in leaving behind a leg that now rendered him jobless and forced her out to work in a tobacconist's.

Granny Beaton was the only woman in the family who had insisted on attending the funeral service.

I'll see Alec returned to his Maker,' Granny had said stubbornly and had set out alone for the Methodist church where Mabel occasionally made the children attend Sunday School. Mabel could not remember the last time she had gone to chapel herself, but she had been grateful for the two hours of peace on a Sunday when Susan marched her siblings along the road to Mr Heslop's classes and she and Alec had been able to draw the curtains and sneak back to bed together.

She felt a great longing for her gentle husband as she realised once again she would never feel his touch under the bedclothes or hear his bawdy whisperings. But it was not customary in their community for the wife to attend the funeral and she had no wish to go. If Alec's old mother wished to make a spectacle of herself, let her go, Mabel thought with irritation.

One other incident that day stuck in Maggie's memory and that was a visit from a foreman at Pearson's where her father had worked for fifteen years. He handed over a huge bunch of flowers, the sort that Maggie had seen presented to important women when they launched ships at Pearson's yard. And there was a large gift wrapped in brown paper.

'Open it, Mam!' Helen had squealed with interest, bored at being kept inside on a sunny afternoon.

The children gathered round their mother in the pristine parlour where a fire had been lit in the gleaming grate and dispelled the fusty smell of death. Helen helped her mother tear open the parcel, then stopped in disappointment at the mundane contents.

'It's a tub,' Helen said in disgust.

'And a washboard - that's useful,' Susan added timidly, trying to be positive.

Maggie watched her mother's face turn from bafflement to a crimson anger.

I've never been so insulted!' Mabel gasped. 'Of all the bloody cheek!'

Aunt Violet tutted from behind. 'They're just trying to be practical, Mabel,' she sniffed, her round face barely hiding her glee. 'After all, you'll have to make a living somehow, with all your bairns. I've found it hard enough just providing for me and Barny. Be thankful for what you're given, I say.'

For a moment, Maggie thought her mother was going to strike Aunt Violet in her fury. Her eyes blazed as she took a step towards Violet and the plump woman retreated.

'Well, I'll not be taking in any washing for anybody!' Mabel declared. 'My husband was a skilled man with a good trade - the Beatons are respected around here. I'll not have my home turned into a public washhouse! Pearson's can keep their bloody washboard; I'd rather go begging to the parish than take their measly charity!'

Violet fled from the room as Mabel picked up the offending washboard and hurled it across the room where it dented the highly polished floor. Susan and Helen gawped at their mother and Jimmy clung anxiously to Susan's skirt, terrified by the outburst.

Maggie ran a finger over the brand new tub; it smelt of virgin wood.

'We could break it up and sell it for firewood, Mam,' she suggested calmly, 'or give it to Aunt Violet as a Christmas present.' Mabel turned to her dark-haired daughter, still shaking with rage, and saw the glint of mischief in the girl's grey eyes. With a smile of gratitude she put her arms round Maggie and hugged her hard.

'That's what we'll do, bonny lass,' she laughed a little hysterically, 'give our Violet the treat she deserves.'

With the funeral well over and a growing family to feed, Mabel's fighting talk began to sound hollow. She spent the last of their savings on a new pair of shoes for Susan who had suddenly sprouted to the same size as herself. On Saturdays she made sure she was out when the tickman called from the furniture shop where they had bought the large dresser for the parlour and which they only half owned. By October, Mabel was two weeks behind with the rent and owed money to the dairy and the coalman, who only gave her credit because she lived in Sarah Crescent and they knew she had possessions she could sell. Granny Beaton seemed in no hurry to return to Glasgow and even the cautious Jimmy had been won over by her stories and Gaelic songs which helped him drift into dreamless sleep. Mabel could not ask the lonely woman to go, but it worried her that she had an extra mouth to feed.

On a dank day in late October, Mabel dressed in her smartest blue gown and matching hat and set off with head held high, a heavy bag at her side, to the pawnshop on Amelia Terrace. She spread out Alec's second-best suit on the counter, fingering the familiar material nervously and praying no one she knew had seen her enter.

'It's worth eighteen shillings, but I'm prepared to take fifteen.' Mabel was businesslike.

The pawnbroker snorted. 'It's fraying at the cuff here, and it's hardly the height of fashion. Not worth more than six shillings.'

Mabel swallowed her indignation. 'It'd be robbery to let it go for less than ten shillings,' she bartered.

'I'll give you eight,' the shopkeeper said, 'or you can take it elsewhere.'

'Eight then,' Mabel said with resignation and gave the suit one last affectionate brush before pushing it across the counter.

The pawnbroker showed more interest in the jewellery that Mabel had to offer; gifts bought by her husband when he had begun bringing in a good wage

7

from Pearson's, whose precious value only she knew.

When Mabel left she was determined that she would reclaim her lost treasures although she knew in her heart that she would never wear them again.

All too soon, the trips to the pawnbroker became a weekly event and out of the house trickled vases, linen, ornaments and china. Her humiliation became public knowledge when the furniture shop came and reclaimed her oak dresser and there was an ugly scene with the rent collector, who waylaid her in the street.

'You'll have to find the money by Friday,' the weary man shouted, 'or Mr Thomas wants you out.'

'We've always been good payers, haven't we?' Mabel answered with spirit.

'Listen, if you can't afford to live here, you'll just have to find somewhere cheaper,' the rentman said testily. 'I'm just trying to do my job.

Mabel turned her back on him and stormed into the house, slamming the door in his face, cursing the avaricious accountant Thomas whom she had never set eyes on, who owned the roof over her children's heads and now threatened to make them homeless. But she still clung to the idea of staying in Sarah Crescent, unable to face the alternative.

To her surprise it was the stoical Granny Beaton who shook Mabel out of her paralysed state and goaded her into action.

'It's only bricks and mortar,' the old woman said quietly that night as they sat in the dark of the kitchen with just a spluttering fire for comfort. 'Not worth going to an early grave over, lassie.'

'But it's where Alec and I have been so happy,' Mabel whispered, unburdening herself for once, now that the children were in bed.

'Aye, but Alec's gone from here and there doesn't seem much point in staying. Do you want the sadness of seeing your little ones turned out on the street in front of all your neighbours?'

Mabel felt tears begin to trickle unbidden down her face. 'Now I know what it must have been like for you,' she said miserably.

Agnes Beaton put her hand over her daughter-in-law's and squeezed it. 'It was different for me because it was happening to everyone around me too. It's hard for you, lassie, because most of your neighbours are just looking on, thanking God it hasn't happened to them.'

'Oh, Mrs Beaton, what shall I do?' Mabel pleaded.

'Flit before they come to throw you out,' the older woman said roundly.

Mabel peered at her in the dark, astonished 'You mean run away from Sarah Crescent?' she gasped 'What would the neighbours say?'

Agnes Beaton's smile was wry. 'They won't be your neighbours much longer, so don't you be bothering what they say. God will guide your steps and lead us to another home.'

'Us?' Mabel queried. 'So you're going to stay too?'

'You need me to look after the children while you find work,' her mother-in-law said matter-of-factly. 'I'm used to getting by on a scrap of meal and a prayer.'

'What can I do?' Mabel asked, still despairing. 'I've never worked outside the home.'

'You've still got your sewing machine,' Agnes pointed out. 'You could take in mending - a bit of dressmaking. Susan and Maggie will have to find wee jobs to help out too. We'll manage.'

Mabel felt a flood of warmth towards Alec's strange mother. She had seen her as a burden and an old blether, filling the children's heads full of fairytales, but Agnes Beaton was showing the strength of character that had helped her survive eviction and near starvation and still bring up her son to be a skilled craftsman.

The next day, Mabel ventured down the hill to the warren of mean streets that packed around the riverside factories and docks and sought out a flat for a lower rent. She steeled herself to enter a dwelling in Gun Street, stinking of damp and excrement from the earth closet in the back yard. Her nerve nearly failed her when she saw the filthy, dilapidated state of the three downstairs rooms she was being offered by the surly publican who owned the building. From upstairs she could hear the squalling of children and the thump of heavy boots which shook the gas mantle overhead.

'How much?' Mabel gulped, glancing out of the dirty window at the drab street with not a tree or blade of grass in sight.

'Four shillings a week,' the publican grunted.

'I'm a widow with four bairns to keep,' Mabel said in a supplicating voice she despised. 'And this place is too small to take in lodgers.'

'Three and six then. I can easy find other tenants who'll show more gratitude than you.' He gave Mabel a disparaging look, seemingly annoyed by her bargaining.

'I'll take it,' she said stiffly. 'We'll move in the day after tomorrow.'

'I need a week's rent up front,' the landlord insisted.

Mabel bit back a retort that no one should have to pay in advance for a hovel such as this and that he should be paying her for the work she would have to do to make it habitable.

Instead she fumbled in her coat pocket for the precious coins and handed them over with a proud look. With relief she hurried from the depressing street, shrouded in dank mist from the river, and climbed the steep streets to Sarah Crescent for the last time.

Borrowing a cart from Mr Heslop, the Sunday School teacher who had been generous in giving her leftovers from his butcher's shop, Mabel had the house cleared of its remaining possessions by the time the children returned from school. John Heslop and Mabel's brother Barny came to help in heaving the two beds and the kitchen table onto the cart, though Barny spent most of the time drinking from a jug of dark mild beer he had brought to fortify them during the task. Heslop politely refused, but Mabel took a glass after he had gone and found that despite its bitter taste it had a reviving effect on her flagging spirits. She was silently grateful that the butcher had made no criticism of her decision to do a moonlight flit; in fact Heslop had been eager to help.

'What's happening, Mam?' Susan asked in astonishment as she ran in from the cold twilight, Jimmy at her heels. She stared around the empty kitchen in bewilderment.

'We're leaving tonight, pet,' her mother answered as calmly as possible. 'I know it's sudden, but I've found somewhere else more affordable.'

Maggie rushed in after her sister and took in the sight of her mother drinking beer with Uncle Barny while Granny Beaton stood over the cooling range, crooked hands outstretched in their black mittens, quietly humming one of her Gaelic songs.

'Where are we going?' Maggie asked, half excited by the idea of flirting. Since her father's death she had hated to see her mother's unhappiness as their home was gradually denuded of pictures and furniture. Perhaps they were going to live in the country in some homely farm with animals all around them and fields to play in like in Granny Beaton's childhood tales.

'You'll find out soon enough,' her mother answered shortly, unable to bring herself to tell them the worst. 'We're leaving as soon as it's dark.'

Mabel glanced anxiously out of the bare window, half expecting that someone would have reported her planned escape to the accountant Thomas and that the police would soon be at her door. But no one had; flits were all too common and no one knew when a similar fate might befall them. An hour later, John Heslop returned and drove the cart off down the hill, the children squashed in among the chattels, silent and subdued. Mabel did not look back at her old home and vowed she would never set foot in Sarah Crescent again until she could afford to live there.

That night she bedded down her frightened children in the kitchen of the Gun Street flat while Granny Beaton coaxed a fire into life in the soot-clogged grate.

'Tomorrow we'll give the place a good scrubbing out,' Mabel told her daughters. 'We'll soon have it looking like home.'

'Does that mean we don't have to go to school, Mam?' Susan brightened at the thought.

'Not tomorrow,' her mother agreed, thinking silently how Susan's school days were numbered anyway. She would be needed to help bring in money. Maggie was a different case; she had brains and Mabel was determined to keep her at school as long as she could.

Then Helen began to cry for her old bedroom. 'I hate it here,' she sobbed. 'I shan't stay! It's all your fault, Mam. I hate you for bringing us here!'

Mabel snuggled down beside the miserable girl and held her close until she wore herself out with crying and fell asleep.

Only Maggie stayed awake long into the night, watching the flames of Granny's fire flickering and throwing weird shadows across the blackened ceiling and listening to the muffled shouts from the room above. She imagined they were the rough calls of the landlord's men come to evict them from their thatched bothy in the Highlands, but Granny Beaton would cast a spell on them and they would not be able to put out the fire that was the heart of the home ...

A boat hooted somewhere out on the Tyne, much louder than could be heard in Sarah Crescent, and Maggie realised there was no escape from their new pitiful surroundings. The dismal flat with its poky slime-covered yard which they must share with strangers was a place of terror, but she must show no fear. She would never blame her mother for what had happened as Helen did; it was the fault of landlords like Thomas and powerful people like the Pearsons who did not care what became of the families of their dead and discarded workers. They would go on living in their big fancy mansion at Hebron House no matter how many riveters fell from their scaffolding while building their ships.

That night, Maggie felt the stirrings of a deep resentment in her troubled mind, a new mood of rebelliousness against the world outside. She was not sure with whom or what she was most angry, but somehow she was going to change things for the better.

With that thought to nurture and comfort her, Maggie finally fell asleep.

Chapter Two

1913

'Votes for Women!' Maggie Beaton shouted as she thrust a copy of The Suffragette newspaper at the people alighting from the tram. 'Equal wages for equal work!'

Most of them ignored her, but a stout man in a bowler hat pushed her out of his way. 'Get off home,' he growled, 'where you belong.'

Maggie was undaunted. 'Penny a copy, madam,' she spoke to the woman beside him. 'Read about the terrible way our sisters are treated in prison - force-fed and—'

'You should be ashamed of yourself, a young lass like you getting mixed up with them sort.' The woman glared at her with disapproval.

'Aye,' her companion agreed with an aggressive jut of his fleshy chin, 'you deserve a good hiding for going against men's authority.' With this he grabbed the newspaper from Maggie and tore it in half, throwing it to the ground and stamping on the Joan of Arc figure on the front.

Fuming at the man's actions, Maggie bent down and picked up the tattered newspaper, blocking his way with her slim, defiant body.

'That'll be one penny, please,' she said in a loud voice that carried over the din of trams and horse traffic.

The astonished man hesitated a moment, his jowled face colouring red as passers-by began to stop and take interest He regained his aggression quickly.

'Out me way! I'll not be spoken to like that by any lass.'

'You took the newspaper, now you'll pay me for it,' Maggie insisted stoutly.

'I'll do nothing of the sort,' the man blustered.

A crowd began to gather round them, amused by the exchange. Maggie's friend Rose Johnstone who had been selling copies of The Suffragette outside a nearby cinema hall hurried over.

'You've wantonly destroyed my property,' Maggie seized her chance for publicity as the number of spectators grew, 'and now you are refusing to pay. It's just another example of how women are badly treated by men. You wouldn't have dared do that if I'd been a man, would you?'

Someone shouted, 'What about you suffragettes destroying public property?'

Maggie rose on her tiptoes and bellowed back, 'We women have to resort to damaging the property of the rich and powerful because they won't listen to our arguments or give us justice. But we pay, all right. We pay with our bodies. Do you know what they're doing to women in British prisons?' Her voice rose. 'Torturing them, that's what!'

'That's right,' Rose Johnstone came to her friend's support, 'women are being brutalised by our own British doctors and prison warders - it's barbaric.' Her face glowed crimson with indignation under her shock of frizzy red hair.

'Aye,' a woman burdened with a large basket of shopping and an infant agreed. 'It's not right what they're doing, no matter what the Pankhursts and them have done.'

'And it's going to get worse,' Maggie continued, feeling a thawing of hostility among the crowd. 'The government have brought in this new law, the "Cat and Mouse" Act, which means that when the women get worn down and ill they send them home, then re-arrest them when they're only half recovered. This

11

way they're trying to keep us lasses in prison for months. We've been outlawed and banned for daring to speak against the government.' Her vital grey eyes scanned her audience as she shook the damaged newspaper in the air. 'But, by heck, they'll not silence our protest with their wicked laws! However many women foot soldiers they lock away, there'll be more to rise up and take their place and carry forward the banner of justice for women. For ours is a just cause and we will have victory!'

Rose cheered and someone behind her started to clap. Maggie's pale face shone as it always did when-roused by her own oratory. Rose marvelled once again how people forgot her friend's small stature and delicate appearance as soon as she began to speak in that loud resonant voice that brought horses to a standstill and children to gawp.

The belligerent man who had provoked the scene attempted a retreat, but the woman with the small child clasped to her drab tweed coat blocked his way.

'You've not paid your debt yet, hinny,' she told him with mock familiarity. 'One penny for the women's cause,' she cackled.

With a foul oath the man dug a coin out of his trouser pocket and hurled it onto the ground. 'I hope the lot of you rot in hell,' he fumed.

'Aye, well, we'll see you there then,' Maggie answered with a flash of a smile. Her aggressor stalked away with his wife bustling to keep up with him.

Maggie bent to pick up the penny and she and Rose quickly distributed newspapers before the crowd dispersed along Grainger Street and into the town's shops and pubs. Rose shivered suddenly in the raw air of the early April afternoon and nodded up the street.

'Two policemen coming - that man's probably complained about us,' Rose said with unease.

'We've done nothing wrong.' Maggie was unconcerned.

'That won't stop them picking us up,' Rose responded quickly, taking Maggie by the arm. 'Let's go back to the office -I need to thaw out anyway.'

Maggie felt reluctant, undaunted by the police or the cold, although her only protection was a thin purple jacket over her coarse green woollen skirt, both scavenged from her mother's second-hand clothes stall. To complete her outfit of suffragist colours she always campaigned in a white scarf which in cold weather she tied over her hat and secured under her narrow chin.

'I've still half a dozen papers to get rid of,' Maggie said, fired with energy from the encounter.

'Well, I need a hot drink,' Rose insisted, 'and so do you, your hands are quite white, so come along.'

Maggie could see her companion's thin lips set stubbornly and knew why Rose Johnstone was so feared and respected by the children she taught at elementary school in Elswick. She was older than Maggie by five years and had been a pupil teacher at the school Maggie had transferred to when they had flitted to Gun Street after her father's death. Maggie and Rose had taken to each other immediately, sharing a passion for books and knowledge. How she had yearned to follow Rose into teaching, Maggie remembered, but her overworked mother and resentful sister Susan had insisted she found employment at fourteen.

Maggie and Rose had remained firm friends; Rose treated her to theatre visits and took her to lectures that released her briefly from the drab poverty of her dank home by Pearson's shipyard and her back-breaking cleaning job. It was Rose who had taken fifteen-year-old Maggie along to listen to Emmeline Pankhurst speak on the Town Moor and lit the spark of her suffragism and interest in politics. Rose had also paid for Maggie's night classes in typing and book-keeping that had led to a better position as typist in Pearson's armaments factory. Maggie knew she owed so much to Rose that the least she could do was allow her to have her own way over trivial matters such as a cup of tea.

'Tea it is then,' Maggie smiled and blew on her hands, suppressing her disappointment that this Saturday's campaigning was over.

Merging into the crowd, they made their way through the shoppers and street sellers to the modest office in Blackett Street used by the Women's Social and Political Union as their Newcastle headquarters. They prided themselves on being the most militant and active of suffragist groups in the area, each member prepared to risk imprisonment for her actions. Since their campaign of defiance had been stepped up, so had the persecution against them. Rose had been arrested for breach of the peace for merely selling newspapers, but released with a caution after the intervention of Miss Alice Pearson, daughter of the shipping and armaments magnate, Lord Pearson. Miss Alice patronised the local WSPU to the disapproval of her father, but in recent months any meetings she attended were broken up before she could speak and Maggie had never met her.

I'm afraid I won't be able to come to Susan's birthday supper tonight,' Rose told her as they hurried up the steep stairs to the office. They had managed to give the two policemen the slip, but a solitary constable watched the office from across the street.

'Why not?' Maggie asked in dismay.

'I'm singing at Miss Pearson's soiree,' Rose said breezily, going ahead through the door. 'It was arranged at short notice. Sorry.' She avoided Maggie's gaze.

Maggie could make no protest as they entered the office which was bustling with fellow unionists, but she could not veil her disappointment. Rose would have been an ally against the carping of Susan and her mother and the snide asides of Aunt Violet about her involvement with the movement. Family get-togethers usually ended with her mother and Uncle Barny having too much to drink and Maggie, goaded by her captious aunt, arguing heatedly about politics. As the unpopularity of the suffragettes grew in the newspapers, so did her mother's disapproval of Maggie's friendship with Rose. Where once her friend had been warmly welcomed at Gun Street, now she was cold-shouldered. No wonder Rose shirked invitations to her home, Maggie thought, preferring to cultivate her acquaintance with Newcastle's well-to-do through her suffragist friends. Most of their comrades were from quite a different class to their own; moneyed, well-educated, middle-class women with the odd sprinkling of upper-class celebrities such as Miss Alice Pearson who added glamour to their social events and opened fund-raising bazaars.

In the office they swapped news and drank tea with the other women.

'Maggie was so brave the way she handled that awful man,' Rose told the assembled, making her friend blush.

'That's the wonderful thing about having a girl like Maggie in the ranks who can rub along with the common people,' said Jocelyn Fulford with a benign smile. 'By the way, how is your mother, Maggie? She hasn't called for a month or more.'

Maggie bit back her annoyance at being patronised by this tea merchant's wife from Jesmond.

'She's not been that well lately,' Maggie answered 'But I'll tell her you were kind enough to ask after her,' she forced herself to add, knowing her mother's second-hand clothes business relied on donations from wealthy women like Mrs

Fulford.

'Well, tell her to call, won't you, dear.' The older woman patted her hand and added in a loud whisper, 'I've several of last season's dresses she might like.'

Maggie thanked her stiffly, hoping that nothing she was wearing came from the Fulford household. At times she was acutely aware of being socially inferior to her fellow suffragists, yet put her in a room with people talking politics and she would hold her own with the Prime Minister if necessary. While they fought the same cause, class difference seemed irrelevant; it was only when they reverted to social chit-chat or returned home to their separate parts of the city that the barriers between them went up again.

Rose came to her rescue. 'I'll get the tram with you, Maggie. You don't want to be late for Susan's party, do you?'

The young women left together and headed towards Central Station, detouring through Grainger Market so Maggie could bargain with the butchers for a joint of brisket and some black pudding to see them through the week. Her purchases made, they headed out of the glass-roofed market with its smell of raw meat and pipe smoke, their long skirts swishing across the sawdust-sprinkled aisles.

'You could join the choir too,' Rose broke the silence between them, 'you've got a good enough voice.'

'I haven't the time,' Maggie said in excuse. 'You know the trouble I get into at home as it is. Imagine the fireworks from Mam and Susan if I was off singing at Hebron House on Susan's birthday.'

'That's not the reason you don't want to come,' Rose challenged her with a direct gaze from behind her spectacles. 'You don't approve of Miss Alice, do you?'

'You can choose to curry favour with the likes of the Pearson's, but I wouldn't feel comfortable,' Maggie said with resentment, crossing the road quickly to avoid a large dray horse. Rose caught her up.

'Don't speak to me in that tone of voice,' she said sharply, grabbing Maggie's arm.

'And don't speak to me as if I were one of your pupils,' Maggie retorted, throwing off her hold.

Rose glared at her, red-faced, but Maggie stood her ground. Unexpectedly, Maggie began to laugh.

'What's so funny?' Rose demanded.

'You are! You look as if you're about to send me into the comer,' Maggie grinned, unable to remain cross with her friend. Rose relaxed and snorted in amusement. They linked arms and continued.

'I know it's difficult for you at home,' Rose sympathised 'I'm lucky that my mother supports our work.'

Maggie nodded ruefully, thinking of Rose's bird-like mother who had once waved an umbrella at the liberal Winston Churchill, demanding votes for women.

'But listen, Maggie,' Rose became brisk, 'Alice Pearson can hardly be blamed for your father's death or the shabby way your family were treated by Pearson's afterwards. Can't you see that women like Miss Alice are fighting on our side so that we can change things for widows like your mother and my mother once we have the vote?'

'Yes, I can see that,' Maggie sighed, feeling contrite and remembering that Rose's comfortable childhood had been shattered too by her father's untimely death at sea and a will leaving all his wealth to a mistress and son in London.

'Still, I don't have time to join the choir.'

Maggie kept the thought to herself that Rose was much more socially assured than she was and that the ladies' choir would probably be horror-struck if Maggie joined their soirees at Hebron House. Bright she might be, but the way she spoke and the clothes she wore labelled her as working class. Maggie knew that, for her, there was no escape from Newcastle's gritty West End But it did not stop her wondering what it might be like to see inside the blackened, decaying, Palladian mansion that stood in its modest grounds, surrounded now by working-class terraces, where the eccentric Alice Pearson continued to live. Her parents and the heir, Mr Herbert, had long since abandoned Hebron House and moved up the valley to their new home, a Gothic castle with acres of grouse moor.

Through the dank drizzle that had begun to chill them, the women hurried on in silence, wrapped in their own thoughts, and reached the tram stop just as a tram clanked into view, blue sparks flying from its screeching wheels. It was crammed with passengers, wrapped in a warm fug of tobacco smoke, and Maggie and Rose had to stand. No one offered them a seat, which was usual when they wore their bold suffragette sashes for all to see.

Maggie did not mind, content to let a comfortable drowsiness envelop her as they jolted along the tramline, the smoky terraces of Elswick slipping past the window. The tram stopped outside a parade of shops on Scotswood Road, their faded awnings giving shelter to late shoppers and inquisitive children. Rose alighted with a farewell wave. 'Best wishes to Susan,' she called.

Maggie waved back, knowing how little Rose thought of Susan. Maggie sighed as she thought of her fussing elder sister, already careworn and middle-aged at twenty-two. Rose had found her dull and unwilling to learn at school and had been constantly irritated by her truancy. But Maggie knew Susan's uninterest in learning was less a mark of stupidity than a sign of her burning sense of duty to her mother and the family.

Ever since their father had died, Susan had mothered her younger sisters and brother while Mabel went to work in the public laundry. With the help of Granny Beaton, Susan had brought them up, obsessive in her mission to turn them out clean, starched, fed and polite to the outside world. Many a time Maggie had sparred with her sister over a dirt-smeared pinafore or lateness for meals.

'Girls don't climb trees!' Susan had once scolded.

'God made trees for lasses as well as lads,' Maggie had replied, unconcerned as she brushed at the offending stains.

'You should be setting an example for our Helen and Jimmy,' Susan's nagging continued.

'I'll show them how to climb trees any time they want,' Maggie had quipped, 'though the day our Tich climbs anything more than the back steps they'll hang flags from the High Level Bridge.'

Criticism of their sickly brother Jimmy always riled Susan. A blazing argument ensued, only brought to an end by a slap from their forceful mother and the gentle intervention of Granny Beaton. Granny was the one family member who stuck up for Maggie no matter what trouble she landed in. Her wizened, becapped Scottish grandmother who attended the John Knox Presbyterian Kirk in Elswick every Sunday was Maggie's quiet ally and the only one who did not criticise her involvement in women's emancipation.

Maggie's musings lasted until her stop, in the shadow of the fortress gates to Pearson's shipyard. She left the warm tram with reluctance and pulled her scarf tighter against the increasing rain as it bounced off the high roofs of the factory sheds. Clutching her purchases and dashing across the tramlines, Maggie was soaked by the splashing of a passing coal cart. Cursing the weather and looking down at her mud-spattered skirt, she thought how Susan would enjoy reprimanding her. Then it occurred to her that she had not bought Susan anything for her birthday. Knowing she could not return empty-handed having spent the afternoon in town, Maggie bent her head and hurried up the steep hill to Alison Terrace, the main street of shops that cut through the uniform ranks of terraced rows with a dash of colour and interest.

Luckily the haberdasher's was still open and Maggie in a fit of generosity spent the contents of her purse on a selection of ribbons and lace and delicate pearl buttons for Susan to lavish on one of their mother's second-hand garments. The light was fading from the dull grey day as Maggie hurried to the end of Alison Terrace. She felt the old familiar churning as she neared the corner, for across the road she could glimpse the start of their old street, Sarah Crescent, where they had all lived so happily until ten years ago. Even in the gloomy April evening, Sarah Crescent wore an air of stylish prosperity, a calm respectability that mocked their impoverished existence in Gun Street. No amount of Susan's painstaking housewifery could change the reality that they lived in a Victorian slum, ten minutes' walk and a social world away from that pleasant Edwardian street.

How different their lives might have been if their father had not died in Pearson's shipyard and their mother had not half killed herself working in the laundry and then clawing a living for them all by setting up her own clothes stall. By determination, persistence, wiles and lies, Mabel Beaton had persuaded the genteel ladies of the town to part with their unwanted clothes in return for spurious fortune-telling and tea-leaf reading that flattered her bored patrons.

If fate had been kinder to them, would she have been able to stay on at school and become a pupil teacher? Maggie wondered, and would Susan now be married and in her own home as she yearned to be? There would have been money for their vain sister Helen to dress in new clothes instead of trawling through rich ladies' cast-offs. And there would have been money for medicine and holidays by the sea for Tich, so that he would have grown into a healthy lad instead of a skinny scrap of a boy with a gaunt, cheeky face and a cough that kept him indoors most of each winter and grated on all their nerves.

If only ... Maggie allowed herself a rare moment of self-pity.

Suddenly a door to a public house banged open just behind her and noise erupted into the street. Maggie turned to see a man being ejected from the brightly lit interior.

'Take these and bugger off!' said the portly aproned barman, flinging a handful of leaflets after the sprawling man. 'I don't want to see you in here again, do you hear?'

One of the leaflets fluttered to Maggie's feet and she picked it up. It advertised a union meeting to discuss pay increases and was advocating strike action at Pearson's shipyard.

'You'll be the one losing out when men can't afford your piss-weak beer!' the young agitator shouted back as he picked himself up off the ground. He was tall and brawny with a bushy black moustache and short-cropped hair. Something about him seemed familiar to Maggie as she watched him rescue his cap from a puddle. His suit was well cut though shabby and his white collar was stiffly starched.

As the door to the bar slammed shut, the young man caught Maggie eyeing him with curiosity.

'What you staring at?' he asked aggressively, embarrassed that she had witnessed his ejection from the Hammer and Anvil.

'Nothing, I just thought. . .' Maggie blushed and handed him the leaflet. The other bills were turning to a sodden pulp on the rain-soaked pavement.

Ta,' he grunted, still cautious.

Realisation dawned on Maggie. 'You're George Gordon, aren't you?' The Gordon boys had been at her elementary school when she had lived up the hill. They were miner's sons from Benwell and well known for being loud and boisterous and rough with their schoolmates. George was the eldest and had stood aloof while the younger ones had plagued her for being studious and goaded her into carrying out dares when she beat them at running. George had left school shortly before her father died and she had barely seen him since. 'Still picking fights, I see.'

'How do you know me?' George asked, squinting through the rain at the slight woman before him. Her neat appearance and the WSPU sash made him uneasy. Her face was shadowed by her wide-brimmed hat and scarf. 'I don't know any of your kind.'

'I'm Maggie Beaton. I was at school with your brothers -the twins,' Maggie reminded him.

'Our Billy and Joshua?'

'Aye. Are they still causing trouble?'

George grunted. 'They haven't the time; they're both down the pit.'

He stepped closer to get a better look and Maggie felt suddenly awkward. She should never have stopped to speak to this man who was almost a stranger, only the leaflet had aroused her interest in him. She turned to go.

'Wait, I remember now. The Beatons who lived in Sarah Crescent' He had a hazy recollection of a restless, talkative girl who was always trying to interfere in their games. 'Were you the clever one?'

'Maybe,' Maggie shrugged, pleased with the comment.

'Aye, the Beatons.' George gave a sudden laugh. 'Your mam was always chasing us away with a rolling pin or worse.'

Maggie smiled. 'Sounds like Mam.'

'Which way are you walking?' he asked her, relaxing. Maggie was at once nervous and stepped away from him. . 'I don't go your way.'

He gave her a quizzical look. 'Just to the end of the street then.' They walked in silence until he said, 'So why are you dressed up like them suffragettes? You're too bonny to be one of them.'

Maggie bristled. 'I'm a supporter of women's suffrage,' she said proudly. 'It's not a carnival parade.'

'Oh, aye?' George smirked. 'You're a right little hell-raiser, I bet.'

Maggie was riled. 'Don't scoff at me, George Gordon. We women know what we want, so why should men in Parliament make laws for us?'

George stopped and considered her, pulling on his moustache. She made him feel suddenly defensive. 'The suffragettes want to give the vote to a load of posh middle-class women who'll vote the bosses in for evermore,' George scoffed. 'You'll still get the ruling classes making the laws for the likes of you and me.'

'No! I'm fighting for justice for all women,' Maggie replied stoutly.

George laughed in derision. 'The only way working-class women will get better conditions is if working-class men are given the vote. Then you'll get better housing and healthy bairns and be able to stop at home and look after them like you're supposed to.'

Maggie was furious. 'Don't tell me what women are supposed to do!' she glared. 'We want equality with men under the law and equal wages for the work we do.'

He gawped at her. He had never heard such nonsense; none of the women he knew spoke to him in such a forthright way.

'You'll never get that,' he told her sternly. 'It's lasses like you who are keeping men's wages down, taking our jobs, because the bosses treat you like the cheap labour that you are.' He brandished the soggy leaflet at her in his annoyance. 'Men are the rightful wage-earners. But how can they take enough home to their families when lasses are undercutting them?'

'We have families to support too! Me mam's struggled on a slave's wage for ten years since me dad died. We deserve better pay and we'll get it,' Maggie said resolutely, standing her ground, 'and the vote. Folk will come to see that it's not right for men to make laws that affect women's work. We pay taxes but we have no say in how they're spent.'

George could hardly believe he was bothering to argue politics in the rain with a mere woman. He was still smarting that she should have witnessed his ignominious exit from the pub. So, unable to beat her in argument, he resorted to abuse.

'I might have known you'd turn into a gobby lass with too high an opinion of yourself,' he said angrily. 'You Beatons always did think you were better than the rest of us, but from what I heard you were taken down a peg or two.'

Maggie flushed. Angrily she turned on him. 'We were "taken down a peg or two", as you call it, because me father had the misfortune to get himself killed and no one cares tuppence-halfpenny about widows like me mam or their bairns. But then I wouldn't expect a pig-ignorant Gordon like you to understand that!' Her eyes were blazing as she berated him. 'Well, I'll never be beholden to any man like Mam was, never! I'll make me own way in the world. So you can put that in your pipe and choke on it, George Gordon!'

With that she turned and stalked off down the hill, her back stiff with anger. Men were all the same, she raged inwardly, whether they were rich Pearsons ready to exploit women clerks at half a man's wage or working men like George Gordon who would make them drudges at home. She had long known that women had to look after themselves. Well, George Gordon could go to the devil!

George stared after her speechless, wondering how she had riled him so quickly. In frustration at his fruitless afternoon and the way she had had the last word, he screwed up the leaflet and hurled it under the hooves of a passing horse. Crossing the road, with collar turned up against the rain, he hoped he would never run into Maggie Beaton again.

Chapter Three

'How do I look, Mam?' Susan Beaton asked her mother timidly as she studied her reflection in front of the mirror in their small parlour.

Turn around, hinny,' Mabel instructed her eldest daughter, eyeing the pink and white dress critically.

It was the best dress she could find, made of soft muslin and patterned with small roses in deep pink. She had mended the tear in the sleeve and shortened the length so that it didn't trail along the floor too much, but its flowing line only highlighted Susan's tendency towards dumpiness. She'll be as stout as I am in five years' time, Mabel thought wearily; already the girlish pink-cheeked bloom that had made Susan almost pretty was fading.

'You look pretty as a picture,' Mabel assured her and kissed her flushed forehead.

'The gown was Mrs Cochrane's from Heaton,' Helen piped up. 'Of course, blouses that flop over the waist aren't in fashion nowadays and it's much too wide in the skirt. The tighter at the ankle the better, this season,' she pronounced.

Mabel glared at her youngest daughter as she helped Susan arrange her long fair hair, the one striking feature that was a legacy from her father. She knew Helen yearned for the dress and was being deliberately spiteful.

'Don't listen to a word of it,' Mabel told Susan, seeing the dashed expression on her face. 'She only wants it for herself.'

'Wouldn't catch me in an old maid's dress like that,' Helen pouted, shaking her fair ringlets and looking at her mother with resentful blue eyes.

'I'm not an old maid!' Susan protested, her round face going puce. 'I've just turned twenty-two.'

'Of course you're not, hinny,' Mabel soothed, hairpins gripped between her teeth.

'Well, the lads aren't exactly queuing up to take you out, are they?' Helen sneered.

'When have I had the chance to start courting?' Susan protested, rising to Helen's baiting. 'I spend every hour of the day looking after the house and all of you.'

'Susan, don't listen to her,' Mabel said, losing patience. She turned to Helen and added sharply, 'Go and find our Tich and tell him to wash before Uncle Barny arrives.' Helen's pretty face was mutinous. 'Or you'll feel the sting of me hand. Go on!'

Still Helen did nothing. 'So who's this Richard Turvey, Aunt Violet's been going on about?' she asked, picking at the crust of a pork pie on the table.

Susan took a swipe at her hand. 'Leave the food, will you!'

'Richard's a nephew of Aunt Violet's, and I don't want you being saucy to him tonight,' Mabel answered shortly. 'Now be off and find your brother.'

'He's manager at one of the new cinema halls,' Susan could not resist saying, betraying her eagerness to meet their mystery guest. 'Aunt Violet said he's worked in variety, travelled all over the country.'

Helen's sleek eyes lit with interest. She was addicted to the pictures and spent any spare pennies she could scrounge or steal from her mother on going to the films at the old mission hall in Glass Street. Or if they had a really good day at Paddy's Market, she could usually persuade her mother to pay for an evening at the Queen's Hall or the Olympia in town.

'Why haven't we met him before?' Helen asked, pushing in front of Susan to glance at herself in the tarnished mirror over the dresser.

'You know Aunt Violet's kin are mainly in London,' Mabel was terse as she rearranged the food where Helen had disturbed it. 'Mr Turvey's not been in Newcastle long. Now stop fussing over your hair and go and find Jimmy.'

'I think ringlets make me look too babyish, Mam,' Helen said, continuing to ignore her mother's orders. 'Can I tie my hair up like our Susan's?'

Mabel advanced on her with a serving spoon, her patience at an end. 'I'll be tying up more than just your hair if you don't do as you're told!' she said with a swipe at Helen's hand.

Helen squealed in protest. 'That hurt!' Tears sprang instantly to her bright blue eyes.

'Oh, I'll go and fetch Tich,' Susan huffed, not wanting her birthday spoilt by a familiar family row. She was across the room, through the kitchen and out onto the landing before her mother could stop her. The stairway snaked off into the gloom and she could just make out the door to the downstairs flat where she knew Tich would be ensconced They had lived there themselves when they had first come to Gun Street but had eventually managed to move to the larger flat upstairs once Maggie had started earning a wage at Pearson's. It was a small but important step out of poverty in Susan's eyes; one day they would leave Gun Street for good and move back up the hill to a respectable house and respectable neighbours.

Descending the stairs, Susan steeled herself to knock on the Smiths' door. Mrs Smith was friendly enough but she was always avoiding the tickman and Susan constantly had to lie about .where the Smiths were while her mother hid Mrs Smith upstairs. She disapproved of Mrs Smith because she was for ever tempting her mother to drink beer with her, catching her weary and footsore on her way upstairs in the evening.

'Fancy a cup of tea, Mabel?' Mary Smith would bob out of her doorway like a furtive mouse. More often than not, her mother would succumb and return an hour later, that stale yeasty smell about her that came from dark mild beer and not tea.

Tich was another one who liked to haunt the Smiths' grubby, cockroach-infested flat because his best mate was Tommy, the Smiths' only surviving child. Mrs Smith had told them tearfully that she had lost three babies since Tommy; Susan could not help feeling that it must be Mary Smith's own fault. She had heard it said that infants died when their mothers were feckless or drank too much or were too lazy to keep their houses clean or went out to work. Well, Mary Smith was guilty on all counts, as far as Susan could see.

She knocked. The door opened and a fug of stale air greeted her with a smiling Mrs Smith.

'Come in, Susan hinny. I hear it's your birthday, the day. Aye, Jimmy's here - not a scrap of bother he's been. I've just been baking. You'll have a slice of me currant loaf, won't you?'

'I can't stop, thanks all the same, Mrs Smith,' Susan said hurriedly. 'I've just come for Tich. We've got company for tea.'

Mrs Smith looked disappointed. 'Well, I'll wrap it up for you just the same and you can have it for your guests. Your Uncle Barny bringing his fiddle over, is he?'

Susan nodded, trying to ignore the expectant look on her neighbour's scrawny face. She turned to Jimmy who was sprawled in front of the fire playing draughts with his friend.

'You look canny in that frock,' he smiled up at his sister.

'Ta, Tich.' Susan flushed with pleasure. 'You're to come home now; Aunt Violet's bringing Mr Turvey this evening, so you'll need to smarten yourself up.'

Jimmy groaned, his thin face reluctant. 'What's so special about this Mr Turvey? Are all me sisters going to pick straws for him or summat?'

'Watch your lip,' Susan reprimanded as he and Tommy sniggered. 'Mr Turvey's an important man in the cinematography business,' she said, meaning to impress Mrs Smith.

'By! Cine-mog-raphy,' Mrs Smith aped inaccurately. 'Fancy that!'

'Aye, he's from London too,' Susan preened.

'A Londoner!' Mrs Smith's curiosity in the glamorous stranger mounted. 'Well I never.'

Tich's round, mouse-like eyes lit with interest too. He liked nothing better than to sit in the warmth of a picture house watching comedies or films about faraway places, imagining he was a brave legionnaire or the daredevil hero.

'Hey, Smithy, he might take us to the films,' he told his friend excitedly. Tommy Smith, who was two years younger and still at school, looked impressed. 'Smithy can come up and meet him, can't he?' Tich asked.

Susan felt dismay at the thought of her birthday supper and her special guest being monopolised by her younger siblings, but she could not dampen her brother's enthusiasm. Jimmy had always been her baby, ever since she had staggered around with him as a newborn infant while her mother spent weeks in bed recovering from the birth. She had loved him instantly and over the years had tried to make up for their mother's lack of interest in her youngest child.

'Of course Tommy can come,' Susan replied, her sigh almost inaudible. 'If he smartens himself up,' she added to Mrs Smith.

Mary Smith did not take offence at the criticism. 'That's canny of you, pet,' she smiled at Susan. 'I'll get him scrubbed. Must be grand having company,' she added wistfully.

Susan hesitated. She was loath to invite her neighbour whom she saw as common and dowdy but felt a gnawing guilt at excluding her. Mary Smith would just be sitting alone with a jug of beer for company, listening to the revelries upstairs. Her husband, Gabriel Smith, was a morose, solitary character who disappeared for days on end and there was no sign of him about the flat at the moment.

'You'll come up as well, won't you, Mrs Smith?' Susan said, relenting.

'Eeh, hinny, I'd like nothing better,' the small woman replied at once. "That's very neighbourly of you. I'll bring me baking. Currant loaf and a meat pie. Don't expect my Gabriel will be back before Monday. Gone off on his wanders. Won't miss owt.'

Susan steered Jimmy out of the flat quickly to escape Mary Smith's effusiveness and the smell of unwashed bodies.

'That's canny of you to invite the old lass,' Jimmy said as they climbed the stairs together. 'Old Smithy's been gone for a week this time. It's a good job Mr Heslop lets her clean his shop else they'd have nowt to live on.'

Susan sighed, letting her arm slip round her brother's bony shoulders. 'Aunt Violet'll probably have a fit, mind.' She grimaced at the thought.

'She'll be happy as pig in swill,' Jimmy giggled 'Someone to turn up her nose at.'

They both laughed as they entered the flat together.

By the time Maggie mounted the stairs, barely illuminated by the spluttering gas lamp, she could hear the sounds of music and singing resounding from her home. With any luck, Susan and her mother would be in too good a mood to notice that she was late and mud-spattered from the filthy streets outside.

She entered the warm kitchen to see Granny Beaton hovering over the range, muttering to herself as usual.

'Is that you, Maggie?' The ancient woman peered round with rheumy eyes. Maggie knew her grandmother could hardly make her out but she would not admit to her frailty or allow Maggie to buy her spectacles.

'Aye, Granny,' Maggie answered, pulling off her soaking scarf and hat and plonking down her purchases on the rough wooden table. 'Has Uncle Barny been here long?'

'This past hour or so,' Granny Beaton said, moving towards her granddaughter with a stooped back. 'You're soaking, lassie!' she cried, feeling Maggie's jacket and suffragette sash as she began to help her discard her wet clothes. She clucked and fussed around her.

'I better change,' Maggie said 'You go back into the parlour.'

'No, no, I'm brewing up a strupach,' Granny Beaton answered, nodding at the warming teapot. 'And there are some in there could do with it to clear their heads,' she added in disapproval.

Maggie heard her mother's raucous laughter rise above the others; the party was obviously well under way. But before she could retreat to the bedroom she shared with her sisters, the parlour door was thrown open and Aunt Violet came bustling out.

'So you've decided to show your face at last,' she sniffed at her bedraggled niece. 'I told your Susan it's a disgrace you not being here at the start, but she wouldn't have you criticised. She's all heart, your Susan. But why you have to go about with those creatures who call themselves women.' Aunt Violet's prim face puckered in distaste.

Maggie turned to her grandmother, ignoring her aunt. 'I went by the butchers' market, Granny. I'll put the meat in the pantry.'

'Let me, lassie,'Granny Beaton picked up the package from the table and tottered off towards .the scullery over the back stairs where a cold stone slab served as a larder.

'You get yourself in the parlour, young lady,' Aunt Violet grabbed at Maggie as she attempted to retreat. 'Your mam's already showing herself up as usual, and that awful Smith woman is smelling the room out. They've polished off a jug between them.'

'And I suppose Uncle Barny's drinking water,' Maggie said wryly, shaking off her aunt's hold. Violet had plagued them all for years eager to criticise her mother's desperate attempts to keep them fed and with a roof over their heads. What did it matter if she took the odd drink or two? But Violet had few good words to say about any of them .except Susan, whom she favoured, because Susan was too weak to stand up to her, in Maggie's opinion.

'Don't you be cheeky about your uncle,' Violet snapped, giving Maggie a shove in the back.

Pulling wet strands of hair from her face, Maggie marched into the parlour. A red-faced Uncle Barny was resting his fiddle on his stiff cork leg, raising a pot of beer to his lips. Beside him, Maggie's mother looked equally jovial, her greying hair falling loose and her stout hands caressing a glass of ale. Glancing about the crowded room, Maggie noticed Mary Smith and her plump son squatting on the floor next to Jimmy. Helen was sitting demurely on a chair, smiling up at a slim man with a thin moustache and prominent teeth who was telling some joke.

'Maggie!' Susan rushed over to greet her sister, her face animated. 'Come and meet Mr Turvey.'

Maggie was surprised at her sister's lack of reproof at her lateness and looked again at the stranger who was the centre of attention.

'So this is the Maggie I've heard so much about,' the man smiled, his accent southern. He stepped forward in an immaculate brown suit and checked waistcoat with ostentatious watch and chain. Holding out his hand he said jauntily, 'Pleased to meet you, I'm sure.'

Maggie looked at him with suspicion, but took his hand briefly. It was warm and he tried to hang on to hers while he fixed her with deep-set hazel eyes.

'Sorry I'm late, Susan,' Maggie turned to her sister, 'but I got you these.' She handed over the lace and buttons and Susan gasped with pleasure.

'They're lovely. Look, Mam, pearl buttons. They'd look canny on your grey blouse.'

'They're for you!' Maggie laughed in exasperation. 'I've not spent all me wages to see you give me present away.'

'Ta, very much.' Susan blushed and pecked her sister on the cheek. 'We've kept some pie for you and Mrs Smith's currant loaf is delicious. You look worn out. Come and sit down. Mr Turvey's just telling us about his travels on the Continent.'

'You must call me Richard, please,' he insisted. 'I don't suppose Maggie is the least bit interested in hearing about my touring days. I hear you're very serious-minded, young Maggie,' he laughed, 'not one for idle story-telling.'

Maggie instantly disliked his smooth, patronising manner.

'Don't be daft!' she replied. 'I've had a day of politics; I'd like nothing better than a bit of entertainment.'

Richard smiled. 'Can't think of anything worse than a day of politics.' He pulled a theatrical face.

This brought giggles from Helen and the boys and a titter from Aunt Violet.

'Heads down!' cried Uncle Barny jovially. 'The cannonballs are going to fly.'

But Maggie was too weary to spar with the aggravating young man and fell into a seat by the table, picking up a sandwich hungrily. Richard Turvey appeared disappointed.

'Well, the least I expected was to be heckled,' he laughed. 'Isn't that what you political ladies are best at? You're a very disappointing suffragette, young Maggie. Of course, I don't see why pretty young girls like you should want to bother with politics.'

'That's what I say,' Violet nodded vigorously. 'It's not ladylike.'

'I agree, Aunt Violet. Pretty girls don't want to waste their womanly charms marching about and carrying banners,' Richard said with a wink at Helen. 'Marching and banners is for soldiers, eh, Uncle Barny?'

'I love the sight of soldiers on the march,' Helen giggled.

Maggie did not know if she was more irritated by his provocative manner or Helen's simpering response. She put down her half-eaten sandwich and gave him a withering look..

'With such an enlightened attitude as that, Mr Turvey, I'm surprised you're not a member of the government. It's such a pleasure meeting you and being reminded just how necessary the women's struggle is.'

'Bravo!' Uncle Barny chuckled. "That's you told, Richard, me lad.'

'Maggie,' Susan remonstrated, flushing with embarrassment. 'I think you should apologise to Mr Turvey.'

'No, no.' Richard held up a hand, attempting to hide his annoyance at being snubbed. 'No apology necessary. I was in the wrong for upsetting the little lady.'

Mabel broke in quickly, knowing Maggie's temper was as short as her own. 'Give us another tune, Barny,' she nudged her brother.

'But, Mam,' Helen protested, 'Richard's in the middle of his story about the Russian prince.'

'Well, he can give his lungs a rest for a few minutes. Sit yourself down, Richard hinny,' Mabel shouted at her guest, 'and stop your gabbing. And, Mary, pour me another glass before Granny forces me to drink her tea.'

Seeing that no one argued with Mabel Beaton, Richard slipped onto the sofa next to Helen, for once upstaged. As Barny struck up a lively jig and Mary Smith passed round the jug of beer once more, he contented himself with witty asides to Helen and winks across the room at Susan, while all the time being aware of how the darkly becoming Maggie Beaton ignored him.

The evening continued with rousing singing and Jimmy was sent out for more beer until Granny Beaton chased the guests away, muttering that the Sabbath would soon be upon them. Mabel and Mary, who were singing The Blaydon Races for the sixth time, had to be prised apart and Mary was helped downstairs by her son Tommy, while an inebriated Uncle Barny leaned on Tich and Susan for support.

'It's me leg,' he chortled, 'can't make it do what I want.'

'It's the booze, more like,' Violet answered huffily, stalking off ahead.

Maggie caught Richard whispering something to Helen on his way out, which brought a coquettish look to her sister's face.

'Grand evening!' Mary Smith shouted up from below and then the downstairs door banged shut behind her.

'Have I told you 'bout the siege of Lichtenburg, Jimmy?' Barny slurred at his nephew.

'Aye, once or twice, Uncle Barny,' Jimmy grinned and rolled his eyes heavenwards at Susan.

'I lost me leg, you know—'

'Our Tich'll see you up the road,' Susan interrupted as they reached the bottom of the stairs.

'No need, young man,' Richard appeared at Barny's side, 'I can manage him.' He smiled at Susan. 'It's been a wonderful evening and I have enjoyed meeting you, Susan. Aunt Violet told me you were the special one and I see what she means,' he winked at her.

Susan flushed with pleasure and surprise, for she had been disappointed by the amount of attention he had paid to Helen.

'It's been canny meeting you too,' she said shyly, her hand going to her neck in a nervous gesture.

He moved closer and dropped his voice. 'I hope I may call on you sometime.'

'Of c-course,' Susan stuttered and beamed with delight.

'Right then, Uncle Barny,' he said loudly, relieving Jimmy of the portly older man's weight. Barny began to sing again as he was steered into the dark damp street.

'I'll get you into the matinee next Saturday, Jimmy, my boy,' Richard promised.

'Ta very much,' Tich replied enthusiastically. 'That would be champion.'

Susan and her brother watched them go, Aunt Violet stalking ahead with Barny's fiddle while the men weaved their way behind.

'He's canny, isn't he?' Tich glanced at his sister.

'I think so,' Susan answered coyly.

'It was disgusting the way Helen was flirting with him all evening, mind,' Jimmy complained as they retreated inside.

Susan agreed but said nothing. After all, it was she and not the brazen Helen that Richard had asked to see again. She was seized by the sudden exciting thought, as they ascended to the flat, that Richard could be their means of escape from Gun Street. She would marry Richard and being an important man he would buy a house big enough for them all to live in. It would be a house with a proper parlour, only used for entertaining, Susan daydreamed, and there would be railings and a gate in front and a door with gleaming brasses. Her mother would no longer have to slog around Newcastle selling clothes and Helen could be indulged with new dresses. Granny Beaton could spend her final days sitting in front of a roaring fire that never went out and Tich would find a good position, working indoors instead of hawking firewood around the neighbourhood. And Maggie...

Susan's imagination failed her when she thought of her other sister. Try as she might, she could not see Richard living happily with Maggie under his roof, a constant critic of all he said and did. No, Maggie would be much happier setting up house with Rose Johnstone or one of her other strident friends. She could visit them for Sunday tea or whenever she wanted, but it would be a far more harmonious household if Maggie was absent, Susan mused, then felt a pang of guilt for the disloyal thought.

The next morning Maggie had just finished dressing her grandmother in the room that passed for parlour and the old woman's bedroom when she heard banging on the front door. Her mother and Helen were still lying in bed and Tich was out early delivering Sunday newspapers. She heard Susan, who was stirring the porridge, go to answer the door.

Instantly, she recognised Rose's clear voice.

'What is it?' Maggie rushed out to greet her friend, knowing it must be something serious to bring her rushing round on a Sunday morning.

'Mrs Pankhurst!' Rose thrust a newspaper at her. 'They've given her three years' penal servitude. Isn't it outrageous?'

Maggie scanned the inside page in shock. Emmeline Pankhurst had been given a three-year sentence for 'incitement' following a mysterious fire at Walton Heath. The judge had ignored the jury's plea to show her mercy and women protesters had been cleared from the gallery for shouting 'shame' and singing 'The Women's Marseillaise'.

'Three years? After all she's been through already?' Maggie gasped. "They're trying to kill the woman. We have to do something, Rose.'

'Don't be ridiculous,' Susan said, hands on hips. 'What can you possibly do? You think you're so important, but you're no better than the rest of us.'

'Something will be done,' Rose said, giving Susan a dismissive look. 'Maggie, can I have a word alone?'

'Come in the parlour.' Maggie steered her friend quickly into the adjoining room and closed the door on Susan's affronted face. Rose glanced warily at Granny Beaton sitting staring at her Bible on the iron-framed bed.

'She can't hear very well,' Maggie assured her friend, 'and she wouldn't tell if she could.'

The old woman glanced up and smiled at Rose who gave her a hasty greeting. Maggie knew her grandmother had always approved of her friendship with the schoolteacher.

They spoke in hushed tones. 'There's to be a meeting this afternoon to decide on a response to the prison sentence,' Rose said.

'Good,' Maggie said roundly, itching to take some action. 'What time?'

'Three o'clock.'

'Not till then?' Maggie felt frustration.

Rose shook her head. 'It was agreed last night, when news was telephoned through to Miss Pearson.'

Maggie suddenly remembered that Rose had been at a soirée at Hebron House and felt niggled that she had not heard about the news sooner.

'I'll come to your house after dinner,' Maggie said. 'We can go up to town together.'

'The meeting's not at the office,' Rose told her softly. 'The police might be keeping an eye on activity there.'

'Where then?' Maggie asked.

'Alice Pearson said we must meet at Hebron House.'

Maggie felt a thrill of expectation. Finally, she was going to enter the mysterious world of the rich and powerful Pearsons and come face to face with the formidable Alice Pearson.

Chapter Four

From the terrace of Hebron House, Alice Pearson could not see the ranks of workers' houses that hemmed in the mansion and its grounds. The view was of dense mature trees coming into bud and rolling lawns interrupted by circular flowerbeds of daffodils and primulas. Cherry blossom scattered across the terrace like soft confetti as Alice descended the steps with her friend Emily Davison.

'It was good of you to come, Pem.' Alice smiled down at the slim woman beside her, noticing a stiffness in her movements as she walked. She had aged dramatically since her last visit to Hebron House, yet her eyes still shone with vitality and the lustre had not quite gone from her golden hair.

'I had to come,' Emily answered forcefully. 'It's monstrous what they've done to Emmeline Pankhurst and I know just what a terrible time they'll give her in prison. We really must hit back as hard as we can.'

She broke off coughing, her face looking pinched and drawn in the blustery spring wind. Alice slipped an arm through hers in concern.

'Would you rather return to the house? It was selfish of me to make you walk outside on such a cold day. I can see how your last spell in prison has—'

'I'm quite all right,' Emily said to the large woman at her side. 'There's no need to fuss.'

They continued across the lawn with Alice's black poodle, Rosamund, padding at their heels and fell to reminiscing. They had been brought together through their membership of the WSPU and would certainly never have met socially otherwise. Alice had found Emily refreshingly lively and outspoken compared to her own conventional family; she enjoyed a party and was accomplished on the piano as well as being dedicated to the suffragist cause. Alice's brother Herbert could not bear her friends, but even he enjoyed being shocked by Emily Davison's outrageous and engaging conversation. Alice's broad face broke into a smile as Emily recounted her escapade into the House of Commons where she had hidden in a heating flue.

'And what about the time you broke the window of Lloyd George's car?' Alice reminded her with a hearty laugh. 'Pity he wasn't in it.'

'Yes,' Emily agreed. 'I'm really rather bad at recognising faces.'

Alice stopped and shaded her eyes as she scanned the view over the treetops to the coil of river beyond. The Tyne looked grey and choppy and unfriendly at that moment, fringed with the chimney stacks and shipping cranes that generated her father's wealth. The wind was blowing downriver bringing the pungent smells of paint and iron and human effluent into the secluded haven of Hebron House. Alice shivered and drew her coat round her bulky shoulders.

'A dramatic gesture is needed,' she spoke sombrely, 'something that will draw attention to the highest in the land -the King even.'

'I quite agree,' Emily was enthusiastic, 'and I think I know what you're going to say.'

'You do?'

'Yes. HMS *Courageous.*'

'HMS *Courageous*?' Alice was taken by surprise.

'Yes, your father's new battleship.'

'I know very well what it is,' Alice answered tersely. 'But what's it got to do with grand gestures?'

'Its launch,' Emily said with an edge of impatience. 'Surely the Royal Navy's most modern battleship will be launched by royalty or a member of the Cabinet at least.'

Alice stopped. 'It may well be, it really hadn't occurred to me.'

'But it's a marvellous opportunity,' Emily enthused, 'and so easy to organise. You'll be able to find out all the details.'

'No!' Alice said instinctively. 'I mean, not at this moment. The launch won't be until later in the summer, we need a more immediate protest. Yes, more immediate.' She took her friend by the arm and steered her round. 'You see, I've been contacted by headquarters. They want a disruption at the Derby, in front of the King and Queen. Now that would really capture the headlines.'

Emily resisted Alice's attempts to marshal her indoors and Alice found herself being scrutinised. She could see she had disappointed her militant friend and she felt vaguely annoyed that she, a Pearson, should be judged and found wanting. She did not take criticism easily and saw no reason why she should have to explain that she felt a pride in the new battleship and would be helping her father to entertain the dignitaries on launch day at Hebron House. She could not possibly sabotage such an important event for Pearson's.

But Alice could not admit that the overriding reason for steering clear of such action was her fear of losing her valued independence at Hebron House. Her father tolerated her eccentric desire to live alone and dabble in the women's movement because she was considered beyond marriageable age and because he could afford it. In return, she helped him with the business as much as she could. While her brother Herbert gambled his wealth away at their mother's card tables, she at least helped Pearson's compete against their powerful rivals.

'The Derby?' Emily said at last.

'Yes, at Epsom,' Alice encouraged.

'So that's what this meeting is about?' Emily asked, her voice flat.

Alice nodded. She saw now how she could distract Emily from plotting to disrupt the launch. 'We need someone of experience and courage to carry out the task,' she said, bending to pick up a whining Rosamund. 'I naturally thought of you. Of course, it'll have to be discussed with the others and put to the vote.'

Emily nodded but said nothing. Alice was too relieved that she had dropped the subject of the launch to notice her lack of enthusiasm.

. 'Let's go back inside,' Alice said brightly. 'The others will be arriving for the meeting shortly and I'd like to discuss the idea further with you before they come.' Alice began to walk purposefully towards the house, clutching the spoilt Rosamund. 'I'll arrange for tea to be served in the drawing room.'

Skirting the summer pavilion with its huge stone urns, Alice marched them back to the house.

Maggie entered the grounds of Hebron House bursting with curiosity, Rose Johnstone at her side.

'Look at the size of it!' Maggie gasped as the gatekeeper clanged the side gate shut behind them. She had glimpsed the roof of the mansion from the top of her school building, but never before had she seen its vast frontage of classical pillars and lofty windows. 'Have you brought a map with you?' she laughed nervously.

'Yes,' Rose teased. 'People have been known to get lost in there and wander around for years without finding a way out.'

'Bet there's folk in there think Queen Victoria's still on the throne,' said Maggie.

They hurried up the drive, moving to the verge as a horse and trap bumped its way past them to the gates. As they approached the house, signs of decay became evident; the paintwork had blistered on the front doors and the window-frames were faded and bleached a silvery white. The stone pillars showed as much black grime as the houses in Gun Street and the paving on the terrace was cracked and weed-choked. Its air of neglect surprised Maggie. For a moment she wished she could have brought Susan with her, knowing how fascinated her elder sister would have been, but the meeting was secret and Susan would have disapproved of it anyway. In front of the house, Maggie recognised Jocelyn Fulford's shiny black motorcar.

Rose pushed her up the steps to the entrance.

Inside they were shown up a vast staircase shrouded by dark portraits of sombre men with hunting dogs and women in crinoline dresses to a bright room overlooking the front terrace. It was as big as the public reading room in the library and loftier than her old school hall. Maggie stared around in wonder at the drawing room crowded with deep easy chairs and huge jardinieres holding exotic palms. A fierce fire blazed in a white marble fireplace overhung with huge mirrors, its mantel decorated with candlesticks. The walls groaned with oil paintings in heavy gilt frames squeezed in among dozens of framed photographs. Maggie had heard that Alice Pearson was an accomplished amateur photographer and glancing at one photograph by the door she saw a charmingly natural image of a pretty boy on a miniature pony.

Rose nudged her forward and Maggie found her buttoned boots made no noise as she crept over the carpet.

'Come in, come in,' Alice Pearson encouraged, waving her arms at them. Maggie recognised the tall, well-built woman with the sweep of chestnut hair and large outspread hands as their hostess. She had an expressive, full face, dominated by a bulky nose and bold brown eyes that never seemed to blink.

Rose had told Maggie that Alice had somehow avoided being married off and was now safely into spinsterhood, following her own pursuits. She can afford to, Maggie thought enviously, unable to stop staring at her surroundings.

'This is Maggie Beaton,' Rose introduced her nervously.

'How do you do?' Alice held out a hand with a warm smile.

Maggie, acutely aware that her hands could have been cleaner, responded awkwardly.

'There's tea on the table and then we'll get down to business.'

All Maggie could do was nod, feeling dowdy in her grey woollen dress and shapeless blue hat. Rose began to chat to one of the others about the soirée, leaving her wondering what to do. A woman Maggie recognised as the militant Emily Davison came towards her with a cup of tea. She had seen Miss Davison's picture in the newspapers on several occasions and realised she was among a very select group of activists, thanks to Rose's recommendation.

'Help yourself to milk or sugar,' Emily smiled at the overawed young woman. 'We're so pleased you've joined us today.'

Maggie smiled back gratefully, hardly able to believe she was in the company of such important women.

Soon, Alice Pearson brought the room to order.

'We all know why we are here,' she said in a clear, confident voice. 'Our sister Emmeline has been wronged by so-called British justice. She has been locked away for three years for inciting voteless women to burn down an empty villa. Where is her crime?' Alice demanded. 'They only acted out of frustration. I say it is those in authority who incited the women; it is they who should have been put in the dock.'

'That's right,' Emily Davison said, rising to her feet. 'They had to blow up Lloyd George's house to wake him up! We have declared war, sisters, and the sword must not be put away until we win the vote. Like Joan of Arc, we'll fight and take the consequences for our beliefs. We'll continue to go to prison, we'll suffer force-feeding, we shall not submit until we have justice!'

Maggie watched her transfixed, stirred deep within herself by the uncompromising words. She knew then that she was prepared to do as much as Emily Davison and Alice Pearson asked of her. Gripped by the rightness of their cause, it no longer mattered that they were from different sides of a social gulf and that the tall upper-class woman was a Pearson. As Rose had said, Miss Alice had had nothing to do with the way Pearson's shipyard had treated her family, she was on their side.

'We want a volunteer,' Alice Pearson was speaking again. 'Someone prepared to make a dramatic gesture that will splash our cause across every newspaper in the land.'

'We think the Derby at Epsom is where we must demonstrate,' Emily joined in. 'The King and Queen will be present, it's a God-given opportunity.'

'One of us will make a protest as the King's horse goes past - brandish one of our banners,' Alice continued. Maggie sensed a hushed tension among the dozen women present.

Emily added, 'And we'll fight on, sisters. God will give the victory!'

'Here, here!' said Jocelyn and approval rippled around the room.

'I have been in contact with our sisters in London,' Alice said, 'and they agree that the volunteer should come from the north - she is less likely to be recognised or detected. Are we all in agreement that this is the course of action we should take?' She swept them with her brown-eyed gaze.

There were murmurs of assent, but Rose tugged on Maggie's arm and whispered, 'We can't take part.'

Maggie, hardly able to contain her excitement at the idea, looked at her friend in astonishment. 'Of course we can.'

'No, Maggie, can't you see—'

'Do you wish to say something, Rose?' Alice spoke across the room. 'If so, we'd all like to hear it.'

Rose flushed deeply but answered in her clear schoolroom voice. 'I'm sorry, but Maggie and I cannot take part in the protest. We have to work for our living; we cannot afford to take off to Epsom. It's not just the expense, but the time. We'd lose our jobs. As you know, I'm a teacher and Maggie is, well, she's a secretary in one of Pearson's workshops.'

Alice nodded in sympathy. 'I quite understand. Such sacrifice would be unnecessary. As a matter of fact, I was going to propose our sister Emily for the task. She has courageously agreed to have her name put forward but of course it must be put to the vote.'

Maggie felt indignant at her friend's intervention and the way in which she had been so quickly excluded from the plot.

She stood up. 'I don't care if I do lose me job,' she said with spirit. 'Pearson's aren't the only employer around here. I'll find summat else, more than likely. I want to do something important for our cause, not just handing out bits of paper on a Saturday afternoon. I've got the bottle to do it I'd throw myself under the hooves of the King's horse if I had to,' Maggie said with vehemence.

Alice was taken aback. 'There's certainly no need for that,' she answered with a nervous laugh, looking more closely at the diminutive young woman with the ill-fitting hat. There was raw defiance in her slim face. She had dismissed this working-class girl as some lame duck of Rose Johnstone's, who was probably only good for handing out newspapers in the rougher parts of town.

'Maggie, you can't,' Rose intervened again. 'It's all very well being full of high ideals, but your family depends on the wage you bring in. There are others here who can undertake the protest -I think Miss Davison is an excellent choice.'

'Quite so,' Alice agreed quickly, keeping the uncomfortable thought to herself that Maggie might also be out of her social depth among the London WSPU. 'My dear, we do appreciate your fervour,' she smiled at the eager young woman before her, 'and we shall find plenty for you to do locally. Now, are there any other proposed names?'

Maggie sat back down, livid with Rose and with Alice Pearson's patronising manner. She watched as the others shook their heads and then voted unanimously for Emily Davison to take on the task. She sat in the seat next to Maggie, quietly composed, an air of fatality clinging to her pale face.

Suddenly Maggie was gripped with foreboding for her; she sensed danger like a powerful smell hanging in the room.

Slowly Emily stood up. 'Thank you for choosing me,' she said. 'I consider it a great honour to be able to strike this blow on behalf of womankind.'

Soon afterwards, the meeting broke up and Rose and Maggie followed the others out, not speaking to each other. Out in the fresh air, Maggie was about to berate Rose for her interference when Emily Davison came hurrying out after them.

'Miss Beaton,' she called, 'I would like to talk to you at greater length. Perhaps we could meet at Miss Johnstone's one evening soon?'

Maggie and Rose exchanged surprised looks. 'Of course,' Rose said, 'I'd be pleased to have you.'

'Why do you want to speak to me?' Maggie asked her warily, suspecting this well-spoken woman was just patronising her too.

Emily flashed a smile. 'Because you've got a strong dose of north country spirit, my girl, and that's just what's needed for a plan of mine.' She glanced over her shoulder and added hurriedly, 'I can't speak of it here but I really do need to talk to you soon. It's of the utmost importance to the cause. Can I rely on you, Miss Beaton?'

Maggie answered without hesitation, 'Aye, of course you can. I'll do anything for the movement.'

Emily Davison fixed her with bright eyes. 'Yes, I thought you'd say that.'

Once more, Maggie had a fleeting premonition of disaster like a tiny shiver across the shoulders, and she suspected that whatever happened to this fearless woman, it would change her own life too.

The following weeks dragged by with no word from Emily Davison and Maggie could hardly concentrate on her office work at Pearson's. She was increasingly reprimanded by her superior, Mr Roberts, for typing errors and was impatient for the end of each day when she could escape the dirty little office in Number 12 workshop.

Two older women worked with Maggie in the same shop's office for ten shillings a week, having replaced a man who had been paid one pound for his clerical services. One was a timid woman called Mary Watson who rarely spoke but the other was a keen-eyed Yorkshirewoman, Eve Tindall, whose foreman husband had secured her the job.

'What's bothering you, lass?' Eve finally asked during their daily half-hour tea break. They sat in the office, for there was nowhere else for them to go, while the men from the factory vanished to the nearby public house. 'Your mind's not on your work. Isn't that a fact, Mary?'

Mary Watson did not look up from her penny romance or acknowledge that she had been spoken to.

'Nowt as queer as folk, and nowt as strange as that one,' Eve said, shrugging and turning back to Maggie. 'Is there trouble at home?'

Maggie was cautious, knowing how Eve liked to know everything about everybody. The secretive Mary Watson drove Eve Tindall to distraction.

'No more than usual,' Maggie grimaced, thinking of Helen's petty bitching towards Susan over Richard Turvey. So far he had called on neither of them and the mounting suspense was proving unbearable to both.

'It's all this business about the suffragettes then?' Eve guessed. 'By, there's been some terror going on - burning down cricket pavilions and setting fire to trains. Whatever next!'

Maggie, too, had read about the spate of militant acts that had flared up around the country after Mrs Pankhurst's arrest. 'Taking action is the only way of getting through to these people,' she answered.

Eve gave her a shrewd look over tiny oval spectacles. 'You mixed up in some trouble?'

Maggie shook her head and slurped at her tea.

'You know summat, don't you?' Eve said excitedly, whipping off her spectacles and leaning closer.

'Don't be daft, I'm just a foot soldier who sells newspapers. I'm not going to know what the big guns are up to.' Maggie tried to keep her voice unconcerned.

Eve breathed hard on her glasses and rubbed off dust particles that plagued their cramped workspace. 'There's devilment afoot and you know about it, Maggie Beaton. You can't fool me with your butter-wouldn't-melt looks.' She leaned closer still, her large bosom squashing on the table top. 'Now are you going to tell Auntie Eve all about it? You know I wouldn't tell a soul,' she whispered.

Maggie leaned towards her and hesitated. She was aware that Mary Watson had not turned a page of her book for several minutes, though she still pretended not to listen.

'Do you really want to know?' Maggie asked in a loud whisper. Eve nodded vigorously. 'Well, if you join the WSPU you'll find out everything!' Maggie grinned.

'You minx.' Eve sank back in disappointment.

'Why don't you?' Maggie laughed. 'It needs sensible ordinary women like you to broaden the campaign. There are too many women hostile to the cause.'

'That's because it's just a load of toffee-nosed madams who have nothing better to do with their time than chain themselves to railings.' Eve snorted.

'Rubbish!' Maggie replied at once. 'If ordinary women like you and me sit back and pretend it's got nothing to do with us, then men are always going to decide how our lives are run, can't you see that? They aren't going to just give up power and hand us freedom on a plate, we have to fight for it.'

Eve looked dubious. 'My Barry says politics is men's business anyway. He says the working man can look after our interests better than we can ourselves,' Eve said, jamming her glasses back on her stubby nose. 'And I think he's right.'

Maggie thought fleetingly of the arrogant George Gordon and felt a surge of annoyance that a woman should be echoing his views. It was men like Gordon who talked women into believing they had no worth beyond the kitchen hearth.

'Well, that's what working men with a bit of power always say,' Maggie retorted. 'I can't believe someone with your nous can accept such nonsense, Eve! You shouldn't believe everything Mr Tindall says without question, you know.'

Eve pursed her lips in offence and Maggie wondered if she had gone too far. Mary Watson turned a page noisily.

Maggie gave a sigh of frustration. 'Sorry, Eve,' she recanted hastily, thinking of the small jovial foreman who was active on behalf of his union members. 'I didn't mean to be rude about Mr Tindall.'

'No, well, we'll speak no more on't,' Eve huffed 'Let's just say we have differing views on what's seemly for women.'

Maggie shook her head as she cleared away their cups, disheartened by the thought that it was often women themselves who seemed to be the greatest obstacle to their own advancement.

Susan was happiest on those rare occasions when she and her mother sat quietly by the kitchen stove, the tea plates cleared and their stomachs pleasantly full. So many times she had gone to bed in Gun Street with hunger cramps and not been able to sleep for thought of food and memories of the well-stocked larder in Sarah Crescent. But since Maggie had been working for Pearson's, there was always jam with her homemade bread and meat three times a week and strong refreshing tea in the pot.

'Please God, don't let our Maggie do anything daft and lose her job,' Susan prayed every night, her greatest fear being that her headstrong sister would come to a sorry end with all this politics.

But this Friday evening all was tranquil. Susan sat embroidering a handkerchief while her mother sorted through a pile of clothes for tomorrow's trip to the quayside market and Jimmy lay stretched in front of the fire reading a battered comic of Tommy Smith's. Maggie had taken Granny Beaton for a walk up the hill to Daniel Park, gifted by Lord Daniel Pearson to the city, while Helen had gone with her noisy friends to see a moving picture about a ragtime band which she said was 'all the rage'.

Susan quelled her feeling of resentment as she .thought of her contrary youngest sister. Helen could delight everyone with her easy chatter and broad smile but she could be very waspish towards her family if she did not get what she wanted. It had always been that way, Susan sighed; Helen loved to question her authority and make her look foolish in front of others. Susan tried to love her like she loved the others, but Helen didn't seem to want her love.

And now the spectre of Richard Turvey rose between them.

Susan suspected Helen had seen him around the town while she was at home keeping the place in order. For all she knew, Helen might be seeing him this evening, yet she was only seventeen and too young to be courting. If only the engaging Richard would pay her more attention, she would soon show him what a model wjfe she would make. But although he had been pleasant towards her when she visited Aunt Violet, he still had not called to see her as he had indicated he would.

'Penny for them,' Mabel said, watching Susan's troubled face and thinking once again that her eldest looked too careworn for twenty-two.

'Nothing, Mam.' Susan blushed and bent to pick up the sewing that had fallen distractedly from her hands.

'You should have gone for a bit of fresh air with our Maggie,' Mabel chided. 'You look that peaky.'

'I'm on me feet all day, Mam,' Susan smiled. 'I'd rather stop here with you and Tich. Anyway, Maggie and Granny just talk about politics or Granny's past life, and I cannot join in.'

Mabel laughed 'Aye, they're clannish, that pair, when they get going.'

'Doesn't it worry you, Maggie getting mixed up with these suffragettes?' Susan asked, frowning again.

Mabel shook out a crumpled lilac linen dress and sucked in her sagging cheeks. Maggie's radicalism did worry her though she knew to say so would only make her daughter more determined. She had so many hopes for her dark-haired girl, seeing her as the one with the intelligence and drive to lift them finally out of their poverty. Maggie was the one who would look after the family when she'd gone, Mabel thought, because she was the breadwinner. If she had had any influence on Maggie, it was to instil in her the determination not to be dependent on a man for a living. Susan and Helen could not think further than marriage; they were no more farsighted than she had been as a girl. But she had encouraged Maggie to study and learn and make her own way in the world, because her education and skills would be their best guard against poverty.

'Maggie can look after herself,' Mabel answered stoutly.

'But what if she got arrested at one of her demonstrations?' Susan persisted. 'We couldn't manage without her wage again.'

'Aye,' Jimmy piped up excitedly. 'She told me she'd be proud to gan to gaol for the cause.'

Mabel snapped, 'She wouldn't be so daft in the head! Our Maggie's worked hard to get her job at Pearson's. She's always had more brains than the rest of you put together, she's not going to fling it all out the window.'

Susan could see her mother was growing agitated, sweat breaking out on her putty-coloured skin.

'Maggie says they torture lasses in prison,' Jimmy continued in fascination. 'I think she'd be brave to gan to gaol - just like Joan of Arc.'

'She's not going to gaol!' Mabel shouted, her breathing laboured. 'Your head's always full of such nonsense, Jimmy.'

'Of course she's not, Mam,' Susan said soothingly, alarmed to see her mother so upset.

A knock at the door brought the argument to an abrupt end and Jimmy leapt up to answer it, glad to escape his mother's anger. He did not know what he had done to upset her but as usual he had succeeded in doing so.

. 'Richard! 'Jimmy beamed with delight at the surprise visitor. 'You've just saved me from a clout around the lugs,' he grinned.

'I'm very glad to hear it,' Richard smiled and stepped into the kitchen, 'but I can't believe these delightful ladies would do you any harm.'

Susan flushed and stood up, her sewing dropping to the floor. Mabel waved him in.

'Come in, hinny. We could do with some company. So where've you been hiding?'

'Business, business,' Richard replied with an evasive smile. 'But all work and no play makes for a dull life, don't you think, Mrs Beaton?' He glanced around the room as he spoke, noting the absence of the others. Susan was too flustered to see the glint of disappointment in his eyes.

'When are you going to take me and Tommy to the pictures, Richard?' Jimmy asked eagerly. 'You promised, remember?'

'Did I?' Richard asked with a vague smile.

34

'Aye, you did!' Jimmy was adamant 'You said—'

'Stop whingeing, lad,' Mabel scolded. 'Can't you see he's a busy man? Susan'll fetch you a sandwich, Richard.' She pushed him into a chair beside her.

'I'll make a pot of tea,' Susan said breathlessly.

'No.' Mabel stopped her. 'Get out a couple of glasses.' She winked at Richard. 'Tich, take the coppers in the tea caddy and gan to the corner for a jug of beer.'

Jimmy did so with a resigned sigh, being used to such errands for his mother and Mrs Smith downstairs. They knew him well at the Gunners where their landlord was the proprietor and Jimmy had long since got used to the ribald remarks about serving Widow Beaton and her haughty daughters.

'That's more like it,' Richard laughed, rubbing his hands together. 'Make it three glasses, Susan. You'll join us for a little taste, won't you?' he winked.

Susan curbed her disapproval and looked at her mother for guidance.

Mabel wagged her finger. 'Just a taste now.'

'Aye,' Susan giggled, not wanting Richard to think her boring. What was the harm of a little drink behind closed doors?

'That's my girl,' Richard grinned and patted the stool beside him, making Susan's heart leap with excitement.

Half an hour and a jug of beer later, the merry group at Gun Street had started to sing and Richard was delighting them with sentimental variety hall songs.

Susan, mellow and slightly tipsy from the bitter-sweet ale, watched him in smiling adoration. Tonight, she thought contentedly, Richard Turvey had come here to court her. It was a new beginning. Despite Granny Beaton's muttered forebodings, 1913 was going to be a lucky year for the Beatons, a year of romance and prosperity. Finally, life was going to get better, Susan thought, flushed with optimism and alcohol.

It was in this state of semi-inebriated sentimentality that Maggie and Granny Beaton found the family on their return from Daniel Park. Granny tutted in disapproval but Maggie did not want to spoil Susan's happy state and good-naturedly joined in the singing. She began 'The Women's Marseillaise' until the others shouted her down.

'No politics, Maggie!' Susan protested.

But Maggie did not care, for she was bubbling with news that she found hard to keep to herself. In the park she had met Rose Johnstone.

'Come round to my house on Sunday afternoon,' Rose had told her in that light, unconcerned voice that suffragettes used to convey their messages in public places. 'I have a friend coming to tea.'

The look of understanding that had passed between them confirmed that Emily Davison wanted to meet Maggie at last.

Chapter Five

'It's not fair!' Helen complained for the umpteenth time. 'I bet Richard came to see me, not our Susan.'

'Button that mouth of yours or I'll skelp you,' Mabel hissed sharply, arranging a man's overcoat on the rug spread out at her feet. Around them, other stallholders were arranging their wares on the worn cobbles.

'And she was drunk when I got in - stinkin' of wallop,' Helen ranted. 'It's disgustin'! And giving him the eye.'

Mabel whipped round and gave her daughter a hard smack across her cheek. Helen screamed in shock.

'Don't you dare speak about your sister like that again! She's a better lass than you'll ever be and you're not going to spoil things for her. Richard's taking her to the rowing this afternoon and you'll keep out the way.'

Maggie watched the scene in dismay as the impact from her mother's hand left livid red marks across Helen's fair cheek. She wished she had not come to help out at the Sandgate market, there had been nothing but argument since arriving, but she had wanted to keep herself occupied to take her mind off the coming meeting with Emily Davison.

Helen was now sobbing uncontrollably, so Maggie put an arm about her shaking shoulders. She hated it when their mother's weary frustration erupted into violence against them as it still frequently did.

'There was no need for that, Mam,' Maggie chided quietly. 'Helen's not a bairn any more.'

'Well, she's behaving like one,' Mabel snapped, her face haggard and sweating in the sunshine. She turned away from her daughter's critical look and Maggie suspected she already regretted striking Helen.

'Haway,' Maggie shook her sister kindly, 'you're driving away custom with all your noise.' She pulled out a handkerchief and wiped Helen's streaming face. 'The foreign sailors aren't going to look twice, they'll just think you're one of the wailing cats around here.'

Helen sniffed behind the handkerchief, peering down towards the quay. 'What sailors?'

Maggie grinned. 'That's more like it. There's a pair coming towards us in yellow clogs, Dutch or Norwegian - big and blond anyway.'

Helen's crying died away as she wiped her face dry and tossed back her ringlets, her eyes on the approaching merchantmen. Composed in an instant, she hurried to her mother's side and began a busy arranging of the shoes in the barrow. 'Let me, Mam,' she insisted with a sweet smile, as if their tiff had never been.

Mabel exchanged a shake of the head with Maggie and they all settled to the business of bartering.

'Come here, hinnies!' Mabel cried at the curious sailors who had stopped at a nearby stall. 'I've just the clothes for fine young lads like you.'

One of them laughed in understanding and stepped closer, eyeing the wares spread out on the ground. He pointed at the black coat.

'Aye, a good choice, hinny,' Mabel nodded. 'Belonged to a bishop, very good quality – I'll not have another one like it. Feel the thickness, gan on.'

Maggie watched in admiration as her mother coaxed the young man to try it on, clucking with compliments.

Helen beamed with encouragement too.

'It suits you,' she said coyly.

The young man was pleased and laughed, exchanging comments in his own tongue with his shipmate.

'I know you're not on a captain's wage so it's yours for sixteen shillings,' Mabel said.

The sailor hesitated and shook his head. He pulled out some money from an inside pocket and laid it out on his palm: There were nine shillings. He shrugged to indicate it was all he had. Maggie saw her mother look disappointed, but Helen intercepted.

'Let him have it, Mam,' she pleaded. 'He's probably only a deckhand.'

Mabel relented. 'Gan on and take it, hinny,' she sighed, 'but tell all your mates where they can buy a fine bargain.'

The sailor handed over the money, winked at Helen and walked off proudly wearing his purchase.

Maggie turned to her mother in amusement 'A bishop's coat, eh? Durham or Canterbury?'

'It's not a word of a lie,' her mother said defensively. 'It belonged to a Mr Bishop in High Heaton.'

Maggie and Helen burst out laughing. Soon the morning's quarrel was forgotten as they competed for custom and tried to outdo each other's wooing of passers-by.

Maggie loved the vibrant life of Newcastle's quayside and the flotilla of merchant ships bobbing lazily in the sun on the silver Tyne. They had to shout above the din of cartwheels grinding over the cobbles and the calls of hawkers and tipsters. A man went past with a placard announcing that the day of judgement was nigh. 'Repent! Repent!' he shouted at them with a fierce look. At a comer cafe, traders and seamen sat smoking reflectively while the down-at-heel sunned themselves on the warming steps of a lodging house, turning pallid faces to the sky.

After a morning's trading, the second-hand clothes merchants began to bundle up their wares and disperse. Mabel led her daughters to the nearby cafe for some tea and cake as a reward for their efforts. She flopped down exhausted and stretched out her aching feet, exchanging pleasantries with Stella the cafe owner whom she knew well from her years of trading. Stella brought them steaming tea in chipped mugs and chatted about the ships that had berthed the previous night. Just then, a gaunt-looking woman with dyed red hair and high black heels passed by the open door, smoking.

'Brazen hussy!' Mabel tutted.

'Aye,' Stella agreed. 'I'll not have them in my establishment.'

'Who?' Helen asked innocently.

'Wicked lasses like that'un,' her mother answered, blowing vigorously at her hot tea. 'She shouldn't be out on the streets in daylight among honest folk. Now stop staring.

'How do you know her?' Helen asked.

'She doesn't, she's a prostitute,' Maggie explained. She had seen them before when John Heslop, the Methodist lay preacher, had led a mission to the quayside and Maggie had volunteered to hand out soup and religious tracts. For a short while she had considered becoming a missionary, but then she had heard Emmeline Pankhurst speak and her life had changed. From that day she had determined that her mission would be women's suffrage.

'A prostitute,' Helen gasped in fascination. 'You mean that one gans with men for money?'

'That's enough,' Mabel said. 'We'll talk no more about it.'

'If lasses had more jobs and better pay, they wouldn't need to serve men for a living,' said Maggie.

'Hush, our Maggie!' Mabel said, scandalised. 'I'll not have you defending whores - they're sinful.'

'Jesus did,' Maggie said dryly.

'Don't you get clever with me, young lady. We've been poor but we've earned a living off honest means, however hard.' Mabel jabbed a censorious finger at the retreating prostitute and looked to Stella for support. 'Her kind wouldn't thank you if you gave her an honest job. That's what comes of wicked living and a bad home.'

'Aye,' Stella nodded. 'Sinners all.'

'If a daughter of mine ever messed with men, I'd hoy them into the street where they belonged.'

Her friend agreed. 'Hoy 'em oot, I say.'

Maggie decided not to challenge her mother further. She glanced at Helen, but her attention was still fixed on the red-headed woman as she strolled out of view in a halo of cigarette smoke.

'You'll come with us, won't you?' Susan pleaded with Maggie. She had dressed in her best pink birthday gown and her golden hair was neatly combed and pinned beneath a straw boater with candy-pink ribbons.

Maggie looked up distractedly from the book she was reading on her grandmother's bed. It was an avant-garde novel, The Story of a Modern Woman, lent to her by Rose, and she wanted to finish it before seeing her friend the next day so they could discuss it. Maggie met Susan's expectant gaze in the parlour minor.

'I've got newspapers to sell this afternoon,'. Maggie countered.

'Oh, Maggie, you must come!' Susan protested. 'Otherwise Helen or Mam will have to chaperone us. Mam's tired and would rather rest anyway, and Helen - well, you know what she'd be like.'

Tich can go with you,' Maggie suggested half-heartedly.

'He's gone fishing with Tommy and old Gabriel.' Susan's eyes swam with sudden tears. 'Please, Maggie.

This is a special day for me and I want it to be canny. I can't go to the boat race if you won't come with me. Me and Richard will just have to stop in the house with Mam and Granny.'

'All right,' Maggie sighed, giving up her plans of a pleasant read or going into town. 'I'll come.'

Susan rushed over and kissed her on the cheek. 'You'll have to put on something smart, mind. And you'll brush your hair, won't you? And please don't wear that hat with the suffragette ribbons round it. You'll not go on about women's rights to Richard either? He doesn't hold with that sort of talk.'

Maggie groaned and closed her book. She had no wish to spend the afternoon trailing around after Susan and the garrulous Richard Turvey, craning over the crowds to get a glimpse of a few rowing boats. But she could see how excited her sister was at the prospect of the afternoon's entertainment and Susan certainly deserved a few hours' respite from the drudgery of Gun Street.

'Haway then,' Maggie smiled resignedly. 'I'll play the meek little sister just this once. What do you want me to wear?'

Taking the tramcar to Scotswood, the party of three alighted close to the Ord Arms and followed the crowd of holidaymakers down to the riverside. Stepping past a group of children playing marbles in the street, they emerged from the uniform ranks of housing onto the banks of the Tyne where a thriving boat club was swarming with spectators.

'Used to go boating a lot on the Thames,' Richard was telling Susan who was clinging to his arm. 'Rowed on most big rivers in Europe, as a matter of fact.'

'Have you, Richard?' Susan looked impressed. 'Thamesmen are supposed to be grand rowers, aren't they?'

Tynesiders are better,' Maggie said, tired of Richard's boastfulness. Susan gave her a warning look.

'Don't listen to Maggie, she just likes to argue,' Susan laughed falsely.

'My, my, little sister,' Richard replied, with an infuriating smile. 'I didn't think you took any interest in rowing.'

'I don't,' Maggie muttered, her irritation mounting. 'I just—'

'You just like to stick up for Geordies, is that it?' Richard said. 'Think I'm being a big-headed Londoner, do you? Well, us Londoners do have a lot to be proud of, you know, little Maggie. But no, I see myself as a man of the world - cosmopolitan, well travelled. You don't want to limit your horizons to one little place on the map, even if you are a proud northerner.' He chuckled, cocking his head to one side under his jaunty cap.

'My horizons aren't limited,' Maggie was stung into answering. 'I've met women from all over the country and I'm just as interested in the rights of lasses in London as Tyneside.'

'Oh, Maggie, you promised not to start on about politics!' Susan protested. 'Can't you just enjoy the afternoon without getting all steamed up?'

'Sorry,' Maggie apologised, swallowing her indignation and turning from Richard's triumphant face. She determined to ignore his jibing and remain mute for the rest of the expedition.

Soon they were surrounded by the crowd and being jostled good-naturedly down to the landings of the boat club. Maggie was not even sure which local teams were in the competition but she assumed by the size of the crowd that there must be several. She knew that most communities along the Tyne had their own rowing club, as did several of the works along the riverfront, including Pearson's.

Rowing had always been a popular local sport and Maggie could vaguely remember enjoying the spectacle of boat racing as a child. She had a memory of being by the lapping river edge, watching the narrow boats cutting through the blue-grey water, the rowers arms stretching and pulling in unison. She had been high on her father's shoulders, up above the cheering crowds and the flotsam of caps and boaters, soaring like a seagull yet safely anchored by her father's large hands. But somewhere in her growing up she had lost her appetite for boating.

'Remember when Father used to take us on the river?' Susan said, echoing her thoughts. 'And you always had to take one of the oars.'

'Always in command, eh, little sister?' Richard teased.

Maggie shrugged. 'I don't really remember.'

'But you must," Susan insisted. 'You loved a trip on the river, just like Father.' She smiled at Richard. 'She was Father's shadow, was our Maggie.'

'Stop going on so, Susan,' Maggie said irritably. 'I hardly remember what me dad was like.'

Glancing at Richard, she noticed him watching her with interest, as if making a mental note of her weakness, the soft underbelly of memories of her father that were too painful to expose. Well, it had nothing to do with this Londoner how she felt about her father, Maggie thought with resentment, and she would not speak about him to Richard. Changing the subject quickly, she said, 'Look, I think something's about to start. We'll get a better view if we push nearer the front.' Maggie pulled Susan after her, squeezing a path through the cheerful spectators and secretly hoping they might lose Richard in the mêlée. Just as they emerged onto the edge of the riverbank, a burly figure in a rowing singlet and shorts pushed by. Maggie stifled an exclamation as George Gordon turned and caught sight of her in the same instant.

For a moment he hesitated, as if debating whether to acknowledge her, then decided to speak.

'Not here to protest at the lack of a ladies' team, are you?' he grunted.

'I'm having an afternoon out with me sister Susan,' she replied coolly.

George nodded amiably at Susan.

'It's George Gordon, isn't it?' Susan squinted at him.

'Aye.'

'Thought it was. You've got the Gordon chin. Doing well at Pearson's, so I hear,' Susan nodded in approval. 'Blacksmith, aren't you?'

Maggie and George both looked at her in astonishment.

'I see your sister Irene at the wash-house every week,' Susan explained with a laugh. 'We always have a bit crack.'

'I might have known,' Maggie sighed. 'There's no one this side of Westgate Road our Susan doesn't know about.'

'Aye, and Irene's the same,' George said, sliding a glance at Maggie. 'There's no one can beat a couple of lasses for gossiping, is there?'

'I always find it's men that like the sound of their own voices,' Maggie retaliated. 'British industry could run off the hot air you lads generate over a few pints of beer.'

'Maggie!' Susan remonstrated.

At that moment, Richard came pushing through breathlessly, throwing Maggie a reproachful look for having left him behind.

'This is Richard Turvey,' Susan introduced him quickly, flustered by Maggie's aggression towards the swarthy rower. 'From London. Richard works in the cinematography business. George Gordon here used to go to school with us, he works at Pearson's.'

The two men nodded at each other suspiciously.

'So which is the crew to bet on, eh?' Richard asked, jangling the change in his pocket.

'Eeh, Richard, you're not going to gamble?' Susan asked, shocked.

'No harm in a little flutter, Susan dear,' Richard answered, amused at her disapproval.

'But the police,' she gasped.

'I'm sure George here can advise me where I can place a little bet,' Richard smiled. 'He looks like a man of the world. Eh, George?'

Maggie thought she saw a flicker of contempt cross the rower's face but he answered courteously enough.

'Over yonder,' he nodded at a riverside pub with blackened opaque windows. 'They'll be happy to take your money. Our crew are as good as any - Pearson's. Now if you'll excuse me,' George said with a mock flick of respect to Maggie, 'we're off next.'

For the first time Maggie noticed the blue and gold colours of Pearson's across his chest and her heart gave a painful squeeze as it conjured up a vivid memory of her father in just such a singlet.

'You row for Pearson's?' she blurted out.

'Aye,' George nodded, surprised by her sudden interest. 'Not going to scupper us as a protest against Lord Pearson, are you?' he grinned. Maggie was surprised George Gordon knew of the magnate's virulent speeches against women's suffrage in the Upper House. Working men of his kind usually took no interest in such debates.

'Perhaps I will,' Maggie responded.

'Well, I hope you can swim,' he joked 'Cos none of these buggers will gan in after a suffragette.'

'Good,' Maggie pouted, her grey eyes flashing. 'I'd rather drown as a suffragette than be beholden to a mere man!'

George laughed out loud and moved off, shaking his head.

'Maggie, how could you be so rude?' Susan scolded.

'He asked for it,' she replied, not in the least contrite. She caught sight of Richard watching her closely once more and felt uneasy under his narrow-eyed scrutiny.

'I don't think Mr Gordon minded Maggie's provocation in the least,' Richard said softly.

Maggie felt herself colouring at his remark and turned away quickly, shielding her eyes from the glare bouncing off the oily water. Her dislike of Richard Turvey was increasing by the hour; she was dismayed at Susan's obvious infatuation with his foxy good looks and glib conversation.

The rest of the afternoon passed pleasantly enough and Maggie enjoyed the holiday mood of the crowd and the warm sunshine on her shoulders as the crews raced along the stretch of Tyne, west of Scotswood Bridge. Being upstream from Pearson's vast shipyard and fortress-like armaments factories, the air was more clear of the ubiquitous pall of smoke and steam that they lived under every day and Maggie filled her lungs full of the lighter air, watching with more interest than she cared to admit, to see how Pearson's crew progressed.

Richard spent a large part of the afternoon in and out of the nearby pub, while Susan tried to hide her disappointment. He was gleeful when the unfavoured young crew from the glassworks on which he was betting beat the mighty Pearson's in the semi-final. But noticing Susan's growing coolness, he quickly pocketed his winnings and bundled them back on a tram to Daniel Park.

'I'm going to treat you to tea at that open-air stall,' he smiled broadly at Susan. 'It's the only reason I wanted to bet in the first place - spend a bit extra on you, dear.'

Maggie found this hard to believe but Susan seemed mollified and slipped her arm through his again. A colliery brass band from Benwell played stirring music under the copper-domed and gilt-painted bandstand as they tucked into cream cakes and a jug of tea in the park. Richard talked expansively. 'I must take you to tea at the new Terrace Tearoom in Fenwick's - they have an orchestra playing every afternoon, you know.'

'Every afternoon!' Susan exclaimed in pink-faced wonder.

'Then we could go and see Houdini at the Empire.'

'Who's Houdini?' Susan asked, through a mouthful of sticky cake.

'Don't tell me you haven't heard of Houdini, girl?' Richard laughed in disbelief. 'The world-famous self-liberator, that's who. Has Helen not told you about him?'

'Helen?' Susan flushed. 'Why should she?'

Richard hesitated, then nudged her playfully. 'No reason, it's just that sister of yours seems to live in the theatre, as far as I can see.'

'She may well,' Susan said with disapproval, 'but I seldom get the chance to go out like she does, though how she finds the money to go to the pictures all the time defeats me.'

Maggie slipped away, musing that money appeared to be no obstacle to Richard either. What exactly was he doing in Newcastle? She wouldn't be surprised if he was just living leech-like off Aunt Violet and making money at gambling, then chided herself for being uncharitable. Just because she disliked him did not mean he made a living by dishonest means. Still, she found it hard to believe that he was anything as responsible as a manager of a prestigious new cinema.

Leaving through the wrought-iron gates, Maggie debated briefly whether to return to Scotswood to see the outcome of the regatta, then dismissed the notion as frivolous. If she walked into town now, she would still have time to sell copies of The Suffragette and on Saturday evening the markets, public houses and cafes were always teaming with people. Pushing thoughts of George Gordon's glistening and muscled arms firmly from her mind, she walked purposefully towards the city.

All afternoon, George had been conscious of the Beaton girls standing on the landing in their pale dresses and straw hats watching the races. Not that that had spurred him on to greater exertions, or been responsible for his crew gaining a well-fought place in the semi-finals of the regatta, but nonetheless he had been aware of their presence. The raising of a pale hand to shade her flint-grey eyes, an amused inaudible comment to her sister, a cat-like yawn in the sunshine were glimpses that had made him conscious of Maggie Beaton throughout the afternoon.

The distraction had been annoying and incomprehensible, and even now he found himself thinking of Maggie's slim, determined face and slender neck framed by her thick, untidy black hair. Now, if she had had Susan Beaton's pleasant feminine manner, he could have understood his stirring attraction. But Maggie Beaton was too forthright and self-opinionated for any man to find attractive and too knowledgeable about manly pursuits such as politics. She would come to no good, that one, George thought, with a shake of his head.

. 'Haway, George man,' said Bob Stanners, a fellow rower, slapping him on the shoulder. 'We're off into town for a few. You coming?'

'Gan on without me,' George replied 'I'll catch you up later.'

. His pale, red-headed friend groaned. 'You going to sulk about losing the cup to Armstrong's for the next year?'

'I'm not sulking,' George insisted, 'just want to stop off at me da's on the way - see how the old bugger is.'

He knew Bob and the others thought him strange for not living at home with his family, preferring to rent a room on his own in a dilapidated house in Rye Hill. But he had always been independent, a very private man, in spite of his capacity for organising others and being a stalwart of the rowing team. He revelled in his one-roomed freedom away from the bursting pit cottage in Benwell where his sister Irene kept house for his father and brothers, his mother having died long since.

'Haven't got yourself a secret woman tucked away in that den of yours, have you, George?' Bob teased, punching him on the chest.

'Wouldn't you like to know.' George caught Bob's fist, delivering a playful cuff on his chin in return. They wrestled for a minute until the others intervened and they parted with cheerful obscenities.

When his friends were out of sight, George turned in the opposite direction and made his way over some derelict land, climbing a battered fence and crossing a field. Later he would visit his old father and help himself to Irene's homemade pies, but first be wanted to walk. Since a scrawny youth he had enjoyed roaming the countryside on the fringes of Newcastle, watching the wilderness retreat before the greedy sprawling mass of hastily thrown up housing and brash new factories.

Small farms and meadows still stood their ground against the grime and smoke and effluent that threatened to poison them with progress. As a boy, George had played among the stooks and waded barefoot through burns, imagining he was an ancient Briton evading the imperious Romans just like in the history book John Heslop, the Sunday School teacher, had lent him. George had long since turned his back on religion, seeing it as a trick of the ruling classes to keep their workers docile and obedient. But Heslop's teaching had fired a love of history that had never been quenched and George would often steal to the institute library after work to read dusty historical tomes and even poetry.

'God forbid - if there is a God - that Bob and the lads should ever find me reciting poetry,' George said aloud as he strode through the young green grasses, stirring up butterflies.

When he was sure he was out of earshot of the receding houses, he pulled a volume of poetry from inside his jacket and began to read Matthew Arnold to the trees and hedgerows as he passed. It was suitably melancholic after his defeat on the river and he boomed out verse after verse. Approaching a farmhouse, George fell silent, enjoying the evening twitter of birds and the bellow of a cow needing milking. He waved at the red-cheeked dairy girl with her raw hands and wondered why he had not been born on the land where he felt most at home.

At least he was not working underground like his father and brothers, George thought with relief. After his mother's death, he had hung around the blacksmith's forge to be near the horses, comforted by the animal smells and the warmth of the forge fire in winter. For years he had watched fascinated as the blacksmith in his leather apron had shod pit ponies and dray horses, his tools ringing harshly as the hot metal glowed orange in his grasp and the forge reeking with the pungency of scorched hooves. Finally the blacksmith had agreed to take him on because he was the strongest of the boys who pestered for a job and he learned quickly.

George gained the top of the hill and looked back down to the Tyne and its hazy industrial sprawl. Church spires poked up hopefully out of the smog, but they were outnumbered by the smoking chimneys and preying cranes. George sighed. He had left the smithy, lured by better prospects in the shipyards, and since then it had been his lot to spend his days sweating in Pearson's forge working its gigantic hammers and hydraulic presses. Although there was satisfaction in producing huge metal sheets that were turned into impressive ships, George often felt he was no more than a tiny ant among thousands, working mindlessly for Pearson's profit.

'Well, ants can bloody well organise!' George shouted down at the miles of factory sheds. 'One day we'll all have a say in our working conditions!' He punched the air as he spoke. No one knew that most of his union speeches had been practised up here. among the indifferent cows. 'One day the nation will own the means of production, not just a handful of men like Pearson. And we'll spend the profits on decent housing and education beyond fourteen and pensions for our old citizens. Never again will they have to fear the workhouse!'

A blackbird came screeching out of a hedge and George stopped to laugh at himself. He was reminded of himself as a young boy, springing out of ditches, brandishing a sword-stick and making battle speeches against the occupying Romans.

Suddenly another voice came stridently into his mind. I'm fighting for justice for all women ... We want equality with men under the law and equal wages...

Maggie Beaton was mad, George declared to himself, and such notions might be a danger to working men whose jobs must be protected and enhanced. Yet he was troubled by Maggie's startling words. Were the suffragettes not asking that women be given the very things that working men wanted - the vote, better pay and improved social conditions?

George mocked himself. What would Bob Stanners and the others think of him if they suspected he was going soft on women's rights? If his friends thought of such things at all, it was with irritation that women dared to set sports pavilions on fire or throw hammers through picture-house windows. When a suffragette had smashed the window of Lloyd George's car in Newcastle, Bob had said, 'If it was my missus, I'd give her a hidin' into next week. Shows lasses aren't fit to vote, doesn't it?'

George had grunted agreement but had been secretly admiring of the woman's courage in confronting the ruling class so brazenly. He was disturbed by the thought that, while the suffragettes got on with their revolution, he and his mates just endlessly talked about it.

Time for a drink, George thought, trying to clear his mind of conflicting feelings. He pushed the poetry book back inside his jacket and strode back towards the town.

Chapter Six

Gas jets were flaring outside the pubs, and Maggie could glimpse smoky interiors behind the heavy brass-handled doors. She was tempted to stride in and shout her slogans over the general hubbub, but she knew she had to be careful. She must do nothing tonight to provoke arrest and miss her important meeting with Emily Davison and she knew the police would detain her on the slightest pretext. They knew all the local militants and watched them like hawks, so she maintained her unobtrusive position at the edge of the Bigg Market, silently holding up a copy of The Suffragette in the hope that some of the Saturday night revellers might buy one.

She was content to watch chattering couples and families walking around the open stalls, lit by a hissing phosphorous light. A father cradled a sleeping girl in his arras, while two boys beside him shared a tub of peas and his wife fingered a piece of red calico in indecision. Rejecting it, the mother moved away, ruffling the boys' hair in amusement at something they had said and Maggie felt a strange sense of aloneness.

She was set apart by what she chose to do, but she was meant to be alone. How else could she do this important work? If she had a husband and family, she would be too occupied with daily chores to have any energy left for the women's cause. She realised that she was lucky to have Susan and Granny at home to take care of the mundane, wearisome tasks of daily life, so that, after her office job, she could concentrate on more important work. Although Granny might think of it like that, she knew her sister did not Yet it cheered Maggie to think that Susan inadvertently helped women's suffrage in this way.

As the market began to empty and the yawning stallholders packed up their goods and went home, Maggie realised how tired and footsore she was. She decided to bundle up her newspapers too.

'Here, hinny.' The toothless pea-seller stopped and offered her a tub from her soapbox on wheels. 'Bet you've had nowt to eat all nigh.'

'Ta, Mrs Surtees.' Maggie smiled gratefully at the stooped woman who often lingered to speak to her, taking the proffered food.

'Too hard for my old gums anyways,' Mrs Surtees cackled. 'Sell 'em to Pearson's as bullets, me old man always says.'

'Taste canny to me,' Maggie said, biting on the hard peas hungrily.

Mrs Surtees began to recount the week's events, her husband's health and the gossip of Sandgate, keeping Maggie entertained while she ate. The square had darkened and fallen so peaceful that the sudden disruption as brawlers spilled out of the Half Moon took them by surprise.

'You're a bloody cheat!'

'I won fair and square. You're too drunk to know the difference.'

'Don't call me a drunk!'

A man was shoved into their path, knocking the remaining tubs of peas onto the cobbles. As they bounced away in front of an astonished Mrs Surtees, Maggie upbraided the sprawling men.

'You big clumsy buggers! You'll pay her for the peas,' she shouted.

A thin-faced man snarled at her to shut up as he took hold of the man at her feet and jerked him round.

Maggie was dumbfounded as she peered into the dark. "Richard Turvey, is that you? What in the world...?'

Richard focused on her with smoke-reddened eyes. 'Help me, won't you?' He doubled up as his assailant kicked him in the stomach. Other men began to crowd round the victim.

'Stop it,' Maggie said, attempting to intervene.

The thin man turned on her aggressively. 'Stay out of this, you silly bitch. He's cheated me of me money and he's in for a good hidin'.'

'And you've cheated this woman of her earnings,' Maggie replied sharply. 'You'll pay for the peas you've ruined.'

The young drunk glared at her menacingly. 'What you interfering for? Who the hell are you anyway?' Suddenly he noticed her suffragette sash and the pile of newspapers. 'You're one of them bloody women,' he spat. 'I'll have you!'

Forgetting the man on the ground, he lurched towards Maggie, grabbing her sash and tearing it off her. In an instant he was followed by others from the pub who turned on her with hostile looks and menacing hands. Maggie froze in terror as Mrs Surtees was shoved out of the way by the riled men. One grabbed her by the jacket, another by the blouse.

'Whore!'

'You've asked for this.'

'Hanging's too good for your kind!'

'Let her have it!'

She screamed in agony as her hair was pulled and someone punched her breast Instinctively she knew that if she lost her footing and went down, that would be the end. She clutched at one of the attackers and held on to his arm, sinking her teeth into his hand. He howled in pain, drawing back his hand, but someone else jabbed a fist into her eye. For a moment Maggie was blinded and as the angry faces blurred before her, she felt herself slipping to the cobbles.

I'm going to die, she thought. I'm going to die in a dirty lane because of these senseless drunken men. And my petty efforts for the cause will be wasted before I've had time to prove myself.

As she went down, Maggie was aware of increased noises and confusion, then her head hit the ground and she blacked out.

George Gordon and Bob Stanners came across the commotion as they took a short cut through the market on their way home. At first they thought it just another Saturday night fight as the pubs emptied, then George spotted a torn sash lying in the debris of rotting vegetables and discarded paper.

Pushing their way into the fight, they saw the old pea-seller crouched and sobbing on the kerb.

'Help the lass, please help the lass!' she wailed at them.

George strained into the dark and saw a young woman on the ground. Filled with fury, he seized the nearest attacker round the neck and pulled him back. Caught off balance, the man stumbled and George helped him on his way with a hard punch. Without hesitation, Bob set about the woman's attackers too. The drunks were no match for the fit blacksmith and his friend and they soon fell back, stumbling away with curses and bleeding noses.

George bent down to help the woman. A lone stallholder hurried over with a lamp and the light flickered to reveal a pale bruised face under the matted black hair.

'Maggie Beaton!' George gasped in horror. 'The bastards!'

'You know the lass?' Bob asked.

'Aye, she's from over our way,' George said, filled with disgust at the attack. He leaned forward and gently lifted her to a sitting position. Maggie's eyes flickered open, but she gave no look of recognition. She moaned and George felt her thin body convulse under his touch.

'It's all right, hinny,' Mrs Surtees tried to reassure her. 'These lads have saved-you. They'll do no harm.'

Maggie still stared at them with confused eyes as a harsh sobbing rose up in her throat.

'Shall I gan for the coppers?' Bob asked.

George hesitated, noticing the torn sash of purple, green and white.

'No, they'd probably just arrest her for selling her papers.'

The truth suddenly dawned on Bob. 'She's a bloody suffragette!'

'So?' George was sharp.

'Probably asked for it,' Bob said disparagingly, 'mouthing off.'

George turned on him angrily. 'No lass deserves to be set on like this, no matter what she stands for.'

'Aye,' Mrs Surtees agreed, stroking Maggie's forehead with her gnarled hands. 'And it only happened 'cos she stood up for a man they were attacking. The bugger didn't even stay to help her. Makes me blood boil.'

George shook his head in disbelief.

'So what do we do with her?' Bob asked glumly.

'We get her home to her family.' George was adamant. 'Help me lift her, Bob.'

Bob muttered, 'All right, but it doesn't mean I agree with—'

'Shut your gob and give us a hand!'

They got Maggie to her feet and George covered her with his own jacket. She was shaking and in shock, saying nothing, as if she did not know him. Mrs Surtees blessed them and waved them away.

In the warmth of the tramcar, Maggie began to revive, becoming aware of curious stares from the passengers. Feeling with her hands, she realised several buttons had gone from her blouse and that the jacket she wore was far too big. What was she doing here? she puzzled. And why was she wearing this jacket? All at once, the memory of the attack flooded over her and she looked around in panic. George Gordon stood looking over her, keeping his balance as the tram jolted them forward.

'You're all right, bonny lass,' he smiled awkwardly. 'We'll see you home.'

Maggie noticed he was in his shirtsleeves. Somehow, the tall blacksmith had rescued her. She closed her eyes again, every bump of the journey jarring her bruised body, though she was thankful to be in the safe fuggy interior of the car.

Later, as George and Bob helped her from the tram and across the road to Gun Street, she was able to discover how they had stopped the assault.

'Thank you,' she whispered.

There was consternation at her arrival, with Susan fussing around her and Granny Beaton instructing her to lie on the parlour bed while they attended to her cuts and bruises. The men withdrew hastily, refusing offers of tea. Jimmy and Helen came in bleary-eyed and yawning and demanding to know what the noise was about. Then Maggie's mother appeared, her greying hair hanging in limp braids over her shoulders and her body shapeless in her nightgown. How old she looks now, Maggie thought through her fatigue as Susan explained what had happened.

Mabel sat on the edge of the bed, holding Maggie's hand 'I should never have let you go out on your own,' she fretted, 'and you shouldn't have put yourself in such danger.'

'I wasn't on my own - Rose was there most of the time too,' Maggie answered. 'She hadn't long gone when -'

'Rose Johnstone!' Mabel grew suddenly angry, withdrawing her hand from Maggie's. 'I wish you'd never met the lass. Turning your head with all this politics -I blame her for this.'

'You were happy enough with Rose when she helped me with me education and getting a job at Pearson's. It wasn't Rose's fault; it was a pack of drunken men who did it!'

Helen gave an impatient huff, jealous of the attention Maggie was receiving. 'There you go again - it's always men's fault for everything. The truth is you've never liked lads.'

'Oh, you silly lass,' Maggie said in exasperation. 'Can't you see there're more important things in life than tappy-lappying after lads? I do what I do because I want to make things better for all lasses - including the likes of you, Helen, believe it or not.'

Helen pulled a face and Maggie sank back again, feeling nauseous from the effort. But Susan was not going to let the matter lie.

'This suffragette business has got to stop, hasn't it, Mam?' she scolded, still badly shaken by what had happened. 'She could have got herself killed.'

'Let the lassie rest,' Granny Beaton chided gently. 'It's nearly the Sabbath. Words can wait till the morning when tempers have cooled.'

But Susan would not be silenced. 'It needs saying now,' she said in high dudgeon. 'Maggie's got to give up this business before it brings the family down.'

'Aye,' Mabel said with a stem look, rising from the bed, 'our Susan's right.'

Maggie felt her eyes sting with tears. 'I won't give it up, Mam, you can't make me,' she answered in a small, defiant voice.

'Yes, she can,' Susan replied heatedly. 'You'll do as Mam and me tell you as long as you live here.'

'I'm a woman of twenty,' Maggie protested, 'and old enough to make my own decisions.'

'You'll do what's right by the family,' her mother said severely, 'instead of inviting trouble.'

All at once, a memory came back to Maggie. 'I didn't ask for trouble - it was all Richard Turvey's fault, anyway. They were after him, not me.'

Susan gawped at her. 'Richard? What are you talking about?'

'Who was after him?' Mabel demanded.

'Some drunks at the Half Moon. I was more angry at them upsetting Mrs Surtees's peas. But Richard was there, sprawling in the gutter.'

Susan went puce. 'Of all the cheek! Dragging Richard's name into this sordid carry-on! He couldn't have been there anyway, he works Saturday nights. No, you're just saying this 'cos you've taken a dislike to him.'

'Aye,' Helen piped up, 'you're just jealous because he doesn't fancy you.'

'I know what I saw,' Maggie answered in agitation. 'He was being chased for money. He asked me to help him and then they turned on me, because of my sash.'

'You're lying!' Helen shouted. 'Richard's a gentleman.'

'It's the truth!'

'George Gordon said nothing about Richard and he would have recognised him if he'd been there,' Susan said sharply.

'He must have run off.'

'Really, Maggie, how could you say such a thing!' Susan was furious.

Mabel clapped her hands for silence. 'Quiet, the lot of you! I don't give two pins for this story about Richard Turvey. What matters is that Maggie's safely home and come to no harm. Now, Helen, get off to bed this instant and take Tich with you.'

Helen scowled, but her mother looked so angry she did as she was told. Jimmy following mutely behind. Mabel turned back to Maggie, determined to wipe the mutinous expression from her face.

'You may think you know best, Maggie,' she said sternly, 'but you don't know the half of it. I was the same at your age, thought I knew the answer to everything. But at twenty you don't. I know what's best for you and I've had enough of this obsession of yours. The likes of you and me can't change the world, so stop trying.'

'It's not an obsession,' Maggie began to protest, but her mother wasn't listening.

'Family comes first, understand? Your duty is to us. If you ever get into a scrape like this again, then there'll be trouble, because I'll not have you risking your job at Pearson's for any fancy notions about equality or votes for women.'

'But Mam—'

Her mother wagged a finger in warning. 'And I'll not have you mixing with law-breakers any more. You stay away from the likes of Rose Johnstone and those other unnatural creatures that call themselves women, do you hear?'

Maggie stared at her mother, appalled. She'd had no idea her mother was so prejudiced against the movement. When she had first joined the WSPU, Maggie was sure her mother had been proud of her showing an independent spirit and wanting to change things for the better. She had always been pushed to better herself. But perhaps Mabel's interest had been superficial; a shallow pride in her daughter's mixing with women of a different social class. Maggie looked into her mother's tired, dark blue eyes and wondered if she believed in anything any more.

Maggie wanted to shout back that her cause was not a childish whim which could be so easily given up. But she felt weak with shock and achingly tired. Her family's opposition overwhelmed her. She knew it would be impossible to give up her friends and her mission, but she did not have the strength to stand up to her mother tonight.

She sighed in frustration, biting back her words of rebellion, and sank back into the pillow.

That night she slept with Granny Beaton, comforted by the old woman's bony warmth and her lack of censure. She fell asleep to her grandmother's soft Gaelic lullabies, just as she had so many times as a young girl, crying noiselessly for her dead father.

The next morning, she woke stiff but rested and was greeted by her smiling grandmother bringing in a cup of tea.

'Here's a strupach to revive you,' she said, putting down the cup with shaky hands beside the bed. 'You're to stay in bed today, so you are.'

'But I can't,' Maggie said at once, wincing as she sat up. 'I have to see . . .' She stopped before Rose's name was mentioned.

'Whatever it is can wait,' Granny Beaton was firm.

'But it's so important,' Maggie cried weakly. 'I'm not going to lie here when I should be...'

'You know your mother won't let you go out as you please any more,' Granny said quietly.

Maggie turned her head away as tears began to fall.

Granny Beaton leaned across in concern, stroking the dark hair away from

Maggie's pale forehead and bruised eye.

'What is it, lassie?' she asked gently. 'You can tell me, right enough.'

Maggie looked into the old woman's crinkled face, full of a lifetime's suffering and wisdom, the faded brown eyes compassionate. She knew her grandmother was the only member of the family she could trust now, after her mother's reprimand the previous night.

Maggie spoke low. 'There's an important meeting at Rose's this afternoon - special work for me to do. If I don't turn up they might think I'm too afraid to do it, they might offer it to someone else. They mustn't think I don't have the courage.'

'Oh, you've got the courage, right enough,' Granny said fondly, placing her smooth, dry old hands round Maggie's face.

For a long moment they looked at each other in silent understanding and Maggie knew the old lady would support her.

'A life of struggle is a hard one to choose,' Granny said in her soft lilt, 'but if that's the one you've chosen, then may God give you strength.' Then she added with a smile, 'I'll take a message to Miss Johns tone.'

Maggie leant over and kissed her withered cheek. 'I don't want to land you in trouble too.'

'Your mother is not a hard woman at heart,' Granny said, 'she just worries for you. As for me, I'm not afraid of trouble because God has always provided. I'll go after Kirk - Miss Johnstone only lives a few minutes away.'

'Thanks, Granny,' Maggie said hoarsely, overcome by the old woman's gesture, and leaned back on the hard bolster. It was routine for her grandmother to go to her own Presbyterian church while Susan led Helen and Jimmy to the Methodist's on Alison Terrace every Sunday, so no one would suspect if the old woman was a few minutes late. They would just assume the sermon had been a long one. Maggie often accompanied her grandmother to the Kirk in Elswick, more out of habit than conviction, knowing that the old Highland lady liked her company walking to church. She knew where Rose lived because on several occasions they had visited the schoolteacher after guild meetings in the Kirk hall.

Maggie dozed and fretted until Granny Beaton returned at lunchtime. She went over in her mind the terrible events of the previous night as if they were the bizarre happenings of a nightmare. She began to doubt if she had indeed seen Richard at all, for if it had been him, would he not have spoken her name? She wished now she had never mentioned him, for it seemed to have inflamed her sisters and set everyone against her. Even Tich was not speaking to her this morning. It sickened her that they should see her attack as being her own fault.

Then Maggie thought of George Gordon's concerned face staring down at hers in the tram and sent up another thankful prayer that he had intervened on her behalf. He at least had not condemned her.

'Miss Johnstone said you're not to worry,' Granny Beaton managed to whisper to her while Susan and Jimmy set the table for lunch. 'She'll send a message when her visitor calls again.'

Maggie took the old woman's veined hand and kissed it. 'Thank you,' she mouthed, swallowing her disappointment that her meeting with Emily Davison had been thwarted.

To Maggie's distress, the family behaved as if the incident had never happened and never referred to it again. On Monday, Maggie struggled to work, pretending she had fallen downstairs and evading the curious questions of Eve

Tindall and the wary looks of Mary Watson.

That evening, George Gordon called. Maggie felt ridiculously tongue-tied and gauche as she sat across the kitchen table from him. He had changed out of his grimy work clothes and was wearing the faded suit she had seen him in when they had sparred outside the pub on Alison Terrace. She remembered how scornful she had been of him then and blushed now at his awkward attempts at small talk.

'Brought you some oranges,' he said, pushing a bag across the rough scrubbed table top.

'Oranges!' Susan exclaimed 'That's kind of you,' she answered for Maggie. "Oranges are that expensive.'

'Didn't know what else to bring,' George said with an embarrassed shrug.

'No need to bring anything,' Susan said, sweeping the package from the table and emptying the bright fruit into their best bowl, usually kept for nuts at Christmas time. 'But thank you all the same.'

Maggie saw her sister look approvingly at George, her suspicion of his visit subsiding. She bustled over to the stove to replenish the teapot.

George cleared his throat. 'You're looking better,' he said.

Maggie smiled. 'Just a bit stiff, that's all.'

Her mother eyed them over her sewing. 'It could have been a lot worse. We're grateful to you, George.'

'Town's a rough place at night,' George grunted. 'Better to sell your papers in the daytime, I reckon.'

'There'll be no more selling papers at any time of the day.' Mabel was sharp. 'Maggie's to have no more to do with the suffragettes.'

George looked at Maggie in surprise and saw her mouth firm into a stubborn line. Her bruised grey eyes beseeched him.

'I can't see Maggie being put off by a bit of a scuffle,' he found himself saying.

Maggie felt the lethargy of the past two days shaken by his words. She had had enough of bowing to her mother's wishes. 'I'm not put off,' she spoke up defiantly, 'and I'll carry on supporting the cause as long as there's breath in me lungs.'

She heard Susan clatter the kettle behind her in shock. Her mother glared. 'I thought I made it clear to you—'

'Aye, Mam, I know what you want,' Maggie said quickly, 'but I can't stop believing in something just because you say so. It's the most important thing in my life, can't you see that?' she pleaded.

Mabel's face puffed out indignantly. 'And what about your family? Are we to take second place behind your hoity-toity friends?'

'Aye,' Susan agreed, 'you've got above yourself with all this nonsense.'

'It's not like that, Mam,' Maggie insisted, ignoring Susan's sour words. 'I joined the movement because I want to make things better for widows like you, for young lasses like Susan and me, so we can have a better life than our mothers and grandmothers had.' She looked at Granny Beaton for support and saw the old lady nod gently.

'Aye, Mabel,' she intercepted quietly, 'the lassie should be admired for trying to change things. And I don't see that selling a few wee newspapers does any harm to anybody.'

Mabel looked at her mother-in-law with annoyance, irritated that she should once again be taking Maggie's side against her. If she had not been such a support to her in the early months after Alec's death, she would have packed her back to Glasgow years ago. She had been too soft in letting her stay, Mabel realised now.

Maggie saw her give Granny Beaton a dismissive look and turn to George for support.

'You're a man, George Gordon,' Mabel wheezed. 'You talk some sense into this daughter of mine. I shudder to think what her father would have made of all this.'

George shifted uncomfortably on his hard chair, bewildered by the bickering.

'Don't bring me dad into this,' Maggie said hotly. 'You don't know what he would have thought.'

'I know he wouldn't have approved of all this violence and carry-on by women,' her mother huffed. 'You don't hold with these suffragettes, do you, George?'

'George has got nothing to do with our quarrel,' Maggie said defensively, afraid of what he might say.

'Let him speak,' Susan said, refilling his cup. 'It's time we heard a man's opinion around here. It might have curbed your rebellious nature, Maggie, if we'd had a man around these past ten years.'

George met Maggie's stormy look. She was quite different from her fair, plump-faced sister or her querulous mother. Maggie's features were slim and feline, her hair dark and wiry, her eyes angry and restless. Whereas the others seemed to have tired, blighted spirits, Maggie seemed full of a fierce energy. He found it exciting, disturbing. He admired the warrior within her and he knew if he joined the censorious band against her he would lose her respect and the possibility of friendship for ever. All at once, he realised that he minded what she thought of him and yearned for the chance to know her better.

'I think Maggie's naive to think giving women the vote will change things for working-class women,' George began cautiously. Mabel and Susan nodded in approval. 'But I don't think there's anything wrong with a bit of militancy. You can't deny the suffragettes have got guts and I admire them for keeping on at the government, being prepared to be unpopular, suffering in prison for what they believe. There're not many men would do as much, least of all those in power. I think Maggie should be allowed to keep on at her work for the women's movement - long as she avoids the Bigg Market on a Saturday night.'

George stopped, wondering where he'd got the courage to speak up against the opinionated Beaton women. He was not used to arguing with women, nor had he ever expressed such support for the women's cause before. He wondered briefly at his motives for doing so, but the look of surprise and admiration on Maggie's face made it worthwhile.

'You see,' Maggie said quickly, swallowing her shock at George's support, 'not all men are against us. Many are coming round to the opinion that we're right, that we must have justice for all.'

'Well, I must say!' Mabel blustered. 'I didn't know you were one of them, George Gordon, or I would have thought twice about letting you through our door.'

'And I think it's a downright disgrace, encouraging our lass,' Susan said with disapproval, removing his cup swiftly.

George decided it was time to leave. 'Thank you for the tea, Susan,' he said, picking up his cap from the table. 'Mrs Beaton.' He nodded at Maggie's mother and grandmother, noting how the elderly Scotswoman gave a faint smile of amusement as she answered his goodbye.

'I'll see you out,' Maggie said, coming round the table quickly.

In the semi-privacy of the landing, she put out a hand and touched George on the sleeve.

'You could have knocked me down with a feather!' she laughed. 'But ta very much, all the same.'

'Surprised myself,' he grinned back.

Maggie suppressed another laugh. 'I'll have you at one of our rallies yet.'

George took her hand briefly. 'I didn't say I was that won over, Maggie Beaton,' he grunted. After a moment's hesitation, he added, 'But I'd be pleased if I could see you again.'

Maggie's amazement was tinged with a shiver of pleasure at the thought. She could hardly believe that the man she had so recently been at loggerheads with wanted to see her again. Was George Gordon asking to court her? Maggie wondered suspiciously. She had never had the slightest interest in being courted by the lads she knew at work or at church and had always dismissed any tentative overtures. She had determined long ago that courting would only interfere with her work for the movement. She was still hesitant about letting any man come close to her, even though George Gordon had shown himself sympathetic to the cause.

'Maybes,' Maggie answered cautiously. 'I've that many meetings, mind, and meetings come first.'

George gave a short laugh and dropped her hand. 'Maggie Beaton, you're a strange lass.'

He fixed his cap over his cropped hair and said goodnight. As he descended the stairs into the gloom, Maggie felt suddenly deflated.

'Maggie, come in now!' her mother shouted fretfully from the kitchen.

'George,' Maggie called after him impulsively. The tall blacksmith stopped and turned, his strong, lively face accentuated by the thick moustache. All she could think of to say was, 'Thanks for the oranges.'

He nodded and waved and was gone into the street.

Returning to the flat, she faced a barrage of critical comments.

'Well, I've said it before, I always thought the Gordons were a wild lot,' Mabel panted and reached for the glass of beer Susan had fetched from the pantry. 'I can see that George hasn't changed - agreeing with lawbreaking and violence, indeed!'

'Aye,' Susan said. 'It makes you wonder what he was doing among the drunks on Saturday night, doesn't it?'

'Mind, they always had a reputation for being unruly, having no mother around,' Mabel added, smacking her lips on the beer. 'And old Gordon's as rough as they come.'

'Aye,' Susan agreed. 'Irene Gordon's got her hands full looking after that lot.'

Maggie confronted them. 'Hypocrites! You were both nice as ninepence to George Gordon until he stood up for me just now.'

'Hark at you!' Susan retaliated 'You're the one who wanted nothing to do with him until he came out with that fancy speech.'

'Well, I was wrong about him,' Maggie admitted. 'He saved me from a bad beating and I'm grateful to him.'

Her mother slurped her beer, suddenly tired of argument. 'He's gone now and that's an end to the trouble. We'll talk no more about what happened on Saturday, do you hear?'

But the dismissive words only served to goad her second daughter. Maggie's irritation erupted at being continually put down by her mother and elder sister. 'He may be gone now,' she told them, 'but you'll have to get used to seeing

George Gordon around this house.'

Her mother spluttered over her drink and Susan asked sharply, 'What's that supposed to mean?'

'Me and George Gordon are courting,' she announced.

As soon as the words were out, she wished they had not been uttered, but she had been provoked beyond endurance.

They all stared at one another, and Maggie wondered which of the three of them was most shocked.

Then Granny Beaton broke the tense silence. 'Gordon. Aye, it's a good Scots name. And George seems worthy of it - a nice laddie.'

Maggie looked gratefully at her kind grandmother and smiled with relief.

Chapter Seven

For nearly a week, Maggie did nothing, hoping that George would call on her. She felt her family watching and waiting to see if her threat about courting the blacksmith was true. On Wednesday she caught her mother and Susan speculating about it on the back stairs in the sunshine when she came in from work. All week, Helen delighted in dropping sceptical remarks about his lack of appearance and by Friday even Jimmy was asking when George was going to call.

'None of your business, Tich,' Maggie told him testily and strode off to work wondering what she was going to do about the mess she had created.

During the half-hour break at midday, Maggie slipped out of the office, saying she had an errand to run. Emerging from the workshop shed, she picked her way over the rail tracks and out of the gates. The forest of scaffolding that marked out Pearson's shipyard was a good quarter of a mile away and she knew she would have to hurry to get there and back within her short dinner break.

The early summer sun was surprisingly warm and beat down on her dark hat and clothing, increasing her discomfort as she set a brisk pace. There were no trees to offer shade along the bare brick streets and as the yard gates came in sight, Maggie's apprehension grew. She had not been down to the yard since her father had died, though as a girl she had often stood at the gates after school, waiting for his release. What would she do once she got there? She had no idea which of the many vast sheds housed the forge or whether she would be allowed to leave a message for George Gordon.

Her courage failed her. What on earth was she doing chasing after a man anyway? She would rather go home and face her family with the admission that she had made up her story of courting George Gordon in a fit of temper. She would take their teasing, Maggie resolved, turning back, it would be better than making a fool of herself in front of the shipyard workers.

But when Eve Tindall suggested a walk through the park after work, Maggie agreed quickly, keen to delay her return home.

'Mr Tindall can wait another ten minutes for his tea,' Eve told her, sitting down on a bench and patting the wooden slats beside her.

Maggie needed no persuasion to linger in Daniel Park and watch the children playing with their hoops and tops. A game of quoits was going on in the distance and the trees were bursting into a lustrous green. Maggie breathed in the fresh air, thankful to be away from the dust and noise of the workplace.

'So, what's troubling thee?' Eve finally asked her, perched on the bench. Maggie stalled by handing over her untouched dinner to the barefoot children who hovered around them.

'Ta, missus!' they cried and ran off with the stale bread and cheese.

'Nothing's troubling,' Maggie answered.

'Tut! Auntie Eve can tell when something's bothering you, so spill the beans.'

Maggie laughed and allowed herself to be coaxed into telling the story of George Gordon's rescue of her and his subsequent visit.

'But I've decided it's not worth the bother,' Maggie concluded 'I'll just swallow my pride and admit I'm not courting.'

'Nonsense!' Eve answered roundly. 'Sounds to me like this Gordon lad is worth going after.'

'I'm not going after any lad!' Maggie said.

'Don't be so stubborn. It's time you had a bit o' fun in your life, Maggie.

You're too serious by half. But I know there's a spark of devilment in your nature; I've seen it now and then. You go and find George Gordon. I doubt he needs much encouragement.'

'And then what do I do?' Maggie laughed. 'Take him to a branch meeting?'

'Course not! Ask him back for tea like any normal lass would.'

'Into the lion's den, you mean?'

'Well, if he survives an evening with your family, nowt will put him off.' Eve gave Maggie's arm a squeeze.

'How do I find him?' Maggie asked 'I'll not go hunting for him among the pit cottages up Benwell.'

'You said he's a rower,' Eve pointed out. 'Well, go to the club and see him there. Now I must be off and get the tea on.'

Maggie wrestled with the idea all the way home. Only when she turned into the lane and spotted Jimmy kicking stones around in boredom did she decide what to do.

'Want to earn a tanner, Tich?' she asked her skinny brother. He nodded eagerly as she knew he would. All his life, Jimmy had run errands for them and been at his sisters' beck and call. It never seemed to occur to him to say no, or perhaps he knew his life would not be worth living if he did. It was hard to think of him as fifteen when he looked no more than twelve and still wore short trousers. His mother had promised him long breeches as soon as he found a full-time job and stopped playing around the streets with the younger boys. But Jimmy seemed content to sell the odd bundle of firewood and fritter away the rest of the day acting cowboys and Indians with Tommy Smith or sneaking into the picture halls for free.

'Come with me after tea to Pearson's rowing club,' Maggie told him.

Jimmy agreed eagerly. 'Can Tommy come an' all?'

Maggie hesitated. Her brother might be more likely to carry out her plan if his thirteen-year-old friend were there to back him up. 'Aye, if he wants to - but not a word about this to anyone. Tell Tommy-to keep his gob shut and I'll give him summat too.'

Maggie tried to ignore the excited look on her brother's face all through tea, sure that Susan would notice and ask the reason.

'Where you going?' Mabel demanded later as Maggie made for the door with her hat on.

'Me and Tich are going down the riverside to look for firewood,' she answered casually. 'It's too nice to stop indoors all evening.'

Her mother looked at Jimmy and he smiled back innocently.

'Be back before it's dark, mind,' Mabel instructed and waved them away.

Jimmy and Tommy hurried beside Maggie, attempting to keep up with her brisk pace.

'Can we go on the tram, Maggie?' Jimmy asked.

'Not if you want paying.'

'What are we going to do at the rowing club?' Tommy questioned, excited to be out of his mother's way for the evening. Maggie knew her mother would use the opportunity of Mrs Smith being on her own to go downstairs for a jar with her.

'You're going to look for firewood,' Maggie told them.

'But that's what you told Mam we were going to do,' Jimmy said in disappointment. 'I thought it was some secret mission for your women's thing - spying or getting a message to someone. It must be summat like that, our Maggie?' He had always admired his rebellious sister for standing up to the family and showing the courage he lacked. Their bullying mother never got the better of Maggie, Jimmy thought, and he would do anything his sister asked of him.

Maggie smiled at her brother's imagination. Well, if that would make the expedition more enjoyable for him, she would play along.

'It is,' she whispered, 'a very special mission. That's why I could trust only you and Tommy.'

'Eeh, will we get into real bother with Mam if she finds out?' Jimmy gasped.

Maggie groaned inwardly to think Jimmy might run off home for fear of their mother.

'She's not going to find out unless you tell her,' Maggie answered severely, 'so you mustn't breathe a word of this to anyone.'

He still looked at her dubiously. 'Not even our Susan?'

'Especially not Susan,' Maggie said sternly. 'Listen, Tich, others are depending on you and Tommy - you're my cover, so that no one gets suspicious. But if you're too scared...'

'Course we're not,' Jimmy answered indignantly. 'We'll do owt you ask us, eh, Tommy?'

'Why-aye!' Tommy agreed and began to whoop with excitement while Jimmy spun imaginary pistols in the air.

'Tell us what it's for,' Jimmy pressed. 'Are you going to blow up the rowing club?'

'No!' Maggie cried.

'Sink one of Pearson's boats?' Tommy asked eagerly.

'No. Now stop making wild guesses,' Maggie said, trying to keep a straight face. 'You have to go and find George Gordon,' she added quickly, 'and tell him I have a message.'

'George Gordon?' Jimmy repeated in surprise. 'Is he mixed up in this too? So Mam was right in saying he's a dangerous radical.'

'Enough said.' Maggie brought a stop to speculation before Jimmy's imagination ran riot. She made them talk of other things until they reached the bank of the Tyne near Scotswood, by which time her heart was hammering. She scribbled a message on the back of a suffragette leaflet, folded it and handed it over to Jimmy.

At first they could find no one down at Pearson's landing, then Jimmy spotted a boat approaching, its oars dipping and splashing rhythmically in the iridescent water. Maggie recognised George's bulky arms before she saw his face. She quelled her impulse to run away and sent the boys down to meet the crew.

'That's him with the black moustache,' Maggie told her brother. 'Ask him to come up and meet me at the tram standard. When you've given him the message, go and look for driftwood until I fetch you.'

'This isn't just a love note, is it?' Jimmy asked, suddenly suspicious. He held the folded leaflet between two fingers as if it might be contaminated.

'Course not,' Maggie answered with a blush.

'That's all right then,' Jimmy smiled and rushed down the bank with his friend following and making whooping noises.

'Pair of daft lads,' Maggie laughed aloud, shaking her head and wondering what had possessed her to come. 'If he refuses me, Eve Tindall, I'll have your guts for garters!'

She waited for what seemed ages at the top of the bank, just out of sight of the boat club. A tram stopped and waited for her to get on, and she waved it away in embarrassment. No one appeared. A second tram came into sight and Maggie was contemplating jumping on it when a voice made her start.

'This is all very secretive, Maggie Beaton.'

She spun round to see George Gordon standing behind her, a faded towel round his bullish neck which still glistened with the sweat of exertion.

'Aye, I'm sorry.' She flushed. 'Our Tich thinks it's some mission for the movement - it's difficult to get away on me own and I didn't know where you lived and I wanted a word, just a favour really. I won't blame you if the answer's no, but I've got myself into a spot of bother with the family.'

'Doesn't surprise me with that lot,' George grunted, folding his arms and watching her, intrigued.

'You see, they don't approve of you since you stood up for me and the movement.'

'I'm flattered,' George laughed.

But Maggie ploughed on, frightened of losing her nerve with him. 'Well, after what you'd done for me, I got mad with Mam and our Susan and I, er, I said - that we were courtin' - just to get me own back at them like. Now they're expecting you to call. So I was wondering if you would accept an invitation to come to tea at our house - Saturday. We could just pretend ...' Maggie's words dried on her lips as she looked up and saw the amusement on George's ruddy face.

'Saturday? Tomorrow?' he asked, pulling on his moustache.

'Aye.'

'Pretend we're courting?'

'Aye,' Maggie whispered, her cheeks on fire. 'I can see now it was a daft idea. Perhaps you could forget what I've just said.' She moved as if to go.

'Hold on, lass,' George answered, putting out a hand to stop her. 'I think it's one of your better ideas, if you want my opinion.'

'Do you?' Maggie looked at him cautiously.

'Well, if it's just pretend, and just for Saturday, I think I could help you out. Just for a favour.'

'Ta,' Maggie gulped, then saw that he was laughing. 'Don't mock me, George Gordon,' she said, lifting her chin. 'I'll not be made fun of.'

'Don't take yourself so seriously, bonny lass,' George grinned, offering her his arm. 'Haway, if we're courting, I can't leave you hanging about a tram standard on your own. Let's go and find Buffalo Bill and his mate.'

Maggie smiled but did not take his arm. They found the boys exploring the shoreline, filling their pockets with a treasure of stones and glass and the detritus of the tide. Maggie felt an unexpected contentment, watching their absorbed play as the sun went down in a smudge of orange beyond the chimneys of the power station.

'They're supposed to be collecting firewood,' Maggie chuckled.

'Leave them be,' George said. 'They're happy as pig in muck. I was the same as a lad - a right little jackdaw. Our Irene would go mad at the rubbish I brought home.'

'But Tich is fifteen now, yet he's still such a bairn.'

'He'll grow up in his own time,' George replied. He turned and looked at Maggie. "Want to walk?'

'Where?'

'Up the hill – Hibbs' Farm,' George suggested.

'The boys ...'

'Won't notice we've gone,' George said, guiding her by the arm. 'I'll show you where I used to play as a bairn.'

'I thought you Gordons just terrorised the school yard,' Maggie laughed.

'No more than the Beatons,' George grinned and led her along the towpath.

He helped her scramble over gates and rickety fences until they reached the edge of Hibbs' meadows and his grazing milk cows. Maggie was amazed at its peacefulness and seclusion so near the grime and smoke of the town. From here, the river looked like a bronze snake in the dying sun, coiling among the hazy rows of houses and silent chimneys. It was so quiet that she could hear the munching of the cows in the long grass and a bird's evensong. Over towards Benwell village, washing hung limp like huge sails becalmed in the soft evening air.

George pointed out landmarks on the Durham side of the river.

'Sixty years ago there'd have been countryside all around here, just farms and little villages and small pits. And the Pearsons were just modest property owners and engineers. Even the river was a different shape - there used to be an island down there, midstream. It was dredged to allow the big ships to be built this far upriver.'

'How do you know so much about the area?' Maggie asked in surprise, watching a laundress gather in the bleached sheets in a distant field.

'Have an interest in history, I suppose,' George said with an embarrassed shrug.

Maggie was intrigued. 'Tell me more, George. I've lived here all me life, yet the only history I know is about kings and queens and boring battles.'

They squatted down in the grass, George picking a strand to chew between his teeth. He told her of old Newcastle with its bustling port and merchants and how industry had spread along the banks of the Tyne with the coming of the railways, deep mining and the inventiveness of engineers like Pearson and Armstrong.

'But all the prosperity counts for nothing if the working man doesn't have a share in it,' George concluded.

'Or the working woman,' Maggie added.

They looked at each other and laughed. 'Or the working woman,' George conceded. 'But don't tell my comrades I said so.'

'I'll make a suffragette out of you yet, George Gordon,' Maggie teased, nudging his arm.

He looked at her slim face under the large battered hat of crushed fake flowers. Gone were the usual frown lines between her blue-grey eyes and her pale full lips were relaxed. Her arms were roped round her green-skirted knees, revealing slim ankles above her worn shoes. If she had sat still and content for a moment longer, George knew he would have bent over and kissed her, but she seemed to catch the intention in his eyes and leapt to her feet.

'Must get off and find our Jimmy,' she said, turning from him and brushing the pollen from her skirt.

She had suddenly become aware of how close they were sitting and of the salty male smell of George, still in his rowing clothes. It made her uneasy. She had no idea how she should behave with a man she was barely courting, but she was sure she should not be sitting alone with him in a darkening field. It had been all right while they had talked of history and commerce, but now in the silence the atmosphere between them had subtly shifted to an intimate and unpredictable mood.

She led the way purposefully back to the riverbank and found the boys building a campfire on a pocket of derelict land. They both looked at Maggie with scepticism as if they realised there had been no special mission. But any disgruntled comments were silenced by the money that Maggie quickly gave them. Cajoled away from the fire, they walked with George to the end of Gun Street.

Tomorrow then,' he said in parting.

'Aye, tomorrow,' Maggie smiled under the light of the gas lamp, then bustled the boys home.

Alice Pearson stepped out of her open-topped motorcar onto the pale gravel drive of Oxford Hall. She dreaded these quarterly visits to her parents' country retreat. It was set amid the rolling hills of the upper Tyne valley among heather moors and lush woods, but the sprawling stone mansion with its bizarre Byzantine turrets guarded by stone griffins was, to Alice, a monstrosity. Unlike her beloved Hebron House, blackened by Newcastle's smoke, the walls of Oxford Hall gave off a glare as if still new after fifteen years. The gardens that spilled away from the terraces were stuffed with gaudy flowers and shrubs, while the ornamental trees were still immature and spindly, betraying themselves as intruders among the long resident birches and ancient elms. The very name Oxford Hall was pretentious to Alice, as the family had no link with the southern town, except that her brother Herbert had failed to get into the university there.

'Alice!'

Alice turned to see her sister-in-law Felicity waving to her from the tennis court. She did not recognise the young woman opponent but guessed it must be one of Felicity's many friends who came to stay and relieve the boredom of country life. Alice waved back. She liked Felicity for her intelligence and wit and felt sorry for her being married to her dull and feckless brother. Yet there was uneasiness between them, Alice always sensing Felicity's resentment at being controlled and hemmed in by the powerful Pearsons. Felicity cared nothing for the family firm but when she showed her uninterest openly, Alice's sympathy for her was strained.

She strode over to the tennis court and Felicity met her, kissing her cheek.

'Glad to see you. Herbert's out shooting rabbits or whatever you're allowed to kill in May. This is my friend Poppy. We were at school together.'

Alice shook hands with an attractive woman, all of her height but slim as a willow in her tennis skirt and blouse. She had intelligent brown eyes and a dusting of unfashionable freckles that spoke of hours spent outside.

'Tish has told me all about you,' Poppy said in a warm, husky voice. 'I'm full of admiration. I just wouldn't have the courage to do the things you do.'

Alice found herself blushing. 'I've done very little really, just lent my name to the cause.'

'Rubbish!' Felicity broke in. 'Herbert's got permanent collywobbles wondering what you're going to do next.' She took Alice by the arm. 'And I'd watch out this visit, he's got a bee in his bonnet about the launch of some boat - thinks you're likely to scupper it.'

'HMS *Courageous*!' Alice laughed. 'Well, he shouldn't go putting ideas into my head, should he?'

'Let's have tea in the summerhouse like children,' Felicity suggested, pushing back strands of wispy blonde hair. 'Your mother's gone to Newcastle shopping and your father's keeping an eye on Herbert - making sure he doesn't massacre the estate tenants by mistake.'

Poppy laughed reprovingly. 'Really, Tish, you're very hard on poor old

Herbert. I'm sure he's not such a bad shot.'

'He's worse than bad; he's a complete liability because he thinks he's good. If we ever go to war with the Boer again, I hope they don't give him a commission.'

They were halfway across the terrace when Poppy said, 'The next war is more likely to be on our doorstep - the Balkans are at each other's throats and the Germans are starting an arms race.'

'Oh, don't be so pessimistic,' Felicity chided.

'I'm so immersed in what's happening here, I don't really take much notice of what's happening on the Continent,' Alice admitted.

'Nothing new,' Felicity said breezily. 'Belligerent Balkans and tired Turks slugging it out. All too far away to bother about, I say.'

'But you don't agree?' Alice asked Poppy. Alice noticed a brief exchange of looks between Felicity and her friend.

'My husband's in the Foreign Office,' Poppy answered. 'He's worried we'll be drawn into a European war.'

'Oh, what does stuffy old Beresford know about Europe?' Felicity cried. 'He won't even let you go over the Channel on holiday.'

'Beresford,' Alice queried, 'is your husband?'

'Yes,' Poppy laughed 'Tish never calls him by his Christian name, John. They've never got on.'

'Stop talking about Beresford,' Felicity ordered, dragging them both forward by the arms. 'It's picnic tea, then swim in the river.'

'Swim?' Alice protested. 'But I've nothing to put on.'

'Who cares?' Felicity cried. 'There's no one around here to see, and no Herbert to huff and puff about our lack of modesty. Come on, girls!'

Alice allowed herself to be propelled across the terrace, knowing that it was useless to argue with her sister-in-law once she had made up her mind.

Tea was ordered and Alice insisted on changing out of her driving suit into a cooler blouse and skirt, while the other women stayed in their tennis wear. Alice was delighted by Felicity's rebellion against changing into formal tea gowns and taking tea inside as her mother would have insisted had she not been away for the day. As an afterthought, Alice fetched her camera and tripod and took photographs of Felicity and Poppy sitting casually on the steps of the summerhouse, tucking into large slices of rich chocolate cake, and later, of the two friends lounging back under the cherry blossom, chatting and unconcerned by the lens that studied them.

Eventually Felicity grew irritated.

'For goodness sake come out from under, that wretched cloak of yours and speak to us. It's like trying to converse with a headless highwayman.'

Alice emerged from under the tripod curtain, laughing.

'I hope you'll give me one of your photographs to keep,' Poppy said. 'I always have such happy times at Oxford Hall.'

This surprised Alice who viewed a week with her family as purgatory, being criticised by her mother and whined at by her brother Herbert. Her father was her only ally. On duty visits to Oxford Hall, Alice spent as much time as possible on her photography and keeping out of the way.

'You can have as many as you like,' Alice answered.

'Now for our swim!' Felicity said, jumping to her feet. 'Race you, Poppy.'

The two young women took off with shrieks of laughter in the direction of the river. As they disappeared through the trees, Alice decided to abandon her camera and follow before she lost them. The undergrowth was fresh and emerald green, with new briars creeping across the old path and a tide of bluebells washing around gnarled tree trunks. She caught a glimpse of white tennis skirts through the foliage and slowed her pace. If she lingered long enough perhaps she would not have to bathe with them. Alice hated cold water and felt rather prudish about discarding her clothes in front of anybody, even her uninhibited sister-in-law.

Picking at some wild garlic, she meandered among the bluebells until she heard the splash of water and a scream of shocked delight. By the time she emerged into the small clearing above the river pool, both women were kicking around in the clear icy water, whooping with delight. Alice was scandalised to see they had completely shed their clothing and had not even left on a chemise for modesty's sake. Then she thought of how outraged her mother would be to see such behaviour and started to laugh.

'Come on, Alice!' Felicity shouted. 'Strip off and join us. We won't look!' The two swimmers giggled and splashed at each other.

Suddenly Alice felt an intruder. It made her uncomfortable.

'I think I'll just go and gather up my equipment,' she shouted back. 'It looks far too cold for me. I'll see you before dinner and after a hot bath.'

'Coward!' Felicity called and waved her away.

As Alice retreated she could hear their laughter and chatter echo round the natural enclosure. She retraced her steps through the bluebells, trying to work out why she had felt so perturbed by the scene at the pool. It was more than just embarrassment at the sight of their naked white flesh shimmering under the clear water. They had seemed so intimate and at ease with each other, Alice was sure they must have swum naked together before. She shrugged. Old school friends often displayed an embarrassing familiarity which she, having never been sent away to school, could not comprehend. Perhaps it was akin to the strong sisterhood felt by some suffragettes, the ones who had suffered together in prison. She, on the other hand, had never felt really close to anyone. She was an observer, happiest looking on rather than fully participating in anything.

She collected her camera and tripod, noticing that the tea things had already been cleared away. What gossip would the servants carry back with the empty teacups? Alice wondered wryly.

Regaining the terrace, she saw a footman struggling up the front steps with a pile of packages from the Bentley and knew that her mother had returned.

'Darling girl!' Alice heard the shriek from halfway up the wide sweep of stairs. 'You shouldn't be out in the sun without a hat or parasol. And what on earth are you wearing? You look like a governess. Come and kiss me.'

Alice did as she was bidden, brushing the flushed powdered cheek that was offered her.

'You've had an enjoyable outing, Mama?' she asked dutifully, feeling a child again as she always did in her mother's presence, despite her thirty-six years.

'Thankful to be out of the city,' Lady Arabella groaned. 'All that smoke and smell - one quite forgets. I don't know how you bear it You'd be much healthier living here with us. You've the complexion of a shopgirl.'

Alice smiled and shifted the tripod under her arm, refusing to be drawn by her mother's familiar jibe. It was tediously predictable that the older woman would spend the next few days bemoaning Alice's wish to live in Newcastle rather than attend to her every wish like a dutiful spinster daughter should.

'You will be staying for the ball this year, won't you, Alice?' Lady Arabella demanded. 'And you'll not sneak off in the middle to take photographs of the servants like the time before? Herbert was furious for weeks after you'd gone and it's always me who has to calm him down, Felicity's absolutely no use. Where is she anyway?'

'In the garden with Poppy Beresford,' Alice answered vaguely. 'And no, I won't be staying for the ball, I have meetings to attend.'

Her mother huffed. 'Really, Alice, you're a law unto yourself. I don't know why we put up with your waywardness. Herbert will be most put out if you don't stay.'

'No he won't, Mama,' Alice answered calmly. 'I only embarrass him with my lack of dancing skills.'

'It might be your last chance...' Arabella looked crossly at her daughter from under her vast hat of silk roses.

Alice knew her mother was referring to her prospects of marriage which had wilted like hothouse blooms many seasons ago, to Alice's relief. But her mother would never give up trying to match her to the decreasing store of eligible bachelors who attended their summer house parties. It was a constant source of vexation that she had once turned down the offer of marriage from the younger son of the Marquess of Lynemouth.

Alice knew that once out of her mother's sight she was largely out of mind and so kept her visits short and infrequent. By entertaining business envoys for her father, Lord Pearson, at Hebron House she secured an ally against her censorious mother. Alice found she enjoyed entertaining foreign dignitaries from China and Turkey and learning about the family business, a far more enjoyable fate than being the wife of a petty coal-owner whose main conversation was horse racing.

'I need to prepare next week for Papa's visitors from Venezuela,' Alice answered sweetly, knowing her mother would raise no objection to this excuse to miss the Oxford Hall ball.

Her mother's pretty blue eyes narrowed in annoyance.

'Go and change for dinner,' she ordered. 'You look such a sight. And try and be civil to Herbert for one evening. I'll not have you upsetting him with any talk of votes for women. You know Asquith is a personal friend of his.'

'Yes, Mama,' Alice said, keeping her temper.

'And that the Prime Minister will be attending the launch of HMS Courageous? her mother went on. 'It's very important for Herbert, now he's considering going into politics.'

Alice stopped very still. Neither her father nor brother had said that Asquith would be at the launch of Pearson's most prestigious and modern battleship, but her mother was incapable of being discreet.

'You did know, didn't you?' Arabella asked, suddenly wary.

'Of course,' Alice smiled.

'You've got that look on your face,' her mother said in a panic. 'You didn't know Asquith was coming here to stay. Now, Alice, I absolutely forbid you to do anything rash. It's Herbert's future. If you spoil anything, I'll have you cut off without a penny.'

'For heaven's sake, Mama,' Alice said impatiently, 'why should I want to do anything that'll harm Papa's business?'

Just at that moment there was a squeal from the landing above and Herbert and Felicity's four-year-old son, Henry, came bumping down the stairs on his stomach. His distracted nanny came rushing after him with fretful words.

'Henry darling!' Arabella cried indulgently. But the boy ignored her proffered cheek and flung himself at Alice.

'Take a photo of me, Aunt Alice. Take it now!'

Alice regained her balance and steadied the bumptious boy, glad for once of his lack of politeness.

'Come outside then, Henry,' she agreed. 'I'll take you by my car if you like.'

The boy hopped in excitement. 'Can I go on it and pretend I'm driving?'

'All right,' Alice agreed, ignoring the protest from her mother and the scowls from Henry's nanny.

The boy clung to her skirt and jumped down the remaining steps in twos, unwittingly helping Alice to escape her mother.

Later, after Henry had tired of photography and been chased back to the nursery, Alice lay soaking in a huge china bath and considered her dilemma.

The launch of the battleship in July and the visit of their adversary, Prime Minister Asquith, would be a golden opportunity for the Tyneside suffragettes to strike at the man who was proving their greatest obstacle to emancipation. And yet...

Alice lay in the warm steam and agonised.

She was afraid of letting events get out of control. It was fine while she felt she had influence over the militants like Emily Davison, choosing what were suitable targets for protest. But to sabotage her father's business? No, she could not allow it, even if it did mean missing the opportunity of harassing and embarrassing Asquith.

Then a memory came into her mind and filled her with unease. Recently, at Hebron House, Emily Davison had urged that they try out the working-class girl from Elswick who had shown such disappointment at not being considered for the Derby Day protest.

'The girl has spirit,' Emily had insisted. 'She was set upon the other night for selling newspapers and her mother's refusing to let her continue. It's time the movement harnessed her commitment before she gets discouraged or goes off and gets married.'

Alice had been unsure. 'She's not much use to us if she won't defy her mother. Besides, this incident may have frightened her off,' she said. 'It's no fun being roughed up and we get so few working-class girls who can stick at it. They have no ambition beyond marriage and spawning a dozen children.'

'They have greater opposition at home to deal with than we do, and no private means,' Emily replied stoutly. 'You mustn't let your prejudice against working women spoil Maggie Beaton's chance to prove herself.'

Alice had been stung by the reproof and began to protest she had no such prejudice, but Emily was already continuing with enthusiasm. 'We need to give her a mission - a touchpaper to light her fighting spirit.'

Alice thought of the small dark-haired girl now. All she remembered was a pasty, undernourished girl, like so many of those from the West End. Yet her eyes had been fierce and her look insubordinate and she had not been afraid to speak out in front of her social superiors, Alice remembered.

She was suddenly afraid that Emily might have the Beaton girl in mind for some sort of demonstration at the launch of HMS Courageous. She would have to scotch any such idea and keep an eye on Maggie Beaton. She was confident she could easily control the unsophisticated girl. And as for Emily, Alice thought with satisfaction, she would soon be off to Epsom.

Chapter Eight

Maggie busied herself resetting the tea table in the front room, annoyed at how nervous she felt at George Gordon's impending arrival. She might have been more composed had Susan not thought to invite Aunt Violet and Uncle Barny round too, which meant that Richard Turvey would also be present. Maggie was sure Susan had done so because she resented her courting. She has no reason to be jealous, Maggie thought; she only looked upon George as a friend. Marriage was out of the question. As for Susan, Maggie felt sure her sister would soon get her wish for a husband and home of her own. If only the wretched Richard would notice how much he meant to her, they might all have more peace around the house.

'Don't touch the table!' Susan flicked a cloth at her sister. 'It's just how it should be.'

'I was only trying to help,' Maggie replied, dropping a spoon.

'Well, don't,' Susan snapped, bending to pick it up.

The flat was stuffy from the heat of the two fires and Susan's mammoth afternoon baking. Maggie looked at her red-faced and irritable sister and realised how tired she must be. She took the spoon from Susan's hand and said, 'I'll brew the tea. You go and have five minutes' lie down. You look all done in.'

Susan looked about to protest, then acquiesced. 'Maybes just for a minute. You'll not let Helen or Tich near the baking, mind?'

'I'll guard the scones with me life.' Maggie pushed her sister from the room.

For a brief peaceful ten minutes, Maggie sat in companionable silence with her grandmother at the open kitchen door while the old woman read her Bible. Maggie watched a sparrow flitting around the wash-house roof and disappear under its eaves. Then her mother and Helen burst in the front door with a blanket full of clothes, with Jimmy on their heels complaining he was hungry.

Helen dashed away to try on a new acquisition from a Jesmond patron, disturbing Susan who emerged bleary-eyed and crosser than before. Maggie was almost relieved when her aunt and uncle appeared.

'Where's Richard?' Helen demanded, preening in her green and yellow dress with an extravagantly lacy collar.

'He's coming later - work to attend to,' Aunt Violet said with a sniff. 'You look dressed for the mayor's ball, not Saturday tea.' She gave Helen a disapproving look. 'Mabel, you spoil that lass something rotten.'

'Fancy, isn't it?' Helen replied, unabashed.

'Mabel, she's too young to be dressed up like that.'

'Leave the lass be,' Mabel sighed, flopping into a chair.

'Mam, you're that tired,' Susan fussed, 'put your feet up. Aunt Violet, you don't mind giving me a hand, do you? Uncle Barny, you go on in the parlour and have a seat.'

'A glass to wet the whistle would be canny,' Barny grinned, hobbling into the front room.

'Grand idea,' Mabel agreed with her brother, ignoring Violet's tuttings.

Susan dispatched Jimmy to the Gunners with an empty jug.

At six o'clock, George Gordon arrived. Susan eyed him with suspicion, Violet and Helen with curiosity.

'Come in, George,' Mabel waved. 'We don't bite.'

'Evening, Mrs Beaton,' George smiled cautiously, removing his cap. An awkward silence settled on the room. Helen continued to gawp.

Violet suddenly spoke. 'Aye, Gordons of Benwell? I know the family - always trouble. Were you the one I threw out the baccy shop for stealing Woodbines?'

Maggie was about to protest when George answered, 'I've never smoked. You must be thinking of Joshua - he's partial to Woodbines.'

Violet clicked her tongue and Susan continued to make tea as if he were not there.

Take him in the parlour, Maggie,' Mabel ordered. 'Show him we Beatons have manners.'

Maggie led the way, trying to cover her nervousness with talk. 'Come and meet Uncle Barny and let him tell you about the siege of Lichtenburg - it's his favourite story. He was with the Fusiliers - lost a leg.'

'Am I ganin' to tell the story or are you?' Barny asked, looking eagerly at the newcomer. 'Sit yoursel' doon, lad, but mind me leg.'

Barny immediately launched into reminiscing, but within minutes George had the old soldier spluttering over his clay pipe.

'What do you mean you've sympathy for the Boer?' Barny demanded. 'They shot me bloody leg off.'

'You were the victim of British imperial aggression,' George continued, oblivious of Maggie's frantic signals to change the subject. 'What business do we have snatching large chunks of Africa from the African any road?'

'We're there to civilise them, of course,' Barny answered, bewildered.

'Herding Boer women and children into diseased camps is civilised, is it?' George was scathing.

'They started the war!' Barny blustered.

'Perhaps you'd like a cup of tea, George?' Maggie asked desperately.

'Anything stronger?' George grinned.

'Jimmy's fetchin' wallop,' Barny growled, 'and by lad I'll be needin' it if I've to listen to any more from this bugger.'

That only encouraged George. 'Haway, man! We're in Africa to steal minerals and use the African as cheap labour. Our ruling classes are good at that - exploiting labour. They've done it here for long enough.'

'Better to have us rule over heathens than leave them to the Germans or Frenchies,' Barny shouted, waving excitedly through his pipe smoke.

'It's all the same, man,' George said, leaning forward. 'The ruling classes all over Europe are scrapping for more land. It makes no difference to the working man. What we need to do is unite with our comrades in other countries and fight for our rights.'

'You mean with Frenchies and the like?' Barny exclaimed, his eyes popping.

'Aye, wherever workers are being exploited, 'George nodded. 'Strength in unity.'

'That's bloody treason. I'll have nowt to do with Frenchies. We beat them at Waterloo - the Fighting Fifth, Wellington called us, my old regiment.'

'That was a hundred years ago,' George said, shaking his head in disbelief.

'Makes nee difference!' Barny shouted, then went into a coughing fit.

Maggie rushed forward and slapped her uncle on the back.

'Are you all right, Uncle Barny? I'll get you a drink of water.' She threw George a severe look. 'Could you not keep your speeches till after tea, George Gordon?'

George flushed and got to his feet. Seeing Jimmy peering in at the door with the jug, he beckoned the boy over.

'Pour your uncle a glass quickly, lad,' he instructed and handed the glass to Barny himself. 'Get that down your neck, Mr Dodds. It'll do you more good than water.'

Barny seized the glass and drained it, belching hard as he finished.

'Frenchies indeed,' he muttered. 'Another one, Gordon!' he ordered, holding the glass out to George.

George obliged, grunting, 'At least it's stopped your imperialist ranting for a minute.'

Barny's bleary round eyes bulged in astonishment and Maggie thought he was about to take another fit. Instead he started to chuckle.

'By, he's a blunt bugger, your George,' Barny said to Maggie. 'You might just survive around here, son,' he laughed and jabbed George playfully with his cork leg. 'Maggie, get George a glass and we'll get stuck into this here jug while I tell him what's what.'

Maggie did so without protest, thankful that George had so far escaped being thrown out of the house. The men continued their argument and Maggie could not remember seeing her uncle so animated for years. Usually he slouched in an amiable half-inebriated state, burbling about past glories and being ignored.

Tea was served by a fraught Susan who kept eyeing the clock on the mantelpiece and glancing towards the door. George drew Mabel's approval by paying for another jug of beer, which Jimmy volunteered to fetch for him. He came back with the foaming jug and plump Tommy Smith, which set Maggie praying that they would say nothing about the encounter at the rowing club.

Barny was in such good humour by the end of tea that he produced his fiddle and they pushed back the furniture to dance. Halfway through the second dance, Susan rushed from the parlour at the sound of heavy steps on the back stairs.

'It's Richard!' she cried in relief. 'Where have you been?'

'Started the party without me, I see,' he teased and staggered .in clutching a large wooden box.

'What is it?' Helen demanded. The women crowded around him in curiosity.

'A gramophone,' Richard announced with a flourish of his hands. 'Bought it today - just for my special girls.' He winked at Helen and put a familiar arm round Susan's shoulders.

'For us?' Susan gasped. 'It must have cost a packet.'

'A gramophone - look, Mam!' Helen squealed 'Does it play anything?'

Richard opened the lid and produced a record from its sleeve. 'A bit of ragtime, eh, girls?'

Helen clapped her hands together in excitement, though Susan looked apprehensively at her mother and aunt.

They all watched, spellbound, as Richard placed the record on the gramophone and wound it up with a golden handle. It crackled and hissed and then the pulsating piano music filled the room. The older women looked quite dumbfounded, Granny Beaton removing her ear trumpet in fright.

Richard caught Helen round the waist and swirled her into a polka. She threw back her fair ringlets and giggled with joy. Maggie caught Susan's pained look and felt vexed with Richard. He was toying with both her sisters and turning them against each other in the process. Glancing at George, she saw him fixed in his seat with the boys at his feet, looking unimpressed by Richard's extravagant gift. Without thinking, Maggie stepped forward, pulling Helen away from Richard.

'You dance with me,' she ordered her sister. 'Richard, it's Susan you should be showing how to polka.'

'Aye, that's right,' Aunt Violet sniffed.

Maggie ignored Helen's petulant face, giving the hesitant Susan an encouraging nod. With relief, Maggie saw her mother push Susan forward.

'Gan on, hinny, dance with Richard,' she wheezed, her face flushed with beer and bonhomie. 'And you keep your eyes off our Helen,' she told the Londoner in her forthright manner. 'She's too young for courtin'.'

And so Richard had little choice but to dance with Susan, which he did with a good grace, Maggie noticed. For the rest of the evening it was Susan who had his attention and they played and replayed the one record until a curious Mary Smith appeared from downstairs looking for her son. At this point, Violet said it was time to get Barny home.

'I'll walk with you up the hill,' George offered at once. Maggie knew he thought nothing of Richard Turvey or his flashy music machine. The two men had ignored each other all evening. She regretted that there had been no opportunity to dance with George to her uncle's fiddle music which had got George's feet tapping before Richard's dramatic entrance.

'Perhaps you'd like to gan for a walk tomorrow afternoon?' George asked Maggie quietly at the door.

'Aye, that would be canny,' Maggie answered at once. There had been no word from Rose yet of a further meeting with Emily Davison, so what harm was there in spending an hour in George Gordon's company?

When he had gone, Maggie felt suddenly tired and was thankful when her grandmother shooed the others out of the parlour, saying she was needing her bed. She brushed the old woman's hair and helped her climb onto the high bedstead, tucking her in.

Granny Beaton touched Maggie softly on the cheek. 'You're well matched, you and the Gordon boy.'

Maggie blushed furiously. 'Granny! We're hardly courting.'

Her grandmother smiled. 'You both have strong beliefs and you're not afraid to speak your mind.'

'Aye,' Maggie laughed. 'He's just as good at upsetting me family as I am.'

Granny Beaton patted her chin like a child. 'That's as maybe. But he's a kind man too - he knew your uncle needed a good blether. Aye,' the old woman sighed wistfully, 'I'm thinking your father would have liked him.'

'Me Da?' Maggie whispered. She so rarely allowed herself to think of her dead father that it came as a sharp pain to be reminded of him now. It was a bitter-sweet thought that George and her father might have been friends.

'Aye, lassie,' Granny nodded and Maggie saw her milky half-blind eyes water. 'He was a man of principles too, right enough.'

Maggie leaned forward, swiftly kissing the old woman, and hurried from the room.

'I blame you, Alice!' Herbert berated his elder sister. 'Felicity won't listen to a word I say any more. You've filled her head full of nonsense about the rights of women and now she just does as she damn well pleases.'

They sat in his study drinking brandy while the sound of laughter from the terrace made Alice impatient to be released. She found these lectures from Herbert so tedious and wondered why she allowed herself to be bullied into his private den. It was hardly a study, Alice thought, glancing once more at the modest bookcase of unread books. Most of the walls were covered in antlers and stuffed animal heads, trophies of his African honeymoon. Poor Tish, Alice thought, in tow behind her new husband as he shot a trail of wild beasts across the African plains.

'How on earth am I responsible for Poppy Beresford overstaying her welcome?' Alice sighed.

'It's your fault Felicity only wants female company these days,' Herbert said petulantly.

'As opposed to yours?' Alice murmured drily.

Herbert's fleshy round face coloured. 'There's something damned unhealthy about this friendship. Poppy's manipulating my wife and you're doing nothing to stop it. You could do - Felicity would listen to you.'

'Oh, Herbert, you are ridiculous. You make it sound like some sort of conspiracy. Felicity and Poppy are old friends and I have absolutely no right to tell either of them what to do.'

'You do if it's affecting the family,' Herbert said, his expression now hurt. 'Tell her it's time Poppy went back home to Beresford.' He swilled the brandy round in his glass and emptied it in one.

'Like a dutiful wife,' Alice teased.

'Exactly,' Herbert nodded, scratching his fat chin and trying unsuccessfully to push a finger between his starched white collar and bulging neck. 'She's been hanging around my wife for weeks.'

'They're old school friends,' Alice reminded him. 'You should be glad Tish has someone to keep her company while you're out shooting.'

'I don't shoot all the time!' Herbert cried defensively. 'You would think I did nothing else the way you go on - just like Felicity.'

Alice put down her brandy glass and stood up, her patience gone. It was always the same when she visited; tossed like a tennis ball between her brother and sister-in-law as one tried to gain advantage over the other. How tedious their marriage seemed; all they did was bicker.

'Don't go,' Herbert ordered. 'This business must be settled.'

Alice sighed and flopped down again. 'Two minutes to put your case,' she warned him.

'They do everything together,' Herbert continued his complaining, heaving his bulky body out of the leather armchair and crossing to the brandy decanter. 'I'm made to feel an. outsider in my own house - not to mention the bedroom.'

'That's enough, Herbert,' Alice protested, feeling embarrassed. 'I don't see that Felicity will take a blind bit of notice of what I say. She'll probably tell me to mind my own business. I'm not sure you're not just imagining the whole affair anyhow.'

'No, I'm not. Speak to her for me,' Herbert pleaded.

Alice felt reluctant. 'If it'll stop your incessant complaining...'

'It will,' Herbert promised. 'Get rid of Poppy Beresford and I'll do anything for you.'

For a moment, Alice was reminded of the eager young boy who used to follow her around Hebron House, irritatingly unable to amuse himself with a book or a game. When he was small she had been moderately fond of her brother, but he had grown into a bumptious bore who bragged about his good shooting and drank and gambled to excess. Yet it amazed her how often he still seemed to get his way and how too often she capitulated to his demands, in the hope of being left alone.

'Anything?' Alice asked, glancing at his empty desk, noticing how even the blotter was unmarked.

'Absolutely, Alice,' Herbert said, waving an expansive hand.

'I want to sit next to the Prime Minister at the launch of *Courageous*,' she answered, fixing him with a determined look.

'Oh God!' Herbert exclaimed. 'How did you know about Asquith?'

'Mama.'

Herbert groaned. 'I can't let you sit next to the Prime Minister and risk you turning the launch into a spectacle for your wretched suffragettes. Father wouldn't allow it.'

'You and I could persuade him,' Alice insisted. 'I merely want the opportunity of talking to him in a civilised manner over a civilised lunch. What is the harm in that?'

Herbert sank another brandy. 'This meeting is important for me now I've decided on a career in politics. You promise there won't be any unseemly goings-on?'

'There'll be no public protest,' Alice agreed. 'After all, I don't want to sabotage the launch of a Pearson ship either.'

Herbert looked dubious.

'Only I can guarantee to keep the local suffragettes in order,' Alice said persuasively.

'Very well,' Herbert answered with reluctance.

'Good,' Alice said triumphantly and headed towards the door. 'And I shall deal with the wayward girls.'

Alice escaped thankfully into the fresh chill air of the terrace, below which Felicity and Poppy were playing croquet in the dark. She watched them tripping over their gauzy evening dresses, feeling a pang of sadness that she had agreed to curtail their happiness. But she had wrested a valuable prize from Herbert, she would have a chance to do verbal battle with arch-enemy Asquith. He alone seemed to stand between women and their suffrage; even his own Cabinet had come round to their way of thinking. Felicity's personal happiness would have to be sacrificed to the greater goal of women's freedom.

All week she looked for an opportunity to catch Felicity by herself, but Poppy Beresford was never out of earshot. Alice began to sympathise with her brother, for it seemed he had not exaggerated his wife's obsessive companionship with her old friend. Alice watched more closely. The young women would get up early and play tennis together before breakfast. After eating a huge amount of kedgeree and toast they would disappear off on bicycles with a picnic lunch or take a rowing boat out on the lake her father had created and swim from the far shore. One day they golfed, another they went for a hike. Always, Felicity pre-empted Alice's attempts to join them.

'I know you hate long walks, Alice darling. See you at tea!'

Or Poppy would drawl, 'I'd love to see you at work in your darkroom - perhaps you'd show me its mysteries when we get back tonight?'

Her exclusion was subtle, Alice thought with admiration, but complete. Felicity appeared to have no time for her husband's family. Lady Arabella chose to ignore the situation and spent her time on shopping trips or visiting her aristocratic neighbours, while Lord Pearson escaped to London and the House of Lords.

Alice tackled her father about the situation before he went and was dumbfounded by his breezy reply.

'Herbert should stop bleating and take a mistress if Felicity chooses to keep him out of the bedroom. He's got his heir.'

'Papa!' Alice was scandalised. 'You make women sound like commodities.'

'Marriage for people of our class is a business contract,' her father said brusquely. 'Felicity has kept her side of it by bringing a dowry and producing Henry, so how she chooses to spend her hours of boredom is her business. Herbert - who is quite happy to spend Felicity's fortune as well as his own -should remember that.'

Alice looked at her tall, distinguished father, still handsome with his iron-grey hair and jet-black eyebrows over keen brown eyes, and wondered if he kept a mistress in London.

'What a depressing picture of marriage,' she grimaced.

'Well, be thankful you've escaped that fate,' Lord Pearson smiled.

'I'd not sign away my liberty to any man,' Alice answered with spirit. 'Wives have no more rights than servants. But once we women have the vote, we'll change all that.'

Her father snorted. 'Poppycock! You'll not get the vote in my lifetime - I at least agree with Asquith on that. Women have no place in politics.'

'We'll win our rightful place, Papa, and you know it.' Alice advanced on him. 'You can stand like Canute and posture, but the tide will turn. There are countless able women whose talents are being wasted by the stubborn prejudice of men like you and Asquith. You know very well I would have made a better heir to Pearson's than Herbert.'

Her father laughed shortly. 'Yes, Alice, you should have been my son. You've the brains for both of you. God got it wrong.'

'No, Papa,' Alice said fixing him with a challenging look, "you can't blame it on God. It's English law that dictates that Herbert inherits rather than me, and laws can be changed by men like you.'

Lord Pearson threw up his hands in submission, 'Alice, that radical tongue of yours will get you into Parliament or prison - I'm not sure which.'

Alice smiled, enjoying shocking her father. Kissing him goodbye she asked, 'You'll come and stay next week at Hebron House?'

'With pleasure,' Lord Pearson nodded and strode from the room.

Alice finally saw her chance at the end of the week. Herbert went off to a neighbouring estate where the fishing and the hospitality were equally abundant, grumbling at Felicity's protestations that she was unwell and could not accompany him. Lady Arabella, who was attracted by the host's card table, said she would accompany him instead as Lord Pearson was to remain in London for several more days. As Alice suspected, Felicity made a dramatic recovery shortly after her husband left.

'Let's take the boat out,' Felicity suggested.

'What a good idea,' Alice answered quickly. 'I'd like to take some photos from the far end of the lake. Perhaps Henry would like to come too. I'll suggest it to Nanny.'

'Oh, Henry,' Felicity said, unsure. 'He's so clumsy with boats.'

But Alice was not going to let her evade taking her son this time. She had observed all week how little attention Henry got from either of his parents and how he showed off to try and gain their approval.

'We can all swim,' Alice answered pointedly, 'so there's nothing to worry about.'

To Alice's disappointment, the day did not go well. Henry was over-boisterous in his excitement at-being invited and soaked them all with the oars before they reached the picnic spot. Felicity was fretful, Nanny petrified and Poppy bored. Alice did her best to jolly the party along with an improvised game of cricket, but Felicity decreed that she was feeling unwell again and made them return early.

She did not appear at dinner and Alice and Poppy dined alone. Suddenly it occurred to Alice that it was Poppy Beresford that she should be speaking to rather than her wilful sister-in-law. But Poppy evaded her suggestion of taking coffee in the drawing room and retired upstairs to read. Alice stood by the blazing fire in the huge stone inglenook fireplace which echoed the orange sunset through the long casement windows. She fumed to think how she had been outmanoeuvred all week. Two brandies later, she decided to go up to Poppy's bedroom and confront her.

The staircase was drowned in an umber half-light from the glass-domed ceiling and all was quiet as Alice ascended. Taking the landing to the left which led to the guest quarters, she thought she heard a door open somewhere behind her, but when she turned there was no sign of anyone. Unsure of Poppy's exact room, Alice knocked tentatively on the end door which was slightly ajar.

'Come, my love,' a soft voice invited her in.

Alice pushed open the door and peered curiously into the darkened room, aware of a pungent burning smell. The curtains were drawn back to allow the remnants of the sunset to suffuse the room with a purplish light. For a moment she thought the room was empty, then gasped in shock at the figure smoking on the chaise longue. Poppy was stretched out naked on the gold brocade with only a cashmere shawl draped across her lower body. Her feline features were tipped towards the window, caught in the fading light. But at Alice's stifled exclamation, she turned and sat up like a startled nymph, pulling the shawl to cover her breasts.

'Good God, you are having an affair!' Alice remarked, still astonished that Herbert's suspicions had been confirmed.

'Shocking, isn't it?' Poppy said, drawing on her cigarette, once more composed.

'I -I suppose it is,' Alice stammered, feeling ridiculous in her formal pearl-grey dress. 'I feel as if I've walked into some French farce.'

'There's nothing farcical about our relationship.' Poppy was defensive. She stood up defiantly, crossed to the unlit fire where she stubbed out her cigarette and picked up a Chinese robe which she wrapped about her nakedness. 'Spying for Herbert, are you?' she accused.

'I wasn't spying,' Alice said indignantly. 'I knocked and you answered. I've been trying to speak to you or Felicity all week, but you've deliberately avoided me.'

'What do you want to know?' Poppy asked tensely, lighting up another cigarette.

'You can't stay here any longer,' Alice said, determined to be business like.

Poppy dropped into a yellow brocade chair. 'Felicity doesn't want me to go. I'll stay as long as she wants me here.'

'That's not the point.'

'And you're going to tell me what is?' Poppy blew smoke at her.

'Yes.' Alice was brisk. 'You've come between Felicity and Herbert. Your relationship with Tish - you don't seem to realise the upset it's causing.'

'Who's upset apart from dreary old Herbert?'

Alice felt annoyed. 'He may be dreary to you - but he's still very fond of his wife.'

'Fond? He's fonder of his damned hunting dogs!'

Alice tried a different tack. 'What about your husband?'

Poppy let out a harsh laugh. 'John doesn't care a fig what I do or where I go, just as long as I put in the odd appearance at diplomatic functions. He tells everyone I go north for the air, for my delicate health.'

'Well, I'm sorry you're not happy, but that's no reason to make things difficult for Herbert.'

Poppy clenched her cigarette and glared. 'Good God, do you Pearsons ever think of anyone but yourselves? You haven't the first idea about being stuck in a loveless marriage. But I know I'm the only person who can make Tish happy. We've always been close, ever since school. We love each other! But I don't imagine you would understand that because you seem incapable of love. What good are all your great causes if you can't feel love?'

Alice flinched under Poppy's scornful look, winded by the accusation. Was she really so unfeeling? Did she not care passionately for her fellow suffragettes and would she not do anything for them if asked? A small voice of dissent niggled at the back of her mind. She hadn't supported Emily in her desire to protest at the launch, the voice taunted her; she'd prefer her to demonstrate far away in Epsom than in her father's shipyard. It struck Alice forcefully that she was a Pearson first and all else was secondary. That's why Poppy Beresford had to go before a scandal broke to harm the family, Herbert's political career, the business.

Controlling her anger, she said, 'A scandal would be harmful to both you and Felicity. Until the rights of married women are improved, you are both dependent on your husbands for your survival. Remember that.'

'You're threatening me, aren't you?' Poppy said, agitated.

'I'm pointing out the facts.'

To her embarrassment, Poppy began to sob. Alice hesitated, not knowing whether to try and comfort the distressed woman. She must not weaken now, the situation was far too volatile to allow Poppy Beresford a reprieve.

'I'll arrange for you to be taken into Newcastle tomorrow. I think it best you should be gone before Herbert and my mother return.'

Poppy gave her a murderous look through her tears but did not protest. Alice turned and fled from the twilit bedroom. She rushed downstairs again, calling for Rosamund. Leading the eager poodle out of the house, she escaped into the chill gardens, willing the darkness to swallow up her revulsion and shame at what she had done.

In the morning, she watched from her mother's upstairs drawing room as the footman loaded up one of her father's cars with Poppy's cases and strapped a trunk on the back. Rosamund barked nervously at the signs of travel. Finally, Poppy appeared with an ashen-faced Felicity at her side. They walked arm in arm, until Poppy disengaged her friend gently and kissed her farewell. Alice looked away but heard Felicity crying as Poppy closed the car door. Suddenly Alice could bear the anguish no longer and raced downstairs to comfort her sister-in-law as the car rolled away down the drive. Alice held out her hands.

'I'm sorry, Tish, but I promised Herbert ...'

Felicity flinched as she came near. 'You've taken away the only person I've ever loved, truly loved,' she said in a flat voice, 'and I can never forgive you.' She turned away and hurried up the stone steps, disappearing into the mansion without a backward glance.

Alice felt herself going cold inside. She had chosen Herbert's side against Felicity although she was much fonder of her sister-in-law. Put to the test, she would always support her family and its business, she realised now. But she knew by doing so she had created an enemy in Felicity.

Alice hurried upstairs again to prepare her own swift .departure, yearning to be back once more in Newcastle among people who did not despise her.

Chapter Nine

The buzzer blared the afternoon release. Maggie, emerging in relief, caught sight of Rose Johnstone waiting for her and her heart sank.

'The meeting's tomorrow,' Rose tersely told Maggie outside Pearson's towering iron gates.

'Not here,' Maggie hissed, glancing at an inquisitive Eve Tindall.

'Then where?' Rose answered impatiently. 'I haven't seen you for three weeks. You've not been to the office, you've not been on the streets helping - '

'Shh!' Maggie ordered. 'I'll come with you now to the park where we can talk.' She raised her voice. 'See you in the morning, Eve.'

Her colleague nodded and they were soon separated in the flood of workers pouring out of the factories. They walked in silence at Rose's brisk pace until they gained the entrance to Daniel Park. Maggie thought how tame and orderly its flowered borders looked compared to the open meadows she had walked with George this past month. The thought made her glance guiltily at Rose, as if she could guess the reason for her truancy from newspaper selling.

Rose sat down abruptly on a park bench and Maggie followed suit like a meek schoolgirl.

'I've even been to your home,' Rose said 'Susan told me you were courting, that you didn't have time for the movement any more.'

'That's rubbish.' Maggie was indignant. 'Our Susan just likes to stir up trouble for me.'

'So you're not courting George Gordon?' Rose asked.

Maggie blushed. 'We've been out together, to concerts and that. He likes Mozart and he reads history and poetry.' George's breadth of interests had been a revelation to Maggie. His words echoed in her mind, 'One day, lass, Mozart and Handel will be for all the people, not just those born with money. When the workers run the world, we'll throw the concert halls open to everyone with lugs to hear.'

'So should I tell Emily Davison that you're too busy to meet her with all this cultural activity?' Rose was scathing.

'Don't be daft. The movement comes first.'

Rose gave her a searching look from behind her spectacles. Suddenly she put out a hand and covered Maggie's.

'I'm sorry,' she said more gently. 'It's none of my business if you're courting this lad. I've just been feeling left out and sorry for myself. If you're happy, then so am I.'

'I am happy,' Maggie admitted, 'but I've been selfish cutting myself off from you and the others these past weeks. I haven't let myself think about it.'

Rose sighed. 'You don't have to go ahead with whatever scheme Miss Davison has planned for you. No doubt it'll be dangerous. There are others who can undertake the task. I don't want you risking everything when you've worked so hard to get where you are and support your family the way you do. If George can offer you happiness and security, I won't blame you for taking it'.

Maggie was surprised by Rose's words and allowed her thoughts to drift for a moment. It would be so easy to fade away from the movement now. She was content in her job, earning enough money for small luxuries above their basic needs, and it would mean no more carping from her family about her involvement in politics. Above all, there would be nothing to stand in the way of her blossoming friendship with George; she could quietly cut the cords of loyalty that bound her to this futile cause for women's suffrage. For was it not futile? Had George himself not told her that the only way to improve the lot of working women was to empower working men who would look after their interests?

Seduced by such thoughts, Maggie's gaze strayed across the park, aware of the families enjoying the sunshine, picnicking in the fresh air while their children played with hoops and gourds. For the first time she entertained the idea of a husband and children of her own one day. Then, with a start, she realised that the man walking past her, grumbling at his wife, was familiar. He was berating her for some domestic imperfection, while she followed, her face resigned.

'That's the man who tore up me newspaper!' Maggie gasped. 'Do you remember, last month, in Newcastle?'

'So it is,' Rose confirmed.

And suddenly it was brought home to Maggie that the working man could not be relied upon to put his womenfolk's interests alongside his own. Whatever women wanted, Maggie realised, they would have to fight for themselves and she must not shirk her part in the battle.

'What time's the meeting with Miss Davison?' Maggie said at last. She saw the relief in Rose's face.

'Come to my house at three o'clock tomorrow,' her friend smiled.

They gripped hands for an instant and then stood up, each departing swiftly through separate gates into the maze of terraced housing.

When Maggie met Emily Davison that Saturday afternoon, her doubts dissolved There was something inspiring about the woman, an energy and conviction that still emanated from her gaunt face and piercing eyes. As she spoke, Maggie felt ashamed of her wavering resolve since her attack in the Bigg Market. This woman had been through countless ordeals for their cause and was about to embark on a dangerous and lonely mission at Epsom, not knowing how an excitable, hostile crowd might react to her protest.

'I would undertake to demonstrate at the launch at Pearson's myself,' Emily was telling her in the quiet civility of Rose's front room, behind the net curtains and the half-drawn blinds. Rose's pleasant, florid-faced mother had made tea for them and withdrawn to the kitchen, not wanting to interfere. 'But,' Emily continued, 'I am too well known in Newcastle and they will be watching for me. And in the meantime, I must protest at the Derby. I may not be here in July.'

Maggie looked sharply at the seasoned suffragette, alerted by something in her voice. For a second time she had a cold sense of foreboding.

'You mean they will imprison you?' she asked.

Emily Davison met her questioning look. 'We must all take the cup of suffering when it is offered, no matter what the consequences,' she answered resolutely. 'This coming week I must drink mine. You must decide if demonstrating at the launch of HMS *Courageous* is to be yours.'

Maggie felt her throat drying as her fear returned.

'I know I'm asking a lot of you,' Emily continued; not allowing Maggie to .glance away. 'It will probably mean arrest. You may lose your job at Pearson's. You will become one of the hunted and the banned. You will get no protection from Alice Pearson - she has already ordered that no action be taken. If you do this, you act alone, without authority from the WSPU. You will be doing it as a favour to me and the greater cause of women's freedom. Alice Pearson is wrong to try and prevent us using this moment when it's rumoured that Asquith himself will be present, along with half of Tyneside. It's a God-sent opportunity. When I met you at Hebron House, Maggie, I knew you were the one to carry out the mission.'

'How did you know?' Maggie asked, excited.

'I recognised the same passion of conviction in you as exists in me,' Emily told her. 'It was like encountering a long lost sister.'

Maggie felt her eyes smart at the generous words. She was unused to compliments and tried to make light of Emily's.

'Sisters! With you so grand and me as common as clarts?' Maggie laughed.

'Not common in the least,' Emily said robustly. 'Alice Pearson may have dismissed you as a working-class girl who wouldn't have the backbone for such action, but not me.'

Maggie's slim face turned crimson. 'She said that about me, did she?'

'Yes, but only because you scared her with your commitment. Alice is a robust campaigner, but she's also a terrible snob.'

'Well, Alice Pearson and all the other ruddy Pearsons have got it coming to them!'

'Maggie, watch your language,' Rose scolded.

'Not on my account,' Emily laughed. She smiled in encouragement. 'I knew you wouldn't let me down, Maggie Beaton.'

That last afternoon in May, Maggie went home with those words of praise from the great suffragette campaigner singing in her ears. Only later did she wonder if Emily Davison had deliberately riled her with Alice Pearson's comments in order to secure her commitment to the task ahead. If so, she had succeeded, for she burned to show the mighty Miss Alice that this working-class lass had twice her courage and fortitude.

Over the next few days she spent her pent-up energy back on the streets selling *The Suffragette*, to the fury of her mother. For the first time in a month she avoided George, unable to decide what to do about him. But by the Wednesday evening when he called at the house, Maggie realised she had to make a choice.

As they walked through the crowded park, George was uncomfortably aware of her distant manner. He asked, 'What's on your mind, bonny lass?'

Maggie did not answer.

'Trouble at home?' George guessed. Maggie shook her head.

'Work then?'

'There's nothing wrong at work.'

'We could gan to Hibbs' Farm,' George suggested, bewildered by her moodiness. 'Lie in the grass and read poetry?' His grin was suggestive.

Maggie felt a twinge of longing at the thought. 'No.' She was adamant. 'We can't. I can't ever again... I'm sorry.' She looked at him unhappily.

Without another word, he took her by the arm and steered her from the park. Reaching a quiet back lane, he demanded, 'Something's bothering you. What is it?'

She looked at the handsome concerned man before her and steeled herself for what was to come. Maggie could no longer deny her growing love for George; she thought of him constantly and longed for his company. But love was selfish and all-consuming, she realised, and her growing preoccupation with the blacksmith was undermining her loyalty to the movement. She could not be true to them both wholeheartedly and so she must give up George Gordon.

'I've been neglecting my duties to the movement,' Maggie answered stiffly, 'seeing you so much. I've been that wrapped up in me own pleasure.'

George smiled in relief. 'I'm glad it's a pleasure. It is for me an' all.' He ran a rough finger down her cheek.

Maggie flinched from the contact, turning away. 'I can't deny I have feelings for you,' she said awkwardly, 'but they can't come to anything.'

George took her hands in the dismal lane, ignoring the boys who played nearby on the mossy cobbles.

'I care for you, Maggie,' he told her. 'It doesn't matter to me that you're a suffragette, even if the other lads give me a hard time. Everyone's entitled to their opinions.'

'But it's not just a matter of opinion,' Maggie protested, drawing away from him. 'The movement demands more than that. It needs total commitment from its members for us to succeed.'

George looked puzzled. 'I've said before, lass, I don't mind you getting involved. You can do your bit when I've got me union meetings.'

Maggie looked at him in dismay. 'You don't understand, do you? It's not just a hobby to fill in time while you're at your important meetings!' she cried. 'I'm a suffragette first and last. Nothing else can be as important - not even us, George.'

He stood back, rebuffed. Searching her face, he found nothing there to reassure him. Her grey eyes were angry, her mouth stubborn.

'Are you telling me you're done with courting?' he asked stiffly.

'Aye,' Maggie gulped. 'I've been asked to do summat important, which you mustn't know about - mustn't even guess.' She looked at him miserably. 'It'd be better for you if you have nothing to do with me.'

George snorted in disbelief. 'Well, I can tell when I'm not wanted. You don't have to make up a fairy story for my sake, bonny lass.'

'It's true,' Maggie protested, stung by his derision. 'I've been given a mission.'

'Oh aye?' George sneered. 'Orders from Mrs Pankhurst herself, is it? Trying to impress the likes of Alice Pearson? Watch your head, Maggie, you'll not get it through your front door.'

'Don't scoff at me,' Maggie was stung. 'I'm just as important as you and all your union mates. You men just sit around and talk about revolution; we women are getting on and starting one!'

George turned away, laughing to hide his hurt. 'I can't wait to read about it in the newspapers.'

'You will!' Maggie yelled after him. 'By God, you will, George Gordon!'

He walked away, furious at her rejection. He had neglected his rowing and his friends for Maggie Beaton, defending her from their derogatory banter. His friends and family thought her far too proud and self-opinionated for a young woman, but George had seen the tender and passionate Maggie who cared deeply about people. In the solitariness of his small lodgings he had yearned for her, impatient for their next meeting. With Maggie he found he could share his poetry and ideals; she was unlike any of the other girls with whom he had grown up and he would have done anything for her. But, George thought bitterly as he strode away, she had not cared for him after all. His friends were right, Maggie Beaton was mad with her own self-importance and vanity and he was better off without her.

Maggie watched him go, her nails digging into the rough brick at her back. Half of her wanted to rush after him and beg him to stay, while the other half smarted from his scathing remarks and cursed his going. So she stayed by the wall, shaking with anger until he was out of sight.

'Arc you all right, missus?' asked a grimy-faced boy who had detached himself from the marble players and was staring at her in curiosity.

Maggie's hands went to her face and found it was damp with tears.

'Aye, Tich,' she answered, wiping the tears roughly with her sleeve. She fished out a toffee for the boy. 'Don't you grow up treating lasses like they're not important,' she said, waving the toffee at him, 'because we are.'

The boy gawped in surprise, then snatched at the sweet. 'Ta, missus,' he answered and sprinted off like a street-wise cat.

Swallowing her misery, Maggie walked resolutely through Elswick towards Rose Johnstone's house. She would discuss tactics for the demonstration that only Rose and Emily Davison were to know about and forget all about the arrogant George Gordon who thought only his interests were important. Thinking of Emily, Maggie felt her optimism return. That brave woman had endured imprisonment, cruelty and pain without complaint, while all she was suffering was a bruised heart. And if George Gordon could not understand why the women's cause was so important to her, then it was better that they parted now before their courtship went too far.

Arriving at Rose's house, she found the heavy black door ajar. The house had once belonged to a wealthy merchant but like many on the edge of the West Road it had been sold and divided into more modest dwellings. Rose and her mother lived on the ground floor, in three rooms of crumbling grandeur, sharing the beautifully plastered hallway and the outside privy with three other families.

Maggie went in, knocking impatiently on the inner door. Mrs Johnstone answered.

'Oh, my dear, come in,' she said. 'Rose thought you'd call.'

'Did she?' Maggie answered in surprise. 'I hadn't intended to.'

Rose rushed forward and hugged her. 'I'm so glad you did. Isn't it terrible news?'

'What news?' Maggie asked, bewildered.

Rose pulled away and exchanged looks with her mother.

'We thought that was why you'd come,' Mrs Johnstone murmured.

'It's in the evening papers,' Rose said dully.

'What is?' Maggie demanded. 'What's so terrible?'

Rose handed her the newspaper. 'Emily Davison threw herself in front of the King's horse.'

It hit Maggie like a thunderbolt: today was Derby Day. Yet she had been too engrossed in her feelings for George to have remembered that this was the day their sister Emily was to face her ordeal at Epsom.

Maggie gasped in horror as she read the report about how their friend had been trampled under the horse's hooves. The reporter seemed more indignant that the race had been ruined by her action than concerned for the woman.

'Is she ...?' Maggie stared at Rose, feeling a cold fear gripping her insides.

'We don't know any more than you,' Rose whispered. 'Perhaps she'll pull through.'

Maggie turned away. 'Perhaps,' she echoed hoarsely.

But in her mind's eye she saw rank upon rank of women in mourning dress and feared that she had foreseen Emily Davison's funeral procession.

Chapter Ten

Alighting from the train at Morpeth station, Maggie and Rose were awed by the crowds of mourners. Emily Davison's coffin, borne from London the previous night, was guarded by suffragettes dressed in white and marked by black armbands, standing at dignified attention.

'So many people!' Rose gasped as they struggled down off the special train laid on from Newcastle.

The platform was covered in a sea of coloured wreaths and floral tributes that the funeral organisers were trying to clear. Maggie and Rose stood in the noon heat in their stiff black dresses and tricolour sashes as more and more spectators poured in on trains and traps and bicycles to join the funeral march.

But Maggie was hardly aware of the discomfort as the procession finally took shape and snaked off down the hill from the station. Thousands of people covered the steep banks and packed the roadsides as they strained for a view of the cortege, inching slowly forward. What were all these people thinking? Maggie wondered. Had Emily's death finally made people realise the injustice women were suffering, or were they just here out of curiosity? Some looked on impassively but there were men who were removing their hats as the coffin went past and Maggie heard one shout out, 'God bless the wild lass!'

Her throat swelled with emotion to see the striking ranks of suffragettes, dressed in flowing white to denote they had suffered imprisonment, carrying Madonna lilies and purple irises, leading the horse-drawn hearse. The coffin was covered in a purple pall, stitched with silver arrows to remind the mourners of Emily's frequent spells in prison, and followed by a mourner carrying a furled union banner, draped in crepe.

'Alice Pearson is holding a leading rope,' Rose hissed to Maggie as they marched alongside members of the Newcastle WSPU.

Maggie peered on tiptoe to see the tall woman, head erect and face visibly upset, walking beside one of the four horses, holding on to a white rope. It struck Maggie that this aristocratic woman's head was bare in a surprising gesture of humility, but she quickly smothered a feeling of sympathy. For was it not Miss Alice who had suggested the Derby Day protest? Maggie thought bitterly.

Emily Davison had lain fighting for life for four days, while Maggie's hopes had hung on a thread. She had prayed feverishly for her recovery but to no avail and now she felt bereft and at a loss without her mentor.

That morning, she had asked Rose, 'What should I do now?'

Her friend had known without asking that the launch of the Pearson battleship was preying on her mind.

'Today we pay our respects to our dead comrade,' Rose had answered firmly. 'We can worry about the future tomorrow.'

Maggie felt overcome now by the sight of the marching women and their banners, stirred by the band from Newcastle that led the procession and played their marching song, "The Women's Marseillaise". There were young girls carrying white lilies, battalions of suffragists in purple and black, and carriages carrying family mourners, and hundreds of ordinary followers who had travelled the country to pay tribute to the suffragette martyr.

Maggie, noticing a photographer recording the event for all time from a nearby inn, felt pride and grief to be processing in front of the gathered thousands, under their banner bearing Emily's own slogan: Fight on and God will give the victory.'

Finally, they reached the path to St Mary's churchyard and the welcome shade of ancient trees under the cloudless sky. The coffin was carried forward through the old lich-gate, the women forming a guard of honour, and then on into the parish church itself. Only family and close friends followed for the brief service, but straining to see who entered, Maggie was sure she saw Alice Pearson's tall figure among the select few.

The tranquil graveyard was so overrun with mourners that Maggie and Rose could not get near to see the coffin lowered into the ground at the Davison burial mound, so they patiently waited their turn among the lofty pines. Some time later they were able to approach the iron-fenced memorial which was almost hidden under the heaps of wreaths and floral messages. The scent of the flowers was overpowering as Maggie tossed her own modest purple iris onto the coffin.

'I'll fight on, I promise!' Maggie whispered, as around her women openly wept.

Maggie shared with them the sense of shock that their friend had sacrificed her life for the cause. It made their efforts seem so paltry, she thought. She was loath to leave the scene of mourning, as if it somehow gave her strength to be near Emily Davison's body. But Rose decided it was time they made their way back to the station.

As they descended the path from the grave, they ran into Alice Pearson. Maggie was shocked to see her face flushed and eyes swollen from crying. She stopped as she saw them.

'Rose Johnstone, isn't it?' she asked with a watery smile.

'Yes, Miss Alice,' Rose said with a deferential nod.

'What a sad, sad day,' Alice sighed.

'Yes,' Rose agreed. 'You must be especially upset to lose a close friend.'

Maggie felt stung. 'She was a friend to us all - an inspiration. Miss Davison wouldn't have wanted us to stand around snivelling over her grave like bairns. She'd have told us to gan on fighting to victory.'

'Maggie, show some respect,' Rose said, aghast at her friend's outburst, but it drew Alice Pearson's attention as Maggie had intended.

'No, your friend is right,' Alice replied, feeling a fresh wave of guilt. 'That's exactly what Emily would have said. We've met before, haven't we?'

Maggie looked at her defiantly. 'Maggie Beaton. I'm in the Newcastle WSPU, same as you.'

Alice flushed at the young woman's rudeness and remembered how Emily Davison had kept on irritatingly about this common girl.

'Well, Maggie,' Alice said stonily, 'if you're such a militant, then it's time you participated more in our local campaigns. I don't recall you've done much so far.'

As soon as she had uttered the reproof Alice felt ashamed, especially as she saw the tears well in the young woman's eyes. If this working-class girl had not made her feel so guilty about Emily's death, she would never have been so unkind. But it was too late; she could tell Maggie Beaton had taken offence.

'Don't you worry, Miss Alice, you're going to see just how militant us working-class lasses can be!'

With that, Maggie stepped past her and stormed off down the churchyard path. In that moment, she determined to risk everything - her job, her home, her family, her prospects of love and marriage - to revenge Emily's death and teach the haughty Alice Pearson a lesson. She would carry out the demonstration at the launch of the Pearson ship and take the consequences.

Having made her decision, Maggie found a new sense of purpose and the days began to pass quickly. She pushed all thoughts of George firmly from her mind and spent her free time at Rose's house making plans for the demonstration over Mrs Johnstone's endless cups of scented tea and pale Madeira cake. Maggie was to dress as an old woman and whiten her hair, so that people would allow the frail widow to the front of the crowds. Once there, she would attempt to clamber onto the launching platform and display a WSPU flag from under her cloak. Maggie grew impatient as she imagined the look of horror on Alice Pearson's face at her action. She would reach Asquith and speak her mind, Maggie determined.

At home, there was bafflement at her abrupt finishing with George Gordon. To Maggie's surprise, her mother appeared disappointed.

'What have you said to put the lad off?' Mabel demanded.

'I thought you didn't approve of him,' Maggie countered.

'You could have done worse,' her mother huffed, 'and at least it kept you away from your demonstrating. Now I don't know what you're up to half the time and you're hardly ever here.'

'She's bringing in a wage. Mam, and that's what counts,' Susan said, coming unexpectedly to her defence. 'If you ask me, I didn't think our Maggie and George Gordon were suited.'

Helen gave a derisory laugh. 'You were just scared she'd up and get wed before you.'

'I was not!' Susan denied hotly. 'I just agree with Aunt Violet that the Gordons are a rough lot.'

'Well, I think George was canny looking,' Helen went on, 'and our Maggie's daft for giving him up. But then Maggie's always been queer about lads. She'll not get another one that easy.'

'Wheesht, lassie!' Granny Beaton interrupted, seeing Maggie's furious look.

'I don't give tuppence for what you all think,' said Maggie. 'It's got nowt to do with any of you what I choose to do.'

She stalked out and went off to see Rose. After that, George Gordon was never mentioned again among the family in Maggie's hearing and she stayed out of the way as much as possible as the evenings grew long and people lived out of doors as much as they could. She hardly saw Jimmy, who disappeared for hours on end, only turning up briefly to be fed.

She felt that her brother was the only one who genuinely missed George's company and sometimes she caught his silent reproachful look. George had taken him out in boats and let him hang around the forge at Hibbs' Farm where he sometimes helped out for no recompense. Maggie had been surprised how George had treated Jimmy as an equal and not as an irritating little brother who was only good for errands. She had laughed when George had given Jimmy an old pair of long trousers, but he had been sharp.

'You all treat that lad like he's still a bairn,' George had said, 'but he's not.'

'He carries on like a bairn,' Maggie had replied. 'Can't do owt for himself.'

'Give him a bit of responsibility and watch the change in him,' George had challenged. 'Your Susan's let him hang on to her skirts too long.'

Jimmy had thrown away his shorts and never taken off his long trousers since. Maggie suspected he still went up to Hibbs' Farm and helped George, but as she never went there herself any more she could not be sure.

Susan, however, was more tolerant towards Maggie than she had been in years and did not scold her for being absent and not helping around the house. Maggie could see this softening in her sister was brought on by her happiness at being courted by Richard Turvey. Susan took extra care with her appearance and was almost skittish in mood whenever Richard was present.

Maggie made a huge effort to be civil and pleasant to the Londoner, although he irritated her with his constant banter and his ingratiating behaviour to her mother and Aunt Violet. And she still did not trust him after the incident in the Bigg Market. Although she wasn't absolutely sure that the man who had run away and left her to be attacked was Richard, she still suspected him of the cowardice. He had protested a wounded innocence when her mother had confronted him and somehow Maggie had been blamed for his upset. Still, Maggie was thankful that he and Susan appeared happy together and Richard had stopped his flirtation with Helen.

On Saturday evenings he would come with his gramophone and records and Uncle Barny would bring his fiddle and pay for a jug of beer and the cramped flat in Gun Street would reverberate with noise, bringing the Smiths bounding up the stairs to join in. Reminded of similar evenings with George, Maggie would make excuses to help her grandmother make tea in the kitchen, but even so she found herself relaxing to the music and enjoying the rare harmony among her family.

As July came and the talk in the office was only of the launch of HMS *Courageous*, Maggie began to grow nervous about her task. Only Rose and her mother could calm and encourage her and she grew even closer to the Johnstone women as the summer wore to its height. Just once did they quarrel, and that was when Rose was outspoken in her relief that Maggie was no longer being courted by George.

'You can do better than a pitman's son with archaic views on what women should be allowed to do,' Rose had pronounced. 'What a waste it would have been to throw away your education and ambitions for such a man.'

'George is no ordinary pitman's son,' Maggie had defended him.

'He's no different from the others, Maggie,' Rose insisted. 'I saw how much he hurt you with his ridiculing of your work. No, I haven't brought you this far to have you throw yourself away for a man who'd keep you at home, weighed down with the drudgeries of married life. Too many of my old pupils have gone that way. I see them scrubbing their doorsteps, old and ill before they're thirty. I'll not let that happen to you, Maggie.'

Maggie had been incensed and a little frightened to think Rose might be ordering her life. 'I'm not your pupil any more,' Maggie had protested. 'Don't treat me like a child who doesn't have a mind of her own. It was my choice to finish with George, not yours, so don't go thinking I do things just because you want me to.'

Maggie had stormed home and stayed away a couple of days, but she missed Rose's friendship and support and had returned to apologise. They had never mentioned George again.

Then three days before the launch. Rose, now on holiday from teaching, came rushing out of the house to meet Maggie.

'The police closed the office this morning! They've seized everything!'

'Why?' Maggie demanded as Rose pulled her into the house and slammed the door.

'It's obvious,' Rose said heatedly. 'They're clamping down on us because Asquith's going to be there. Jocelyn Fulford sent a note to say she's been ordered to stay indoors for twenty-four hours while the Prime Minister's in

Newcastle. We're all likely to be banned from the town during his visit.'

'At least they'll find nothing about our planned demonstration,' Maggie said with relief.

'But they'll have the names and addresses of all our members,' Rose reminded her. 'You'll have to make yourself scarce, Maggie, else all our plans are out of the window.'

Maggie felt apprehensive but answered stoutly, 'They'll not bother with a lass from Gun Street. If they find my name they'll probably just think I'm the cleaner.'

'We can't risk it. You'll have to find a safe place to stay before the protest.'

'But I have to carry on at work, else they'll be suspicious,' Maggie replied.

'Go sick tomorrow,' Rose ordered. 'Now we need to think of somewhere for you to go. We can't risk you coming here and being caught - they may put a watch on the house.'

'Don't be daft,' Maggie laughed.

'It's not daft, Maggie,' Mrs Johnstone broke into the conversation. 'The police are extremely jittery after the recent spate of attacks on public buildings. They'll not want anything happening to the Prime Minister while he's in Newcastle.'

'And Pearson won't want a sniff of suffragette unrest to spoil the launch - he's probably ordered the clampdown,' Rose added.

'We've scared them, haven't we?' Maggie said with glee. 'We've finally got the buggers scared!'

Mrs Johnstone cleared her throat politely.' I have a suggestion about who might help Maggie.'

'Go on, Mother.'

'Mr John Heslop, the lay preacher at the chapel.'

'You mean the old butcher?' Maggie laughed 'Why should he help me?'

'He's sympathetic to our cause, and you used to attend his Sunday School, I believe.'

'Few year ago,' Maggie admitted. 'He was good to Mam after me dad died - helped us flit. Aye, and I once went on his mission to the quayside, an' all. But —'

'There you are,' Mrs Johnstone interrupted 'John Heslop has a strong sense of what's right. I think we should trust him.'

Rose looked doubtful. 'Being sympathetic is not quite the same as agreeing to harbour someone about to deliberately breach the peace.'

'I don't have to tell him what I'm going to do,' Maggie said, 'and then he's not responsible. I'll tell him I've had a row at home - he'll believe that quick enough.'

'You'll have to hide your disguise there,' Rose said. 'You can't risk coming back here until it's all over.'

Maggie felt suddenly overwhelmingly alone. None of them knew when they would meet again or how her actions in three days' time might change things. Mrs Johnstone carefully packed the sombre navy dress she was lending Maggie into an old box, along with the powder to whiten her dark hair and make her look older. Maggie would also wear one of her grandmother's lace caps and voluminous capes.

She kissed the placid widow and hugged Rose tightly.

'I'll make you proud of me,' she promised.

'I've been proud of you for a long time, little sister,' Rose smiled fondly and kissed her forehead. 'Whatever happens, you always have a home here with us,' she added gently. 'Never forget that, Maggie.'

' Thank you,' Maggie gulped and turned quickly, picking up the box. She hurried out of the house without looking back.

At the end of the street her courage wavered and she almost dropped the box and ran to the haven of the Johnstones' decaying, civilised home. But Rose's disappointment in her would have been far worse than her present apprehension and she craved her friend's approval above all others. So Maggie steeled herself for the lonely days ahead and the uncertainty beyond, with angry thoughts of Alice Pearson hobnobbing with the hated Prime Minister and betraying her sisters-in-arms.

That night, she got Granny Beaton to hide the box under her bed in the parlour. Her grandmother asked no questions and Maggie felt a flood of affection for the old woman for standing by her without judgment.

The next day seemed the longest in Maggie's life. She could hardly settle to her work and Eve Tindall's curious questioning began to tell on her nerves.

By three o'clock, Maggie was genuinely able to say, 'I'm feeling that bad, Eve, I think I'll have to stop off tomorrow.'

'You've never missed a day!' Eve answered astonished. She squinted at her behind her glasses. 'Perhaps you're sickening for something. It's the hot weather, there's always sickness going about in hot weather. You take care of yourself now. Best not to come here spreading it around if you're poorly. I don't want to miss the launch.' She went back to her work and did not approach Maggie again that day.

When the hooter blew. Eve hurried out ahead, mumbling she had shopping to do.

'Ta-ra, Eve.' Maggie watched her go. She would probably never work with Eve Tindall in this dusty office again, Maggie thought. She said a mental goodbye to her office job and her ambitions as secretary and forbade herself to fret about the future. The most important job she might ever have to do was to carry out her protest in two days' time; she must concentrate on that alone.

As Maggie turned up Gun Street, she stopped in her tracks. A police constable stood hovering in the entrance to their stairs. A moment later another one emerged from the doorway and began to talk to him, thumbing over his shoulder at the Beatons' flat as he spoke. Maggie was aghast they had bothered to track her down; she had thought Rose was being over-dramatic about a police threat. Any minute now they would glance along the street and see her standing there indecisively. Would they recognise her? Had they come to arrest her or just issue a warning to stay off the streets?

Just as she pondered the thought, the constable who appeared to be in command turned and looked down the street. He ordered the other one to stand at his post by the door and began to walk towards her, his nailed boots ringing on the cobbles. Maggie's heart thudded in alarm. If she fled now she would give herself away and she would never be able to outrun this lanky policeman. Yet somehow she must get rid of him.

As he approached, Maggie began to sway and sing.

"Hello, hinny!' she called at him and rolled her eyes drunkenly. There were plenty of women around Gun Street she could ape, including her mother on occasion, and Maggie played the drunk with zest.

'Gis us a kiss, hinny. Gan on,' she cackled.

The constable slowed down as he neared, suddenly unsure if this was the woman they were after. Maggie, through hooded eyes, could tell what he was thinking. Suffragettes might be awkward and abusive, but the young woman they were seeking could not be this common drunk. He must not get too good a look at my face, she thought . 'Eeh, hinny,' she screeched, 'just a minute.'

She staggered a few steps up the street and turned her back on him. Then planting her legs apart and lifting her skirts above her ankles, Maggie half lowered her drawers and began to urinate over the cobbles. So nervous was she that it came in a great flood, splashing her boots and the hem of her skirt and running in crazy rivulets towards the unsuspecting policeman. Even Maggie was shocked by what she had done and glancing over her shoulder she saw the horrified disgust on the young constable's face as the steaming urine trickled around his boots.

He cursed her foully and stalked past, shoving her roughly out of the way. Maggie flung an obscenity after him for good measure, then turned and weaved her way down the street as quickly as she dared, praying that none of her neighbours or family had witnessed the spectacle.

Once out of sight, she began to laugh hysterically at the thought of the man's polished boots stained with her pee, elated with relief at her escape.

'Votes for women!' she shouted at an organ grinder and his monkey as she hurried onto Scotswood Road. She did not stop laughing until she was two tram stations distant from Gun Street.

When the euphoria of tricking the police had subsided, Maggie realised with a sudden panic that she could not return home until after the launch. The police might tire of waiting for her, but her family would not let her out of their sight if they suspected she was up to something. Disguise or no disguise, she would carry out her mission, Maggie determined, so there was nothing for it but to throw herself on the mercy of John Heslop whom she had not seen to speak to for the last four years.

The unassuming butcher lived alone in a flat above his shop on Alison Terrace and Maggie remembered visiting once or twice for singing evenings when she had attended his Sunday School. She remembered him playing the piano with coat tails hanging over the stool, glancing over his shoulder with a genial smile of encouragement to the squalling choir from the chapel. Maggie had been fascinated that the thick sideburns that grew down to his chin were copper red while the hair on his head was black.

She recalled that for a time John Heslop had come regularly to tea on Sundays to Gun Street and she and Susan had discussed whether he was going to marry their mother. But the visits had dwindled and eventually stopped and the girls only saw him at the chapel. Susan had taught in the Sunday School and Maggie had been enthusiastic about Heslop's mission to the poor of the quayside. But her mother had been furious when Heslop had taken her to the dark, disease-infested alleys along the quay and forbade her to go again. Luckily a battle of wills had been avoided by Maggie's sudden conversion to suffragism. She had railed at Heslop for the church's message that people who suffered in this world gained their rewards in the next; she wanted the burdens and oppression of women to be lifted in this world and in her lifetime.

She had argued with Heslop and left the Methodist chapel on Alison Terrace, abandoning religion for a while. Gradually, her grandmother had coaxed her into accompanying her to the Presbyterian Kirk in Elswick and she had begun to look forward to the Sunday escapes from the wrangling in Gun Street and enjoyed listening to her grandmother's fervent high-pitched hymn singing.

Maggie had never patched up her differences with Heslop and she had avoided using his shop out of embarrassment at the way she had lectured him as an outspoken sixteen-year-old. She was quite prepared for him to shut the door in her face, but there was no harm in trying.

For a couple of hours, Maggie skulked around the back lanes and sat in the park, until the shops on Alison Terrace emptied and people were busy indoors with domestic chores. She walked past the entrance to the butcher's three times before she was satisfied that the two assistants had departed on bicycles and no one was left except the butcher. Then she went inside.

'Maggie Beaton?' John Heslop gasped as he emerged from the back, wiping his knuckled hands on a cloth. He was thinner and more gaunt than she remembered, his cheekbones prominent above the thick red side-whiskers. His dark hair was greying at the temples and in retreat, but his brown eyes were as lively and welcoming as ever.

'Aye, it's me,' Maggie said, blushing and suddenly unsure.

'Grand to see you, Maggie,' Heslop replied. 'I get news from your Susan at chapel, of course, but it's good to see you're well. Can I get you something?'

She was astonished at his open, friendly manner when his last impressions of her must have been of a rude, censorious girl, still in ringlets, condemning his old-fashioned beliefs with all the conviction of a new convert.

'I haven't come to buy anything,' Maggie said.

'No?' Heslop raised his bushy eyebrows a fraction. 'And I take it you haven't just come for some debating? By heck, I missed our discussions once you left the mission.'

'Did you?' Maggie was taken aback.

'Yes,' Heslop laughed, 'and the mission needed people like you who weren't afraid to go in there and preach the word. But Susan says it's politics you preach these days. And I don't blame you. Stick up for your rights, I say. I don't hold with violent revolution, of course, but injustice is the curse of our society. All the wealth of our glorious empire counts for naught when there are people begging on our streets and living in darkness under our very noses.'

Maggie gawped at him. She had forgotten how John Heslop liked to talk and would tackle the thorniest of subjects with customers concerned only with the price of his meat. Their preoccupation with brisket or scrag end faintly annoyed him, while he wheeled his sharp blades and put the world to rights.

'You believe in votes for women, then?' Maggie asked cautiously.

'Universal suffrage, I say,' Heslop nodded 'You're one of God's children; you've as much right to representation as I have.'

Maggie searched for words to express her amazement, but floundered.

The butcher chuckled. 'You think I've queer notions for a man of my advancing years, eh?'

'Aye, I suppose so,' Maggie blushed. 'And you not having .... not being...'

'Being a single man,' he finished for her. She saw a muscle working hard in his cheek under the bushy sideboard and for a moment thought she saw a flicker of anger in his eyes. But then he smiled. 'So what do you want with this crusty old bachelor?'

Maggie looked at him hard and decided to be candid. 'I need somewhere to stay for two nights. The coppers are watching out for me - all suffragettes are under a banning order until after the launch. I wondered if you could let me sleep in the back of your shop - somewhere to shelter after dark. I'll make meself scarce during the day.'

John Heslop looked at her for a moment, showing no surprise. 'Are you going to tell me what it's about?'

'No, Maggie said. 'I can't.'

'But you don't want to be housebound on the day of the launch?' he asked wryly.

They exchanged looks. Maggie nodded.

'You can stay in the flat. I'll sleep in the back of the shop,' he offered.

Maggie shook her head. 'Mary Smith, my neighbour, cleans for you. I couldn't risk her seeing me and telling Mam. She'd be up here like a shot and dragging me off by the ear. I 'don't want to bring you any trouble.'

Heslop grunted. 'Your mother doesn't hold me in much regard anyway.'

'I never understood that, after the way you helped us when me dad died,' Maggie said.

'No,' Heslop sighed. 'Well, we had words. Anyway, that's water under the bridge, as they say. Your problem is to have somewhere safe to stay and to escape detection from friend or foe until after Saturday.'

Maggie smiled. The butcher tugged on one of his side-whiskers as he thought.

'I know just the place. No one will come looking for you - but you'll have to do me a favour in return.'

Maggie looked at him suspiciously. 'What favour?'

'You can stay at the mission hall on the quayside - and help give out sustenance.'

Maggie laughed. 'You're a trier, Mr Heslop.'

'Do we have an agreement?' he asked.

'Why-aye!' Maggie answered.

'I'll take you down in the van,' he said briskly, not hiding his delight. 'Just sit in the back shop a minute while I finish off.'

'There's one other thing,' Maggie said, stopping him. 'I need a box of clothes from Gun Street.'

'Who can you trust?'

'Granny Beaton, but she's too blind and frail to find her way across town.' Maggie thought hard She dismissed Helen and her mother immediately. Susan might take pity, but she would look in the box and discover the disguise and tell their mother anyway.

'Tich,' Maggie said 'I trust Jimmy to do an errand and not blab.'

'I'll send word with Mary Smith then,' Heslop replied. 'Jimmy sometimes brings me bundles of firewood - I'll say I'm needing some.'

'Thank you,' Maggie smiled at him, 'it's more than I deserve.'

'Oh, I'll make you work for it.' He grinned through his whiskers like a brindled cat.

Twenty minutes later they were setting off for the quayside, Maggie secreted inside the butcher's dusty horse-drawn van. She was entering the unknown, she thought nervously, choosing to leave behind the relative security of Gun Street for ever. She had delivered herself into the hands of an eccentric, radical preaching butcher and in two days she would break the law attempting to ruin a prestigious ship launch.

Sitting among the sawdust with the smell of blood in her nostrils, she already felt like a fugitive.

Chapter Eleven

The mission hall was a leaky cellar in the bowels of an antiquated warehouse. John Heslop abandoned his van on the quayside where two boys were paid to tend the horse and keep watch, while he and Maggie made their way through a warren of alleyways in the slum area of Sandgate.

Maggie knew the open area of Sandgate where her mother took clothes every Saturday to sell, but she had seldom ventured into its dank and overcrowded hinterland. Only at the start of the mission had she visited some of the tenements with Heslop, appalled at the evil-smelling, almost pitch-black dwellings where children teemed around the stairwells like rats and mothers' shrill voices competed over the wails of babies and hacking coughs of the unseen. Maggie thought she knew poverty, but never in her worst nightmares had she seen or smelt such degradation.

'The hall has been gifted by the merchant who owns the building,' Heslop told her as they entered.

'How generous,' Maggie answered, pulling a wry face at the spartan cellar as her eyes grew accustomed to the gloom. The bare stone walls glistened with damp in the spluttering light from oil lamps that hung from low beams over rows of wooden tables and benches. The hall was already filling up and Maggie tried not to gag at the stench of unwashed bodies and paraffin fumes. Men and women of all ages were occupying the wooden forms, exchanging subdued comments. After the noise and bustle of the Sandgate outside, where families were sitting and playing in the dust, chatting, knitting, shouting, spitting and courting, this twilight place seemed unnaturally quiet.

'How do you get so many to come to your service?' Maggie whispered, astonished by the mix of vagrants, sailors, prostitutes, hawkers and elderly. Some appeared respectably dressed but their neatness was frayed, their faces careworn and ill.

'Word soon gets round if there's a bowl of soup on offer,' Heslop replied candidly.

Maggie glanced towards the curtained-off area in the corner which she had assumed was a store of hymn books and tracts. Now she noticed the steam rising from behind the hangings.

'You're running a kitchen?' Maggie asked in surprise. 'You're not just preaching at them?'

Heslop tugged at his sideburns. 'Most of these people are destitute,' he growled. 'We attempt to sustain their bodies as well as their souls. You can't transform people's lives on empty stomachs. We don't give them much, but it'll keep some of them out of the workhouse a while longer.'

Maggie felt humbled. She knew from first-hand experience that the greatest fear of the poor was to be consigned to the workhouse where families were separated and treated like prisoners, carrying out menial tasks with little prospect of escape. It was the perpetual humiliation of the workhouse, Maggie thought, which weighed heaviest in the minds of these people. It was the spur that had driven her own mother to find work at all costs and provide shelter for her family after Pearson's had cut off their security so abruptly on the death of her father.

She wanted to say something encouraging to Heslop about what he was attempting to do here but he had already crossed to the makeshift kitchen and disappeared behind the curtain.

Maggie looked around, feeling awkward in her neatness. A woman caught her eye and gave her a guardedly hostile look. Maggie recognised her as the prostitute who had drawn her mother's censure outside Stella's cafe. Closer up, her painted face looked old and weary, as if here at least she did not have to pretend to be young and appealing. There was an air of watchfulness, almost expectancy, about the patiently waiting dozens. Maggie escaped behind the curtain.

'Here, give me something to do,' she said.

Heslop was in conversation with a stout woman in her middle years and a girl with a delicate waxen face.

'Stir this, hinny,' the older woman said, handing her the ladle.

Two minutes and we'll begin,' Heslop said, after introducing his helpers as Millie Dobson and her daughter Annie.

As Maggie stirred a broth of bacon bits, peas and potatoes, which gave off a welcome aroma in the fusty hall, she heard Heslop calling his congregation to attention. Annie was dishing out hymn books with an anxious smile, while her mother hacked at a pile of loaves with a blunt carving knife.

'Mr Heslop's a good'un,' she panted over her task, 'Doesn't turn up his nose at us like other do-gooders.'

'You're not from the chapel, then, Mrs Dobson?' Maggie asked.

The woman gave a loud cackle. 'Me from the chapel! Eeh, that's a laugh. Never been inside a church since me baptism.' She saw the confusion on Maggie's face. 'I came here to give my Annie some nourishment, hinny. She's always been thin as a reed. I like a bit sing-song and Mr Heslop was that canny, we kept coming back. Then he asks us if I'd like to give a hand -extra bowl of broth in it for my Annie, an' all. Been working here for a year now, taking care of the hall.'

Maggie glanced over at the lean butcher and smiled to herself at his pragmatic approach to saving souls.

He led his flock in a rousing hymn which most of them sang and then said prayers and gave a short address, through which a couple of foreign sailors fidgeted and yawned. After a final hymn, there was a clatter as the assembled sat down and shuffled in anticipation on the benches. Heslop tapped two men on the shoulder and they got up and went to help carry out the bowls of soup for Annie. Maggie joined them, doling out hunks of ragged bread to the grimy hands that reached out to her.

All the while, Heslop went among them, talking and listening and sharing a joke with his motley congregation. Maggie noticed him in conversation with the prostitute and wondered what the respectable ladies of Alison Terrace Methodist Church would say if they could have seen him in such company. What, Maggie wondered wryly, would her own mother mink, for that matter?

With the food finished, people began to drift away and the hall to empty. Maggie helped the Dobsons to clear away and wash the bowls and spoons in a half-barrel that did for a sink.

'Miss Beaton will be sleeping here tonight,' John Heslop told Mrs Dobson. He turned to Maggie. 'Mrs Dobson and Annie are my caretakers, they live above.'

'No need for the lass to stay on her own, Mrs Dobson said at once. 'She's welcome to share with us.'

'Ta very much,' Maggie smiled with gratitude, 'if it's no bother.'

'No bother at all, hinny,' she insisted. 'Only too pleased to help a friend of Mr

Heslop's.'

Locking up the hall, John Heslop bade them goodnight and left. Maggie followed the women up to the next floor. What must have been an old office, still with a large marble fireplace, was now the living quarters of the two Dobsons. A large bed stood in one corner, a horsehair sofa in another, a dresser with a tin washbowl and chipped china jug, along with a small gas stove, filled the remaining space. From one large opaque window the room was washed in a muted green light. By the proud way Mrs Dobson showed Maggie their home, she realised they must have come from somewhere infinitely worse.

'We'll have a little nip before bed, eh?' Millie Dobson chuckled, going to the dresser and producing a small bottle of brandy, almost empty.

'Mam,' Annie said fretfully, 'Mr Heslop would hoy us out if he knew you were drinking.'

'Brandy's medicinal,'Millie Dobson replied, pouring the contents into a teacup and handing it to Maggie. 'Have a sip to help you sleep, hinny.'

Maggie hesitated. She knew Heslop disapproved of drink and according to Susan it was the reason why he had not married their mother. Yet it might help take her mind off the ordeal ahead. She sipped and then nearly spat it back out as the alcohol tore at her throat. Seconds later, warmth flooded into her cheeks and she felt better. Annie left the room in disapproval, taking the jug to fetch water.

Millie Dobson cackled. 'Annie doesn't like it, but it's got me through many a night's whoring.' She drained the rest of the brandy.

Maggie stared at her, wondering if she had heard correctly.

'Didn't Mr Heslop tell you what I was?' Millie laughed. 'Suppose you won't want to stop with us now.'

'Makes no difference to me,' Maggie answered, trying to hide her shock.

'Well, what could a widow like me do but gan on the street?' Mrs Dobson said, suddenly defensive. 'Me man died at sea. I had nee money and a sickly bairn. I wasn't going to sit back and watch my Annie die an' all!'

'I understand,' Maggie said quickly.

'How can a lass like you understand?' the older woman said bitterly.

'Because me mam was widowed too and had to bring up four bairns on her own. She was lucky, Mr Heslop lent her a bit of money to set up a second-hand clothes business and she had a few household things to sell. But it's been a struggle.'

'Ah, Mr Heslop! He's given me a hand up off the street with this mission, and Annie too. I want Annie to do better than me, have a future, respectable like.'

'But doesn't it make you boil that women like you and me mam have to rely on the charity of men like Mr Heslop?' Maggie asked, emboldened by the brandy. 'Widows should have more security - and the families that depend on them.'

'Aye,' Millie sighed, 'but there's nowt we can do about it, hinny.'

'By heck there is!' Maggie cried. 'We can fight for the vote, then we can begin to change the laws to suit us women.'

Millie Dobson looked at her with eyes that sagged in a liverish face. 'Are you one of them militants?' she asked suspiciously.

'Aye,' Maggie admitted proudly, 'and if there were more of us, we'd have the vote sharpish. Women have bowed their heads and carried their burden without a fuss for too long. Even Heslop thinks we should have the vote.'

'Does he, you bugger!' Millie exclaimed in astonishment She peered hard at Maggie. 'Are you in bother with the coppers or summat? Is that why Heslop's hiding you?'

'Not yet,' Maggie said with a grim smile.

'Tell us what you're up to, hinny.'

Maggie found it a relief to confide in the woman who sheltered her, for her aloneness was at times overwhelming. Even if Mrs Dobson was indiscreet, who would take any notice of a talkative old prostitute? She outlined her planned protest.

Millie cackled with glee. 'Eeh, and you just a slip of a lass! Good on you! I wish I had summat stronger to give you, but it'll have to be tea we toast you with, hinny.'

She went to the stove and lit the gas under a blackened pan of stewed tea and condensed milk. When the dubious mixture had boiled, Mrs Dobson poured it into two cups with their handles missing and handed one to Maggie. 'To us lasses!' she toasted.

Maggie clinked cups. 'To us lasses!' she echoed and took a gulp. It was thick and sweet and the most revolting tea she had ever drunk, but with the broken-toothed Mrs Dobson grinning at her in encouragement, it tasted strangely comforting.

On the day of the launch, Alice Pearson rose early. Dressing in an outdoor skirt and jacket, she slipped out of Hebron House as the maids were still laying the fires downstairs. Her dog Rosamund padded eagerly from her basket in the flower room when Alice called her. Together they set off across the terrace and down the front steps onto the dew-soaked lawn. Mist lay like a shawl over the treetops, obscuring the view of the river and its docks, but in its damp chill lay the promise of its evaporation and a hot day ahead. The smell of coal fires wafted over the high park walls, reminding Alice of the teeming humanity beyond her oasis of green trees and flowering bushes.

Rosamund returned and shook droplets of water over her skirt, the hem of which was already soaked with dew.

'This is going to be a great day!' Alice said aloud, reaching down to fondle her poodle.

She thought of her father in the east wing, sleeping off the grand dinner she had thrown for those involved with the Pearson's enterprise: the chief engineers, their business suppliers, the local coal-owner, their financial partners, agents and bankers. Alice had been determined to impress them all with Pearson hospitality, so that it would be the talk of the business world for the next year. They had dined on Scottish salmon, delicately clear soups, massive sides of beef and pork, a dozen different vegetables, strong cheeses and soft puddings that sparkled with spun sugar and spectacular decoration. They had drunk sherry and wine and port and Madeira and the dining table had groaned under the weight of silver candlesticks and gleaming tureens and cutlery and bright crystal. The downstairs rooms had been filled with fresh cut flowers whose perfume had filled the old mansion with a warm heady scent in the evening sun. Daniel Pearson had been delighted with it all.

Alice looked up at her father's curtained rooms. Why was he so liberal towards her as an individual, she pondered, while so reactionary in his attitude to women in general? He encouraged her involvement in Pearson's and resisted her mother's attempts to have her married off and yet he scoffed at the idea of women having a share in political power. Perhaps he was merely posturing to his political allies and business associates, Alice thought. One thing she was sure of was that he valued her companionship and conversation more than that of his wife or son and, for her part, she would do anything to please him.

Alice shot an uneasy look at the unseen, ordered rows of terraces that muscled against the walls, of the estate. To please her father she had co-operated in the subduing of the local suffragettes for the duration of Asquith's visit. More than that, she had provided the police with details about Maggie Beaton.

'The girl is unstable!' she said aloud to Rosamund. 'I could tell from the way she ranted at me at Emily's funeral. Very bad form!'

The dog barked at the sound of her mistress's cross voice.

Talking of what Emily would have wanted as if she had been a friend - quite insulting! And making threats about taking action. No, it was important the girl be warned off.'

No doubt a visit from the police would have scared her from acting rashly, Alice thought, and if not her, then certainly her family.

'She mustn't be allowed to spoil my plans, Rosamund,' Alice said to the dog as they returned to the house.

Her father had promised that she would he seated next to the Prime Minister at lunch and would have an opportunity to do some discreet lobbying. Alice did not allow herself to dwell on what her fellow suffragettes might think of such a passive approach, for she had convinced herself that she could do more for the cause using her position of influence than they could throwing missiles or protests from afar. Anyway, she did not care about making herself unpopular, as long as she achieved what she wanted, she thought stubbornly.

'Come, girl!' she ordered Rosamund. 'We've work to do today.'

No one was taking any particular notice of the two women and the pasty-faced girl making their way along Scotswood Road among the crowds. One was small and old, stooped under a large black cape and lace cap, the other stout and coarse-looking in a drab brown dress and battered orange hat

'You'll have to take those flowers and that stuffed bird off the top!' Maggie had protested at Millie Dobson that morning. Millie had been quite offended.

'I paid good money for that hat. It's not just any old bird, it's a nightingale.'

'It's nowt but a spuggy,' Maggie had contradicted, looking at the dusty, pathetic sparrow. 'You'll draw attention. I'm supposed to be an old widow, not part of a vaudeville act.'

'All right,' Mrs Dobson had huffed and given the offending hat to Annie to unstitch.

On Friday evening, John Heslop had handed over the box of clothes to Maggie, saying, 'Jimmy got these out the house without a problem, or so he says. He's itching with curiosity to know what you're doing - and so am I."

'You'll know soon enough,' Maggie had answered, grinning. Then just as he was leaving, Maggie asked him, 'I know Mam and Granny'll be worrying over me. After it's all over, will you go and tell them I came to no harm and I'll see them when I get out.'

John Heslop had studied her a moment and then nodded, seeming to understand that Maggie was heading for imprisonment. 'I'll go and see your family,' he had promised and departed.

There was a festive air about the crowds making their way towards Pearson's shipyard Maggie had to force herself to slacken her pace and remember that she was a frail elderly woman in Mrs Johnstone's dark blue dress and her grandmother's enveloping cape.

'This is a canny day out,' Millie Dobson declared, infected by the high spirits around her. 'I've never been this far upriver in all me life.'

Maggie grunted 'People don't come down here unless they have to - it's not exactly Gosforth Park, is it?'

'Looks a fine place to me,' Mrs Dobson replied, looking about the bustling street. But Maggie noticed that Annie was coughing in the dusty, smoky air, her face pale as china. She seemed to have difficulty keeping up with even their stately pace.

'Not long now,' Maggie smiled at the wan girl. 'See the spiked gates over there? That's Pearson's.'

Maggie felt her stomach churn as she said the words. Her moment of immortality was approaching, she thought. Round her waist the suffragette flag was fastened by a cord and one pull on the bow would release it. If she never did anything worthwhile in her life again, Maggie thought, at least today she was going to make history. It never crossed her mind that she might fail in her protest, for she had dismissed Rose's fears that the crowd would not let her through, or that she would be arrested before displaying her banner, or that Asquith would never notice her. Maggie was inspired by an inner conviction that her cause was just and therefore she would succeed.

About her, voices chattered and hooters on the river blew in anticipation of the event. Yet the yard seemed strangely hushed Maggie suddenly realised that the usual noises of industry had ceased for this short special time, while all the workers and their families came to see the launch of their ship. The ringing clang of plates falling into position and the din of hammer on metal had stopped. For a moment she was reminded of an occasion in her childhood when her father had proudly taken her to see the launch of a passenger ship he had helped to build. Swung high on his shoulders, she had been nearly sick with excitement as the men threw their caps in the air and her father had shouted, 'Go, you bonny boat!'

The huge bulk had slid into the water with a screech of chains and snapping ropes like some primeval beast roaring out of its lair of scaffolding, to dip and roll triumphantly in the murky green water. Maggie had stared in wonder as her father described the luxury of its vast interior. 'Like a palace, Maggie - and the nearest we'll ever get to one!'

As they jostled forward now, Maggie looked round at the expectant faces, the array of flags and coloured bunting around the distant makeshift stand for the launching party. These people - her people - were just as excited as she had been as a child to see the birth of their ship. Briefly she wondered where George Gordon was. Probably boozing in the pub, she thought disdainfully. Well, she would show him and all of Pearson's other workers how deluded they were. This ship was not their ship, it belonged to Pearson's who cared nothing for the men who had sweated and toiled over its creation and would soon sell it to a government that kept women vote- less and powerless.

Maggie's anger ignited at the thought of how her father had died building one of their ships and she realised that she was not just protesting about the vote. She yearned to strike a blow at the heartless Lord Pearson and his haughty daughter. They were to blame for her family's misfortune. The deep sense of loss for her rather and the humiliation felt for her mother on the funeral day when Pearson's had sent her a washboard and bucket engulfed her once more. For years she had nursed her anger and bitterness at the injustice they had suffered and she had to restrain herself from dashing forward at that very moment and tearing into the assembled Pearsons like a frenzied dervish.

They were near enough now to make out the figures on the platform. The men were dressed in well-cut coats and top hats, the women in a blaze of colourful summer dresses, all frills and lace and crowned with elaborate hats of feathers and ribbons. Maggie tried to peer over the heads of the crowd to make out the figure of Alice Pearson.

'Haway, lads!' Millie Dobson cried at the men around them. 'Make way for me old mother. She's walked all the way from Newcastle to see this. Give her a bit space, hinnies.'

Mrs Dobson's ploy worked instantly; a path opened up before them and people pushed aside for the bent old woman and her family. Maggie knew she must gain the launch platform itself if she was to make any impact at all. As they approached through the heaving press of bodies, she could see the steps were well policed and the crowds were being kept back. But thanks to Mrs Dobson's persistence they were as close to the launch party as they could get and she could clearly identify the tall imposing figure of Alice Pearson in a frock of mint green and cream and a hat of ostrich feathers. Was that Asquith next to her, or Lord Pearson? Maggie was suddenly unsure. Neither of them looked like the pictures she had seen of the Prime Minister in the newspapers. She realised with a jolt that, even if she came across him in the street, she would not know what Lord Pearson looked like and yet he controlled the lives of all around him. The only man she recognised was Herbert Pearson, Lord Pearson's son, whom she had glimpsed on a rare visit to her workshop and who was standing at the far end looking bored.

'You'll have to cause a diversion,' Maggie hissed at Mrs Dobson. 'They must be about to start now the band's playing.'

Above her, the gentry nodded and smiled in their finery and a bottle of champagne hung ready in its gaudy ribbons to smash on the battle-grey hull of the ship. HMS *Courageous* towered overhead as men in overalls swarmed over the unfinished boat. Later they would fit it out with its guns and trimmings, but now they were about to glory in its baptism, pride mixed with anxiety that the lumbering metal monster would float.

Maggie was filled with awe as she gazed up at the ship, then felt a lurch of panic at what she was doing. She was about to ruin the moment for scores of riveters and platers, joiners and smiths . . . Forcing the image of an outraged George Gordon from her mind, she elbowed forward towards the cordon of police. A tall, long-nosed man was starting to speak on the platform and Maggie realised the moment must be now.

It all happened in seconds and yet to Maggie it felt like the slow motions of an interminable dream. Beside her, Annie Dobson began an alarming coughing and choking, doubling up in agony. Her mother, Millie, cried for help. For a moment Maggie stopped in concern, but Millie pushed her roughly out of the way. Not knowing if Annie's distress was genuine or a theatrical diversion, she crouched lower under her bonnet and hobbled towards the steps, clutching a battered posy of flowers. Gripping the arm of the nearest policeman, she gabbled, 'Help the lass, she's having a fit, please help the lass!'

He turned to look at the gasping Annie and stepped forward to help. Another constable by the steps did the same and opened up a gap in the protective cordon. No one on the platform seemed to have noticed the small commotion taking place beneath their dais and the man continued his speech. The policeman nearest to her now was watching the dignitaries, unconcerned by the fuss in the crowd over the fainting girl.

Maggie slipped past him, muttering about her flowers, and gained the steps. In seconds she had unhooked her cape and pulled the cord round her waist.

Shaking the flag free, she dashed up the remaining steps and raised it in the air.

'Votes for women, Mr Asquith!' she shouted, pushing her way among the astonished party. Someone shrieked and behind her Maggie heard the thud of boots on the wooden steps. A man stepped into her path and attempted to hold her, but Maggie resisted and struggled free. She threw herself headlong at the aghast speaker, waving the purple, green and white banner in his face.

'You can't throw us all into gaol, Mr Asquith! Stop killing Mrs Pankhurst and give us the vote now!'

She felt a foot go out to trip her. She landed painfully on her outstretched arm and then gasped in agony as the hobnailed boot of a policeman pinned her hand to the ground. Hands seized her and dragged her up. She was aware of a ripple of noise from the crowd below and as she staggered to her feet, Maggie caught sight of Alice Pearson's thunderous red face. The aristocrat's brown unblinking eyes glared at her with astonished fury.

'Remember Emily Davison!' Maggie managed to shout, before being yanked round and pushed down the steps by her captors.

She saw no sign of the Dobson women but the mood of the crowd was openly hostile. People jeered and spat at her as she was led swiftly away behind the platform. One man came at her and punched the side of her head, spewing out a string of obscenities. The two constables gripping her did nothing to stop the assault.

With head pounding and nauseous from the blows, Maggie was dragged away, pursued by a crowd of onlookers baying for her blood like dogs. She was thrown roughly into the back of a Black Maria waiting by a side gate and was locked into a closet-sized cell in which she could not stand up. Slumping into a crouched position, her hand bleeding and pulsating from where the constable had ground his boot, she closed her eyes and fought back the urge to cry. As the horse-drawn police van lurched off over the cobbles and threw her against the opposite wall, she could hear and feel the banging of men's fists as they angrily pursued.

Maggie was shocked into numbness by their hatred. Her noble gesture had turned into an ignominious scuffle that had hardly disrupted the launch. She had been dragged through the crowds like a common criminal, removed from the sight of the gentry and politicians as a piece of dung is tossed on the midden. Maggie felt humiliated and defiled. She began to shake and could not stop. She ground her teeth together to stop her sobs and wished for oblivion.

Then above the sound of the ringing hooves and fading abuse, Maggie heard it: not the jaunty tune as the Pearson shipyard band struck up but the triumphant screech as HMS *Courageous* stirred and juddered down the slipway. The launch was going ahead, contemptuous of her attempts to halt it. Nothing, she realised with desolation, could stop the might of the Pearsons.

Chapter Twelve

Alice felt her father's fury in the brief look he gave her as they stepped off the launch platform; it was ice-cold. He said nothing to her as they left the shipyard with their guests, and Asquith was ushered into the waiting Bentley to take him to Oxford Hall.

Only Herbert spoke to her in indignant tones. 'How could you, Alice! And after you'd promised nothing would happen. There'll be a fearful row over this.'

Her mother ignored her, but Felicity gave her a malicious little smile as if she had enjoyed the drama and Alice's embarrassment. Alice said nothing but inwardly she seethed. How could that common little upstart, Maggie Beaton, evade all her measures to gag her and carry out her startling protest? She had ruined everything. Now her father would never let her near the Prime Minister and he would not hear her well-rehearsed and persuasive arguments for enfranchisement, Alice fumed.

She drove her own car through the smoky streets of West Newcastle and out into the winding lanes of the Tyne valley, following Asquith's police escort. The hedgerows and meadows were burgeoning with flowers and butterflies fluttered up as she roared past, her rage making her blind to the beauty.

'She's set back our cause!' Alice railed at the road. 'Girls like Maggie Beaton making unseemly protests will only confirm Asquith in his belief that we're not fit to be trusted with the vote. I hope they lock her up for ever, damn her!' Rosamund barked, confused by her mistress's anger.

By the time Alice reached Oxford Hall, her temper had subsided and she was once more in control of herself. She would not let her family see how much the incident had upset her.

As she suspected, she was seated well down the table from Asquith and the conversation was kept light and trivial. She tried to gain her father's attention after lunch, but he politely rebuffed her.

'I shall visit you at Hebron House next week,' he told her, 'and we'll discuss things then.'

As Herbert seemed in a huff and Felicity was deliberately ignoring her, Alice decided to leave. Even her mother did not try and persuade her to stay for dinner and the night. They all wished to punish her for the spectacle at the launch, Alice thought, so she would not stay to be humiliated further.

'They can all go to hell!' she muttered as she drove off down the crackling gravel drive lined with orderly saplings.

That night she went to bed early, but could not sleep. She tried to read, but could not concentrate. It struck her then how no one from the movement had attempted to contact her for weeks. Where were all her friends? she wondered in bewilderment How alone she felt.

Dressing again, Alice went out onto the terrace and sat on a wrought-iron chair staring at the hazy orange sunset over the trees. She could just see the gantry lights of the riverside cranes winking in the descending darkness.

What was happening to Maggie Beaton at this moment? Alice wondered. She had exhausted her anger over the girl's actions and admitted, in the quiet of the evening, to a stirring of shame. That unsophisticated working girl had done something astonishing; she had risked everything to protest for a few moments today, in front of a crowd that would have gladly lynched her. Maggie Beaton had shown a courage that Alice could never have summoned. The girl would probably be imprisoned and certainly lose her job at Pearson's, while she, privileged and powerful, had turned from the cause in fright of losing her independence and privileges.

Alice covered her face with her hands. Her guilt overwhelmed her. She had betrayed her fellow suffragettes. Was it any wonder that they had stopped calling at Hebron House since Emily's funeral? She had not encouraged them and they in turn had not invited her to their homes or soirees. It had been easy to put her name to the women's cause when it was just a matter of lending money and prestige. She had been happy to attend their fund-raising events, revelling in shocking her mother and brother with her radical show of independence. But never in a thousand years, Alice told herself brutally, would she have the courage to throw herself under the King's horse or disrupt a launch for an *ideal*. That kind of moral fortitude took her breath away.

Alice saw again, behind her closed eyelids, the spectre of Maggie Beaton being hauled through the crowd, kicked and spat upon like a traitor.

'My God,' Alice whispered. 'I'm the traitor!'

And then the tears came.

Maggie spent the night in a stifling cell at the police station. She lay for an eternity on a plank bed with a stained straw pallet and listened to the maudlin cries of a drunk in the next cell. For some reason the stranger's erratic, tearful singing reminded her of Uncle Barny and she yearned suddenly for the crowded security of Gun Street and her family. What would they be thinking of her now? she wondered. Would they have seen or heard anything of her protest or would John Heslop have gone as promised to explain her absence?

Her mother and Susan would probably be distressed and furious. Helen would be unconcerned and already arguing for her clothes, while Jimmy would most likely boast of his part in the plan and be walloped. Only Granny Beaton would understand why she had done it and Maggie knew the old woman would be missing her companionship.

Maggie curled up tighter and tried to shut out the drunk's singing. On Monday morning she would appear before the magistrates and be sentenced. She longed to see her friend Rose and hear what the other suffragettes thought of the surprise protest, frightened now that she would be cast out of the movement for acting on her own. And what of the Dobsons? Maggie fretted, hoping that they had not been caught up in the scuffles.

Her fears and doubts raced around her mind as the hours dragged by and the daylight never seemed to come.

Richard Turvey woke with a thumping head. It took him several minutes to work out where he was and when he remembered, he groaned and closed his eyes again. He had a vague recollection of the last bar he had been drinking in and the game of cards in which he had lost the last of his money - or rather Aunt Violet's money. There had been a lot of hard drinking after the launch of the battleship, to which he had not gone, but he had entered into the spirit of the day.

Too much so, Richard thought, wincing at his hangover. Somehow he had got involved in someone else's brawl, over someone else's girl, and the last thing he recalled was being bundled inside a van and brought to the police station.

'Well, that's curtains to my job at the Olympia,' Richard groaned. He should have been there last night calling for customers outside the doors and he was on his final warning from the long-suffering manager. He would have to think up a good story for Aunt Violet too, for his indulgent aunt would not turn a blind eye to his waywardness for ever, Richard was sure. As for Susan ... Richard sighed when he thought of the plump-faced, fussing, affectionate young woman who seemed determined to have him. He was far more partial to her saucy younger sister Helen, but Susan was a better home-maker and more likely to provide him with a comfortable life than pretty, moody Helen. After all, there would be the mother's business to inherit, Richard mused, and judging by the way the old lady drank and wheezed with ill health, it might be sooner rather than later.

A key rattled in the lock and the duty sergeant brought in a mug of tea.

'Looks like you could do with this, lad,' he grunted.

Richard nodded and took the mug. To his dismay the policeman seemed in a mood to chat.

'You'll be going up after they've dealt with that suffragette lass on Monday,' the constable told him.

'Oh no,' Richard murmured, his head thumping with the effort of sitting up. How would he explain his prolonged absence to Aunt Violet?

'Doesn't look the type to say boo to a goose, if you ask me,' the portly sergeant continued. 'Makes you wonder what gets into them.'

Richard became aware of a young voice singing robustly from a cell down the corridor.

'That's her making a racket,' the sergeant nodded. 'She'll not be so happy when they put her away for a spell.'

Something about the singer's voice made Richard ask, 'What's the girl called?'

'Margaret Beaton, from down Elswick.'

Richard spluttered over his tea.

'Do you know her or summat?' the policeman asked.

'Me? No, don't recognise the name.' Richard's denial was too quick. The sergeant gave him a speculative look.

'Might do you some good if you did,' he said quietly.

'What do you mean?' Richard asked, his mind like a fog.

'She's caused a right stir that one - upsetting the Pearsons and the Prime Minister. Now if someone was able to give a bit of information on the lass - keep an eye on her once she's out, that sort of thing - then there might be something in it for that someone. We can't have these militant women terrorising our town, now can we?'

'You mean spy on her?' Richard asked slowly.

The sergeant said nothing, but continued to watch him.

'Who would pay for such information?' Richard whispered.

The policeman shrugged. 'The Pearsons are wealthy folk. Now it doesn't look to me like you've got much to rub together, lad. And there'll be a hefty fine for your brawling.'

He was right, Richard thought desperately. He had no money of his own, only debts. He pretended to his relations that he had a good job at the Olympia, but he was merely the caller who tried to entice customers off the street. If he did not get some money from somewhere quickly, he would have to disappear from Newcastle in a hurry. But could he deliberately betray Susan's sister Maggie? After all, she had saved him from a beating on that earlier night of trouble in which he had denied all involvement.

For a moment he fought with his weakening conscience, then gave up. Maggie had brought this upon herself with her high self-opinion and desire to be infamous. She brought nothing but trouble to the Beaton household anyway, Richard decided. It would be better for Susan and her mother and Aunt Violet if

Maggie was kept under control. Easier for him too, for Maggie's uninterest in him had been infuriating and it disturbed him that she was the only one who seemed to see through his play-acting and suspected him for the lazy opportunist that he was.

'Come to think of it, perhaps I do know something about the girl,' Richard answered, feeling himself reviving with the tea.

'Thought you might,' the sergeant grunted and glanced out of the cell. 'I'll see what I can do for you.'

The court appearance passed in a bewildering rush. Maggie stood pale in the dock, surrounded by a sea of curious faces while two policemen gave evidence against her. She felt paralysed and unable to speak. When the time came to defend herself, Maggie could not think of a single thing to say. Then she heard the magistrate sentence her to six months' imprisonment and her head began to spin. It stretched ahead in her mind like a lifetime of captivity and she felt real fear - fear of unknown horrors awaiting her in prison, fear of loneliness and isolation, fear that her old life would never be recaptured.

As she was led away, Maggie thought she caught a glimpse of Rose in the gallery. For a few seconds the sighting of a friendly, supportive presence lifted her spirits. She turned and shouted at the magistrates, 'Votes for Women!'

Her escorts grabbed her and ushered her roughly from the court.

Later, inside Newcastle prison, Maggie found herself among a motley group of petty criminals waiting to be dealt with by the wardresses. Still dazed, Maggie was astonished to hear one of the women call her name. It was the toothless pea-seller, Mrs Surtees, from the Bigg Market.

'Got you at last did they, hinny?' Mrs Surtees tutted.

'Six months,' Maggie whispered, still unable to believe her own words.

'Eeh, never! A young lass like you - it's a scandal!'

Mrs Surtees, it appeared, was in for stealing a purse from another stallholder.

'I just needed a lend of some money till I got down the pawnshop,' Mrs Surtees said with a baffled shrug, 'but he didn't see it that way.'

Then a tired-looking head wardress came in with two helpers and demanded silence. The prisoners were unceremoniously stripped and searched and weighed, then forced to take a tepid bath, while their paltry possessions were bundled up and removed. A couple of the women laughed and put on a show of bravado until the wardress upbraided them, but Maggie was sunk in a dispirited numbness.

Without protest, she put on a scratchy prison uniform, a starched cap and voluminous apron and was led away to a dismal cell. She stood in the middle of the stone floor for a long time, staring at the barred window and the patch of blue sky beyond as if it was a distant unattainable paradise.

What had she done? Maggie asked herself miserably. What had she achieved by her reckless protest? She had lost her liberty and her family had lost her precious wages, for which she would probably never be forgiven. Worst of all, women were no nearer to winning the vote than they had been two days ago. She had imagined herself as a romantic martyr to the cause, just like Emily Davison, but no one would remember the working-class Maggie Beaton, she told herself harshly. Heroines did not come from mean dwellings in Gun Street and common widows' daughters did not get themselves into history books, Maggie thought with self-mockery.

Sometime towards evening, her cell was unlocked and food brought in. Maggie's depression lifted to see the steaming mug of tea and her mouth began to water at the aroma of suet dumpling wafting from the tin. The wardress dumped the meal on the floor.

Maggie hurried over, her stomach hollow with hunger. She realised she had eaten little more than bread and tea since breakfast with the Dobsons two days ago. She grabbed the mug and the wardress cackled.

'Didn't take you long to give in to temptation, did it?'

Maggie gave her a suspicious look. 'What's that supposed to mean?'

'Thought proper suffragettes went on hunger strike,' the woman mocked. 'Still, you don't look tough enough for that carry-on. You'll last the six months, you will. Probably looking forward to it, I bet. Better food in here than at home, eh? That why you done it?' She let out another belly laugh.

The woman's scorn was like a slap in the face. Maggie gasped with indignation. How dare this wardress treat her like common muck? she fumed. She was just as dedicated as any of the others in the movement and she would show this ignorant, sour-faced gaoler how tough she could be.

'I'm just as strong as any posh suffragettes you've had in here,' Maggie answered sharply. 'Take your bloody suet dumplings and stick them up your backside! I'll not be eating them!'

Maggie kicked the tin violently towards the door and the astonished prison warder. The woman retreated hastily and slammed the door, shouting, 'You'll have to clear up your own mess, you filthy bitch.'

Maggie hurled the mug of tea at the metal door and watched the brown liquid splatter onto the walls and floor.

'I'm a political prisoner!' she cried 'I demand to have me own clothes back. I'll not clear up my mess or any other bugger's! I'm no criminal. The criminals are the coppers who put me here, aye, and that fat magistrate! And the male politicians who won't give us the vote. Let them clear up the filth!'

Maggie carried on ranting, long after the wardress was out of earshot. But she did not care, her words gave her courage and shook her out of her former despair. It did matter what insignificant Maggie Beaton did, she told herself. For it was only by the acts and sacrifices of scores of individuals like herself that their cause would be advanced. They could starve her and humiliate her, but she would not be broken, Maggie vowed. They would never break her!

George Gordon paced around the streets of Newcastle wondering what to do. He entered a public house, but left before ordering a pint. Eventually he retraced his steps to Carliol Square and looked up at the grim walls of the prison. Where was Maggie being held? he wondered. Was she here at all or had she been taken to another gaol? How would her delicate young body stand up to six months of prison life? he fretted. Worse still, would she refuse food and starve herself to death?

He ground his teeth in the agony of not knowing. It was nearly a week now since her sentencing and that depressing morning in court, which he had skipped work to witness. She had seemed so alone and vulnerable, George had wanted to shout at the censorious well-to-do magistrates for being so vindictive. And yet he had gone there himself to see Maggie brought to justice, to make sure she got her comeuppance for spoiling their launch. He had wanted her punished.

It should have been a special day of celebration for all the workers, a moment of pride when the ship broke its shackles and took to the water, proving their craftsmanship. But Maggie's unseemly protest had belittled the occasion as if it were of no importance whatsoever. He had been astounded to see her appear in the centre of the launch party, brandishing her banner in their horrified faces. She seemed to be telling the world they had missed the point, that their day of celebration was nothing more than a silly child's party compared to the long vital struggle for justice to which she was vainly drawing attention.

'Oh Maggie!' He grimaced at the fortress walls in frustration. He lit a cigarette. It pained him to think of how he had scorned her suffragism, of how they had parted so acrimoniously because he would not take her political activities seriously. He had tolerated her ideals because he fancied her and wanted her company, but now he could see how his condescension had angered her.

He had gone to the court for revenge, hoping to see her suffer because she had rejected him. Instead, he had been shamed by her courage. Watching her contemptuous silence in the police court and her defiant cry when being led away, he had been filled with admiration. Maggie Beaton, lowly clerk and working-class girl of no more than twenty, had taken on the Establishment - the Prime Minister, the Pearsons, the police - and lost, but lost with dignity.

George shook his head. She had not cared how unpopular her suffragism made her with her family or workmates, or with him, she had still gone ahead and done it. He knew of no brothers in the union or at work who were so single-minded and it made him feel shame for the way he and other unionists belittled the concerns of women like Maggie.

Grinding the cigarette beneath his boot, he came to a decision. It took him half an hour to find where Rose Johnstone lived, the suffragette friend Maggie had often talked about. It turned out to be not far from where he lived in Rye Hill. A diminutive, pink-faced woman answered his knocking, who turned out to be Rose's mother.

'Rose is out,' she told him cautiously.

He asked if he could wait. She left him to sit in silence in a neat, threadbare parlour, spotlessly clean and smelling of lavender. George was unnerved enough to rest his boots on his cap for fear of dirtying the red and gold patterned rug.

Rose appeared just as he was contemplating flight. He stood as she came in, rescuing his soiled cap. She regarded him suspiciously.

'Have you seen her - Maggie?' he asked immediately.

'No, they won't allow visitors.' Rose remained standing. 'Probably because of the state they'll have reduced her to.'

She watched his face pucker in concern. It was a handsome, square face, dominated by a thick moustache and hooded eyes that hinted of sensuality. Rose could understand what had attracted Maggie to this man, yet she was jealous to think he had tried to win away her protégée and distract Maggie from her work.

'What state?' he asked anxiously.

Rose decided to be brutal; why should he be spared the anguish that ate away inside her? 'She'll have been without food for a week - they'll be force-feeding her by now. Don't you know what that does to a woman?'

George gave an exclamation of horror and sat down, covering his face with his dirt-ingrained hands.

Rose felt a twinge of pity. 'What is it you've come for?' she asked.

George looked up at the severe schoolteacher and shrugged helplessly. 'I don't know. I just wanted to do something for her - makeup for...'

'For not taking her seriously before?' Rose demanded 'You hurt her greatly by scorning her beliefs. She wanted your approval, couldn't you see that?'

'No,' George admitted quietly. 'I didn't see the half of it.' He looked at her accusing bespectacled eyes and felt the awkwardness of a scolded child. He did not much like Maggie's friend, but it would do no good to argue with her. He imagined few people did.

He stood up to leave.

'Wait,' Rose suddenly stopped him. "Have some tea with us.'

'No, ta,' George replied, eager to be gone.

'Please,' Rose insisted. 'I didn't mean to be so sharp with you - it's just the worry over Maggie. It'd be nice to talk to someone about her. Her mother and sisters won't have anything to do with me, you see. Please stay.'

George nodded. 'They're a stubborn lot, the Beatons,' he grunted.

Rose smiled at him for the first time. 'And Maggie's the most stubborn of them all.'

George sighed. 'Aye. And look where it's got her.' They were silent for a moment, each contemplating Maggie's ordeal. 'I just want you to know, Miss Johnstone,' George spoke with sudden passion, 'that when she comes out I'm here to help if she needs me. You will tell her that, won't you?'

Maggie was filled with dread at the ominous rumbling sound of the trolley approaching her cell. The first time she had not known what it signified, but she had barricaded the cell door with her chair and bed anyway. It had taken them twenty minutes to break in and four irate wardresses to pin her to the floor. Burdon, the hard-faced wardress who had taunted Maggie on her arrival, had shouted at the others, 'Lie on the stupid bitch!'

Panting and swearing, they had finally overcome their writhing victim and the four hefty women had her spread-eagled on the ground. Then two doctors had entered the cell, dragging the grim trolley with them. While Burdon gripped her shoulders, one of the doctors had wrenched her head back by the hair and begun to ram the stiff nozzle of a rubber tube up her left nostril.

Maggie had screamed in agony as the tube was shoved further and further in, until it felt as if it had reached inside her eye and would force it from its socket.

'You don't have to endure this,' the doctor told her coldly. 'If you behaved yourself and took your food, you'd save us all a lot of trouble.'

Maggie had been in too much torment to answer. All she could do was to stare in wide-eyed terror as the other doctor calmly lifted up the funnel attached to the other end of the tube and began to pour in his evil concoction of cocoa and Bovril and medicines designed to keep her alive.

As the liquid gushed up her nose and down her gullet, Maggie had felt sure she would choke and drown in the brown liquid. It seemed to go on for an age. She wanted to vomit, but could not.

Finally the torture stopped and they all left abruptly, leaving her sick and dazed and quivering on the cell floor. She had lain bruised and aching for what seemed like hours, before dragging herself onto her bed and crying herself to sleep. That had been two weeks ago and they had come every day since. Now Maggie listened with fear and disgust for the sound of the doctors' trolley and prayed feverishly for delivery.

She heard the cell door being unlocked and gripped the pipe that ran along the floor with what strength she could. She knew the wardresses found her resistance weakening with every visit, so this time she had planned a surprise for them and the disdainful doctors.

'Bloody hell, there's a stink in here!' the young wardress, Stevens, cried as she entered.

'Look what she's done, Dr Shaw!' Burden shrieked in disgust. 'She's worse than an animal.'

Maggie watched them move aside like worried sheep to make way for the stout, balding figure of Dr Shaw. She felt a moment of triumph as a look of appalled distaste creased his jowled face.

'My God!' he exclaimed.

The other doctor, the younger one who stood and dispassionately poured liquid down the tube, came in to look. He stared curiously as if she were some outlandish species he had never studied before.

Here she was, exhausted but still defiant, her prison clothes smeared in the liquid faeces that her force-feeding had produced. She could hardly smell her own excrement for her sense of taste and smell appeared to have wasted away with her appetite and strength. But she could tell that this time, for a brief, triumphant moment, she had defeated them.

'I'm a political prisoner, Dr Shaw,' Maggie croaked. 'I demand the right to be treated differently. I want visitors. I want justice. How do you sleep at night after your dirty work, Dr Shaw? I thought doctors were healers not torturers...' Her voice broke.

'Oh, you'll be treated differently,' the furious doctor snapped. He turned to young Stevens. 'Fetch a bucket of cold water and wash her down. You,' he spoke to Burdon, 'summon the head wardress. After we've fed this Jezebel I'm sure your superiors will see fit to lock her in the punishment cell.'

Burdon moved at once, but Stevens hesitated, aghast at what she was being asked to do.

'Couldn't we just leave her for a bit, doctor?' she asked, her plump cheeks scarlet.

'Do as Dr Shaw says,' Burdon ordered with a shove, 'or you'll be hoyed out on the street.'

They all left and locked the door, leaving a half-hysterical Maggie rocking with laughter. She began to sing *The Women's Marseillaise.*

'To Freedom's cause till death - we swear our fealty. March on! March on!' The effort made Maggie breathless. 'Face - to the Dawn. The dawn ... of... Liberty!'

By the time the feeding party returned, grimly determined to have their way, Maggie had little energy to resist. Stevens drenched her in a deluge of cold water that left her spluttering and gasping for breath and then the women grabbed her arms and legs and held her down.

Dr Shaw seemed to take a delight in forcing the tube up her swollen and bloodied nose and Maggie screamed as if the pain would kill her. The brutality of the feeding and the shock of the cold water made her faint. She could feel consciousness ebbing from her in sickening waves. At one moment she was acutely aware of the young doctor's pale, emotionless face above her and the relentless trickle of liquid down her throat; at the next, her hostile attendants were wavering and indistinct.

Maggie wondered if this was what it felt like to die. At least the pain will stop if I do, she thought. Her whole body shuddered and ached in an uncontrollable spasm and she could not recall what it felt like to be intact. Her battered body had no memory of a time before this violation. She cried out to be left alone, but no words came from her flooded throat.

Then the tube was wrenched out like a hot knife and Maggie passed out with the pain.

Chapter Thirteen

Mabel Beaton laboured half-heartedly with a wooden spoon in the large cracked bowl. She sighed and put down the cake mixture, her arms aching from the effort. Why was it, she thought with vexation, that she was not more pleased with Susan's engagement to Richard Turvey?

The young Londoner had approached her and asked for her daughter's hand in marriage with all his usual charm. These days he wore a new air of prosperity about him since he had secured a new office job down on the quayside. Susan had been delighted with his move from what she saw as insecure and dubious employment in the entertainment world to respectability, and Mabel was encouraged by this show of responsibility too. Richard had been vague about his new job, but from what she could gather, she understood it was to do with exporting armaments for one of Pearson's subsidiary companies. Yet she had never quite trusted him after Maggie's attack in town in which she privately suspected he had been involved in some way.

But perhaps it was just the upset over Maggie's arrest and the exhaustion of the past weeks coping without her wages that had left her feeling weak and depressed, Mabel thought. At first she had been worried at Maggie's disappearance, then furious at her brief notoriety at the launch and in the local press after her court appearance. Mabel had refused to let any of the family attend and had given Jimmy a severe beating for conspiring to get clothes to Maggie. She had refused to speak to Granny Beaton for a fortnight on discovering she had squandered her expensive cape on the escapade and told the old woman that she did not care if she froze this winter as a result. Her mother-in-law was becoming an increasing burden since Maggie's arrest, with her mind withdrawing into a haunted past.

But it was now two months since Maggie had been imprisoned and Mabel's anger was spent. She missed her daughter and fretted over her treatment and knew that old Mrs Beaton did too. Yet it still perplexed her why Maggie had so readily given up her good job and secure future for this obsession with women's rights. Mabel had invested all her hopes in her brightest daughter and now they were as spent as the ashes in the grate.

'Let me finish that, lassie,' Granny Beaton interrupted her thoughts, hobbling across from the fire where she had been sitting in a reverie.

Mabel took up the spoon and began to beat again.

'I can manage,' she said shortly.

'Why don't you go and lie down for a wee bit?' her mother-in-law suggested gently. 'You look tired.'

'I'm all right,' Mabel answered crossly, hating attention being drawn to her ill health. Last week she had taken to her bed for two days with pains in her chest and arms, and Susan had to help Helen with the clothes business. Her thick hair, of which she had been so proud, was now completely silver and thinning on her scalp. When she looked in the mirror she saw a puffy grey-faced woman of nearer sixty than her forty-eight years. These days she felt old as well as looking it.

'What are you making, dearie?' Granny asked, staring half-blindly at the bowl.

'The cake for Susan and Richard's betrothal party,' Mabel said, pausing again. 'I told you before.'

Granny Beaton looked at her vacantly for a moment

'Don't tell me you've forgotten already, Mrs Beaton?' Mabel said in irritation.

'Susan's getting married?' Granny Beaton asked.

'Aye, to Richard Turvey, the lad from London.'

'Richard?' For a moment the old woman seemed to struggle with her memory, then, 'Och, aye. The boy from London.'

The old wife! Mabel thought impatiently. She doubted her mother-in-law would remember Maggie when she finally came home. Then the older woman surprised her with a moment of lucidity.

'I think we should've waited for Maggie to be with us before having a party. They're just young and it wouldn't harm them to wait a wee bit. You won't let them marry while Maggie's still in prison, will you, Mabel?'

'Don't fuss, Mrs Beaton, they'll not be marrying before next summer,' Mabel answered shortly, though she silently shared the old woman's concern. Susan was full of haste and seemed to have rubbed Maggie from her mind, for she never spoke about her absent sister.

The next moment Susan bustled in at the back door, putting a stop to Granny Beaton's anxious questioning.

'Look at this, Mam!' she cried breathlessly, tearing at a package she was carrying before even unbuttoning her coat. 'Richard bought it for me - at Fenwick's!'

The name of the grand department store brought Helen rushing out of the parlour where she had been reluctantly sewing on buttons.

'What've you got?' she demanded, tossing back her fair ringlets to stare at her sister's purchase.

'A new hat!' Susan tore feverishly at the soft paper wrapping inside the box.

'A new hat in its own box!' Mabel exclaimed. 'I've never seen one o' them before.'

Susan discarded her old wide-brimmed hat and lifted the new one carefully from its nest of tissue paper. It was a neat black and white toque with two brilliant feathers of vivid green and china blue. She perched it on the front of her head while the others gazed in awe at her sudden chic appearance. It drew the eye away from the plumpness around her chin and highlighted the curve of her cheeks and brow, whereas her old, all-enveloping hat had accentuated her dumpiness.

'What a bonny picture you look!' Mabel gasped at her eldest child. 'You look a grown woman, our Susan.'

'Well, that's what I am,' Susan preened. 'Eeh, we went to that new Terrace Tearoom an' all. Had a real orchestra playing and proper table linen on the tables. And Mam, you should've seen the cups and saucers - gold trim.'

Mabel caught the look of speechless envy on Helen's face and answered swiftly, 'Well, you better get laying our battered old crockery or there'll be no party the night. And you just watch your step with that young man - you're barely engaged.'

Yet she was pleased to see Susan so animated and happy. Hers had been a long, dull growing up, with few treats and too many family burdens and it was time, Mabel thought, that she had a bit of fun.

'Can I try it on?' Helen gulped, trying to hide her admiration.

Susan looked unwilling. 'You might damage the feathers... '

'I won't,' Helen insisted. 'Just for a minute. Haway, Susan.'

'Oh, all right,' Susan agreed with reluctance and Helen had it on her head in an instant. She dashed straight into the parlour to admire herself in the mirror.

'It suits me, don't you think. Mam?' Helen demanded through the open door. 'White and black are all the mode this autumn,' she added with affectation.

Mabel silently agreed. Above Helen's large blue eyes with their startlingly dark brows and lashes, the effect of the expensive hat was striking.

'It suits an older lass like Susan better,' Mabel lied. 'Don't you go thinking we can afford hats like that for you. Now give it back and help your sister set the table.'

Helen's face turned sulky. 'Why do I always have to wear my sisters' cast-offs? Why can't I have something new for a change?'

'Just be grateful for what you've got,' Mabel snapped wearily.

'Well, I'm not!' Helen shouted. 'Why should I be grateful for carting a load of smelly old clothes around town while our Susan's having tea with the posh lot in Fenwick's?'

'Don't you speak to Mam like that!' Susan scolded, grabbing her hat from Helen. For a moment Helen held on and they tussled with it when suddenly the bright blue feather became detached and fluttered in a crazy zigzag to the scrubbed wooden floor.

They both stopped their struggling and stared in horror at the damaged toque. Helen seemed as aghast at the crime as her sister and immediately released the hat. But it was too late.

'Look what you've done!' Susan shrieked and instantly burst into tears, running into the bedroom and slamming the door behind her.

Susan so seldom cried that the sudden show of emotion upset her mother. Mabel dropped the wooden spoon and lunged round the table before Helen could escape, raised her hand and slapped her daughter hard across the face.

'You selfish little madam! Why do you always have to spoil things for our Susan? And after the way she's brought you up and looked after you!'

Helen glared back, nursing her cheek and trying not to cry. 'I never wanted her to! You're me mam - you should've been there to look after me, not that bossy cow. But you've always put Susan and Maggie before me, ever since me dad died. You've never cared about me! None of you ever cared about me!'

Mabel was appalled by this outburst. She had done everything she could to keep her family together after Alec was killed and she was still working herself into an early grave so that they would never again be homeless or hungry. It was not her fault if she had been unable to give the demanding Helen the attention she constantly craved. She had done her best and the effort had wrung her dry of all reserves of energy and love. The injustice of Helen's words made Mabel's pulse race furiously.

She seized the girl by her curly hair and propelled her towards the back door which stood open to let in the fresh September breeze.

'Get out of my sight, you ungrateful little waster!' she shouted.

'Ah-ya, Mam! Please don't,' Helen wailed.

Pushing Helen down the steps, Mabel hauled the hysterical girl across the moss-covered yard to the coal shed.

'You can stay in there till you learn some manners.'

'No, Mam! I'm sorry!' Helen screamed. 'Please, Mam. I hate it in there. It's dirty ...'

Mabel flung her inside and banged the door shut, forcing across the two bolts. She walked away shaking with her own violence, shutting out her daughter's terrified wails, and wondered how her life had ever come to this.

Once, long ago, she had loved all her daughters with a possessive passion. Now they filled her with worry, disappointment and fatigue that reduced her to locking her youngest in an outhouse to keep order.

As she mounted the back stairs, ignoring the curious stares of the Smiths from their kitchen window, she thought herself no better than the gaolers who kept Maggie imprisoned and wondered again about the fate of her other rebellious child. She had gone once to visit, but they had not let her in and being semi-illiterate she had been too embarrassed to leave a note.

Re-entering the kitchen she found only Granny Beaton sitting staring into the fire, sucking her gums and mumbling to herself in Gaelic. Mabel was suddenly seized with panic that her family was collapsing in on itself like poor baking.

'It mustn't happen,' Mabel said aloud, 'or all the hard graft has been for nowt!'

Granny Beaton looked up at her in confusion. 'What was that, Peggi?'

Mabel had no idea who the old woman thought she was. 'I said it's time we got that cake in the oven, Mrs Beaton. We're going to give Susan the celebration she deserves.'

'Susan?' Granny asked with childlike interest. 'What is the lassie celebrating?'

Mabel sighed and went back to her mixing.

Maggie had no idea how long she spent in solitary confinement, but it came close to breaking her spirit. There was nothing in her cell; even the bed was removed at the start of the day. In the ordinary cell there was a high window that let in the light and to whose ledge tame birds would come and sit and twitter for food. But the punishment cell was like a tomb which shut out the light and the noise of other prisoners until Maggie lost all sense of what day or hour it was. The force-feeding continued relentlessly and eventually she put up no opposition to the assault.

After what seemed like an eternity, Maggie was returned to the main landing and a degree of liberty to shuffle around the larger cell and talk to the sparrows who darted into view.

One day, young Stevens lingered behind to clear up the spillage and bile from a feeding session.

'It's daft, this carry-on,' she said. 'Nobody gives a dickybird what happens to you in here. So what you ganin' on for?'

Maggie just looked at her with silent contempt, too weak to argue, but Stevens persisted, with a nervous glance over her shoulder.

'You see, everyone outside's forgotten what you did. If you'd been a posh lady they might have taken more notice and got you out by now, but who gives a toss about ordinary lasses like us, eh? If you died the morra no one would make a fuss, would they? So why don't you just tell them what they want to hear?'

'And what's that?' Maggie croaked.

'Say you were wrong to do what you did. Say you'll give up being a suffragette,' Stevens urged in a whisper, 'then they'll leave you alone and you can gan home. I tell you, me and the other lasses are pig sick of forcing you to drink that muck every day. It's not right making us do that to another lass. Them doctors aren't right in the head, they've worked too long with people they think are worse than animals.' Stevens darted to the door to make sure she wasn't overheard.

Maggie felt her resolve disintegrating with the girl's concerned words. She had weathered the abuse, the humiliation and the violence and had resisted the temptation to give in, even as her body withered before her sunken eyes. In the dark of the punishment cell, Maggie had clung to the certainty that her cause was just and that her friends outside would be willing her to keep faith. At times she had felt their presence like a comforting pair of arms holding her up and giving her courage.

But now, to be told that the world did not care about her or her sacrifice was shattering. After all, no one had written to her, not even Rose and her mother and she had had no news from any of her family. Maggie felt an overwhelming sense of failure and bitterness at being abandoned.

How pathetic that her only friend appeared to be this solid, anxious wardress who had the humanity to worry over her and wish her ordeal to end. Maggie hung her head and felt painful tears prick her eyes and water her swollen throat. How easy it would be to give up the struggle now, she thought. And why shouldn't she? She had suffered for over three months and could endure no more. Nobody could demand more of her.

'Eeh, Maggie,' Stevens said in concern, 'are you crying?'

A dry harsh sob wrenched itself from Maggie's throat. 'I can't...' Maggie tried to voice her despair but could not.

'Burdon says you've never cried,' Stevens said, putting an arm about her skinny shoulders. 'Says you're not human that way.'

'If I agree to say - what you said,' Maggie gulped, 'will that be an end of it? Will they let me go home?'

'That's what Miss Holland says, and she's head wardress.'

Maggie suddenly yearned to be free and at home, she longed to be forgiven and taken back into the heart of her family, made a fuss of by Granny Beaton and hugged by her mother. She felt faint for want of physical contact and loving arms to nurse her back to life.

'If only someone had written,' Maggie sniffed, 'I could have borne it if just someone had written to me.'

'Aye,' Stevens nodded, 'you've Burdon to thank for that. Now, can I tell Miss Holland you've agreed to sign the papers and you can tell them doctors to go pick their own noses?'

Maggie looked up in confusion. 'What did you say?'

'About signing the papers.'

'No, about Burdon,' Maggie asked.

Stevens stood up and gave a nervous glance towards the door. 'I shouldn't really say.'

Maggie put out a scrawny hand and gripped Stevens with what strength she had left. 'Tell me!'

'You did get letters but Burdon threw them out, said they would only encourage you to be difficult. Don't you dare say I told you, mind,' Stevens said sharply.

Maggie closed her eyes in relief. How close she had come to betraying her friends.

'Go away,' she ordered. 'I'll sign nowt!'

Stevens looked vexed. 'You're bloody daft.'

'Gan on,' Maggie hissed. 'I'd sooner die a suffragette than give in to them bastard doctors.'

Stevens hurried from the cell.

For the next three days, Maggie clung to the knowledge that she had not been forgotten, that someone had tried to keep her spirits from flagging by writing to her. She adamantly refused to sign any papers renouncing her allegiance to the WSPU. But her physical strength was ebbing rapidly.

Finally, in the fourteenth week, when she was too weak to stand, a third doctor was called in to check her heart.

'If you carry on with the feeding, you'll kill her,' he grimly told the prison governor.

The next day Maggie was unceremoniously told she was to be released on licence until she was strong enough to carry out the rest of her sentence. She knew this was how the infamous 'Cat and Mouse' Act kept suffragettes at the mercy of the authorities for months or years as they were shunted in and out of prison. But she felt a lifting of her spirits to think she was about to see the outside world again and smell its vitality after the months of incarceration.

She was given her old clothes to dress in; they hung on her gaunt frame like those on a scarecrow. That afternoon she was bundled into an ambulance and escorted out of the prison. She lay terrified by the speed of the motor vehicle and wincing with pain at the jolts it gave her bony body. She was too exhausted by the journey to notice in which direction she was driven and so it came as a shock to find herself being carried out of the ambulance in front of a large white-bricked house surrounded by trees shedding their coppery leaves. She looked around in panic and confusion.

'Where am I?' she whispered in fright to a round-faced woman with a starched cap and apron who leaned over her in the sunlight. 'This isn't me home. I want to gan home.'

'You're in safe hands,' the woman assured her with a kind smile. 'I'm Sister Robinson.'

Alice Pearson paced along the edge of the water garden, beneath the golden willows. Autumn had a grip on the trees and the wind blowing up from the Tyne was raw with the smell of oil and cinders and the promise of icy rain.

But Alice hardly felt its coldness as she squelched through the mud in her leather boots, Rosamund snuffling happily behind her among the fallen leaves. There was too much occupying her mind.

Should she go and see Maggie Beaton at the convalescent home in Gosforth or not? she fretted. Sister Robinson had said it was too early for visitors and that her patient was in an extremely weakened state and so Alice had an excuse to stay away. She was partly thankful to do so; she did not want to draw attention to her links with the WSPU at this moment, but part of her longed to see Maggie Beaton and try to make amends for her punishing imprisonment.

Not that she was in a strong position to help the girl, except to give her moral support. Perhaps when this storm with Herbert and Felicity had blown over, she might be able to offer Maggie a job in her household ...

'Ruddy Felicity!' Alice growled aloud. She knew that her sister-in-law was at the centre of the family battle to curb her independence and bring her to heel. Alice recalled with anger the way her beloved Hebron House had been appropriated by her brother and his pretty, vindictive wife. She despised Herbert all the more for sending their father to do his brutal work for him, but then that was so like Herbert to hide behind the actions of others, Alice thought with disdain.

She had known that something was wrong when her father turned up unannounced and refused to stay for dinner as he was accustomed to do.

'You've disappointed me, Alice,' Lord Pearson had said curtly, firing his words across the length of the upstairs drawing room. It had been a hot day in August and the room had been flooded with light and warmth that made the air smell of dusty fabric and polished wood.

Alice had stood with her back to the huge marble fireplace and looked at him steadily with her prominent brown eyes.

'I had nothing to do with that girl's protest, Papa,' she told him for the umpteenth time.

'I may believe you but the Prime Minister does not,' her father snapped. 'It's done untold harm to our reputation. We're seen as being a potential target for further sabotage. So,' he said, turning to scrutinise something through the long sash window, 'I've decided we must keep a closer eye on your activities. I'm not going to force you into marriage as your mother wants, but you can no longer live here alone.'

'You're going to find me a suitable companion?' Alice asked mockingly. 'To keep me in check?'

'I won't need to,' he answered in his most businesslike manner, turning from watching a gardener weeding the beds below. 'Herbert and Felicity have decided to move back to town where Herbert can pursue his political career. It might even encourage him to take more interest in the business and stop spending the Pearson fortune, so I've agreed to the plan. They will take over the running of Hebron House at once.'

Alice had gawped at him in shock. She had expected to be chastised for the affair at the launch and was even prepared to spend more time at Oxford Hall at her mother's endless social gatherings, but she had been quite unprepared for this intrusion into her private life.

'You mean Felicity will take over the running of my home?' Alice spluttered. 'She's behind all this, isn't she? She's never forgiven me for doing Herbert's dirty work and getting rid of Poppy Beresford, her lover!'

'Don't be so vile,' her father shouted. 'Felicity is a charming girl and the mother of my grandson - the heir to my empire. If she finds the country too quiet and wishes to return to town then you'll not stand in her way. Remember, Alice, this is my house and you live your liberated life here at my discretion. Don't give me cause to change my mind about that. You'll welcome Felicity here and curb that tongue of yours.'

They had glared at each other, while Alice choked on words of anger.

'If,' her father had continued more evenly, gripping the back of a flowery chintz-covered sofa, 'you prove that you have no more to do with your militant friends and that you can live here peaceably with your brother, I will see that you have more to do with the business. I might even consider a place on the board - all in due time, of course.'

Alice had almost spat the offer back at him. She was furious at the humiliation and being spoken to like a naughty child. She was thirty-six! How dare he speak to her like that! But as always, she backed down in the face of his opposition, comforting herself with the thought that she would still be living in the house she loved and still able to work in the business, albeit unofficially.

Now, standing looking back at Hebron House, its windows winking in the autumn sun like eyes in the soot-blackened elegant building, she cursed her cowardice. Felicity ran the house with a vigour and style that she had never had and it was she who now arranged the entertaining for Lord Pearson's clients and business associates. The two women stood at an uneasy truce, with Alice keeping out of Felicity's way and retreating more and more to her photography and the darkroom she had created out of a former pantry under the servants' staircase.

Sometimes she caught Felicity watching her with resentful pale eyes and knew that she would never be forgiven for getting rid of Poppy Beresford. Although members of Newcastle society came and went, Felicity did not seem to have any close friends and in that respect, Alice thought, they were alike.

Two women adrift in a hostile sea, each trying to cling to the successful Pearson fleet and grab at what rich flotsam came their way.

'Neither of us has any freedom of choice,' Alice said bitterly to the panting Rosamund. 'No matter what our class, we women are ruled and restrained by men.'

It made her think again of the convalescing Maggie Beaton and this time Alice decided she would risk being found out and go and see the invalid.

Maggie spent her first two weeks at the discreet Gosforth nursing home in torpor. She could do nothing to shake off her depression after the initial euphoria of being released. The kind and patient Sister Robinson coaxed her to eat, but Maggie had lost all sense of taste and food held no interest for her.

'Try and remember what it tasted like before,' the nurse suggested as she presented Maggie with a small plate of poached fish.

'Never had fish this good,' Maggie smiled wanly, pushing it away and closing her eyes.

'Drink the tea then,' Sister Robinson said patiently. 'You must try and regain your strength.'

'Who's paying for all this?' Maggie asked, waving a bony hand at the large airy bedroom with its view out over a rambling garden secluded by large beech hedges. Maggie's one pleasure was to sit in the bay window and gaze out over the trees as the autumn wind tore off red and gold leaves and scattered them across the lawn like confetti. It was her only activity and it occupied her for hours at a time.

'The Movement,' the nurse answered after a moment's hesitation, 'so you mustn't worry about how long you stay here.'

'They shouldn't spend their money on the likes of me,' Maggie said forlornly. 'I'm not worth it.'

'Of course you are!' Sister Robinson was brisk. 'The Movement values you highly, and we want you to get better so you can go on fighting.'

'I can't fight any more,' Maggie whimpered. She had never felt so listless. Despite the brightness of her surroundings, it was like living in shadow where everything she saw or touched was a deep dull grey. 'I just want to go home.'

Sister Robinson removed the tray of food and came to sit beside her, taking Maggie's hand gently in her own warm grasp.

'Dear girl,' she said softly, 'you can't go home. You're still, to all intents and purposes, a prisoner. You've seen the constable standing at the front entrance every day - they're watching you in case you try to escape. As soon as they see you walking around again, you'll be re-arrested. If you run home, that's the first place they're going to look for you.'

'Oh God!' Maggie moaned and covered her gaunt face with her hands. 'I'm so alone! If I can't go home, why does no one come to see me here?'

'They won't allow it. And it wouldn't be safe for your militant friends to visit - they would only be followed and questioned and harassed and watched to see if they tried to help you leave.'

'So - I'm a fugitive?' Maggie asked in bewilderment. 'I'm never going to be allowed to lead a normal life again, am I?'

Sister Robinson shook her head slowly. 'You stepped over the line when you stood up to the Prime Minister. Until we women get the vote, they will carry on hunting you and locking you up and treating you like a pariah.'

Maggie crumpled as she covered her head with her arms and buried her face in her lap. Then, for the first time since prison, she cried aloud, deep racking sobs that rose up from her guts and filled the room with her misery. How could she carry on living, she thought desperately, if she was never to see her family or friends again? For the bleak choice appeared to be to submit to further torture in prison until her sentence petered out, or go on the run and attempt to hide from the police, always looking over her shoulder in fear.

She became aware of the nurse's arms about her, trying to comfort.

'You do have friends, Maggie,' she insisted, 'and they're not going to desert you. We'll think of a way to get you out of here to a safe house where you can recover your spirits. It's perfectly normal to feel depressed after what you've been through. But you must believe that what you did was worthwhile to the movement and worth all the sacrifice.'

Maggie had little recollection of the following days, except that the nurse's staunch words kept on coming back to her, until a week or so later she found her interest in small things returning. Tea began to taste pleasant and she started to comb and pin up her dark hair. She dared to look in the mirror and instead of staring at the garden from her bedroom window, she ventured across its dank lawns for her first walk, leaning heavily on a stick.

She nearly fainted from the heady scents of newly turned earth, heavy dew and the sweet acrid smell of burning leaves. As nature began to droop and turn in on itself for the winter, Maggie found herself emerging from her depression and rediscovering a will to live.

She ate. Her appetite returned and she finally began to regain weight. Sister Robinson observed that it was time to act.

One frosty morning, Maggie was completing her circular walk round the garden and contemplating joining the other elderly residents in the sitting room when Sister Robinson beckoned her inside.

'You have a visitor,' she told her, unable to keep the excitement from her voice. 'She's waiting for you upstairs.'

Maggie hurried for the stairs, but the watchful nurse took her arm and helped her up. At the top, Maggie was breathless but carried on in a fever of anticipation. Surely it would be Rose come to see her at last with news of the outside world. Or maybe even her mother had sought her out...

'Good morning, Maggie,' a cultured voice spoke as she pushed open the door with her walking stick.

There before her stood Alice Pearson.

Chapter Fourteen

Maggie stood in disbelief. Alice Pearson was the last person on earth she wished to see.

'How are you?' the tall aristocrat asked. She was dressed in expensive day clothes: a green velvet cape with a black Medici collar and a belted lilac dress. Maggie wondered bitterly if the suffragette colours were deliberately chosen.

'Why are you here?' Maggie asked stonily.

'Maggie,' Sister Robinson interrupted from behind, 'Miss Alice has come at great personal risk. There's no need to be uncivil.'

'Oh, I'm sorry,' Maggie answered with disdain, 'and me thinking she'd come to spy on me for the Pearsons.'

Sister Robinson was about to protest again when Alice asked for them to be left alone.

'Please let's sit down,' she said when the nurse had gone. Maggie stayed leaning on her stick, her anger ready to boil. Alice hesitated, unsure, and then lowered herself onto a straight-backed chair by the window.

'I can't say how sorry I am for what you've been through. My life has changed too. I'm constantly watched by my family and no longer free to associate with the movement,' Alice told her hostile listener.

'I got the impression you'd turned your back on us anyways,' Maggie said, her whole body tense. 'The last I saw of you, you were hobnobbing with Asquith.'

Alice's powdered face flushed at the accusation. She was about to deliver a stinging rebuke to the young woman before her for daring to speak so insolently, when she checked herself. Maggie was so thin and vulnerable, her wasted face and body like that of a child and it made Alice ashamed of her robust size and health. This woman had started with so little in life and yet had been prepared to sacrifice what freedom and security she had for the millions of women better off than her, even for those women who despised her for trying.

'You're right,' Alice answered with a meekness that cost her greatly, turning to stare out of the window, unable to face the girl's huge, haunted grey eyes. 'I pretended to myself that I, the great Alice Pearson, could reason with the Prime Minister, that I alone could persuade him to change his mind about women's suffrage. Others had tried and failed, but *I* would cause his Damascus, a blinding conversion. What vanity!' Alice mocked herself.

She caught sight of a rabbit running across the frosted lawn and disappearing under the root of an oak. It would be so easy to run away now without telling the whole truth, Alice thought, but somehow she felt compelled to confess to this working-class woman. She was startled to realise that she wished to win Maggie's approval.

'So I went along with police plans to keep the local militants quiet,' Alice continued in a low shaky voice. 'I played into their hands. I did what my father wanted. I told myself it was for the good of the movement, but deep down I knew that it was a lie. I did it for myself, for my own self-aggrandisement and that of all Pearsons. But then you evaded and defied us all,' Alice said, turning round to look at Maggie. She saw that the young woman had moved quietly to sit in the armchair opposite.

'I wondered why the police had bothered to search for me,' Maggie said, as realisation dawned. 'You put them on to me, didn't you?'

Alice nodded bleakly.

'Was I that much of a threat to you?' Maggie asked in bewilderment.

'Oh, yes, Maggie. I could tell the first time we met that you were dangerous - outspoken, unafraid, subversive. Emily saw it too. She said you had the makings of a fearless militant. Deeds not words, she used to say to me and, by God, she was right.'

Maggie smiled weakly. 'Miss Davison put me up to it - disrupting the launch. She approached me before she went to Epsom. After she died - well, I had to carry it out, didn't I?'

'Oh, Emily!' Alice cried, 'I suspected as much.' She looked at the remarkable girl before her but could not bring herself to confess how she was burdened by the death of Emily Davison, weighed down by guilt at despatching her to the Derby so that she would think no more of the launch. Dear Emily, how she had wrought her revenge, Alice thought with regret as she remembered her friend.

'Why have you told me all this?' Maggie asked, still suspicious.

Alice gave her a frank look. 'I wanted you to understand the remorse I feel at what you've had to endure while I remain in relative ease and freedom. No one else knows what I've told you. I thought if I explained everything to you, you might trust me. You see, I want to help you.'

Maggie sat mutely wondering whether to believe a Pearson. Perhaps it was some elaborate game she played to ensnare her and send her back to prison.

'Give me a reason to trust you,' Maggie challenged.

Alice leaned forward eagerly. 'I come as a messenger from Rose Johnstone. I've been in touch with her and we've concocted a plan to get you away from here.'

In spite of her reluctance to be won over by the powerful Alice, Maggie felt her interest quicken. Over the past days she had come to dream of escaping the clutches of the police, dreading the thought of returning to prison. A life in hiding was preferable to a creeping death in gaol.

Tell me,' Maggie demanded. 'Please.'

Alice, sensing Maggie's distrust towards her thawing, smiled with relief.

'First, let me call for Sister Robinson. We need her co-operation.'

A few days later, word got out that one of the residents at the nursing home was seriously ill. A sister and niece came to visit their dying relation and exchanged a few anxious words with the policeman at the gate.

'Poorly, very poorly,' the sister told him tearfully as she left. 'Mary doesn't know who I am. Me daughter's staying to help nurse her for a day or two. Eeh, poor Mary...'

A week later, the constable was told that the old woman had died and that the gates must be opened for the undertaker. Flicking through the Newcastle Journal announcements on his break, he found a touching tribute to Mary Halliday from her sister Millicent and family members. The funeral was to be held at a church in Fenham.

Later in the day, the undertaker and his helper arrived in a horse-drawn hearse and carried an expensive polished coffin into the nursing home. The constable was glad of the diversion after days of cold and boredom keeping a watch on the wretched pampered criminal sheltering inside. He could see her now, a thin stick of a young woman, sitting in the upstairs window, half-hidden by the curtain, reading. He saw her every day, creeping around the garden, looking as if one gust of wind would blow her over. Whatever they had done to her in prison, he thought, had punched the stuffing out of her. She wasn't going anywhere fast, of that he was sure.

One of the maids brought him out a cup of tea and chatted with him for a minute while the undertakers emerged, shouldering their burden.

'Old lady's sister's taken it badly,' the girl confided. 'Wants to have the coffin at her place overnight so family can pay their respects.'

The constable grunted. 'Funny how they all get upset after the old wife's gone. I've never seen that sister visit once since I've been here - not until Mrs Halliday was at death's door.'

'Aye,' the maid agreed. 'Most likely after what's in the will. You see it happen all the time.'

The policeman slurped his tea gratefully and watched the undertaker with the bushy side-whiskers climb back on the hearse while the other man led the horse gently round by the bridle. The constable followed them back down the short drive and made sure the gate was bolted behind them. Glancing up at the far bay window, he saw the suffragette still engrossed in her book and went back to pacing the pavement and stamping his feet to keep warm.

The hearse trotted down the tree-lined avenue, crossed over the busy high street and veered into a back lane. John Heslop jumped down, but his helper was already prising the lid off the coffin.

Maggie gulped for breath as strong hands reached in to pull her up. Blinking in the daylight, she gasped with shock to see George Gordon peering at her in concern.

'Are you all right, Maggie?' he asked.

She stared at him with a mixture of disbelief and joy. She had thought she would never see George again to talk to or touch and yet here he was somehow involved in her escape.

'George, I . . .' she stammered, then saw John Heslop watching them. 'Mr Heslop. Miss Alice told me you were going to help. Thank you. I don't know what to say!' She grinned, light-headed from the sudden rush of fresh air and the startling appearance of George Gordon.

'Maggie,' John Heslop said, smiling but businesslike, 'I'm to take you to Millie Dobson's in my van - it's waiting up the lane. George will return the hearse that Miss Alice hired. We must move quickly before the police discover that the figure at your window is really Annie Dobson.'

George took Maggie's arm and helped lift her out of the coffin. She felt exhilarated by his touch and resisted the urge to bury her face in his chest and cling to him. Instead she allowed him to place her on the cobbles and merely rested a hand on his arm as he walked her to Heslop's meat van.

George was shocked by her appearance. He had expected to find her affected by her ordeal but not this waif-like thinness, the almost translucent face and hands. Only her dark grey eyes, which were huge in her wasted face, shone with familiar spirit. Her voice, too, had the same strong richness of tone that he remembered and it gave him hope that Maggie would recover.

'You'll come and visit me, won't you, George?' she asked him. 'So that I can thank you properly. I don't have a clue why you've helped me, but I'm that grateful.'

'I did it 'cos you showed me up, Maggie Beaton,' George grunted in embarrassment, yet relieved she seemed genuinely pleased to see him. 'What you did, standing up for yourself - well, it was bloody marvellous.'

Maggie gave him a wide smile. 'Does this mean I've made a convert?' she teased. 'I hope so, 'cos I'd hate to think three months in prison were for nowt.'

'By heck! Not for nowt,' George insisted. He wanted to say more, that he had missed her and was sorry for quarrelling, but Heslop was beside them now and impatient to be away.

'Come on, Maggie, we mustn't linger here, it's not safe,' John Heslop advised. 'George can come to the mission sometime soon.'

'As long as you don't expect me to pray,' George answered gruffly.

'No,' Maggie laughed, 'we can do that for you.'

He helped her into the van and waved her away, envious of the lanky, middle-aged butcher into whose protection she gave herself without question. George felt a fierce desire to care for Maggie himself, to see her grow strong again so that they could once more walk up to Hibbs' Farm and talk poetry and politics and ... He forced himself to end his daydreaming. No one quite knew what lay ahead for Maggie, except the certainty that she was wanted by the police and could not enjoy such simple pleasures as walking or going to the music hall without the risk of re-arrest. Deep inside, George was filled with foreboding for Maggie.

Maggie and Millie Dobson hugged each other warmly in the safety of the Dobsons' tiny flat.

'How can I thank you?' Maggie laughed, close to tears.

'Eeh, ninny, I enjoyed every minute of it - having that copper on about me dying sister. I tell you, I should've gone on the stage!'

'There's still time, Mrs Dobson.'

'Call me Millie. We're partners in crime now, hinny,' Mrs Dobson cackled.

'But what about Annie?' Maggie asked in concern, flopping down thankfully on the bed.

'She'll come out after dark dressed in a maid's outfit - they'll have changed coppers by then - and the dozy buggers won't notice the difference,' Millie reassured her. 'Tomorrow they'll start to wonder where the hell you've got to, but they'll have a job finding you. My Annie's good with the scissors and a spot of hair dye. Your own mam won't recognise you once we've finished.'

Maggie thought suddenly of her mother and the heartache she must be causing her. Yet, perhaps in Annie's disguise, she might be able to return and visit briefly, Maggie comforted herself with the thought.

Millie poured brandy into two chipped mugs and handed one over.

'Get that down your neck and feel it do you some good,' she ordered, swigging greedily at her own.

Maggie did as she was told, spluttering as the liquor burned its way down her throat and set fire to her chest. Yet with it came a feeling of elation that she was free and had hoodwinked the authorities. They had tried to destroy her body and soul with imprisonment, force-feeding and degradation. But they had not succeeded in breaking her, Maggie thought with fierce pride, and she would regain her strength to fight. She was filled with a new sense of purpose, finally seeing a way out of the terrible blackness of the past weeks.

To us lasses!' Maggie raised her mug again. She clinked it against Millie Dobson's.

To us lasses!' Millie echoed and let out a joyful cackle.

By December, Maggie's health had improved dramatically under the care of the Dobsons and the nutritious fresh food regularly brought by John Heslop. The butcher was kind and concerned and tried to divert Maggie's impatience at being inactive by encouraging her to help at the mission.

'You have great talents that could be put to good use,' Heslop told her. 'Such enthusiasm, and a wonderful singing voice. You've done your bit for women's suffrage, Maggie. There are other equally worthwhile causes.'

He seemed pleased whenever Maggie appeared from the Dobsons' hideaway and lent a hand in the kitchen. As Christmas drew nearer, Maggie threw herself into organising a special meal for those who were out on the streets, enjoying the rousing carols being sung at the mission meetings. It all helped to occupy her mind which was increasingly drawn to thoughts of her family preparing for the festive season. She had heard from Heslop that Susan was engaged to Richard Turvey and despite misgivings about the man, she was pleased for her sister. Through Heslop she had conveyed messages to her family that she was safe and well and hoped to see them before long.

John Heslop was reticent when Maggie asked him what Susan had said at chapel about her escape.

'I'm sure she's reassured to know you're well cared for,' he said rather awkwardly. 'You'll understand that at the moment her thoughts are rather occupied by her engagement to Mr Turvey.'

'Aye, of course,' Maggie replied, disappointed.

Several times, Maggie slipped out of the Dobsons' flat and mingled with the Saturday crowds on the quayside, edging towards Sandgate market where she knew her mother would be selling clothes. On the first occasion it had taken all her willpower to restrain herself from rushing over and flinging her arms round her mother. She had looked quite old and grey-faced, her movements slow as she bent down to spread out her wares. But Helen had been with her and Maggie did not trust her sister to be discreet, so she had crept away in frustration. The market was quite possibly watched. They might be expecting her to contact her mother there.

Since then, to Maggie's concern, her mother had not been at the Saturday market. Helen had been in charge of the secondhand clothes and shoes, though she appeared more interested in gossiping with the other stallholders than attempting to sell her stock. Maggie's alarm had increased when, on one occasion, she spotted Richard Turvey emerge from a nearby public house and help Helen load the unsold coats and dresses onto the barrow. She was too far away to hear what they said, but their manner seemed teasing and over-intimate.

When she told John Heslop of her worries, he was dismissive.

'Mr Turvey is soon to be one of the family, isn't he? It's very commendable that he's willing to help out when your mother is ill.'

'How ill is she?' Maggie asked in real concern, forgetting her unease at Helen's behaviour.

'A chest infection, Susan tells me,' the butcher replied, 'but nothing to worry about. They're just being cautious keeping her indoors during this cold spell.'

She was restless and Millie Dobson began to complain it was like having a wild cat pacing around her room. She was a cheerful, kind-hearted woman but Maggie could tell she was getting on her nerves, cooped up with not enough to do. Her daughter Annie, however, was tired with the cause of women's rights after her involvement in Maggie's escape from the nursing home and constantly shadowed Maggie. It was like having an earnest and attentive ghost, silently following and watching her every move, she told George Gordon on one of his visits. For it was his visiting, and that of her friend Rose and even Alice Pearson, that kept Maggie sane in her cramped, fusty hideout.

'Teach her something,' George suggested, amused.

'I'm not a teacher,' Maggie laughed.

'You've all the makings of one - intelligent, bossy, loud-voiced...'

Maggie took a playful swipe at her companion as they meandered among the maze of tenements near the quayside. He grabbed her hand and locked it into the crook of his arm.

'You could teach her book-keeping, shorthand or whatever you clerks do.'

'Did,' Maggie corrected wryly.

'Well, here's a chance to keep up your skills - teach them to Annie. Her mam would kiss your feet if Annie managed to get a good job.'

'I suppose I could,' Maggie considered. 'She's a bright lass. Thanks, George,' she smiled up at him, 'it'll give me summat to do till the movement comes up with some real work.'

He felt troubled as he watched her determined face with the restless, searching eyes looking beyond him. He had grown used to the new Maggie with her neat wavy blonde hair framing her brow under an enveloping hat, although it gave her a misleadingly placid look, like her sister Susan. Blonde or dark, the sight of her lively upturned face still filled him with longing.

'You're serious about wanting to do more for the movement then?' George asked.

'Course I am,' Maggie answered roundly. 'I'm already the wrong side of the law so what does it matter if I carry on breaking it for the sake of greater justice? I need a new mission - not just brick throwing, something bigger.'

'Heslop's mission not enough for you then?'

'You know I don't mean that kind of mission,' Maggie retorted. 'Anyone can peel tatties and sing hymns; not everyone can be a militant protester.'

George sighed. 'I worry for you, bonny lass. But this time I won't try to stop you.' He leaned over and kissed her cold pink cheek and saw the colour deepen.

'Ta,' Maggie answered with a smile and tightened her grip on his arm. She was flooded with sudden tenderness for him, a deeper feeling than the physical ache that his nearness always provoked. Outwardly, George Gordon was a blunt miner's son, a hard-grafting blacksmith, rower and drinker like many working-class lads with whom she had grown up. But inwardly he nurtured a passionate belief that their brutal world could and would be bettered, if the common people were empowered to change things. He was a romantic, Maggie suddenly realised, with his secret love of history and poetry and music and his whimsical idealism. And standing in the cold damp fog that stole in from the Tyne, she was certain that he cared deeply for her, as she cared for him.

Without another word they walked on contentedly, arm in arm, listening to the cry of the chestnut-seller whose brazier glowed orange through the December mist.

It was Christmas Eve and Hebron House was spectacularly bedecked in holly wreaths, sparkling tinsel and large coloured baubles, and an enormous Christmas tree filled the hallway with glittering waxy light from dozens of candles.

Richard Turvey was hardly aware of Felicity's elaborate gestures to prove to the world that she was mistress of the Pearson mansion as he was hurried down a dimly lit passageway and through a series of doors to a smoke-filled study.

He had met Herbert Pearson on a previous occasion, when the portly businessman had been chummy and offered him a cigar in this trophy-filled private room. Richard had thought fleetingly that it looked like a props room for some exotic play, with stuffed heads, spears and rifles pinned against the walls. He had almost made a joke about it, but stopped himself in time, recognising that his employer had little sense of humour.

Tonight, though, there were no cigars on offer and no boastful chat about hunting in Africa or being on the verge of a glittering political career. Herbert Pearson was inebriated and aggressively threatening.

'*Nothing?*' he demanded.

'I have some idea—'

'Idea? I don't want your bloody ideas, Turvey! I want this woman found and locked up. You're engaged to her sister, for God's sake. A halfwit would have found her by now!' He poured himself another brandy, his breathing laboured, then continued, 'There's been a hammer thrown through the window of our quayside offices with a copy of *The Suffragette* wrapped round it. That picture house I opened a month ago had a brick thrown into the foyer in the middle of the night. It's a blatant attempt to sabotage my election campaign. Don't you read the bloody papers?' Herbert threw a copy of the *Newcastle Journal* at Richard's feet and gulped back the large brandy.

Richard wished it was for him, he was desperate for a drink himself. Restraining the urge to grab the heavy bulbous glass, he picked up the newspaper and adopted an expression of concern.

'Terrible.' He shook his head. 'But how do we know it's Maggie Beaton?'

'We don't!' Herbert snapped. 'But the other militants are under careful watch. It's got to be Beaton - and she's got to have friends protecting her. Her stupid antics are damaging our business as well as my political hopes - people are beginning to ask why we're a target. You would think she had some personal vendetta against us, but I'm told we used to employ the little baggage! Terrorism scares people, Turvey, especially business people. So get off your arse and find her. Otherwise you're fired.'

Richard was jolted by the threat. He looked around the comfortable, ostentatious room with its leather sofas and wool carpets and the roaring coal fire that could have heated all the ranges in Gun Street. He was sick with envy for this over-fed, overbearing man who could have every luxury he cared-for without thinking twice about how to pay for it. All his life he must have got what he wanted, when he wanted it, and Richard was determined he was going to grab a portion of his wealth.

After all, he deserved it, Richard thought resentfully. He had fed back information on a rival export business by befriending an elderly clerk and getting him drunk and with Helen Beaton's help he had the potential to blackmail a prominent councillor. Yes, Helen Beaton had been a useful find. She was impressionable and desperate for love, and it had been easy convincing her that there would be rich rewards if she did as he asked and compromised the respectably married councillor. It was their secret, he had told her when he had seduced her that afternoon in the modest Jesmond hotel; they would work together in secret and one day they would be rich enough to run off together, to London or Paris or Florence... She had been seduced by the very names and he had found her the easiest conquest of his career.

But the fat Herbert, Richard thought with disdain, was ungrateful for all his hard work so far. He was obsessed by the wretched Maggie and the damage she inflicted upon his Pearson pride.

'She's bound to come sneaking round now it's Christmas,' Richard said. 'They're clannish, these Beatons, for all they're at each other's throats half the time. She'll not be able to stay away. Don't you worry, sir.'

'Well, you better be right,' Herbert growled, dismissing him with a wave. 'Now go, and don't return until you've found her. If you don't deliver her by the

New Year, you're out on your arse, Turvey, and back in the gutter where we found you.'

'Yes, sir.'

Richard left, inwardly fuming at his master's rudeness. He would hang on to Pearson like a leech and suck the bastard dry of his wealth, he determined. But first he would have to flush out the elusive Maggie. He would get to her through her family, he vowed.

Deep in thought, he nearly walked straight into a tall woman emerging from what looked like a broom cupboard under the back stairs. He moved aside just as she moved aside, blocking each other again. Her face was completely shadowed in the dim corridor and he took her for some maid.

'Look at the mistletoe!' he said, gesturing above. As she looked up, Richard grabbed her behind the neck and kissed her roundly on the lips. 'Happy Christmas darlin'!'

He walked on, whistling 'Alexander's Ragtime Band'.

Alice stared after the thin young man in the loud checked suit, speechless with outrage. She was further mortified to note that there was not a single sprig of mistletoe to be seen in the passageway. She had no idea who he was, only that he had presumably come from the back entrance to Herbert's study. Some ghastly drinking friend, she assumed, shuddering with distaste, who had taken her for one of the servants.

Perhaps it had done her good to know for an instant what it was like to be treated as an inferior woman, Alice thought. No wonder Maggie Beaton was so at war with the world. Well, she had a present to warm her militant heart this Christmas, Alice smiled, locking the darkroom door behind her to keep her secret safe.

Chapter Fifteen

Maggie experienced a strange thrill as she re-entered the streets of West Newcastle for the first time in months. It was like stepping back into a world she had lost long ago; a vibrant, cosy, thrusting world. Every comer gas lamp, shop and cobbled lane was comfortably familiar and yet she had been away long enough to be struck by things she had never before noticed.

The entrance above the steam laundry was embellished with two fat cherubs, blackened with soot, and there was a clock above the nearby ironmongers that must have been there for years. She had never taken the trouble to look around her home streets as she did this day. Anonymous in an old brown coat and her battered hat, she walked on delightedly past shops decorated with tinsel and colour in their windows.

Horses jangled past in the afternoon twilight as traders delivered final orders and customers rushed about in search of last-minute bargains. The trams trundled and sparked along their lines, disgorging travellers while the pubs filled up with men finishing work for the holiday.

She passed the Gunners with its grubby attempt at jollity - a faded Chinese lantern hung above the door - and then she was outside the entrance to her old home.

All at once Maggie was terrified. She had no idea what her reception might be after such an absence, or whom she might encounter. Then she thought of Granny Beaton and young Tich who never held a grudge - and her mother whom she yearned to see again. No matter what she did, Maggie instinctively knew her mother would stick by her. She mounted the stairs swiftly and without a sound; over the past weeks she had perfected the art of stealth.

Jimmy answered the door, releasing a fug of warmth and light onto the dark stairway. He strained to look at her, failed to recognise his missing sister and asked, 'What you want, missus?'

'A smacking big kiss, kiddar!' Maggie threw her arms round her brother and embraced him.

'What!' Jimmy spluttered 'Who the ...?'

'Maggie, you daft lump!' she answered 'Let us in, man Tich, it's brass monkeys out here.'

'Maggie?' he gasped. 'Eeh, Mam, it's wor Maggie!'

He pulled his sister into the flat and banged the door behind them. The first person Maggie saw was her mother half rising from her chair by the fire. Maggie was shocked to see her dress hanging off her usually stocky figure and her face sunken with ill health. The older woman mouthed her utter astonishment, but no sound came out.

'Mam!' Maggie rushed towards her and enveloped her in a hug. 'I've missed you that much.' She felt her mother's frail arms go round her and cling on.

'Maggie,' she croaked 'Eeh, Maggie.'

For a moment neither of them could trust themselves to speak and they held on tight, tears spilling down their cheeks.

'I don't believe it!' Susan's indignant voice broke in. Maggie pulled away to see her eldest sister staring at her across the kitchen.

'Susan!' Maggie smiled at her and stepped round her mother's chair to greet her sister. 'It's grand to see you - and you're looking bonny. I heard you're betrothed.'

But Susan held herself stiffly away.

'All this time, all this worry, and you just swan in like Princess Muck. Can't you see the state Mam's in? You've half worried her to death with your goings on.'

Maggie was taken aback by her hostility.

'That's enough, Susan!' Mabel silenced her with something of her old authority. 'Don't you go blaming my illness on your sister. My health was ruined long ago, but it's not going to get the better of me. I'm a tough old boot, so don't you go talking about death. Now, tak' that hat off, our Maggie, and let's get a look at you.'

Maggie did as she was bidden, revealing her short blonde hair.

'What in the world have you done, lass?' Mabel shrieked.

They all stared at her in horrified interest.

'You look like one of them lasses in the films,' Jimmy said in admiration. 'I wish Helen was here to see you.'

'Where is our Helen?' Maggie asked.

'Up at Violet's,' her mother answered. 'She spends more time there than at home these days.'

The comment seemed to infuriate Susan who lashed out unkindly, 'You look like a tart, Maggie.'

'Shut your mouth, Susan,' her mother ordered, 'or I'll—'

'Or you'll what, Mam?' Susan challenged her. 'Beat me? Lock me in the netty like Helen? Not any more, you won't. The only reason there's still a roof over our head since Maggie got herself arrested is because of my Richard. Tell Maggie how he's paying the rent now - how he's paying for a goose this Christmas and all the treats. We'd be lucky to have rabbit otherwise.'

'Goose, eh?' Maggie exclaimed. 'And how's Richard Turvey managing that when he's only a caller outside the Olympia?' Maggie had meant only to tease, to dispel the tension, but Susan rounded on her in fury.

'My Richard's got a good job - in an office. He's got prospects. He's earned more in three months than Mam can in three years of peddling old clothes! Anyways, my Richard's never been a caller, so don't you go putting him down. You're just jealous, I can see that.'

Maggie laughed outright. 'Jealous over that trickster? Don't be daft! A friend of mine said she'd seen him touting for business outside the Olympia.'

'Oh, aye? A gaolbird, no doubt!' Susan sneered. 'I wouldn't believe a word of one of your friends - we don't know who you're mixing with these days, anyway. Richard's the best thing that's happened to this family. We'd all be heading for the workhouse without him.'

'Lasses, stop your fighting!' their mother protested wearily.

Maggie was silent. It had been in prison that she had learned from Mrs Surtees the pea-seller that Richard had merely been a tout for the picture house. She had remarked to Maggie that she had seen the man who had run away that night in the Bigg Market and left her to be assaulted. The description had fitted Richard exactly. But Maggie was more dismayed by the influence he obviously exercised over her sister. Along with her smart blue dress, Susan wore a new arrogance and disdain towards her family that upset Maggie. A few months ago, she would never have spoken to their mother in such a cruel way.

She saw Jimmy looking at them in misery and confusion and stopped herself giving Susan a mouthful, turning her back on the older girl.

'Well, our Tich,' she forced herself to be bright, 'I've brought you summat. It's not much but I know you like them.' Maggie handed over her brown paper package which Jimmy tore at eagerly.

'Sorry, I haven't got you owt, Maggie. Didn't know you'd be coming.' His immature face registered surprise, then disappointment as four oranges came tumbling out. 'Oh, ta.'

'Well, I said it wasn't much, but it's all I could afford.'

'It's fine, hinny,' her mother assured, coughing and spitting into a bowl at her side.

'Richard's already given me a pocket watch. Says I'll need to keep good time in me new job. Do you want to see it?' Jimmy grinned.

'You've got a job, our Tich?' Maggie asked, delighted.

'Aye, a proper job,' Jimmy nodded proudly. 'I'm going to be a runner for some merchants down the quayside - start after Christmas.'

'Richard got him the position, of course,' Susan added.

'I'm sure Tich would've got something anyway,' Maggie answered swiftly. 'You've always been a good fetcher and carrier for us.' She ruffled her brother's spiky hair playfully. 'I'm pleased for you, kiddar.'

Just then a figure shuffled slowly into the kitchen from the open parlour door. Maggie saw her dear grandmother squinting blindly across the room.

'Still not wearing specs, Granny!' Maggie teased and moved round the kitchen table to meet her.

The old woman stopped at the familiar voice and cocked her head 'Is that you, Peggi?' she asked.

Maggie felt a stab of disappointment. She raised her voice. 'No, it's me, Maggie, remember?' She took hold of her grandmother's dry, papery hands and squeezed them.

'Divn't worry, hinny,' Mabel consoled her daughter, 'she's away with the fairies half the time. Keeps on about a wife called Peggi.'

'Peggi was her sister,' Maggie whispered. 'She sailed to Canada after the village was broken up and Granny's never seen or heard of her since.'

They all waited in silence as Maggie clung to the old woman and watched her crinkled face to see if the mist of confusion in her myopic eyes would lift. Maggie's heart twisted to think how lost and lonely the old Highlander must be, retreating into a past life, searching for her beloved sister, contused by the strangers around her.

'Maggie?' her grandmother finally asked.

'Aye, Granny,' she encouraged, 'your granddaughter.'

'Maggie,' Agnes Beaton repeated with more conviction. 'You've come home at last.'

'I have,' Maggie smiled, 'but just for a visit.'

'You've been away such a long time,' her grandmother accused.

'She still thinks you're Peggi, I bet,' Susan remarked.

Granny Beaton looked between the two of them, then said clearly, 'I know it's not Peggi. It's your sister Maggie. The hair - it made me think...' She leaned on Maggie's arm and patted her hand. 'And how did they treat you in that terrible prison, dearie?'

Maggie gave Susan and her mother a triumphant look. 'I survived, Granny.'

It was dark by the time Maggie left. She stayed for a cup of tea but her mother could not persuade her to stay the night and share the goose with them on Christmas Day. She felt restless and uneasy in the tense atmosphere of Gun Street and did not relish the prospect of watching Richard and Susan lording it over her family and Aunt Violet simpering with satisfaction that it was her nephew who was saving the Beatons from destitution.

So she went, kissing her mother and grandmother tenderly and promising to keep in touch via John Heslop. She gave Jimmy her return tram fare and told him to buy new shoelaces for work. Susan merely nodded at her when she wished her a happy Christmas and Maggie left feeling depressed that her sister had changed so quickly from a fussing but kind-hearted girl into this preening, self-satisfied woman.

When she got back to the Dobsons she found a visitor waiting.

'Maggie, my dear.' Alice rose from the bed in relief. 'I thought I was going to miss you.'

'I've been home,' Maggie explained, unpinning her hat.

'All's well, I hope.'

'I'm worried about Mam,' Maggie confided. 'She's got this bad chest.'

'I'm sure it cheered her to see you again,' Alice smiled.

'Aye, I think it did,' Maggie sighed 'I miss her summat terrible.'

'Here,' Alice held out a parcel, 'I think this will cheer you up. I wanted to give it to you in person, before I go up to Oxford Hall to join my parents.'

Maggie took the present and unwrapped it cautiously. Nestling in the tissue paper was a pair of miniature silver frames. Maggie turned one over to reveal the thoughtful, half-smiling face of Emily Davison in a large boater.

'To inspire your great efforts,' Alice smiled at Maggie's astonished expression.

Maggie looked at the other one and gasped in delight. It showed her sitting with George; she happy, he glowering with embarrassment.

'My birthday,' Maggie recalled, laughing. 'George hating the idea of having his photograph taken. Oh, they're canny presents. Ta very much, Miss Alice. I'll treasure them always. But I've nothing for you.'

Alice waved a hand 'It's enough to see the pleasure on your face, Maggie.' She rose. Below she could hear the sound of carols being sung at the mission Christmas Eve service where the brandy-smelling Mrs Dobson had gone to help out. Alice wished that Maggie did not have to live in such squalor and was determined that, when Maggie was no longer hunted by the police, she would find a position for her within her own household.

'I may not be able to visit you for a while,' Alice said, pulling on her gloves. 'I intend to go south and visit friends after Christmas. With my brother and his wife spending January on the Continent as usual, the house will be locked up. For the first time in years I think I'm actually glad to be getting away from Hebron House. It doesn't feel like my home any more.'

Maggie nodded, tempted for a moment to tell Alice of the dangerous mission she must undertake. But she resisted. The leadership no longer trusted Alice after her collusion with the police to stifle protest at the launch of HMS *Courageous* and although Maggie no longer blamed Alice, it was best if she knew nothing of her plans. However, it was a relief to hear her confirm that Hebron House would be empty for several weeks.

Alice put a hand on Maggie's arm. 'You will take care of yourself, won't you? I know that you'd do anything for the movement, but I can't save you from prison.'

Maggie was defiant. 'I don't expect you to.'

'No,' Alice sighed and dropped her hold. As she turned to leave, Maggie spoke.

'Whatever happens in the future, Miss Alice, I want you to know how much I've appreciated what you've done for me these past weeks.'

Alice smiled in surprise. "Thank you, Maggie.'

'And you don't have to keep feeling guilty that Miss Davison died and you

125

didn't,' Maggie added quietly. Alice was astounded by the young woman's perceptiveness. 'And you don't have to keep making it up to me. I don't expect anything from you except your comradeship and I can't give you anything but mine in return. At least in that respect we're equal, Miss Alice. But it's probably best if you don't visit again. It's too risky - they might be following you. You've been canny coming down here; I know it can't have been easy. And I want you to know I've been glad of your friendship.'

Alice gulped back a surge of emotion for the straight-backed, dignified woman before her who was telling her gently to go and leave her alone. It was beyond her comprehension why she should find herself wanting the companionship of this lowly woman and her friends - the schoolteacher Rose, that earnest girl Annie and the gruff, well-read blacksmith George. But her visits to the quayside had become more real and vital to her than any of Felicity's tedious soirées or her own attempts to occupy her boring days. Herbert was obstructing any attempts to become more involved in the business, so Alice found consolation in her photography and her radical friends. But now that avenue of interest was to close.

'If that's what you wish - though I'll miss you,' Alice answered hoarsely. Maggie nodded but said nothing. Alice turned and opened the door for herself, then added, 'If you ever need me, you won't be too proud to ask, will you?'

Finally Maggie smiled. 'I'm not one for asking favours,' she said wryly, 'but thank you anyway.'

Alice smiled back. She wanted to hug Maggie, but suspected such a familiar gesture would not be welcome. 'Goodbye, Maggie.'

Ta-ra, Miss Alice,' Maggie replied.

After her visitor had gone, Maggie sat for a while on the bed gazing at her two photographs. She was thrilled to own them and it had not been easy saying goodbye to her benefactress. She had grown to admire, even like, the tall, energetic lady with her extraordinary talent for photography. She had come to see that Miss Alice was not just a conventional, privileged boss's daughter concerned only for her own kind. It took imagination and kindness to think of such a gift - framed memories of the suffragette who had inspired Maggie's radicalism and of the man she loved. But it was best, Maggie thought, that she now distanced herself from Alice Pearson before she undertook her most daring mission yet. And it would be better for Pearson's daughter to be safely away and untainted by the deed.

Maggie kissed the picture of George and hugged it to her chest, then she put it under the pillow she shared with Annie and went downstairs to join the carol singers.

Christmas Day was an unexpectedly happy day for Maggie. Instead of brooding over thoughts of her family tucking into roast goose without her, she and the Dobsons held their own party in the mission hall. Heslop provided a joint of pork which he came and shared with them after a service at the Methodist chapel on Alison Terrace. Rose Johnstone and her mother were invited and George came later after a visit to his inebriated father and brothers and inquisitive sister.

'You're going with someone, aren't you?' Irene had questioned. 'That's why you'll not stop five minutes with your own folk. You've always been the same - Mr Secretive. Just hope she's a better catch than that bad'un Maggie Beaton. I didn't cry buckets when you finished with her, I can tell you!'

George had been relieved to escape, he told Maggie afterwards as they sat round a trestle table, their stomachs full of pork and stuffing and vegetables, wearing party hats and streamers that Maggie and Annie had made out of brown paper. Still to come were Mrs Johnstone's spicy mince pies and ginger wine.

At the head of the table John Heslop sat cracking nuts, while Millie Dobson cracked jokes which grew more unsuitable by the minute. She had been drinking brandy since breakfast, despite Maggie and Annie's protestations, and any minute now they knew she was going to burst into song. Maggie could tell that Rose was curbing her disapproval with difficulty, so she moved to intervene.

'Rose, give us a tune on the piano,' she requested.

'Yes, do, Rose, that would be nice,' Heslop agreed quickly. 'And perhaps you would sing for us, Maggie? You have such a beautiful voice.'

Maggie blushed and glanced at George who winked his encouragement. Without further persuasion the two young women embarked on their repertoire of traditional songs that Rose had taught at school and the pair had absorbed during their growing up. Sad romantic ballads were followed by lively north country songs in which Millie Dobson joined raucously.

The dim, cavernous hall took on a homely air as the party congregated round the old upright piano, their faces flushed in the lamplight, their voices blending together, from Mrs Johnstone's quavering high-pitched notes to George's rumbling bass.

Maggie felt a flood of gratitude towards the compassionate butcher for looking after them all and she smiled at him warmly as he stood close to Rose's mother. For a moment she thought how nice it would be if John Heslop and Mrs Johnstone ended up finding companionship together, for she suspected both were lonely. The genteel and placid Mrs Johnstone would be a less turbulent choice than her own intemperate mother would have been, Maggie mused.

Finally the party broke up. As Rose and her mother left with Heslop, George took Maggie by the arm and steered her towards the door after them.

'I could do with some air after all that nosh,' he smiled. 'Come with me.'

Grabbing her coat, Maggie followed eagerly into the salty dusk of the quayside. Linking arms they walked along the riverside, past warehouses and tenements and the merchant vessels bobbing on the high tide.

'You're up to summat, aren't you?' George guessed. 'You've got another job on, haven't you?'

'Aye,' Maggie admitted quietly. 'Headquarters have been in touch.'

'"What's it this time? Customs House? Town Hall? I can't keep giving you all me hammers, Maggie, I'll have no tools left for work.'

Maggie laughed to hide her apprehension. 'I'm not going to hoy hammers through windows this time, Geordie.' It was the nickname she called him by and it gave her comfort using it.

'What then?' George asked, pulling her round to look at him.

'I've told no one, not even Rose.'

'Maggie, you can tell me,' George insisted Trust me!'

She looked at him steadily. 'Arson,' she said quietly.

George swore in disbelief. 'Where?'

'Hebron House.'

'Bloody hell!'

'Herbert Pearson is campaigning against us in his by-election speeches. We must do all we can to give him a rough ride,' Maggie defended stoutly. 'The house will be empty until well into the New Year - Miss Alice said so - so no one's life is at risk.'

'*Your* life is, Maggie! The plan might go wrong - it sounds too dangerous.'

She leaned up on tiptoes and silenced him with a kiss on the lips. It was the first time. George stared at her, speechless with surprise. Maggie laughed.

'Never been kissed before, bonny lad?' she teased.

'Not like that,' George grinned and pulled her to him in the dark, planting another one vigorously on her mouth.

They clung together, excited by their own daring, Maggie blushing in the dark to think how her family would disapprove at such carrying on. But she was now beyond the protection of her family and free to make her own mistakes. Maggie revelled in the feel of his arms about her and the warmth of his breath on her face, the moistness of his mouth. She was intoxicated with the feel of him, the closeness, the urgency of his kissing, and she did not want the embracing to end.

A couple of sailors went past. 'You'd think you'd not eaten for a week!' one joked. 'Warmer between the sheets, darlin',' the other laughed bawdily.

Maggie pulled away, scandalised by their ribaldry, but George just shouted back a derogatory comment as the men weaved their way down the quay. Now filled with awkwardness towards him, Maggie insisted it was time she returned to the Dobsons. George reluctantly agreed. He took her arm and turned back.

As they neared the old warehouse, wrapped in an intimate silence, they became aware of a commotion at the door. Instinctively, George pushed Maggie into the black void of a nearby close. The shouting increased, interspersed with the screams of women as a struggling group emerged from the warehouse.

Straining to see in the dark, Maggie gave a stifled cry as George put his hand about her mouth. They both saw Annie Dobson being dragged away between two policemen, with Millie screaming obscenities at them in their wake.

'You've got the wrong lass!' Mrs Dobson yelled, quite hysterical. 'Leave my Annie be!'

George held on to Maggie tightly, to prevent her dashing out into the lane. When the police van had gone, leaving Millie Dobson sobbing on the cold cobbles, he let her go.

'They were after you, Maggie,' George said grimly.

'We should have helped her!' Maggie hissed at him.

'And let you both get arrested?' George snapped. 'What good would that have done?'

Maggie was shaking with fright and anger, but she knew George was right.

'I must go to Millie,' she said, listening to the woman's anguished sobbing.

George caught her arm again. 'You can't go back there, Maggie. They know where you've been hiding - there might be someone waiting inside.'

'Oh, poor Annie!' Maggie groaned, thinking of how terrified the girl would be. 'It's my fault they've taken her.'

But he shook her impatiently. 'Maggie, you've got to get away from here.'

'Where can I go?' she asked in bewilderment. 'Someone's betrayed me.' She gave an anguished moan, her mind trying to grapple with the implications of her near arrest. Who knew of her hideaway? Heslop, Miss Alice, Rose...

'Nowhere's safe now,' she gulped in fear.

George stared into her face, his eyes intent. 'I'm the only one you can trust. Come with me, Maggie,' he urged. 'You'll be safe with me.'

Chapter Sixteen

On a cold, sharp, black night just before New Year, the sky above Elswick lit with the brightness of daylight. Yet it was a sinister, lurid light that leapt and danced in the inky dark and brought the jangle of fire engines and horses to disturb the sleeping townsfolk.

People came out of their houses in the early hours, wrapped in shawls to gaze at the conflagration beyond the fortress walls of the Hebron estate. Rumours spread like the fire.

'It's a canny blaze!'

'A fire in the woods?'

'Looks close to the house ...'

'It's the house itself!'

'It's punishment for them that've got above themselves!'

The comments of bystanders grew bolder and more inventive as the firemen fought to bring the fire under control. By daylight the blaze had exhausted itself into a damp smoulder, filling the winter morning with an acrid stench of charred wood and stone.

The evening newspapers ended speculation as to the damage to the Pearson mansion. They reported that the fire had mysteriously started in the summer pavilion which had been gutted, but Hebron House itself was untouched.

A day later, a suffragette bill was discovered pinned to a nearby tree, decrying the Cat and Mouse Act and proclaiming, 'The Liberal Cat - Electors Vote Against Him! Keep the Liberal Out!'

The local newspapers over the following week were not slow to make the connection between Herbert Pearson's bid as the Liberal candidate in the pending by-election and the burning down of his summerhouse. The fire was now being treated as arson and the search for the suffragette arsonist intensified.

And Richard Turvey was a worried man.

For the past ten minutes he had stood in Herbert Pearson's study and listened as his paymaster hurled vitriolic abuse on his character and competence as an informer. He seethed inwardly that Maggie should have escaped arrest so narrowly on Christmas Day. He was sure that the prostitute in his pay had given him accurate information that Maggie was helping out at Heslop's mission and that a garrulous, half-drunk, former whore called Dobson was harbouring her.

On his last frantic visit to the seamier parts of the quayside on Christmas Eve, trawling for news of the elusive Maggie, he had finally heard the indiscreet old hag for himself, boasting in a bar that she knew the lass who had brought the launch of the battleship to a halt. Richard's fury that he had missed Maggie at Gun Street by less than an hour had turned to triumph at Millie Dobson's words. Others confirmed that a blonde-haired woman called Maggie was living with the Dobsons and it suddenly dawned on Richard that Maggie must have changed her appearance and so made his descriptions of her useless.

He had gone to the police with the Dobsons' address, gleeful that Pearson would be receiving an extra Christmas present and would reward him well. Richard had enjoyed the excess of food and drink and flirtation at the Beatons' that Christmas Day, knowing that Maggie would soon be under lock and key once more and he would be many pounds the richer.

But Maggie had escaped, Pearson's private pavilion had been destroyed, his election campaign was foundering and the suffragettes had achieved stunning publicity for their cause once more. Furthermore, Maggie's elusiveness and militancy was growing into a local legend and Richard was beginning to take her defiance as personally as Herbert Pearson was.

'We still don't know it was Beaton,' Richard pointed out.

'Don't try and make excuses for your balls-up, Turvey. Of course it was Beaton. She's a thorn in my side. And no one seems to care that my pavilion's in ruins. Instead the press are running stories about the treatment of suffragettes in prison as if it's all my fault! By God, I'd have her hanged, drawn and quartered if it was left up to me. Force-feeding's too good for the likes of that common trollop!'

Richard let him rant on for another ten minutes until he'd exhausted himself.

'So give me one good reason why I shouldn't throw you out without a penny?' Herbert spat the words, puce in the face.

'Because, sir, I found her. If the constables had been a bit quicker on Christmas night, we would have caught her right and proper,' Richard complained. 'I want to get this girl for you, sir, honest I do. She's bad news for both of us - stirring things up among the family against me, she is.' Richard assumed his most earnestly willing look. 'I know how to bring her out the woodwork, sir. I'm going to hurry on my marriage to her sister Susan. Blood's thicker than water, sir. She'll not be able to stay away, believe me. And she may not like me, Mr Herbert, but she can't think I've got anything to do with her near arrest.'

Herbert snorted 'I suppose you have a point. And I don't have much choice, do I? Very well, I'll give you a bit longer to deliver. But by God, you better deliver and I better get elected, else I'll hang you from the Swing Bridge, Turvey!'

Maggie sat curled by the small coal fire, her head resting against George's knees while he read to her. Sometimes he read essays or plays by the Fabian, G.B. Shaw, or novels by Dickens and Scott, but tonight he had borrowed a translation of a Russian novel by Turgenev. After a faltering start, George lost his inhibition at reading aloud and was delivering the story of a nihilist hero with some passion.

Maggie gazed into the fire, mesmerised by its flickering warmth and George's resonant voice. The hearth tiles were cracked and the fender dull with age, while the mantelpiece held only a packet of spills and matches and Maggie's two photographs. Thankfully, she had been carrying them with her in her coat pocket to show George the night of her attempted arrest.

The dinginess of the room was banished into the shadows as George read by candlelight in the one armchair. Hidden in the dark were a small round table and three stools, a mattress which George used as a bed and a cumbersome dresser which held his collection of books and pamphlets, clothes and crockery.

In a tiny box room beyond was Maggie's bedroom with its three-quarter-sized bed and an upended wooden crate that served as a chair cum table.

It was their second 'home' since Maggie had taken refuge with George, for he had thought it unwise to stay in lodgings where his family and friends might call. They had moved east and north, to an area of the city known as Arthur's Hill where they were unknown. George continued to visit his family without telling them he had moved and if he met his friends on a Friday night to go drinking, the arrangements would be made at work. But increasingly he was reluctant to go out and leave Maggie on her own. He watched the firelight glinting off her now red-dyed hair and could not resist pausing to stroke its burnished softness.

To the outside world they were Mr and Mrs Gordon and kept to themselves, paying the rent promptly and causing the neighbours no upset. Maggie had taken a position as a part-time clerk for a coal merchant, while George continued to work in the giant forge at Pearson's. They could have afforded something more spacious and genteel than the poky rooms in Arthur's Hill but did not want to draw attention to themselves.

Inside their home they maintained proprieties by sleeping in separate rooms, yet Maggie knew how scandalised her mother and sister Susan would be at such an arrangement. For herself, she felt no guilt. Glancing up at the man now stroking her hair, she smiled in contentment and found it hard to think of a time when she had felt so secure or at peace with life. Yet each day was so uncertain and shadowed by the threat of re-arrest that Maggie thought only of here and now, grateful for the snatched happiness of these stolen weeks with George.

She was living the double life of the fugitive, working quietly in the coal merchant's draughty shed every morning, then returning home to await instructions from the movement. Yet the idea that someone had betrayed her to the police preyed on her mind at times, though George had pointed out that many people came and went at Heslop's mission hall and could have been paid to find her. Heslop himself was reported to be very upset at the arson attack and at the arrest of Annie Dobson who was now serving a two-month sentence for window-breaking. Maggie felt wretched for the hapless Annie and had made sure that she would be cared for by the WSPU on her release. As for Alice Pearson, there was no way of knowing what her reaction to the fire was; it was too dangerous to try and make contact with her.

But if Maggie regretted anything about her new life, it was the way Rose had turned her back on her after the arson attack. Maggie blanched to think of the scene her former friend had made at their lodgings.

'You've gone too far with your violence, threatening the Pearsons like that,' Rose had cried. 'How could you betray Miss Alice?'

'It was a symbolic attack on a summerhouse!' Maggie had protested. 'Alice Pearson should understand that even if you can't. You're only this upset because the Pearsons are rich and upper class and it flatters your snobbishness that Miss Alice pays you attention. You wouldn't be half so bothered if I'd bombed a poor man's house or a public building.'

'How dare you!' Rose had shaken with fury. 'You've stepped over the line, Maggie. Just look at yourself living in cheap rooms with a man you're not even married to. I'm ashamed of you now.'

Maggie had glared back. 'So that's what's really bothering you, isn't it, Rose? That I've chosen to live with George as well as carry on being a militant. You're jealous because I'm doing things my own way now, instead of doing what you think is best for me. And you're jealous of my love for George, aren't you?'

Rose had stormed to the door, puce with indignation.

'Do what you want, Maggie, I really don't care any more. But this thing with George Gordon is wrong - hiding like a rat in a hole. It'll come to no good, but don't depend on me to be around to pick up the pieces!'

It had been a horrible, horrible argument, Maggie winced at the memory, and she had seen nothing of Rose or her mother since.

Maggie sighed.

'What's bothering you, pet?' George asked, closing the book.

Maggie laid her warm cheek on his knee. 'How long can we go on like this before I'm discovered?' she asked

'They'll not find you,' George tried to reassure her, stroking her face. 'If you're worried we could leave Newcastle - go abroad where no one'll know us. Isn't it Paris the suffragette leaders gan to when there's bother?'

Maggie chuckled. "The ones with money, maybes.'

'Aye, Paris.' George began to daydream aloud. 'A place of revolution - we'd fit in there, bonny lass. We could join in the workers' struggle with our French comrades.'

'And how much French can you speak, Geordie?' Maggie teased, twisting to look up at him.

'Nowt!' he laughed. 'But revolution is the same in any language.'

'Oh, George, you really would leave with me, wouldn't you?' Maggie smiled in amazement.

'If that's what it takes to keep you,' George answered earnestly.

Maggie regarded him fondly, wistfully. 'Sometimes I wish we could run away,' she said quietly. 'But that's the coward's way, isn't it? We've got to try and change things here, for our people, haven't we?'

George gazed into her troubled grey eyes, like dark pools in the candlelight.

'By, Maggie, you're a strong lass. You inspire me, you do. More than ten speeches or a bucketful of beer.'

Maggie smiled and stretched up her hand to caress his face. 'I wish it could always be like this, Geordie,' she said tenderly.

Suddenly he bent and kissed her full on the lips and felt her answering passion. Their arms went about each other and he pulled her up into his hold.

A banging on the door startled them out of their embrace and sent the candlelight flickering crazily.

'Get in the bedroom,' George ordered immediately.

Maggie hid herself in the other room, straining to hear who the caller was as George opened the door. The draught nearly blew out the candle and it seemed an age before the door closed again.

'It's all right, Maggie,' George called. 'It's Mr Heslop.'

Maggie emerged from the box room, feeling bashful and bewildered to see the lay preacher standing in her secret haven, muffled in a large black coat and clutching his bowler hat.

'Will you sit down and have a cup of tea with us, Mr Heslop?' Maggie asked in a strong voice that belied her nervousness at his unexpected arrival.

'No thank you, Maggie.' He cleared his throat, appearing just as awkward to be there. 'I just come with a message.'

'How did you find me?' Maggie gulped.

George intervened. 'Rose told him.'

'Rose!' Maggie exclaimed, indignant.

Heslop held up his hand. 'I know you've argued and gone your separate ways, but Miss Johnstone still worries for you. She knows I would never give away your whereabouts to the police and I wanted to tell you the news in person.'

'What news?' Maggie was suddenly anxious. 'It's not Mam?'

'It's not bad news.' John Heslop smiled for the first time. 'Your sister Susan and Mr Turvey are going to be married on Saturday at the chapel.'

'I see,' Maggie said. "That's all very sudden. I suppose Susan has asked you to find me and tell me to come.'

'Not exactly,' John Heslop said, clearing his throat once again.

'Maggie can't go,' George broke in, grim-faced and feeling resentful of the older man's intrusion into their privacy. 'It's too dangerous. She'll be picked up straight away.'

'It's hardly a society wedding,' Heslop answered dismissively. 'It's a simple chapel service and it's been arranged so quickly that I doubt that anyone in authority will link it with Maggie.' He turned to stare at Maggie. 'I think you should go. It's an opportunity to be reconciled with your family. As you know, your mother is not well and it would cheer her greatly to see you. Susan too, I'm sure, would want you to be there.'

'I can't,' Maggie answered bluntly, 'and I don't believe Susan would want me to spoil her day by appearing like the prodigal either.'

Heslop stepped towards her and took her hands in his.

'That's it, Maggie. The prodigal. Go home to your family where you belong - where you're needed. Give up this destructive life you've fallen into, this militancy. They'll forgive you.'

'Forgive her!' George shouted 'There's nothing to forgive. You've got a bloody cheek coming here and preaching at her like some fallen woman.'

Heslop turned on George. 'It's not right, her living here like a criminal. You're protecting an arsonist, remember.'

'If that's what you think of me, why are you here?' Maggie asked, furious at his condemnation of them both. 'And you used to be full of such praise for the women's movement and equal rights. You hypocrite!'

John Heslop flinched at her scorn. 'I did believe in those things - I still do. Your non-violent protest was brave and right, but not this burning and breaking of people's property. I want to save you, Maggie. Go and see your sister married and then give yourself up.'

Maggie shook him off, horrified. 'Do you know what you're asking? You're asking me to admit defeat, to go back into that prison and submit to their torture.'

'Not if you renounce your militancy,' Heslop urged. 'Admit that you were misguided and that you won't have any more to do with violent protest or terrorism. Then you'll be free to go home. You have so much to offer the world, Maggie, I can't see you throw your life away, here with this man.'

George cursed in anger, but Maggie grabbed the hand he raised at the butcher and held on to it.

'George Gordon is a good man,' she answered with passion, 'and he's stood by me when everyone else turned their backs. This home of ours may be damp and poor, but it's not a place of sin, Mr Heslop. It's a place of love and warmth, where I'm cherished for the lass I am, not the lass others would make me. And I'll carry on with me work to free women from the slavery they're in even if it meets with the hostility of me family and so-called friends.'

Heslop looked at her dumbstruck, but her tirade continued.

'I never expected the struggle to be easy but I've chosen to struggle rather than submit to an easy life, to letting things go on as they are. I know you came here with good intentions, Mr Heslop, but I don't want saving from the life I've chosen. And if it means ganin' back to prison then I'd gan, but at least I'll know I've not betrayed me own beliefs or the sisters I fight for!'

She watched the expression on his face turn from angry frustration to bewildered resignation. He jammed on his hard hat, tight-lipped, and strode to the door, exchanging a look of animosity with George.

'Mr Heslop,' Maggie said as he reached for the door handle. 'Please give Susan my love and best wishes for Saturday.'

He gave her the curtest of nods. Then George blocked his way with an arm on the door.

'If you betray Maggie to the police or anyone else, I'll come after you,

Heslop,' he threatened.

Heslop glared back. 'I've already given my word that I'll do nothing of the sort.'

George stood back and Heslop dived for the open door, slamming it behind him. The candle snuffed out.

For a moment, Maggie stood staring at the place where her old family friend had been and felt an acute wave of loneliness engulf her like the sudden darkness of the room. Then George's arms went about her and pulled her into his warm hold. She leant against him and sobbed quietly into his rough jacket as he caressed her head.

'Don't leave me, Geordie,' she whispered.

'Oh, Maggie man, I'll never leave you,' he promised fervently, clinging to her tighter.

She looked at him with haunted eyes in her tear-stained face. 'No, I mean tonight. Don't leave me alone tonight.' For a moment he seemed not to understand. Then he bent and kissed her gently on the lips.

'I'll do whatever you want, pet,' George whispered into her hair.

Maggie took him by the hand and led him into the bedroom.

That night was a startling awakening for Maggie. Faint gaslight filtered in from the street through the dirty skylight, but hardly penetrated the blackness of the box room. They undressed in an awkward, expectant silence, each as bashful as the other to be seen naked. In the end they got into bed still in their undergarments, shivering at the touch of the chilled bedding, and reached for one another, thankful of the dark.

For a while they simply lay and held each other, wondering what to do next. Maggie, having invited the intimacy, had no clue how to act. In the raciest film she had seen, the actress just lay on a couch looking furtive. Perhaps this lying together in the same bed was sex, she thought in bafflement.

George lay, overcome with nerves. He had only had lasses standing up in back lanes, never lying down. They had been older girls, doing it for coppers or food and he had hardly touched them. Sex had been a quick gratification, for mutual self-interest, a transaction carried out and quickly forgotten, a bodily function like eating or urinating. But here he was, lying next to the woman he had desired for months, petrified she would find him disgusting, would turn her face to the wall in boredom or disdain like the other girls he had penetrated. He was paralysed, yet already aroused.

Maggie spoke softly. 'Kiss me, Geordie, man!'

George felt relief as he began to cover her hair and face with gentle exploring kisses. Soon their kissing became more urgent, the exploration more daring and the lovemaking began.

Maggie, who had not even seen her own brother naked, was fascinated and aghast at George's body. The touch and smell of the man was quite alien and the way her own body responded to his caressing was terrifying and thrilling. Under the warming bedlinen they wriggled out of their clothes, eager to experience more.

Awkwardness was forgotten as they gave way to pleasure and excitement on the ancient iron bedstead.

'I love you, Maggie!' George whispered.

Maggie held him fiercely and responded, 'Don't ever leave me now.'

'Never!' he promised and kissed her tenderly.

Later, George fell asleep, his arm resting across Maggie, heavy and protective. But she lay awake, staring up at the skylight, thinking of her sister about to embark on the same experience with Richard Turvey.

Was Susan lying awake nervously at this same moment? Maggie wondered. Would Richard be as affectionate and passionate a lover as George? She could not help thinking that Susan would probably be revolted by the mess and intimacy of the marriage bed and for a moment worried for her elder sister.

But after tonight, Maggie knew she could not possibly return to her family as if nothing had happened. They would look at her and know.

No, Maggie thought with only a twinge of regret, she had put herself beyond the pale of society, just as Rose had accused. She was not only an arsonist and a criminal, as Heslop had said, she was also a fornicator. It sounded such a harsh, unforgiving word, she thought sleepily, denying the depth of love she felt. Yet that is how the world would judge her for giving herself unreservedly to George Gordon, the loving, strong man at her side.

Maggie kissed his sleeping face, comforted by the feel of his regular warm breath on her cheek, and fell asleep.

Chapter Seventeen

Susan woke on her wedding morning to see snow lying like a sprinkling of sugar over the densely packed roofs and cobbled lanes around Gun Street. It gleamed in the dark and for an instant she was delighted by the dazzle of whiteness covering the grime of the back yards and listened to the silence that had descended with the snowfall. It seemed an omen of good luck; of purity, of a fresh beginning. Then Helen spoke from the bed they shared.

'It'll ruin our shoes,' she yawned and complained at the same time. 'We'll be slipping all o'er the place. And the slush on me new frock—'

'Belt up!' Susan shouted at her crossly. 'You're not going to spoil me wedding day with your whingeing on.'

Helen stepped out of bed, unconcerned. Susan eyed her warily as she began to unbraid the rags that were twisted into her hair, her bare legs protruding from the too-small nightgown that pulled tightly over her developing breasts. Susan was struck again by the air of defiant confidence, of knowingness that hung about her sister these days. She was just seventeen, yet Helen had the scent and sleekness of an older woman which made Susan feel as awkward as a schoolgirl.

For the first time, Susan was glad that she was marrying today. She had thought Richard too hasty and would have preferred a respectable period of betrothal while he progressed in his new job until they could afford a house of their own. As it was, they would have to live with Aunt Violet and Uncle Barny and Susan would have to defer to her fussing aunt in all things domestic, instead of running the household as she was used to doing. But Richard had swept aside her doubts, assuring her that he would soon be earning good money and she could have any house in the west of Newcastle that she desired.

And she did desire. Susan longed and dreamed for the day when she could live again on Sarah Crescent and leave behind the filth and stigma of Gun Street for ever. So she had agreed to Richard's hasty marriage plans, flattered that he was so eager to become her husband.

And this morning, with Helen so moody and giving her those superior looks, Susan felt a new urgency to be married and regain her status over her sisters. She only allowed herself a fleeting thought of Maggie, for Maggie's outrageous behaviour was too painful to contemplate. She had brought shame on the family with her extreme politics. To have a sister who deliberately went to prison and now ran from the police and was rumoured to be the one who carried out the arson attack on the mighty Pearsons - Susan shuddered. She must marry Richard with haste in case he changed his mind about marrying into such a family.

Dressing in work-a-day clothes and hurrying into the kitchen, she found her mother was already up. She had lit the lamp and made a fresh pot of tea and was toasting stale bread over the fire.

'Mam, you should've stayed in bed a bit longer,' Susan admonished, kissing her mother with sudden affection. Her recent illness had been a constant irritation and worry to Susan, but now that she would be leaving her for the first time in her life, she felt a keen nostalgia for the days when her mother had been the solid dictatorial woman to whom they had all clung - obeying, fearing and loving in equal measure.

'I'll not lie in me bed on the day me eldest lass is to be wed,' Mabel protested

'I've dreamed of this day for you, hinny.'

'Have you, Mam?' Susan asked in surprise, delighted to see her mother so robust on this special morning.

'Aye,' her mother nodded, unbending from her task for a moment and turning the heel of bread. 'I've wanted to see you wed more than any of the others.'

Susan flushed with pleasure. 'Why, Mam?'

'You're a home-maker, Susan hinny,' her mother smiled. 'Maggie got all the brains and Helen the looks, though it'll bring them nowt but bother.' Mabel shook her head and sucked in her weathered cheeks. 'But all you've wanted was to mother folk. Now you'll have a chance to mother your own, and you deserve it. I know you've taken the brunt of bringing up your sisters and brother and it's time you thought about yourself. I just wish you didn't have to live in with that complaining old wife Violet.'

'Mam! Aunt Violet's canny really,' Susan protested. But she was touched by the sudden concern, the unexpected tenderness. She put her arms about her mother's burly shoulders and hid her face in the sour-sweet warmth of her neck.

'Mam, I'm sorry I've been a bit sharp with you lately. I didn't mean any of those things about Richard saving the family from the workhouse. You've always done your best by us, I know you have. You've been the canniest mam we could've had.'

Mabel shook her off, embarrassed. 'Eeh, haway with you. Gan and help your gran get washed and dressed.'

The brief intimacy between them was over but Susan would not forget it quickly. How often, when the younger ones had seemed to be getting all the attention, had she yearned for a hug and a confiding word from her mother.

Mabel had already bent again to her toasting.

'You'll not drink too much today, will you, Mam?' Susan asked, her mind once more on her wedding day. She was desperate for it to go well and fearful that it would not.

But her mother just grunted, 'You may be about to become Mrs Turvey, but you're still my lass and you'll not tell me how to carry on.'

Susan's heart sank as she disappeared into the parlour, noticing at once the smell of her grandmother's incontinence that would have to be disguised with disinfectant and polish before the wedding party that afternoon. The stench of incontinence and the fear of her mother's behaviour combined to increase her apprehension.

Mabel stared into the fire and thought of her long dead husband Alec. How he would have relished the wedding day of his firstborn and the excuse for a party. She still saw him as young, as he had been on the day he strode off to work whistling - and never came back. She had watched him from the scrubbed and chalked step of their neat, prosperous home and thought how lucky she was to be married to the tall, broad-backed Scot who commanded such respect in the street. It should have been Alec's privilege to deliver his daughter into Richard's care and not John Heslop's, who would be taking his place in the chapel that day, at Susan's request.

Mabel coughed and spat into the flames. John Heslop! The man who had given them friendship and help when she was first widowed and struggling to make ends meet, yet had drawn back from marrying her, Mabel thought bitterly. She had even promised to stop her drinking and to attend chapel if he would take her on for the sake of the children. But he had seen in her eyes that she did not love him and he told her as gently as possible that he did not love her either. So, humiliated, she had thrown him out and sworn that she would rely on no man's charity; she would raise her children and survive in the world without a man in the house interfering.

The memory made her defiant. Today she would have a good skinful of booze and the devil take the long-faced teetotallers. Then she could forget that Susan was marrying a fly talker and spendthrift. And she could forget about Maggie and where she might be and what she might be doing, and the soreness in her heart would be dulled for a day.

'What about me, Mam?' A sleepy voice in the corner disturbed her thoughts. She had forgotten Jimmy asleep on the truckle bed.

'What about you?' Mabel answered shortly.

'If Maggie got all the brains, Helen the looks and Susan's the home-maker, what's special about me?' he demanded.

The little bugger had been eavesdropping, she thought in exasperation. Mabel snorted. 'You, Jimmy? You're just a daft lad.'

'Mam, I'm serious,' Jimmy answered in annoyance. 'Tell us what was different about me?'

Mabel thought, but could only remember how ill she was the eight months she carried him and the terrible birth, after which she swore she would have no more babies.

'You were the sickly bairn,' she told him. 'We expected you to die. But your father wouldn't let you. He sat up all night and fed you teaspoons of whisky and said the Lord's Prayer over and over till the sun came up.' Mabel grunted. 'So you'll either be an alcoholic or a priest or both. Now get yourself up and gan and get some water from the pump if it's not frozen.'

Jimmy got up and pulled on his trousers and jacket, his look bitterly disappointed. But Mabel had turned again to the fire and did not notice.

Susan looked around the room at the glowing faces. Her wedding day appeared to have gone well enough, she thought with relief. She knew she had looked becoming in her new outfit of blue and cream with the matching hat and gloves for which Richard had insisted on paying. Jimmy had managed to last until after the service before soaking his new trousers in a snowball fight with Tommy Smith, and Helen had looked demure in pink. Even her mother had made an effort to smarten her hair and looked quite handsome in a yellow dress and mustard tweed coat that she had salvaged from the secondhand stall.

Not that she was smart now, Susan thought with disapproval, eyeing her mother as she leant against the piano, her hair falling from its pins, her face flushed with drink as she ordered Richard to play another music hall score.

But no one else seemed to care, even Aunt Violet was clapping at the music and her quavering voice was joining in with Mary Smith's. Uncle Barny was wedged in the corner with his cork leg, singing two bars behind the others, his nose a red beacon in the fading light. Behind the horsehair sofa Jimmy and Tommy were swigging beer out of the best china cups and giggling at their own jokes, while Granny Beaton sat beaming vacantly by the fire, sipping ginger wine. John Heslop had stayed only briefly to toast their union in tea and with his departure the wedding party's inhibitions had relaxed.

Even so, Susan could not shake off the feeling that something was wrong. Richard, since the chapel service, had seemed preoccupied, almost sullen. He banged aggressively at the keyboard and was drinking twice as much as everyone else. Perhaps, like her, he was just emotional and exhausted. She wished they could now be alone together, so she could have him to herself.

'Give us "The Blaydon Races", Richard hinny!' Mabel shouted, thumping her new son-in-law on the back.

'I told you before, don't know it, Mrs Beaton,' he said curtly.

'What! Don't know... How long've you been in Newcastle? Eeh, Violet, get this lad of yours taught quick. He's a Geordie now.' She thumped him on the back again.

Susan stepped forward, sensing her husband's irritation, and placed a possessive hand on his shoulder. She was sorry none of Richard's own family had been able to attend the wedding, but if he had felt any disappointment he had not shown it.

When Susan had expressed regret at not meeting his mother, he had laughed 'She thinks the Eskimos live up here, darlin'. Too far and too cold for the old doll to travel at this time of year.'

'Perhaps we could travel down and see her in the spring,' Susan had suggested tentatively, eager to meet Richard's mother and visit London.

'We'll see,' Richard had replied evasively.

Now Susan said, 'It's getting on, Richard. Perhaps we should be going.'

He looked round at her. 'Go? We've just started celebrating, doll.' His laugh sounded harsh.

'Aye!' Mabel waved at her daughter. 'Gan and make some tea if you're tiring. You'll need to keep your strength up for the night. Eh, Richard?' she cackled and slapped him playfully.

'Mam!' Susan exclaimed, blushing furiously. The thought of being left alone with Richard set her stomach churning with nerves, but she wanted to get the first night over with quickly, so that people would know she was fully a wife and a woman of the world and Helen's smug smirking would be wiped from her face. It annoyed her that her sister was sitting close to Richard, balanced on the edge of his stool, flirting, and it niggled that Richard did not seem to mind.

Mary Smith surprised Susan by leaving the group around the piano and taking her by the arm.

'You and me will get the kettle on, hinny. I'm parched and the beer's running out. Haway!'

Susan felt a rush of gratitude towards their neighbour and regretted that she had so often dismissed Mary Smith as an inadequate mother and slovenly housekeeper. She had led a hard life with her strange, moody husband who was more often absent than present and yet the woman was always cheerful and generous with what little she had.

They made tea and brought out rice cakes and more sandwiches and the party continued. It grew dark and the beer and spirits ran out.

'Let's go to the Gunners!' Richard suggested, to Susan's dismay.

'Richard...'

'Don't be a spoilsport, Susan,' he cut off her protest, his smile tight. 'If you don't want to come, you go on home with Aunt Violet. Me and Uncle Barny will follow on. Eh, General Dodds?'

' With a ta-ra, ra-ra, ra!' Barny sang and waved in agreement.

'Aye, Mary,' Mabel cried, loud with drink, 'we'll gan an' all. Have a little jug in the snug, eh?'

Susan saw that her mother was hellbent on a drinking session and wondered if she was deliberately trying to blot out her disappointment that Maggie was not here. John Heslop had been apologetic in failing to persuade Maggie to attend, but he would not disclose where she was hiding and this had annoyed her mother intensely. The whole question of whether Maggie would turn up for the wedding seemed to have irritated Richard too.

'If the silly cow can't be bothered to see her own sister married, then she's not worth a farthing,' he had snapped. Susan had firmly agreed, but she suspected her mother was drinking to forget about the wretched Maggie.

'I'm right behind you, Mabel!' Mary Smith cackled. 'A hug in the snug!' And she grabbed her son Tommy round the waist.

'Gerroff, Mam!' He wriggled out of her hold, embarrassed.

Violet loudly disapproved of the idea and the party soon collapsed into argument as to whether they should continue celebrations in the pub. Finally Richard got his own way and left with the drinkers. Violet stayed to help Helen and Susan clear up. She huffed and sniffed continual condemnation of her sister-in-law, blaming Mabel for leading her husband and young nephew astray. Jimmy and Tommy were scolded for draining the dregs of stale beer and escaped downstairs.

Helen sang and smiled infuriatingly as if nothing was wrong and Susan, on the edge of tears, announced that she was too tired to wait and would Aunt Violet please take her home? They left, carrying a small bag of clothes and possessions, with only a sleepy Granny Beaton and a smirking Helen to wish Susan goodbye. Trudging over the icy pavements, Susan could not help shedding tears of disappointment in the dark.

'That's men for you,' Aunt Violet complained. 'They think only of themselves and where the next beer's coming from. I've put up with it for nearly forty years.'

'Richard's not like that normally,' Susan sniffed, determined not to believe her aunt. 'It's just because it's his wedding day -I've got to make allowances.'

Violet snorted in disbelief. 'Richard can charm the birds off the trees, but when it comes to taking a drink, he's just like any other lad. Before he got that good job he was for ever borrowing off me and your Uncle Barny to go supping in the town.'

Susan looked at her, disturbed. 'You never said anything about his drinking,' she accused.

'I can't be blamed if you don't keep your eyes open, lass. You've known him as long as I have.' Perhaps something in Susan's dejected walk made her aunt feel a twinge of sympathy, because she added, 'Never mind, that lad of yours is bringing in a good wage now and he's generous when he's got the money. You could have done a lot worse.'

Susan sighed. 'Why didn't any of your and Richard's family come up from London, Aunt Violet?'

Her aunt shook her head and pursed her lips. "We're not a close family, Susan. Haven't been in touch with Richard's mother for years. Me sister Ida's moved about that much, so Richard says. I did write about the wedding, mind,' Violet sniffed, 'but Ida didn't have the decency to reply. In fact she never even bothered to tell me Richard was coming to Newcastle last year - he just turned up on my doorstep all bright and breezy. But then Ida married into a bad lot - the Turveys.'

Susan felt her spirits plunge at her aunt's depressing revelations.

Later, as she sat on the bed in the room she was to share with Richard, brushing out her fair hair, she told herself not to listen to Violet's moanings. Her aunt never had a good word to say about anyone and seemed to thrive on other people's misfortunes. She would just have to put up with living here for a short while until they could move into a house of their own.

Susan must have dozed off with fatigue, because she was startled awake by the door banging open and Richard stumbling through it in the dark. The waft of stale whisky as he came to peer over her made her feel nauseous.

'Susan, doll,' he slurred and lunged down to plant a wet kiss on her face.

'Richard, the door ...' Susan sat up in a panic. 'My uncle and aunt can hear.'

'A bloody cannon going off wouldn't wake your uncle,' Richard laughed. 'The old bastard's well pissed.'

'Please, Richard,' Susan pleaded, affronted by his language, 'shut the door.'

'I can't see you if I shut the door,' Richard answered. Susan fumbled to light the candle at her bedside. As it flared, Richard staggered over and slammed the door shut.

He turned round and ordered, 'Take your nightdress off.'

Susan sat rigid.

'You're my wife now, do as I bloody well say!'

Shock seized her, paralysing her movements. Then he rushed at her, foul-mouthed and threatening. Susan, galvanised by fear, stood up and began to fumble with her nightgown. Richard watched her as he began to discard his wedding clothes about the floor.

She stood shivering in the cold, a sob lodged in her throat. Once naked, he ordered her into the bed.

The consummation was over quicker than a cup of tea, Susan thought in bewilderment. Seconds later, Richard rolled off her, slumped across the bolster and began to snore.

Susan lay quite appalled at what had taken place. No one had warned her of the ordeal. She lay in pain, too shocked by the assault to cry. How could she possibly endure such a disgusting act again? She would never be able to enter this icy room without thinking of the humiliation and animal behaviour that sex with her husband appeared to demand. She saw the nights stretching ahead to eternity, dreading the darkness and fearing the touch of this man whom she thought she loved.

Why was he so different in bed from the witty and charming man who had courted her? Then a worm of doubt wriggled in her mind. Perhaps he had not courted her at all; perhaps it was she who had done all the running and he had merely succumbed to pressure from the family to marry her as the eldest rather than the pretty but immature Helen. Maybe Richard had just been too lazy to resist, or perhaps he thought he could have them both . . . After what Violet had said about him, she wondered if she knew her husband at all.

Susan lay, torturing herself with doubts and fears about Richard. But she refused to cry. Thousands of women before her must have endured as much without complaint. She would just have to become pregnant as quickly as possible and then she would be left alone. With that small shred of comfort, she turned her back on her unconscious husband and prayed for the delivery of sleep.

Chapter Eighteen

The early weeks of 1914 were the happiest Maggie could remember. She was an outcast from her old life in the teeming streets of West Newcastle, yet she was experiencing the greatest freedom of her life. It seemed to mark the dawning of a new age of optimism and progression. Ready to continue her campaign of militancy when instructed by headquarters, she felt increasingly that they were winning the fight for the vote. More and more politicians were speaking out on their behalf and the publicity given to the treatment of women prisoners was beginning to sicken citizens with a conscience. She had been told to lie low for several weeks, until the furore over the arson attack at Hebron House had died down.

Yet she managed to meet other suffragettes in discreet tearooms in the east of the city, in parlours of sympathetic supporters. She frequently wondered what Alice Pearson thought of her now, but all she could learn about the magnate's daughter was that she was touring on the Continent.

Maggie continued to work part-time for the coal merchant and in the evenings she looked forward eagerly to George's return from the shipyard.

Sometimes she shook her head in amazement at how they had been thrown together in adversity. She had thought it impossible that she would find such a soul-mate in a man, least of all in a man like George Gordon, raised in a tough community that took men's superiority over women for granted. But beneath his brawny, aggressive stance, George was as much an idealist as she was.

At night they would curl up by the small fire and express aloud their dreams of how they would better the world together. Sometimes they went to the house of a friend of George's, a Jewish musician called Isaac Samuel who attracted around him a small group of intellectuals. George had met him at the Pearson library and been amazed by the thin, bearded Russian who had fled persecution and arrived on a merchant vessel up the Tyne. He scraped a living by giving music lessons, while his sister Miriam took in sewing.

Maggie enjoyed the cosy evenings in Isaac's over-furnished rooms, sitting among chairs strewn with music and books, arguing with the others about religion and imperialism, capitalism and the new Bolshevism seeping out of Russia. She was the only woman who took part in the discussions; the enigmatic Miriam chose instead to read or embroider by the corner lamp, unperturbed by their arguing.

'Lenin's right,' George announced one evening. 'The workers need to organise more into a revolutionary force. Organise and protest - disrupt production if necessary. Not like our lot who allow the bosses to divide them into different classes, so each thinks they're a step above the others.'

'But your bosses,' Isaac Samuel said with a wave of his long bony hands, 'allow a great freedom of speech among the working classes. You have open-air meetings and say things that would get you shot in my Russia.'

'There's precious little freedom of speech for us lasses,' Maggie interjected.

'Ah, the lasses,' Isaac nodded his bearded face. 'In Russia they are respected once they are old and toothless.'

Maggie laughed and shook her head.

'But the working classes here have been bought off,' George said, returning to what preoccupied him. 'Every time we organise and push for more rights, they build us a park or an institute or a church to keep us quiet and grateful.'

'Or a library to read in,' Isaac mentioned with the ghost of a smile.

'Or a rowing club to compete in,' Maggie added, grinning at their host.

George, realising they were teasing him, grunted. 'All right, I'm just as easily bought as the next man. But reading and sport should be there for everyone, not dependent on the whim of some patron whose money was made by the sweat of the workers any how.'

Miriam rose and poured them all tea from a huge hissing and steaming machine they called a samovar and the discussion changed to religion. George would have none of it in his workers' Utopia, while Maggie and Isaac demanded complete freedom to worship without persecution.

'The Sabbath was invented to occupy the working classes, so they wouldn't cause trouble on their day off,' George announced, playing devil's advocate.

'If it wasn't for God and the Sabbath,' Isaac parried with a smile, 'the working classes would not have their day off.'

'It's hardly a day off for the women anyway,' Maggie reminded them quickly. 'They still have to dress the bairns in their Sunday best and slave over the stove making the Sunday dinner, then clear up while the men sleep it off.'

'Sounds like paradise, doesn't it, Isaac?' George winked.

Maggie gave him a playful push. Miriam promptly invited them to lunch on Sunday without glancing up from her sewing and Maggie realised that the quiet, grey-haired woman had been listening all along.

Later, stamping through the raw, dimly lit streets, oblivious of the cold and energised by their debate, they hastened to bed and made love.

At times Maggie felt utterly free and fulfilled by her new life, but at others she was overwhelmed by a desire to see her mother and family and return to the streets where she grew up. The wanting would start as a dull nagging, like mild toothache, then worsen into a sharp pain of needing that left her irritable and restless. As the winter wore on with no missions to undertake for the WSPU, Maggie felt her inaction and creeping guilt about neglecting her family grip her like a malaise. Worst of all, she found she could not talk to George of her mixed feelings towards her family. He bristled when she mentioned them and bad-mouthed them for rejecting her, so that it was better to keep her worries to herself.

But every so often, George would catch her lifting the window blind and gazing out over the rooftops, preoccupied.

'What's wrong, pet?' he asked one dark Saturday in late February. The sky was the colour of gun metal and had never grown more than half light all day.

She let the blind drop and sighed.

Her bouts of restlessness made George nervous, his greatest fear being that she would tire of her restricted life with him and return to her family. He wanted them always to be together, would have proposed marriage if she had not declared so forcefully that marriage was a form of enslavement for women that needed thorough reform in law before she would entertain it. They seemed to be of one mind on so much, George thought irritably, and yet he was aware of her holding back from him - not physically - but somewhere deep within her being.

'Nothing's wrong,' she answered glumly.

'It's your mam, isn't it?' George said, a note of irritation creeping into his voice.

'Aye,' Maggie admitted abruptly. She was tired of pretending that nothing was wrong. 'The last time I saw her she looked that poorly.'

'We'd have heard if anything had happened.'

'Geordie!' Maggie was hurt. 'Am I supposed to wait around until I hear she's kicked the bucket? Wait for Mr Heslop to come creeping round like a ghoul with bad news?'

'If that preacher sets foot near here again, I'll kick his self-righteous backside into next week!'

'You shouldn't speak about him like that,' Maggie reprimanded, crossing her arms in front of her like a barrier. 'Mr Heslop came here out of the best of reasons, to try and get me to gan to Susan's wedding. And perhaps I should've - I feel that bad about it. I haven't spoken to me sister or even sent her a gift - I've done nothing for her.'

'And why should you?' George replied indignantly, remembering how Susan had shown her disapproval of him. 'She turned her back on you when you went to prison, remember,' he said, his temper growing with his anxiety. 'Why should you bother with her now?'

Maggie was annoyed to be reminded of how her family had been quick to disown her over the launch episode. She realised suddenly how much their rejection hurt, not just her sisters' open hostility but her mother's seeming acceptance that she was no longer part of the family.

'It's not just Susan and me mam,' Maggie answered crossly. 'I want to see Granny - and Tich. I -I miss them.'

'Am I not enough family for you then?' George asked, at once hating his carping words.

'That's not fair, Geordie. You can go and see your family any day of the week. It's not my fault if you're not close to them and don't visit from one month to the next.'

George was stung with guilt and anger at her words. 'The only reason I've stopped going regularly is to protect you! They don't even know where to find me if me old man drops dead.'

'They can fetch you from work,' Maggie pointed out harshly. 'But I might as well be dead for all my family know about me.'

'Perhaps that's the way they want it,' George said in a quiet, hard voice. 'Then they can forget the shame you've brought them.'

Maggie stared at her lover, wounded by his words and the awful realisation that they might be true. After all, none of her family had tried to contact her, only Heslop had come seeking her and been shocked by what he found.

'Is that what you think?' Maggie hissed. 'That I'm someone to be ashamed of?'

'That's not what I said!' George answered crossly.

'But it's what you mean!' Maggie cried in panic. 'It suits you to keep me cooped up here in secret, doesn't it? I'm just a fancy bit that you don't want your family or workmates to know about, is that it? My God, you're just as conventional as the rest of them, George Gordon!'

George was furious; furious at the accusations and furious that this row had blown up so unexpectedly and uncontrollably.

'How could you even think that was all I wanted you for?' George shouted. 'Well, gan back to your precious family if you think they'll have you! But don't blame me if they turn you over to the coppers as soon as you get there.' He stopped pacing about the tiny parlour and grabbed his jacket from the nail behind the door.

'Where're you going?' Maggie demanded, not wanting him to leave but too upset to say so.

'Out - anywhere. To see me old dad that you say I've neglected and then maybes for a pint with Billy or Joshua. Aye, I feel like having a skinful. And what's it matter to you if I do?' he glared.

'Matters nowt!' Maggie shouted back at him. 'That's the way you lads always save the world, isn't it? Over a bucket of beer!'

George raised a menacing finger and stabbed the air. 'And when has breaking windows ever benefited anyone except glaziers?' he said full of scorn.

'Aye, gan on and mock me!' she cried, advancing on him. 'But it's the closest you'll ever get to revolution, Geordie. You're all talk and no action. You're as conservative as they come.'

George cursed and slammed the door in her face. She heard him running down the stairs away from her. Shaking, Maggie slumped to the cold bare floorboards, angry and hurt and bewildered by their sudden argument that had flared out of nothing.

No, not nothing, she thought. It had been simmering for weeks. Ever since Heslop had burst into their haven and fuelled her guilt at abandoning her family ...

Maggie realised with a heavy heart that she could never escape her past and the messy tangle of obligations and emotions that bound her to her relations. No matter what lengths she went to erase her former life, she was still a Beaton.

Shivering in the cold gloom of the room that suddenly seemed lifeless and depressing without George, Maggie yearned for the chaotic comfort of Gun Street. Picking herself up from the floor, she knew she had to go there. At that moment she wanted her mother's solid arms about her more than anything in the world.

It was late afternoon when Maggie reached Gun Street and to her bafflement and disappointment no one answered her knocking at the upstairs flat. As she hammered for a third time, Mary Smith popped her head out from the flat below.

'No one's there, hinny,' she called at the shadowy figure. 'Can I help?'

'It's me, Mrs Smith. Maggie.'

For a moment there was silence, then Mary Smith screeched, 'It's never!' She advanced out of the door and up the first few steps. 'Where have you been hiding yourself, hinny? Your mam's been that worried. Eeh, and you missed Susan's wedding. She looked a picture.' Mary reached out and pulled Maggie by the arm. 'Come in an' have a cup of tea with me. They'll not be long. Your Susan's giving them all their tea at your Aunt Violet's.'

Maggie needed little persuasion to keep her old neighbour company. She could not bear the thought of returning to the empty rooms in Arthur's Hill and no longer knew if she was welcome there. They sat by the stove, drinking tea while Maggie listened to Mary Smith chatter on about the family and Susan's wedding and how well Mr Turvey was doing.

'Always so nicely turned out, is Mr Turvey,' she said in approval. 'And Susan's never too busy to visit her mam. Over here every day, she is. Course she's always been close to her mam - a real one for family.'

Maggie winced at the unintentional criticism but let the garrulous, lonely woman continue.

'That Helen's full of mischief, mind. Needles your Susan whenever she can. If you ask me,' Mary said, leaning closer and dropping her voice as if someone might hear, 'she shows Mr Turvey too much attention when he comes round. She's going to be a terrible one for the lads. Don't say a word of this to your mam, mind. She's got enough to worry about with Granny Beaton and Jimmy.'

'What do you mean?' Maggie asked in concern.

'Well, with your grandmother wetting the bed all the time and wandering off like a bairn. And Tich packing in his job because he thinks he can get summat better. He's turning into a right tearaway - he's out now somewhere with my Tommy. The devil knows where they get to.'

Suddenly Maggie could not stay another minute. She wanted to rush out and find her mother and hug her and ask forgiveness for the worry she had put her through.

'Mrs Smith,' Maggie said, putting her cup down on the hearth, 'ta for the tea but—'

A door banged open in the hall.

'That'll be your mam back, I expect,' Mary Smith said with a nod.

Maggie jumped up and rushed to the door, opening it without another word. Under the fuzzy gas light, she made out three wrapped figures, the one with a stick being helped in by the other two.

'Mam! Granny Beaton!' Maggie cried and dashed forward. 'Helen!'

For a moment they all gawped at her as if they had seen a ghost, then her mother put out a hand and clutched her arm as if to convince herself she was real.

'Maggie?' she gasped. 'Eeh, Maggie, you little bugger!'

Her mother's arms went about her in a cold damp hug of delight and Maggie clung to her, not sure whether she was laughing or crying.

'Get yourself upstairs this minute,' Mabel ordered her daughter, pulling away with a sniff, 'and you can tell us everything.' She shouted at her mother-in-law, 'It's Maggie, Mrs Beaton, she's come home. Maggie,' she repeated to the deaf old woman.

'Oh, Maggie,' her grandmother smiled, understanding. 'Dear lassie.'

Maggie was delighted. 'Let me help you, Granny," she offered.

Helen harrumphed. 'Typical! You blow in like a bad smell from goodness knows where and get all the attention. But what have you done for the family but get us a bad name?'

'Hold your tongue!' her mother ordered. 'You're beginning to sound like Susan.'

'How is Susan?' Maggie asked, ignoring Helen's resentful words. 'I wish I'd seen her wed. But - it was too risky.'

'Eeh, hinny,' Mabel sighed as she mounted the stairs, 'what sort o f life are you leading?'

'Different,' Maggie said, blushing in the gloom.

They helped Granny Beaton upstairs and Mabel went over to light the lamp with a taper from the banked-up fire.

'Mam,' Helen spoke again, this time more sweetly, 'shall I go and fetch our Susan? I'm sure she'd want to see Maggie.'

Mabel gave her a suspicious look. 'What are you up to, offering to run errands?'

But Maggie interrupted eagerly, 'That would be canny of you, Helen,' she smiled. 'I can't stay long.'

'You'll stay the night with us, hinny?' her mother pleaded. 'You can't turn up here after months of being missing and run off into the night again. You can share with Helen the night.'

'Aye,' Helen agreed 'I don't mind for a night.'

'Well,' Maggie considered, thinking it might give George time to calm down, 'maybes just for the night.'

'Shall I go then. Mam?' Helen asked, buttoning up her coat again.

'Aye, be off with you. But don't breathe a word to Aunt Violet or we'll have the police round before you get back.'

Helen was already at the door, tossing her fair ringlets in a habitual gesture.

When she had gone, Mabel sighed. 'She can't bear to be still for two minutes, that lass.'

'Is she helping you with the business?' Maggie asked, discarding her hat and coat over the back of a kitchen chair.

Mabel snorted. 'It's a constant battle to stop her wearing half the clothes we collect. She's got an eye for what's fancy but she's a better spender than shopkeeper.'

Maggie automatically set about warming the teapot and reached up for the tea caddy on the mantelpiece. She noticed that her grandmother was content to rest silently by the fire, her knuckled hands lying loosely in her lap as she stared vacantly into the flames. It was as if her spirit had quietly slipped out of her ageing body and wandered off, leaving a pale likeness of the once intelligent and compassionate woman who had captivated the young Maggie with her tales of the Highlands.

Her mother seemed to read her thoughts.

'She's quite happy just sitting there all day long,' she said quietly, 'dreaming her dreams. She did well recognising you downstairs - she usually calls people names from her past life in Scotland.'

'I wish I could look after her,' Maggie sighed, 'like I used to.'

'So where are you living, Maggie?' her mother asked and Maggie saw the worry shadow her dark blue eyes. 'I know you're not with that teacher Johnstone 'cos I had it out with her. She said you'd rowed and she didn't see you any more. But I knew she was keeping summat back. What was it that prim schoolmistress didn't want me to hear, lass?'

Maggie was surprised to discover her mother had tried to trace her, but could she tell her about George? And if she did, would she throw her down the stairs in disgust, as she was capable of doing? Maggie felt her face go hot.

Mabel suddenly grabbed her hand. 'Hinny, I wasn't born yesterday. It'll tak' a lot to shock me, so you can tell us and know I won't go blabbing to all the neighbours. You're living with a man, aren't you?'

Maggie looked at her mother in astonishment.

'I thought as much,' Mabel grunted.

'Did Mr Heslop tell you?' Maggie asked, her throat quite dry.

'No,' Mabel shook her head, 'he told me nowt, but I could tell he didn't approve of what he'd found.'

'He didn't,' Maggie admitted, flushing deeper, 'and I doubt you will either. I've been living with George Gordon. As she confessed, Maggie raised her head with a defiant jut of her chin, then added, less sure, 'He might not have me back, mind - we argued over me coming here and risking being caught.'

For a moment she thought her mother was going to slap her, and she flinched as Mabel pulled her close, but instead found her mother's arms encircling her tightly.

'Eeh, me darlin' bairn. Just let them try and tak' you away - over my dead body!' she cried.

Maggie clung to her mother and let the tears of relief stream from her closed eyes. For a moment she felt like the ten-year-old Maggie who had hugged her mother for comfort after the death of her father, drawing strength from the warm protective hold, the smell of cheap soap and mothballs and her rough love. Her mother had always been there to turn to; vital, permanent, sharp-tongued and forgiving.

'Will you marry the lad?' Mabel asked, rocking Maggie in her arms.

'No,' Maggie said firmly. 'I'll marry no one. Marriage does nowt but hold women back.'

Her mother sighed, 'Aye, you might be right, hinny. But if you love the lad ...'

'Who says I do?' Maggie bristled.

'I can tell by the way you're carrying on, pretending you don't mind that he threw you out.'

'He didn't throw me out!' Maggie declared, pulling away. 'It was my choice to come back here.'

Mabel laughed. 'Eeh, Maggie. We Beaton women just don't seem to click with men, do we? Since your father died, I couldn't be bothered with a man interfering in the house. And there's poor Susan, tappy-lappying behind Richard Turvey, doing whatever he tells her and getting her head bitten off if she doesn't. The times I've wanted to shake him by the neck. But she doesn't complain, speaks up for him if I try to interfere, so what can I do?'

'Nothing, Mam,' Maggie smiled wryly. 'Susan chose Richard of her own free will. I warned her about him, but she wouldn't listen, so now she's just got to make the best of it. From what Mary Smith says, she's enjoying spending his money and bragging about it round the houses.'

'Aye, maybes,' Mabel shrugged, 'but I'd put money on it that she's not happy. Perhaps I should've let Richard tak' wor Helen off me hands after all.'

'Helen's just a bairn!' Maggie replied.

'I sometimes wonder,' Mabel said with a roll of her eyes. 'Anyhow, get that tea poured, hinny.' Her mother pushed her gently away and went to poke the fire.

Maggie poured the tea and placed a cup carefully in her grandmother's lap. The old woman smiled and thanked her, but without any recognition.

'So what's our Tich been up to, packing in his job?' Maggie asked.

Mabel huffed and stabbed the fire harder with the poker. 'That lad's a loser if ever there was one. Lasted a month in that job Richard got him down the quayside. Said it was too long hours and too little money and he could get summat better - not that he has, mind. And he fights with Helen like cat and dog or disappears off with Tommy Smith - probably thieving. Well, I wash me hands of that lad. He's neither use nor ornament!'

'He's still young, Mam,' Maggie defended her brother. 'He'll grow into summat in time. Jimmy's not a bad'un at heart.'

'I know why you're defending him,' her mother snorted, 'cos he helped you in that daft carry-on at the launch.' Mabel scrutinised her. 'Is it true you set fire to the pavilion at Hebron House an' all?'

'Aye,' Maggie confessed, 'but you mustn't tell a soul.'

To her surprise, her mother gave a cackle of laughter. 'Good on you, hinny!' she grinned 'I wish you'd sent a few Pearsons to heaven with it.'

'Mam!' Maggie was shocked. 'We're not murderers. I only agreed to do it 'cos I knew the place was empty.'

'No?' Mabel questioned. 'Well, you're a better lass than me.'

Maggie smiled. 'Mr Heslop doesn't think so. I'm nowt but a fallen woman in his eyes.'

'Heslop!' Mabel ridiculed. 'That man's always trying to save us Beatons.'

They sat by the fire and talked for an hour, reminiscing and confiding and drinking tea. Maggie could not remember her mother being so open with her before, talking about her father with unusual tenderness, while Maggie told her of the past secretive months. She sensed her mother was just as relieved to unburden herself as she was.

Then Jimmy returned and was immediately sent out again to fetch a jug of beer before his astonished questions could be answered. A few minutes later Helen returned and the intimacy of the evening was broken.

'Susan won't come,' she announced with a glint of glee, keeping to herself the unholy row that had erupted at Aunt Violet's at the news of Maggie's return.

Maggie was dashed.

'What do you mean she won't come?' Mabel asked crossly. 'Did you not tell her who was here?'

'Aye,' Helen pouted, 'but she doesn't want to see Maggie. Said if she couldn't be bothered to see her wed, she couldn't be bothered to come out on a cold night and see her now.'

'By, she's got above herself, that one!' Mabel fumed. 'I'll have words with her the morra.'

'It doesn't matter, Mam,' Maggie intervened. 'I can understand why she's not speaking.'

'Well, I can't!' Mabel shouted. 'She's changed that much since she wed Richard Turvey.'

Jimmy's return with the jug of beer quelled Mabel's wrath and she settled down by the hearth to drink it. Helen went to bed, telling Maggie not to wake her when she joined her, and Jimmy lay on the truckle bed playing with some lead soldiers he had had since childhood. Maggie tried to talk to him, but he was moody and unapproachable, so she gave up.

Later, she helped Mabel get Granny Beaton to bed in the parlour and kissed the old woman goodnight, leaving the candle burning.

'She sees things in the dark,' Mabel whispered, 'that frighten her, so I leave the candle burning till I come to bed.'

Maggie was struck by the concern in her mother's voice.

'You care a lot for Granny, don't you, Mam?'

Mabel was brusque. 'Someone has to, and she did enough for me when your father died. I'll not see her end up in the workhouse.'

Maggie felt reluctant to turn in. She sat by the fire while her mother drank and dozed, wondering if George had returned to find her gone. Perhaps she would stay, a few more days at Gun Street. If she drew no attention to herself, she would be safe enough, she decided. George would have to realise that she had other obligations in her life and would not be beholden to him for taking her in. If they were to live together again it must be on equal terms.

Maggie closed her eyes in the dark warmth of the kitchen, aware of Jimmy's even breathing in the shadows and her mother's gentle snoring at her side. She felt safe and content as her limbs and eyelids became leaden and overcome with sleep.

Susan leant over and was sick into the tin bowl by the bed. Richard did not even turn round as he buttoned up his trousers.

'I told you. You're not well enough to go running off to see that wayward sister of yours. Let her come to you if she's so keen to see you.'

Susan fought off another wave of nausea, thinking that if her husband was so concerned for her health he would stop subjecting her to the nightly ordeal in bed.

'Where are you going?' she croaked, her throat stinging from the bile.

'Out, darlin',' Richard said offhandedly. 'I'll be back at closing.'

'Don't wake me up then,' Susan answered huffily.

In a second he had whipped round and leaned across the bed to seize her arm. She winced in pain. 'Don't nag, Susan,' he threatened, 'or I might take up with someone else.'

She stared at him bleakly, half wishing that he would be unfaithful so that she would be spared his attentions in bed. She still thought he was handsome but her fondness for him had gone. Looking at him, she felt only irritation at his selfishness and a quiver of fear at what he might do if he did not get his way. So she let him go without protest and curled up in the dark, feeling wretched and sick and frustrated at not seeing Maggie.

Of course, she told herself, she was furious with her sister for abandoning the family and failing to come to her wedding. Yet she longed to see Maggie again, to discover what she had been doing, to hear her acknowledge her married status and be impressed by how well she had done ...

'Oh, Maggie!' Susan cried noiselessly and felt the tears hot on her face. 'I wish we could go back to how it was before - just the family!' She pulled the covers over her head to deaden the noise of her sobbing and thought she had never been so unhappy.

George woke stiff and cold. He had let the fire go out. The after-effects of the beer made his temples throb and his throat was thick and parched. He groaned and pulled himself out of the chair. Glancing in at the bedroom he saw at once that nothing had been disturbed since his return in an alcoholic haze earlier that evening.

Maggie was gone.

He pulled a blanket off the bed and wrapped himself in it. Lighting a candle he began to flick through a book on philosophy lent to him by Isaac, but found he had no concentration.

She must have gone to see her mother, George kept telling himself, and it had grown late and she had decided to stay. Who could blame her after the way they had argued? But she would come back, he assured himself, when that Beaton temper of hers had simmered down. He would be magnanimous and forgiving and they would have a loving reunion ...

George gripped the arms of the chair. But what if she didn't come back? What would he do?

The thought was so bleak, so unanswerable, that George forced it from his mind. He would go to bed and stop thinking of Maggie until the morning. They were invited to the Samuels' for Sunday dinner and she would not miss that, he thought.

But George found he could not move. He was frozen with foreboding. He sat on in the icy flat, lit faintly by the gas lamp in the street, and waited for Maggie to return and fill the room with her warmth.

He watched the door and waited, but she did not come.

Chapter Nineteen

Maggie woke with a start. Someone was banging heavily on the front door. At first she was disorientated, thinking she must be at the flat in Arthur's Hill, then she caught sight of her mother's solid figure, slumped in the chair next to her.

'Mrs Beaton!' a man shouted.

Maggie shook her mother from her sleep.

'What the devil...?' the older woman asked groggily.

The hammering continued. Maggie was on her feet.

'Do you want to break me bloody door down?' Mabel shouted back. 'Who are you?'

'Police. Let us in, Mrs Beaton.'

Mabel sprang from her chair as if she had been scalded and pushed Maggie towards the back door.

'Scarper! Quick!' she ordered.

Maggie looked at her wide-eyed. 'It might not—'

'Course they're after you,' Mabel hissed. 'Who else? Get down them stairs now!'

A blast of cold air hit her face as Maggie wrenched at the back door and flung it open. She looked back at her mother and for a moment held her gaze, wordlessly, no time for farewells. Then Maggie was bolting down the damp steps to the yard below.

As she reached the gate, she heard a commotion in the flat above. Her mother was protesting, someone was screaming and voices argued back. Maggie slipped on the cobbles, picked herself up and, lifting her skirt, began to run up the dark back lane.

Her heart was thumping furiously and her breathing was loud in her ears. For a few minutes she ran aimlessly, like a hunted quarry, too terrified to think about direction. But when no clatter of boots pursued her, she began to take note of where she was. She skirted the walls of Daniel Park and headed uphill. Alison Terrace was deserted. For a moment she agonised over whether to pound on Heslop's door and beg for sanctuary, but she could not muster the courage to confront him. Maggie ran on.

A milk cart nearly mowed her down as she darted across the road by the Presbyterian Kirk. She slowed to a brisk walk, breathless and wheezing, but growing optimistic that she had escaped. Ten more minutes' walking and she would be safely back to Arthur's Hill and George. That thought gave her comfort.

She paused for breath under the arc of a street lamp and heard a van lumbering up behind her. Dazed by a light, she was too slow to recognise the hunched black vehicle of a police van. Minutes later, Maggie was under arrest again and on her way to the police station.

Later that day, Mabel heard that Maggie had been caught. It was splashed across the evening newspaper that Mary Smith brought back from Heslop's after work.

Without hesitation she turned on Helen and grabbed her by the hair. 'You told Violet that Maggie was here, didn't you?' she shouted.

Helen screamed in pain and fright.

'I didn't!'

'Divn't lie to me, you little bitch!' Mabel cried, pulling her about the room by her hair. 'You told Violet and she went to the police. How else did they know to come knocking here in the middle of the night? Unless you shopped Maggie yourself?'

Helen screamed again, so loud that Mary Smith tried to intervene, but Mabel shoved her away.

'I didn't!' Helen whimpered. 'But Susan and Richard had such a row about it - Aunt Violet heard everything.'

Mabel flung her to the floor. 'I knew it! That bloody woman's been interfering with me life and me family for years. Well, Violet's got it coming to her now!'

Without stopping to put on her coat or hat, Mabel marched from the kitchen and down the back stairs, leaving Helen crying into Mary's shoulder.

'I hate her!' Helen sobbed 'I wish she was dead.'

'No you don't, hinny,' Mary said, cradling the distraught girl. 'You mustn't say such things about your mam.'

'She's never loved me,' Helen cried hysterically. 'She blames me for everything. None of them love me! I hate them all!'

Mabel laboured up the hill to Benwell, gasping for breath in the dank, smoky air. She became aware of Jimmy running up beside her in the gloom but did not slacken her pace.

'Mam, wait!' he called. 'I think I know who told the coppers about Maggie. It's not who you think.'

'I know who told them!' Mabel shouted back. 'And I don't need you getting in the way. I've a few scores to settle with wor Violet.'

Jimmy lost courage and stopped pursuing his mother. He did not want to witness a scrap between his relations or hear the arguments, so he turned round and skulked away.

Mabel entered without knocking. They were all sitting round the tea table, eating in silence. Susan looked up, pale-faced and astonished. Before Violet had time to defend herself, Mabel was laying into her physically and verbally. The frustrations and petty jealousies and slights of years came pouring out in one incoherent, savage attack.

Mabel's brother Barny hobbled onto his good leg and tried to intervene, shocked to see his sister so riled. She was screaming about Maggie and betrayal, calling his wife evil and vindictive. Violet was wailing in terror. All the while Richard and Susan sat watching, stupefied by the scene.

'Do something, Richard.' Susan shook him, horrified to see her mother in such a state. She had seen her lose her temper before, but this time she was apoplectic with rage, her face a livid crimson. Richard rose half-heartedly, murmuring placations, but obviously reluctant to come between the women.

'Mam, what are you shouting about?' Susan said, rising in agitation and moving round the table to reach her.

Mabel's blinding fury seemed to abate for a moment at the sound of Susan's voice.

'Where were you when your sister needed you?' Mabel accused. 'You couldn't be bothered to come, could you?'

'I wanted to, Mam,' Susan answered, unable to bear her mother's withering look, 'but Richard—'

'Well, you're too late,' Mabel cut off her excuses. 'Maggie's been arrested again. This time it'll probably kill her! And all because Violet couldn't keep her big nose out of it!' Mabel screamed.

'I never! I never!' Violet gasped, crouching from her sister-in-law's raised hand. 'Barny, tell her I've done nothing wrong.' But her husband had collapsed into his chair, too shocked to act.

It was Susan who stepped between them and grabbed her mother's fist. 'When was Maggie arrested?' she demanded

'In the middle of the night,' Mabel cried, trembling with rage and exhaustion. 'You couldn't even wait till morning, could you, Violet? You've always picked on my Maggie because she was special to me.'

Susan flinched at the words. 'It couldn't have been Aunt Violet,' she said angrily. 'She never went out until this morning. One of your neighbours must have seen her and—' Susan stopped. Richard had gone out last night, unexpectedly, she remembered. Normally he slept well after intercourse and lay in until after breakfast But last night he had returned late and this morning he had disappeared to work early. She looked at him, wondering. He was quite capable of betraying Maggie, especially if there was money in it for him, she thought. But she could never accuse him in front of her mother, just as she could never admit her mistake in marrying him in the first place.

But Mabel caught her look of suspicion and turned on Richard. Could it be that Jimmy had been trying to tell her about Richard? she suddenly wondered. Was this smiling, selfish, handsome man who had wheedled his way into her family really Maggie's betrayer? He had manipulated and charmed them all: Susan, Helen, Jimmy, Violet, Barny, even herself - all except Maggie who had shown open contempt for him. Oh, yes, Mabel thought with bitter anger, Richard Turvey was quite capable of betraying her beloved Maggie!

Mabel lunged for Richard, her mouth open in accusation. But no words came out, just a strangled sound. Mabel clutched herself as pain shot up her arm and across her chest. She groped for support and latched onto Susan, trying to speak. A look of incomprehension crossed her face, alarm and disbelief.

'Mam, what's wrong?' Susan asked in fright. '

Her mother doubled up and then slowly, gracefully, crumpled to the floor.

'Mam! ' Susan screamed and knelt beside her. But her mother did not answer.

'Fetch the doctor, man!' Barny shouted at Richard and waved his stick in agitation.

Long before the doctor arrived, Mabel Beaton was dead. Susan touched the cooling skin, draining of life, and wailed in distress. Violet, not knowing what else to do, went to fetch Mrs Liddle, to help lay out the body.

Mabel was buried the day Maggie began her new term in prison. She had three months still to serve of her previous sentence and a further two years for admitting the arson at Hebron House. This time she was taken to Durham gaol and so did not learn about her mother's death until nearly two weeks later when John Heslop was permitted to visit in order to tell her the sad news.

Already weakened from hunger strike, she sat pale and stunned by the news. A heart attack ... all very sudden . . . buried the Saturday before last . . . crocuses out ... Susan looking after the family.

She hardly took in Heslop's conversation, but this last piece of information reached her.

'Susan?' Maggie asked in bewilderment. 'But she's married...'

'Susan and Richard have moved back to Gun Street,' John Heslop explained. 'They will take care of your grandmother and Helen and Jimmy, so there's no need to worry. I gather there was friction between the young couple and your aunt, so it's worked out for the best.'

'The best?' Maggie echoed dully.

Heslop reached forward and briefly touched Maggie's clenched hands. 'I was fond of your mother too,' he said quietly. When Maggie did not speak, he asked, 'Is there anything I can do for you?'

But she just stared at him with large, desolate eyes and shook her head. He was worried for her, but felt powerless to help. Glancing around at the narrow interview cell and the surly wardress with the heavy bunch of keys, he was suddenly moved to pray.

Heslop prayed out loud for Maggie, though he was certain she did not hear him. She had withdrawn into some inner hiding place to nurse her pain.

Leaving the prison and returning to a world of spring buds and birdsong should have come as a relief, yet he felt a great weight on his spirit at the thought of Maggie left alone in her misery. All the way home on the train, Heslop wrestled with the problem of how he could help her. By the time he reached Newcastle, he had determined to undertake the task he least wanted to do - go and visit her lover, George Gordon.

The visit was a disaster. The young blacksmith was angry and bitter at Maggie's re-arrest and John Heslop found himself indignantly denying that he had betrayed her.

'How do I know it wasn't you who went to the police?' George accused. 'You wanted Maggie to give herself up before, didn't you?'

'Yes, but only if it was of her choosing,' the butcher answered, offended. 'I would never have betrayed her, no matter what she'd done. I respect and care for her too much.'

But this seemed to inflame the younger man all the more.

'I'm the one who cared for her when you all turned your backs, remember! And I'm the one who'll take care of her when she comes out - *if* she comes out of Durham alive!'

'I can see there's no point in staying and being insulted,' Heslop said stiffly. 'I only came out of friendship for Maggie to tell you that I had seen her and that she looked as well as could be expected.'

For a moment they glared at each other in dislike, then George forced himself to apologise.

'I'm sorry. It was good of you to come.' He swallowed hard and asked hesitantly, 'Did she ... did she ask you to come?'

Heslop shook his head and saw the bleak look cross the blacksmith's face. So he added, 'But she asked me to send you her fondest regards.'

It was a lie, but he felt Maggie would have sent such a message if she had been in any state to speak. Besides, he did not like to see the young man suffering, despite their differences.

'Thank you,' George murmured, flushing with embarrassment.

'I'm sure they would let you write to her,' the butcher suggested, 'or I could send a letter on your behalf.'

'Thank you, but I can write for mesel',' George bristled.

Heslop decided it was best to leave and did so, promising to pass on any news he received of Maggie's welfare.

After he had gone, George sat for a long time by the dying fire in the poky flat, thinking of Maggie and rueing their bitter row. He had been jealous of her family who still seemed to have a hold over her and instead of going with her to see them and protecting her, he had derided and rejected her so that she had run home anyway. If they had not argued she would not have been caught, he tortured himself with the thought.

George cried out in his agony and loneliness. He could not stay here alone in this flat that reminded him constantly of Maggie. Her clothes and suffragette newspapers lay around reproachfully and even the scent of her seemed to linger in the room. He would give notice and leave at the end of the week, George decided. He would find somewhere quite different, somewhere for his sore spirit to recuperate and where Maggie could come and live with him when she was released. Somewhere that would not remind them of the hurtful things they had said to each other. The thought gave him new comfort and hope.

And George came to another startling decision. He would tell his family about Maggie. They would disapprove strongly, but there would be no more hiding and lying about his relationship with her. There would be no more shame.

Alice Pearson disembarked from the London train with three porters in her wake carrying her luggage. Two further trunkfuls of new clothes purchased in Paris and London had been sent ahead to Hebron House. Alice had come hurrying home after Herbert's message that their father had suffered a stroke - Herbert blaming it on the distress caused by the arson attack. But Maggie Beaton had been caught and sentenced for her part in the arson attack and was safely incarcerated in Durham prison. Herbert insisted that he needed Alice to help in the final run-up to the by-election and she found she needed little persuasion to return home.

She revelled in the smells of steam and smoke around Central Station, the bustle of railwaymen, flower-sellers and shoe-shine boys. The Pearson Bentley was waiting for her outside the vast arched entrance and she settled into the comfortable leather seat, eager to watch the sights of busy Tyneside as they nosed their way past trams and drays and rolleys.

Two months had given Alice time to reflect on the outrage carried out at Hebron House. Her initial fury at Maggie's actions which had caused her to flee Newcastle had now abated, but she still felt the arson was a personal betrayal. She had shown the Beaton girl friendship and support yet had been repaid with this wicked attack on her family's property. The WSPU could have chosen any number of targets without picking on Hebron House and she had immediately severed all ties with the suffrage movement. She agreed now with Herbert that she must stand firm with her own class, to protect their own interests against this creeping threat of anarchy, of socialism, of empowering working-class women like Maggie who would only use it to bring them down.

It frightened Alice that these people had no sense of deference to those who ruled them, no sense of loyalty. For without a sense of place, the world was turned on its head and anything could happen. She firmly believed that there were those born to lead and those born to follow; reducing all to the same level would provoke anarchy - revolution.

'God forbid!' Alice said aloud in the purring motorcar.

She could now admit to herself that her commitment to women's suffrage had been superficial, a flirtation with ideals of equality in which she did not really believe. If she was brutally frank with herself, she had espoused the cause because she had enjoyed the attention, being in demand socially for fund-raising luncheons and bazaars. She had delighted in shocking her parents and brother too, because it made them notice her and take her more seriously.

But she would never have the appetite for sacrifice that Emily Davison or Maggie Beaton had; indeed, she did not want equality with women such as they.

Over the past two months, Alice had come to this startling revelation about herself. She was a Pearson, one of the elite in British society, and she believed in and wished to uphold their system of class. She would work with her brother to further his political ambitions and consolidate the Pearson dynasty and in return would demand political rights for women of her class, those who could be trusted with power. Intelligent, articulate women such as herself should be given the vote and greater freedom in law, but such freedoms should be based upon property and privilege. They were not for the masses or the likes of Maggie Beaton who terrified her.

The high wrought-iron gates closed behind the Bentley; early daffodils at the edge of the drive bowed their heads in the breeze. Beyond, Alice could see scaffolding around the damaged summer pavilion; the roof was being renewed and the windows replaced. Workmen crawled over the scorched stone like ants, busily restoring it to its former glory.

Alice felt overwhelming relief.

Herbert greeted her at the entrance and later, in his study, bubbled over with news of his campaign.

'There's a dinner at the Assembly Rooms tonight. Felicity doesn't want to go, so I want you to accompany me. And there's a luncheon at the Liberal Club tomorrow and I want you to organise a dinner here on Saturday.'

'What does Tish say about that?' Alice asked warily.

'She's going to London for a week - staying with the Beresfords,' Herbert said, avoiding his sister's look. 'She's been quite a help really, but politics doesn't interest her like it does you.'

'I see,' Alice replied. And she did. Her brother wanted to forget their past differences and use her skills at organising and entertaining politicians and businessmen. Felicity's reward for playing the loyal wife and social hostess to Newcastle society was to be allowed the occasional trip to stay with Poppy Beresford. As long as Poppy was kept safely at a distance, Herbert could pretend she did not exist.

Alice smiled, glad that she was to have a free rein in her own house again, even for a short while. Tomorrow she would drive up to Oxford Hall and see her father, whose recovery was proving slow and would probably only be partial, Herbert told her.

After tea, Alice went to her darkroom and did a thorough clear-out of drawers and folders. Dispassionately she looked at the pictures of her former friends in the WSPU. Reduced to mere black and white images, Alice could forget that she had once had feelings for them. Now they were just specimens captured by her camera. She took the photographs into the drawing room and watched them burn in the fireplace. Then she went to pour herself a brandy. The WSPU had been part of a dangerous episode in her life, when she had dabbled with viewing the world differently, as if from the wrong end of a lens. Ridding herself of the images helped Alice restore her old set of values and reinforce her comforting sense of place.

In the end, it was an unnervingly close race. The Labour Party fielded a candidate who played on the shipyard workers' dissatisfaction with their pay.

'We're producing more tonnage than ever before!' the Labour hopeful shouted from the hustings. 'But the buying power of the sovereign in your pocket is getting less!'

He told voters - the prosperous, property-owning skilled men who could swing the result - that earnings among most trades had not improved in fifteen years and were not likely to if a Pearson became their MP.

To Alice's bitter indignation, the local WSPU threw its weight behind the Labour candidate as he had made vague promises about women's suffrage. She redoubled her efforts to court and win the middle-class vote for her brother, speaking on Herbert's behalf at open meetings and dining businessmen and local politicians at Hebron House. Felicity stayed away until the day of the election and Alice had a free rein in the Elswick mansion.

Right up until the votes were counted at the Town Hall on election night, no one was quite sure of the outcome. Herbert stood anxious and perspiring amidst the hubbub of the count, while Felicity sat cool and aloof, hardly concealing her boredom with the whole affair.

Alice, on the other hand, found the experience electrifying. She had worked tirelessly for three weeks, entertaining, lobbying and organising on Herbert's behalf, and paced around all evening, fully enjoying the suspense and anticipation. She smelt the scent of victory before the announcement and when Herbert was finally declared the new MP, her elation was intoxicating. For a split second she daydreamed that it was she who had won the honour of representing the west of Newcastle in Parliament, then she set her mind on enjoying Herbert's victory. She began to invite supporters back for a late supper at Hebron House.

George Gordon and Bob Stanners, standing on the steps of the Town Hall, learned with disappointment that their candidate had missed an historic victory by fewer than a thousand votes. It seemed the dominance of the Pearsons in West Newcastle could not be shaken, economically or politically.

The friends retired to a nearby pub to drown their frustration.

'Here's to the working man!' Bob grunted and drank.

'Here's to revolution!' George muttered.

'Bugger revolution,' Bob spat. 'Just give me a better wage, a rich lass and a few more o' these.' He raised his glass again.

'It'll happen,' George predicted, spreading his hands wide. 'International socialism - across Europe. Brothers together.'

'What about sisters?' Bob teased.

George knew it was a dig about Maggie. He flushed, feeling a pang of anxiety.

They drank silently for a minute.

'If we had solidarity with other workers abroad,' George continued his theme, burying his worries about Maggie, 'we could have change tomorrow. They couldn't stop us, we'd be too many. The Pearsons of this world would have to graft like honest men, aye, and throw their mansions open to families who can't afford a roof over their heads.'

'Like a posh workhouse, you mean?' Bob grinned.

'There'd be no need for workhouses any more,' George enthused. 'Everyone would have a right to a job and a share in the profits. The workers would run the industries, the mines, transport - just think of it!'

'Aye, that's all very well, but what about these foreigners?' Bob sniffed. 'I don't like the sound of fraternising with foreigners.'

'Not foreigners,' George replied stoutly, 'just French brothers and German brothers. We've all got the same needs and concerns underneath,' he insisted. 'They just talk different.'

'French brothers!' Bob ridiculed 'You're full o' daft ideas, George man!' his friend laughed.

'Not daft at all,' George said and slurped his pint. 'Workers unite! Aye, and do it before some halfwit emperor picks a fight with another and drags us into a war.'

'Now you're really talking daft,' Bob laughed. 'The King's related to them all, he's not going to allow a scrap.'

'Haven't you heard of families scrapping?' George grunted 'They've been at it in the Balkans again and the race is on with the Germans to build ships - that's obvious at Pearson's. That Kaiser's itching for a fight.'

'Shut your gob, George, and buy us a beer,' Bob groaned. 'You're like a prophet of doom and I've had enough of that the night. Haway and gan to the bar!'

In Durham prison, Maggie held out for ten weeks before hunger striking and force-feeding broke her. This time she was prepared for the struggles and torture and hostility of the prison authorities, knowing how weak and listless she would become. But she was not prepared for the overwhelming blackness that engulfed her with the news of her mother's death.

She was filled with grief and guilt. If she had not visited and brought the police to Gun Street, perhaps her mother would still be alive, she accused herself. Had the strain of their emotional reunion and the shock of her flight and arrest killed her mother? Over and over, in the dreary grey cell, she replayed that visit in her mind and imagined her mother's death.

Heslop had said she had died at Aunt Violet's. What had she been doing there? Reprimanding Susan for not coming to see her? Accusing Violet of betraying her? And who was it who had tipped off the police about her secret visit? Maggie wondered day after day, with nothing else to occupy her thoughts. Helen? Violet? Susan? Mary Smith? But none of it made sense.

Maggie tried to visualise Gun Street without her mother, but could not. And she wept at the thought that her mother would never achieve her dream of returning to Sarah Crescent and living out her old age in dignified comfort as she had wished.

Then, lying in pain on the narrow bed, her throat and mouth and tongue swollen from the force-feeding, thoughts of George and the flat in Arthur's Hill came to haunt Maggie. Had she really lived there with him for those brief happy weeks or had it just been a dream? Her memories swum like elusive fish in her head. She missed him desperately, but did George think about her now with any affection? He had not written to say so.

At the beginning of May and quite unexpectedly, John Heslop came to visit.

He could not hide his shock at what he found; a grey-faced, emaciated woman who looked nearer fifty than her twenty-one years.

'They're going to release you again on licence,' he told her, 'and I've come to make arrangements for your transfer.'

'How kind,' Maggie managed to say in a voice as dry as parchment. 'No need ...'

'Dear Maggie,' he said, taking her hand. 'I'm afraid there is a need. You see,' he cleared his throat awkwardly, 'you can't go back to Gun Street. They won't - there's no room for you. The Gosforth nursing home can't take you in because,' he hesitated, again sounding awkward, 'well, it's a matter of funding. And I can't provide for you at the mission. Sadly, Millie Dobson has returned to the streets - all that business over Annie's arrest turned her back to drink so there's no one there to nurse you. And you simply must have someone to look after you. Can you think of anyone you can go to to convalesce?' He held his breath, wondering if she would think of him as someone to whom she could turn.

But Maggie's mind felt dense like putrid water. Her family would not have her back was the only thought in her head.

'Perhaps the Johnstones?' John Heslop suggested hesitantly.

Maggie shook her head slowly. 'Rose and I fell out after that fire business,' she croaked.

'Would you like me to make enquiries among the congregation?' Heslop tried again. 'I could help you ...'

Maggie's eyes filled with tears at his show of concern.

'You're very kind, Mr Heslop,' she said weepily.

'I'm more than willing,' he assured her, 'and I want to help.'

Maggie searched his face, wondering how much she could ask of this man, who for some unfathomable reason kept wanting to befriend her.

'Will you do something for me?' Maggie asked, her large, shadowed eyes pleading.

'Of course, anything,' he promised.

Silence hung between them like a web while Maggie hesitated. Shadows flickered across the cell floor as the spring sunlight tried to penetrate through the narrow window high up in the wall. Her mother had loved the spring. But her mother was dead, Maggie thought in desolation. She realised suddenly that she did not want to return to Gun Street anyway; it could never be home again without her mother there. The thought spurred her on to release the words trapped inside.

'Please go and ask George Gordon if I can come home to him,' she whispered. 'He's the only one I've got.'

John Heslop turned from her to hide his disappointment. He would have taken her in if she had asked, even if it had provoked the censure of his fellow chapel-goers. But she saw him only as a family friend showing her kindness, a messenger, nothing more.

Chapter Twenty

Against his better judgment, John Heslop carried out Maggie's request and sought out George Gordon. He finally tracked him down through the rowing club to a cottage beyond Scotswood, on the edge of Hibbs' Farm. Delivering Maggie's message without enthusiasm, he was unprepared for the young man's arrogant delight. Of course he would take her in, she was his lass.

Heslop pointed out that he could not possibly nurse her and would have to engage help. George insisted he would care for her himself.

Heslop left in a turmoil of doubt that he had done the right thing. Since Mabel's death, he felt doubly responsible for Maggie, especially since the rest of her family wanted nothing to do with her. Yet he was delivering her back into a sinful existence with the atheist blacksmith.

On a mild day in early May, with the young green foliage bursting on the trees around the prison, he collected Maggie Beaton in his van. She lay in the back on a makeshift bed of mattress and blankets while they jostled their way to Newcastle under police escort. Not that the prone, silent woman was in any condition to escape. Her eyes were dull and lacklustre, her hair thin and limp, her limbs like twigs. She found it difficult to speak and seemed to have lost her appetite for words as well as food.

George was aghast at her deterioration. She seemed bewildered by her surroundings as they helped her into the cottage and laid her on a bed in the corner of the room, next to a lit fire. Although it was May, there was still a chill in the air and the thick-walled cottage had not yet dried out from the spring squalls.

'She needs coaxing to eat,' Heslop said severely. 'Simple things like milk and soup.'

"I get milk from the farm,' George told him, 'and there're plenty vegetables in the plot to make broth.'

'I still think you should employ someone,' Heslop fretted. 'I could help pay—'

'I can manage on me own,' George replied stubbornly. 'I've fended for mesel' since I was little more than a nipper. Maggie's all right wi' me.'

Maggie watched them dumbly as they discussed her as if she were not there. But then that was how she felt - detached. She was drained to her very core, clinging on to life and sanity by her broken fingernails. She had no interest in her surroundings, only that she was out of that miserable cell and that George was with her. Yet the blackness of the past weeks was wrapped as firmly round her as ever, stifling her thoughts and actions. She was too weary to speak, too weak to cry. All she wanted to do was sleep and sleep …

Heslop left and the police withdrew, satisfied that their charge was in no state to attempt an escape. George went over to the bed and gazed at Maggie. She was sleeping, her body so frail it hardly made an impression under the covers. He stroked the dark hair away from her gaunt face and kissed her softly on the forehead. Her ragged breathing altered a fraction, but the strained set of her features remained.

If he had believed in a God, he would have given thanks for this second chance to care for Maggie, to make her whole again, for that was the task be set himself. But he did not believe, so he strode back outside and busied himself in the allotment.

Maggie's recovery was uneven. After two weeks she was sitting up in bed drinking watery soup. At the end of the month she could sit in a chair in the doorway, sheltered from the wind that whipped around the hill, and watch George tending the garden after work. She had progressed to bread soaked in milk and mashed vegetables and stewed apples like a small child learning to eat. But there were still days when she took to her bed and lay paralysed by the blanket of blackness that lay over her, unseen but smothering.

George had again given up his rowing to look after her and she was amazed at his patience and resourcefulness. He cooked and washed up and took their clothes to the laundry, as well as tending the fire, feeding the hens that pecked around the house and harvesting the early rhubarb and runner beans. At haymaking, he lent a hand after work on Hibbs' Farm and was paid in milk and cheese and butter.

And in the evenings, as the sun lay down below the western hills, he would settle Maggie by the fire and read to her by flickering candlelight. He did not seem to mind if she did not listen, or curled up on the bed in the grip of a black mood and cried at nothing. He neither chided not rebuked her; he did not storm off as he had once done, and his gentleness was a revelation.

Slowly, like one of his tenderly nurtured plants, Maggie emerged from the dark soil of her depression and stretched into the light. She was overwhelmed with gratitude for his loving care as she became aware of her surroundings and began to take an interest in life again.

June arrived and she delighted in the small dilapidated cottage that he had discovered on the lip of the farm, with its plum trees and ragged garden, burgeoning with George's vegetables and the trespassing hens. From here she could see right down to the River Tyne and its cranes and factory chimneys and ranks of terraces, stacked up on its banks like dolls' houses.

To the west she could gaze upriver to the rich green valley of the upper Tyne, beyond the grazing animals and peaceful fields of Farmer Hibbs. Late one tranquil summer evening, she sat contentedly in the garden and watched the sunset wavering like a banner in the sky while George read and talked and listened to the sounds of dusk.

'Arcadia,' Maggie nicknamed their new home.

'Just wait till winter,' George teased, 'and see how much you like it then.'

'I can wait,' Maggie laughed.

And she revelled in the thought, because winter seemed an age away and it made her content to think they had all this time stretching ahead together. She tried to banish from her mind that her licence ran out at the end of July and that she must deliver herself back to prison by then and was only reminded of this by occasional visits from the police, checking on her whereabouts. This time she was not going to be forced into hiding.

So they kept up the pretence that they could make plans into the winter, each unable to contemplate what another stint in prison might do to Maggie's health.

That evening, Maggie stood in the doorway as the half-dark crept over the garden, reluctant to go inside. She kept glancing beyond the gate and down the hill, her mind alert to something as yet unidentified. After months of malnutrition in prison she thought her 'feelings' about things had been numbed, cauterised by the trauma. But tonight they tingled down her spine and made her uneasy.

'Come in, pet,' George beckoned from inside their cottage.

Maggie sighed and shrugged to herself. Perhaps the ghost of her mother was passing... Then she saw it: a dark, darting shadow on the path below, skirting

161

the hedgerow.

'George,' she called, 'someone's coming.'

He came to stand by her as the figure drew nearer, anxious to protect Maggie and constantly watchful that she should not be taken before her time expired.

'He's alone, whoever he is,' Maggie murmured.

By now they could hear his panting as he ran the last stretch up the hill towards the cottage. A gangling figure appeared in the gloom by the garden gate. Maggie peered. She began to walk towards him.

'Maggie!' George cautioned, but she was quickening her pace.

'Jimmy, is it you?' she cried.

He burst through the gate and flung his arms round his sister in answer.

'Will you tak' us in?' he gasped. 'Please, Maggie, will you have me?'

'Of course,' Maggie answered without hesitation. 'But what in the world brings you up here?'

'Heslop told me where you were,' Jimmy panted, still clinging to her. 'I had to get away. It's terrible at home. I cannot gan back. Never!'

'You don't have to gan back,' Maggie assured him, deeply troubled. 'Come inside.'

She glanced at George as she steered her brother round and her lover nodded his silent assent.

In the candlelight they saw the blood on his cheek and the swelling around his left eye.

'Who the devil's done this to you?' Maggie demanded angrily, sitting him down on a chair.

Turvey,' Jimmy spat out the name.

'Richard?' Maggie asked in astonishment. 'Surely not.'

'Aye, he did,' Jimmy said, wincing at her probing fingers. 'And I'm not the only one he's raised his fists to an' all. I could kill 'im for what he's done to our family!'

Maggie and George exchanged worried looks.

Later that night, after hearing Jimmy's disturbing story, they put the exhausted boy to bed on a mattress of hay in the loft. Then they went to bed, too troubled to talk of what they had learned, and held each other close. Maggie knew now that she would have to be strong for others as well as herself; her time of recuperation was over.

And so is Arcadia, Maggie thought with regret, as she burrowed further into George's comforting arms.

Susan ducked as a shoe came flying at her head.

'Do you call these polished?' Richard shouted.

'I did polish them,' Susan answered fearfully.

'Well do 'em again, you stupid cow!' Richard hurled the other one at his wife.

Shaking, she bent down to pick them up, feeling a flutter inside. The baby, she told herself, I must protect the baby. For there was no doubt now that she was pregnant; her swelling womb was beginning to show and her breasts had enlarged, so that all the new dresses that Richard had bought her no longer fitted. But instead of being happy about becoming a father, he seemed to be annoyed that she no longer looked elegant and did not have the energy to accompany him to tea dances and theatres. Instead, he took Helen, dressing her up in Susan's old clothes and flaunting her around the town. It had been the cause of a fearful row with her sister which had resulted in Richard punching Susan for accusing him of adultery with Helen.

'Don't ever talk to me like that again!' he had shouted as she fell against the table from the force of his blow. She could smell the drink on his breath.

'Just promise me you'll not touch her,' Susan had sobbed.

This had enraged him further and he had seized her by the arms and threatened, 'Well, you better start acting like a dutiful wife in bed, doll, then I won't have to go looking around, will I?'

Susan was left with a strange feeling of guilt. It must have been something she had done, or not done, that had turned Richard into the selfish, manipulating man who now bullied their household. She strove to please him, to placate his moods, avoid confrontations with Helen. But nothing she did seemed to be enough in her husband's eyes. She yearned for his approval, for kind words and affection, but they grew rarer.

Susan bore the cuffs and the humiliation because she did not know what else she could do, and there was the baby to consider now. Respectable women did not leave their husbands, especially after six months of marriage, she thought miserably. Besides, she had nowhere else to go. She would have to put up with the insults and assaults and attempt to bring her unborn child safely into the world.

But what a world! Susan thought bitterly. A violent, unpredictable father and a pathetic, cowering mother, still living in lowly Gun Street. They could afford better, Susan knew, if only Richard did not squander all he earned on gambling and drinking and taking Helen to shows. They had argued about money. They had argued about Helen. Even skinny, ineffectual Jimmy had tried to stand up to him but had been kicked out of the house for his trouble.

Now she had no ally, Susan thought wretchedly. Aunt Violet had not spoken to them since her mother's death, except when they passed in the street and she demanded the money that Richard owed her. But Susan was becoming immune to the daily humiliations. She would bear them for her baby, because that was the only thing in her world that was worth striving for.

Alone, she ran her mother's old clothes stall while Helen went goodness knows where. The girl was beyond her control, obeying only Richard. Resisting Mary Smith's temptations to go and drink with her downstairs as her mother had done, Susan relied on a frail and increasingly demented Granny Beaton for company. But her grandmother had become a burden to them all and her senile ways a constant irritation.

'The old bag's got to go,' Richard had threatened after the elderly woman had nearly set fire to the flat trying to light the paraffin lamp. It was the night Jimmy had left.

'Go where?' Susan had muttered.

'The workhouse,' he had answered at once. 'The old bat's going to the workhouse if she singes any more of my furniture.'

Susan's frayed nerves had caused her to snap back, '*Your* furniture? It was Mam's best chair she burned. You've never spent a farthing on this place.'

He had slapped her hard for speaking her mind and Jimmy had finally intervened, sickened by the months of abuse. Richard had given him a black eye and thrown him down the back stairs. Susan had screamed after him in the dark to come back, but all she heard was his sobbing as he ran away up the back lane.

For three days now she had not gone out for fear of the neighbours gossiping about her bruised face and she did not want to miss Jimmy if he attempted to return. She was only thankful that her mother was dead and could not see in what hell she was living.

'That feeble brother of yours been back yet?' Richard demanded to know as he straightened his tie in the parlour mirror.

'No,' Susan answered wearily. 'He'll not be back in a hurry.'

'Good,' Richard grunted 'I don't want him sneaking round here for food while I'm out, do you hear? He's not getting any more of my charity, the little toe-rag.'

Susan did not reply as she reached mechanically for the shoe polish and brushes in a box by the hearth. She polished Richard's shoes again, wondering where Jimmy had gone. No doubt she would hear soon enough through Tommy Smith, for the two lads could not be separated for long. All her life she had taken care of Jimmy and the pain she felt at his going was far worse than her aching face.

Richard came and stood over her. She put his shoes on for him and tied the laces. Then, in a flash of unpredictability, he leant over and stroked her cheek.

'You look done in, doll,' he smiled in concern. 'You should go and lie down. Got to keep your strength up - think of our baby, eh?'

Susan smiled back in relief. Just when she was thinking evil thoughts about Richard, he surprised her with a tender remark and she felt wicked for having wanted to be rid of him. It filled her with hope that he would be a loving father once the baby came and everything would be all right again between them, like it was in their courting days. Perhaps she expected too much from him. She had been tired and short-tempered with him lately, so was it any wonder that he chose to stay out and drink until closing? And it was only in drink that he was cruel and uncaring.

Richard kissed her on the head. 'Fetch me dut then, doll.'

Susan got to her feet and crossed to the dresser where Richard's bowler hat sat in pompous state. She gave it a possessive brush with her hand and fixed it on his head. Without another word, Richard reached for his ebony walking cane and left by the front door, whistling.

Susan sighed. Richard was her husband and she had promised to stay with him for better or for worse and that is what she would do. One day, life really would be better, she determined. The dream of a respectable house, full of clean respectful children and a husband who was content to stay at home after tea, wavered before her. Where there's a will there's a way, her mother had always said. She would make it happen.

Susan looked across at her grandmother, dozing and mumbling in her chair. Over the past weeks Granny had risen in the night and been found wandering the streets in her nightgown, attempting to hang out washing in the moonlight. For the first time, Susan entertained the idea of putting Granny Beaton in a home. After all, she reasoned, once the baby was here there would be precious little room and she would have no time to look after the old woman as well. Would she not be better off in a home with other old people for company? And it would please Richard. Life would be so much easier for them all...

Susan dared to think the unthinkable. The old woman was so feeble-minded it would make no difference to her where she lived out her dwindling days. She did not know where she was most of the time.

Having broached the idea in her own mind and justified getting rid of her grandmother for the best of reasons, Susan set about sorting piles of clothing for the Saturday market in the morning. Life must go on, she told herself sternly, and she must make some money at the market to pay for Richard's extravagances.

Maggie put off going to see Susan until the middle of July, not wanting to think about her sister's predicament and wary of interfering. Besides, she told herself, she had been too involved with suffragist matters. Along with other local members of the WSPU, she had been part of a deputation to the Bishop of Durham. In the grand, opulent surroundings of the bishop's palace, Dr Moule had listened to them give details of forced feeding in British prisons. As her energy returned, Maggie felt a growing need to be politically active again.

'If you gan about protesting again, they'll throw you back in the nick sharpish,' George had fretted. 'Keep your head down, Maggie man, then they won't touch you till your licence runs out.'

'It's not a protest,' Maggie had replied breezily, 'it's a deputation - all very proper. So stop worrying.'

But increasingly George seemed to worry about the slightest of things, Maggie thought impatiently. The assassination of some foreign archduke at the end of June had put him in a mood and he came home every day now with a newspaper to scan the news from the Continent.

When she tried to tell him about their interview with the bishop, he only half listened, his attention fixed on an article headed 'The Austrian Tragedy' and detailing the funeral of the archduke and his 'consort'.

'What's it all got to do with us?' Maggie demanded in annoyance. 'They're always bumping people off in the Balkans.'

'Aye, but if the Austrians retaliate against the Serbs for this murder, that brings in the Russians to defend Serbia and the Germans to support the Austrians,' George explained.

'So?' Maggie sighed, thinking it was all so trivial and irrelevant to their political work here.

'The Russians are in alliance with France and us,' George said, his voice rising. 'We're at the whim of our ruling classes and their despot friends.'

'Geordie man, we're not going to get into a war over some dead Austrian royals!' Maggie said dismissively.

But George had not been mollified and had taken himself off to see Isaac Samuel and discuss politics with his friend.

That evening, Jimmy caused consternation by arriving home with excited talk of an attack on Whitley Bay by foreigners.

'They were trying to blow up our ships at Elswick. There were ambulances everywhere and lads on stretchers - they were takin' them into this church ball in Jesmond.'

'Jesmond?' Maggie asked in bewilderment. 'What were you doing over there?'

'Me and Tommy followed them. They said they'd come by train from Whitley to Walker, then on ambulances and carts.'

'Who said?' Maggie demanded

'The wounded soldiers!' Jimmy cried.

'Have you gone potty, Tich?' Maggie gasped 'Are you telling me we've been invaded?'

Her brother grinned. 'No, they were just acting - rehearsing for a real invasion.'

Maggie picked up an apple and threw it at him in her annoyance and relief.

'Don't you go giving me a heart attack, you little bugger!'

Jimmy caught the apple and began to munch. 'But it's what'll really happen if them foreigners try and land at Whitley Bay. They wouldn't be practising if it wasn't likely to happen.'

'Don't talk daft.'

'I'd join up the morra if there was a war,' Jimmy declared.

Maggie snorted 'You're too young - and too tichy. They'd not have you.'

But the incident shook Maggie and the future suddenly seemed even less certain than before. She decided it was time to make her peace with Susan.

Maggie found her alone in Gun Street one Saturday afternoon. Susan appeared nervous and jumpy at her sudden appearance.

'What are you doing here?' she demanded suspiciously.

"Thought it was time to come and see you - give a hand with things while I can,' Maggie offered.

'Why should I need any help? I've always managed just grand,' Susan answered stiffly. 'Even without Mam ...'

'Aye, Mam,' Maggie said sadly. 'I've been to her grave... Oh, Susan, it was terrible not being there when it happened.'

Susan winced. 'It was terrible being there, you mean. There was nothing I could do. If you'd been there, it might never have happened. She was arguing over you!' And she burst into tears.

Maggie felt winded by the accusation, but it was no more than she deserved. To her dying day she would feel guilty for bringing the anxiety and strain upon her mother that had caused her death. She tried to pat Susan's shoulder in comfort, but her sister turned away from her as if she could not bear her near. Susan blew hard into a handkerchief and wiped her face.

'You shouldn't have come,' she muttered. 'If Richard finds you here, there'll be hell on. Your name's muck around here.'

But Maggie would not be got rid of so easily. 'Good things grow out of muck.'

Maggie glanced about, noticing the differences for the first time. There was a new dresser in the comer and curtains at the window. Their mother's worn, comfortable old chair was gone from the fireside and Jimmy's truckle bed had been replaced by a wooden crib. In the comer stood a baby's high chair. Maggie's jaw dropped open and she turned to scrutinise her sister.

'You're going to have a bairn?' she gasped.

Susan's head went up proudly. 'Aye, I'm six months gone.'

Maggie stepped forward to hug her but felt her sister flinch at the contact once more.

'That's grand! I'm that pleased for you, Susan,' Maggie smiled, despite her sister's coolness. 'Tich never said anything about you expecting.'

'Tich?' Susan questioned sharply. 'You've seen him?'

'Aye, he's living with me and - and George Gordon.' Maggie felt herself blush.

'George Gordon?' Susan gasped. 'When did you wed?'

'We didn't,' Maggie told her defiantly. 'We don't believe in the slavery of marriage.'

'You should be ashamed of yourself!' Susan answered in shock. 'Living out of wedlock - and corrupting our Jimmy with your wicked ideas. You send him back here at once!'

'He won't come.' Maggie was blunt. 'He's had enough of Richard Turvey knocking him about. And he's told me all about how he treats you like dirt and carries on with our Helen. You don't have to put on any airs for me and pretend everything's rosy - I'm your sister, remember? Why don't you kick him out? I'd not put with such carry-on and you shouldn't have to either.'

Susan turned hot with outrage. 'How dare you tell me what to do! You're nowt but a trollop and a criminal - you should still be locked up! Well, you'll not go causing trouble round here! My Richard's a good husband and treats me canny. I can have anything I want,' she declared, waving at the new pieces of baby furniture. 'You're just jealous that I'm married and having a baby and getting on in the world, while all you've got to show for your life is a prison record and a man who doesn't respect you enough to marry you!' Flecks of spittle spattered Susan's chin from her vitriolic attack. Maggie watched, astounded.

'I'll not stay here to be insulted,' she declared. 'I only came here to make amends and see if I could help you. But you're beyond help, Susan. You're a stuck-up, narrow-minded prig who can't admit the mistake you've made marrying that waster, Turvey. I'd rather die in gaol than have your life any day!'

'Get out!' Susan screamed.

'Not before I've had a word with Granny Beaton.' Maggie stood her ground.

Watching, she saw the colour drain from Susan's puffy cheeks. Suddenly, it struck Maggie that there was no sign of her grandmother. The fireside chair was gone; the smell of her had vanished.

'Is she in the parlour?' Maggie asked.

Susan shook her head

'Where is she?' Maggie demanded in alarm. 'She's not d- '

'She's in a home,' Susan answered curtly. 'We couldn't cope with her here any longer.'

'What home?'

Susan felt alarm at the sight of Maggie's horrified look. She gulped. 'St Chad's.'

Maggie advanced on her furiously. 'You've put her in the workhouse?'

Susan backed into a chair. 'Don't upset me!' she trembled. 'I must think of my baby first.'

Maggie halted. She suddenly saw before her a weak and frightened woman, lashing out through her own misery and guilt. Maggie no longer knew who this woman was, for she was not the caring, fussing, elder sister with whom she had grown up. Infuriating and nagging she may have been, but the old Susan would never have considered banishing their grandmother to the workhouse. Maggie thought of her dear, confused Granny Beaton wandering the unfriendly corridors of St Chad's, trying to find a way home. It made her want to weep.

She did not utter another word to her sister but turned and left abruptly.

Susan sat shaking in her chair, dry sobs struggling to escape her throat. Maggie was gone, but her look of condemnation haunted her. She placed her hands protectively against her swelling womb and sought comfort from her baby's kick. Yet she could not rid her mind of Maggie's accusing eyes.

With Jimmy's persuasion, George agreed that they could look after Granny Beaton even if Maggie were to return to prison. So Jimmy and Maggie went to collect their ancient grandmother from St Chad's Institution for the Poor. Maggie shivered with unease as they waited in a draughty hall being scrubbed by three scrawny women of indeterminate age. Its bleakness was only relieved by the occasional religious tract nailed to the wall and the summer sun hardly penetrated the high windows. It reminded Maggie all too much of prison and she was nearly physically sick at the thought.

Old Agnes Beaton had no idea who the young people were who led her from the workhouse, but she followed trustingly.

'The fire,' she muttered, as they supported her out of the gates. 'They've put out the fire. The fire is the heart of the home - there must be a fire.'

Maggie tried to calm her fretfulness. "There's a grand fire at home, Granny, don't you worry yourself.'

'No, they put milk on the fire - the last of our milk,' the old woman wailed. 'What will my baby drink? There's no fire. We have to go.'

But the dark images that haunted their grandmother seemed to subside once they had her at the cottage and sitting in front of the warm range. It was a hot July day and they would not normally have stoked up the fire so vigorously, but George had done so to welcome the old woman.

They gave up their bed in the corner and moved into the loft, while Jimmy slept on the sofa in the cottage.

'I 'll make us a proper bed,' George promised as they nestled down in the straw.

'I love you, Geordie,' Maggie murmured into his shoulder. 'You're a canny, canny man.'

They left the skylight open to the mild night air with its scents of roses and clover and newly cut logs and chickens and gazed up at the stars. For two weeks they continued to enjoy their rustic freedom and the dry balmy evenings. After the sweat and toil of the forge, George would hasten up the hill and out of the dusty, hot streets as fast as he could, while Maggie stayed close to home, attending her grandmother and impatient for his return.

He stopped bringing newspapers home, as if that could stem the rumours of war and the quickening excitement flowing out of the town. Jimmy would return with reports of activity at the barracks and grave talk along the quayside and he elected to sleep outside wrapped in a blanket, saying he was preparing for a life on the march.

'Well, you can forage for your own food then, Private Beaton,' Maggie told him. 'I'll have no talk of foreign wars in my house.'

After three days of thunderstorms, Jimmy beat a retreat inside and spent the next two days sneezing by the fire, his head disappearing under a blanket to infuse the steam from a bowl of hot water.

'It'll not be that wet abroad,' Jimmy muttered at Maggie's amused face. 'You don't catch your death in hot countries.'

Maggie shivered at his words and told him sharply to eat some soup.

But the following day, Jimmy's war games were overshadowed by the arrival of the police. Maggie had not reported back at the expiry of her licence and they had come to re-arrest her.

It was all so calmly and politely done compared to the awful scene at Gun Street. George was at work and Jimmy was out in the garden, digging up some vegetables. He came running in to gawp at the policemen. Maggie bent and kissed her grandmother on her capped head and said mildly to her brother, 'Take care of Granny till I come back.'

She kissed him too as she passed and walked meekly out of the cottage that had become such a dear home to her and George. As she said a silent farewell to Hibbs' Cottage, Maggie was thankful that George was not there. She could not have borne such a parting.

That day the view from the hill was clear, a strong west wind blowing the smoke from the chimneys downriver. The Tyne snaked and shimmered in the strong sun like a coil of steel, binding the communities on both its banks - Scotswood to Blaydon, Elswick to Dunston. They all lived off its strength, Maggie thought, feeling a pull of belonging yet already detached from the world before her.

Somewhere down in the bustling industrial sprawl at the river's edge George was labouring over a new ship for Pearson's. Perhaps it would be used in the war that everyone was talking about as if it were a certainty. But one day it would either rust or break up on the sea bed. Maggie was struck by how transitory human existence was. All the struggles and desires and achievements - what were they for?

As they approached a waiting van at the bottom of the track, Maggie looked at the river for the last time, trying to imprint its curves and patterns in her mind. There was the symbol of permanence that she sought, right before her very eyes, she realised. The River Tyne. Whatever happened, she comforted herself, the river that had been a part of her existence since her earliest memories would always be there.

Chapter Twenty-One

Alice went out with her camera to the High Level Bridge to capture the excitement. It was a bank holiday and the town was full of people standing around the streets talking and speculating. Rumours of war abounded. This morning's newspapers had reported Germany's declaration of war on Russia and France and it was believed the Germans were sweeping through Luxembourg towards France at this very moment.

Alice found the bridge guarded by soldiers and as soon as they saw her with her tripod and camera, they warned her away.

A paper-seller beside her spat and spoke. 'They've arrested a lad this morning. Marched him off to the guardroom at the station.'

'What was he doing?' Alice asked.

'Drawings of the bridge,' the man answered with a sombre nod.

"That's hardly a crime,' Alice said in astonishment.

'Aye, but he was spying!' the man said with glee. 'Doing drawings for the Kaiser.'

Alice shook her head in disbelief and strode off towards Central Station where crowds were gathering. Reservists had been asked to return to the colours and there was worried talk down on the quayside that boats and cargoes abroad had been seized by the Germans. But around the entrance to the station, all were in a state of joyful frenzy. A special train was leaving for Chatham with naval reservists on board and they were being given a tumultuous send-off. Women wept, boys threw their caps in the air and men clapped them on the shoulder and wished them luck.

'And war hasn't even been declared,' Alice said under her breath, quite overwhelmed by the passion of the people.

She felt a stab of envy for the ordinary townsfolk, showing their uninhibited support for their men. For a moment she revelled in being a part of the show of patriotism, proud to be there at the departure of the first sailors and soldiers. It gave her a sense of belonging after the months of aimlessness following Herbert's election to the House of Commons. Her brother had soon made it clear he had no more need of her and Felicity was running Hebron House once more. Herbert was away all week in London, while Felicity entertained her friends, filling the house with loud ragtime music and acrid tobacco smoke. At weekends they threw extravagant parties and gambled late into the night.

Alice felt she was tolerated rather than welcomed at such affairs and so chose to dine alone in her rooms or take herself out to the theatre. She felt bitter at her rejection by Herbert but even angrier that he had not kept his promise of involving her more in the business. Increasingly she escaped to Oxford Hall where she pushed her invalid father out in his wheelchair and talked politics, while a delighted Rosamund barked and chased after butterflies.

On her last visit, her father had struggled to say, 'If there's a war with the Kaiser, Herbert will need your help. We won't be able to make ships and armaments fast enough. Your time will come, Alice.'

She had sensed his frustration with his half-paralysed body and his slurred speech and had bent to kiss him tenderly on the head.

'He'll need your advice too, Papa,' she assured him, though they both knew Herbert would never do anything his father advised.

Standing now among the smell and press of scores of bodies, Alice felt ambition stir for the first time in months. If war broke out as everyone predicted, she thought, she would do something to help. As yet she did not know what, but she would do something.

Emerging from the station into the light of a sunny August day, she saw a silver-haired man being marched between two soldiers, with a gaggle of booing boys in their wake.

'Spy! Spy!' they taunted the frightened man. 'Dirty rotten Hun!'

Alice felt a moment of misgiving, then shrugged it off. It was necessary to be vigilant against the enemy and there were bound to be Germans living in Newcastle who would be sympathetic to the Kaiser. They must learn swiftly that Great Britain with her mighty empire would not be cowed by German aggression and that every Briton would rally to the country's defence if war were declared.

George was digging in the garden when a breathless Jimmy came scrambling up the path shouting, 'We're at war with Germany!'

George paused for a moment to push back his cap. 'Bloody daft!' he muttered and carried on digging, aware of Jimmy's deflated look.

Jimmy said, 'Don't you want to come and watch the soldiers leave?'

'No,' George replied curtly. 'I've better things to do with the holiday than watch folk gettin' hysterical over uniforms.'

'That's not very patriotic,' Jimmy answered in disappointment. 'You should be proud of our lads going to fight for our freedom.'

George thrust his spade into the soil and looked up.

'Freedom? What freedom?' he cried savagely. 'We're wage slaves to the bosses and now the bosses are packing us off to fight against the German working man. Aye, that makes me really proud!'

George saw the look of incomprehension on the youth's face and wanted desperately to make him understand.

'Can't you see, Jimmy? It's not a war about our freedom, it's a power struggle between rulers and bosses wanting more land, more power. The likes of you and me are just cannon fodder in their daft war. We should have nothing to do with it, let alone be supporting it! The only fight that concerns the working man is the one the trades unions are fighting against the bosses. That's the only struggle I'm bothered about - and I don't give a toss if they're British bosses or German!'

But by the hostile look on Jimmy's face, George could tell the boy understood nothing of what he was trying to say. He sighed and went back to his gardening.

'I always thought you were brave,' Jimmy said accusingly, 'but you haven't got the stomach for a fight, have you? You're all talk. Well, I'm proud to be English and I'd join up the morra if I was old enough!'

'Be thankful you're not,' George grunted.

'Well, I'm not thankful,' Jimmy huffed 'War'll be over before I can gan. It's not bloody fair!'

'Stop your moaning and gan to the fish shop for some herring,' George ordered with a friendly cuff. He pulled a sixpence out of his pocket. 'Your gran likes a bit herring, and we'll have some o' these new tatties, eh?'

Jimmy took the coin with a scowl. George watched him stomp off down the hill, hands thrust into his over-large jacket, and realised he had proved a great disappointment to Maggie's young brother.

The boy had shown his affection and admiration since coming to live at the cottage, eager to run errands for him and learn what he could about the work of a blacksmith. George had approached the smith at the forge where he had learned his trade and the man had allowed Jimmy to watch him and do small jobs around the smithy. But Jimmy was still so scrawny and immature; George was worried that the boy's head might be turned by all this war hysteria. What if he were to run away and try to join up while Maggie was still in prison? He felt responsible for the lad and did not want to see him come to any harm.

'Oh, Maggie,' he sighed to the sky, 'I need you here, lass.' Then he went on digging.

By Friday and the return to work, George could no longer cut himself off from the quickening pace of war preparations. The shipyard and the pubs buzzed with the news. There were lengthening queues outside the co-operative store and the bakers, as panic buying of flour and sugar and other staples spread.

By Saturday, Newcastle was declared a 'prohibited port', with no one allowed off ship without a permit from the Customs House. Schools were taken over as billets for the army and recruiting offices were mobbed by volunteers. Cinemas advertised special films entitled *England's Might* and *Boys of the Bulldog Breed* which Jimmy rushed off to see. Motor wagons were requisitioned for ambulances and horses were taken over by the military in large numbers. Soldiers were given free train travel and George was disgruntled to notice that those in uniform were admitted free to the baths.

The unwelcome news that HMS *Amphion* had been struck by a mine and sunk with over a hundred men lost was swiftly followed by jubilation that a German cruiser had been sunk off the Tyne by a British destroyer, HMS *Lance*. Young boys dashed around the back streets, shooting each other with imaginary revolvers and falling mock-dead at George's feet, but he was more concerned by the jingoism that had led to a German pork butcher's shop being set on fire at New Bridge Street. The town seemed gripped by a fever.

A visit to his family had ended in a blazing row with his father and siblings about the war. Billy, already in the Territorial's, had reported to the depot and Joshua was eagerly talking of joining up. A heated argument had flared, with his sister Irene telling him to wash his mouth out with soap and water for saying King George was nearly as German as the Kaiser. His father had called him a traitor and told his brothers to 'hoy 'im oot!' Punches had been exchanged and George had left with a bloody nose and the neighbours jeering.

In search of sanity, he had gone the next evening to Isaac and Miriam's, but found them tense and nervous in their small flat and reluctant to let anyone in.

'But you've nowt to fear,' George had said in astonishment, 'you're Russian!'

Isaac gave a dispirited shrug. 'Simple people do not know the difference. They hear my accent, my name, and they think I'm a spy. Everywhere there is suspicion - and ignorance. It is just as it was in Russia for us Jews. Now we are not wanted here.'

For once Miriam was vocal. 'Isaac was arrested last week on his way to the synagogue,' she told him. 'They came here and went through all his papers before he was allowed to go. But they found an old ticket from Hamburg - it's where we got the boat for Newcastle when we escaped. I didn't even know we'd kept it. But they kept on at Isaac to produce a return ticket, still thinking him a spy. When they couldn't find one, they left.' Miriam shuddered deeply. 'But they said they might come back.'

George looked at his elderly friend, appalled. 'If they give you any more trouble, I want to know,' he answered angrily. 'This war's turning England into a police state. They've already made it plain at the shipyard they want no agitation. This war's a godsend to the bosses.'

Isaac sighed. 'I don't know about that. All I do know is that your people do not want a foreign music teacher any more. My students are joining up or staying away. Perhaps it is time for Miriam and me to move on.'

'But where would you go?' George asked anxiously. 'Russia is at war now too.'

'We'd never go back to Russia,' Miriam said with feeling. 'But we have a cousin in New York. Perhaps if we sold everything...'

George looked at their bleak, resigned faces and did not know how to reassure them. He could stand up for himself, but how could he defend his friends from the creeping prejudice and rumour that was choking their livelihood? As for the tide of patriotism rising in the country, it threatened to drown all opposition to the war. Even in his own home it lapped around them, causing a growing gulf between himself and Jimmy.

A week after the start of the war, the boy came home brandishing a newspaper at George.

'Your King and coun-try needs you,' he read out haltingly. 'A call to arms. Kit-chen-er is con-fid-ent it will be res-ponded to by all - those - who have the safe-ty of our Em-pire at heart. God Save the King!'

'Aye,' George grunted, 'that's all they're bothered about, saving the empire.'

'The first soldiers have sailed for France,' Jimmy announced, ignoring the remark, 'Uncle Barny said.'

George looked up. 'You been seeing your uncle and aunt again?'

'Aye. Uncle Barny's been telling me stories about the Fusiliers. That's who I'm going to join.'

'Well, look what happened to your uncle - got his leg shot off for his trouble,' George pointed out.

'I'm not scared of getting' wounded,' Jimmy said with disdain. 'I'm prepared to die for me country. Me and Smithy, we've made a pact to join up together.'

'Smithy!' George laughed. 'He's just out of short britches.'

Jimmy threw down the newspaper. 'Don't laugh at us!' the boy cried and stormed out of the cottage.

That evening, George went for a long walk across Hibbs' fields, up the valley, among the ripening corn. He had paid one of the dairymaids to come in and bathe Granny Beaton and sit with her twice a week so that he could have the odd evening to himself. The old woman was becoming too much for him to look after and Jimmy was increasingly absent and of little help. Soon he would have to consider taking Agnes Beaton back to the workhouse.

The future seemed so grim for them all and with war occupying his mind, George turned morosely for home.

It was half dark by the time he reached Hibbs' Cottage and all was quiet. He called for Jane, the dairymaid, but no one answered. Cursing the girl for having slipped away early, George strode into the cottage and saw the old woman lying asleep in the corner bed.

'And where the devil have you been?'

George started at the voice. A figure rose from the chair by the dying fire and turned to face him.

'Maggie?' he gasped.

'Aye, Geordie, they've hoyed me oot.' He could not see her face clearly in the gloom, but the amusement in her voice was clear.

She stepped towards him and in a moment his arms were about her, squeezing her close to him so that she protested she could not breathe.

'Maggie! Oh, Maggie!' He picked her up and swung her round. 'It really is you!'

'Well, I hope you wouldn't be doing this for that lass from the dairy I found here,' Maggie teased.

'Only on Saturdays,' George teased her back.

They kissed in relief and delight.

'But why didn't you send word you were being freed?' George demanded. 'You're under licence again?'

Maggie shook her head. 'I'm not going back this time, Geordie. They've given us all a pardon - Mrs Pankhurst, all of us. It all happened that quickly. Mind you, it's a bit of a cheek - pardon indeed! It's the government should be asking us for a pardon!'

George laughed and hugged her to him again.

'That's me fighting lass!'

'Aye, well, that's what Mrs Pankhurst is saying we should be doing now,' Maggie told him, 'fighting with the government and not against them in the war effort. She's told us to be loyal to them and the country. At least that's what it says in the paper the prison governor showed me.'

George sighed. 'And is that what you think you should do?'

Maggie sank onto a chair, the excitement of being reunited with George leaving her suddenly weak. 'I don't know. It's been so sudden. One minute I'm an enemy of the state, serving a two-year sentence and starving myself to death for me beliefs, then the next minute I'm free and being told by me leaders that I've got to support me persecutors.' Maggie looked at him in bewilderment. 'What's it all been for? All that struggling and pain, and now it's suddenly over and we haven't won an inch in the fight for the vote. I really thought we were coming close to winning the battle, Geordie, but this war in Europe's put a stop to everything. I feel cheated. I want to go on fighting for women's rights, just like I've always done, but the leadership's gone, so what can I do?'

George knelt down beside her and put his rough hands round her face. 'You can gan on fighting, bonny lass,' he said. 'There'll always be summat worth struggling for. Don't give up just because the ruling classes are closing ranks - that's nothing new. As long as there's breath in your body you can fight for what you believe in, Maggie.'

She felt a rush of gratitude towards him for understanding how she felt and for giving her the strength to go on. The past few days had been so confusing that she had not known what to do or who to believe. But George had shown again that he loved and accepted her for who she was and it filled her with warmth.

She raised her face and kissed him tenderly. 'Us against the world then?' she joked.

George laughed softly as he helped her to her feet. 'Aye, you and me, lass,' he agreed, 'that's all that matters.' And he carried her up the ladder to their bed in the rafters.

Chapter Twenty-Two

Surprisingly, Maggie found she settled into the mundane chores of daily life, despite the extraordinary events occurring far away in Flanders. Her strength returned and she devoted her time to caring for her grandmother and the household while George worked increasingly long hours at the shipyard and Jimmy got odd jobs fetching and carrying down at the station, for many porters had rushed to enlist.

The usual shop sales and regattas continued that strange hot August, the war somehow unreal and remote, and there was talk of it all being over in a couple of months as news filtered through of a Russian advance and the Kaiser's troops being repulsed.

'Even them Belgian lasses have seen off the Hun,' Jimmy proudly told his sister. 'Hoyed boiling water over them in the street, Uncle Barny said.'

Maggie wondered about those factory workers who had armed themselves in the face of invasion and tried to imagine what she would do if Newcastle was ever threatened. Would she forget her strong leanings towards pacifism and rush to defend her home town? Like George, she believed this war was about imperial gain and that the people had been cruelly tricked into supporting it by crude appeals to their patriotism. Nevertheless, if foreign imperialists tried to storm Newcastle from the North Sea and overrun them, Maggie knew she would not be able to stand by. She would fight.

By September, the first lists of war casualties began to be published in the local newspapers. At first it was the officers who were named and other ranks were merely listed as figures of killed or wounded. There were thousands.

Appeals were made for ex-NCOs to join for the duration of the war and reports began to describe the situation on the Western Front as being 'not quite satisfactory'. Hundreds from the pit villages round about flocked to the recruiting stations and the streets of the town were flooded with raw recruits who encamped on the Town Moor in leaky tents. They trained with wooden dummy rifles and wore civilian clothes with coloured cord round their right shoulders because there was a shortage of uniforms.

Jimmy went to watch them drill the new service battalions with names like the Tyneside Scottish, Tyneside Irish, the Commercials and the Pioneers. He had taken to wearing Uncle Barny's old military jacket, which swamped his narrow shoulders, and tried to cultivate a wisp of a moustache on his soft upper lip.

Winter arrived and a week before Christmas three German battlecruisers crept in from the North Sea and shelled Hartlepool. The war was suddenly too close to home and the shock was followed by outrage as news broke of civilian casualties. One hundred and nineteen men, women and children had been killed. Recruitment posters appeared again, portraying dashing cavalrymen - and volunteers flocked once more.

Jimmy's seventeenth birthday was two days before Christmas and Maggie baked him a special cake. When he did not return from the station by seven o'clock, she sent George out to look for him. He returned two hours later, supporting an inebriated Jimmy crying into his shoulder.

'Tommy Smith told me where to find him,' George grunted. 'In the Forge and Hammer.'

Maggie cuffed her drunken brother and demanded, 'Tich, what you makin' an exhibition of yourself for?'

'They wouldn't have me,' Jimmy sobbed and staggered outside to be sick.

George explained. 'He tried to enlist with the Tyneside Scottish - went down to the camp at Newburn. But they didn't believe him when he said he was nineteen and they told him he was too small anyway - wouldn't pass the medical.'

Maggie saw her peaky-faced brother appear in the doorway.

"The lads laughed at me,' he whispered miserably.

'Oh, man, Tich;' Maggie said, holding out her arms to him in comfort. But he flinched away from her.

'Don't ever call me Tich again!' he shouted and staggered back outside.

Christmas passed quietly, with Jimmy spending his time increasingly away from the cottage, roaming the town with Tommy Smith and getting into fights on a Saturday night, returning with his eyes blackened and lips cut more often than not.

Maggie despaired of her brother but George would intervene and tell her to leave him alone, recognising the deep anger and frustration within the boy. When the spring came, he coaxed Jimmy down to the rowing club and by the early summer the youth was coxing in four-oared races on the Tyne.

But the war increasingly began to intrude into Maggie's quiet haven at the farm. One afternoon a gang of boys came up the hill and started to shout at the gate. Maggie went out to discover the cause of the commotion.

'What do you want?' she demanded.

'You're spies, aren't you?' one of them shouted.

'Don't be daft!' she laughed. 'Be off and don't pester me.'

'We've seen the old hag you're hidin' in there,' the tall vocal boy persisted. 'We know she's Boches. We've heard her speakin' funny.'

'You mean me granny? She's Scots and she speaks Gaelic not Kraut,' Maggie snapped in annoyance.

'Same difference,' the boy jeered. 'Scotchie or Boches, we don't like her here. You're spies and that man you live with is a coward for not joining up like me dad and me uncles.' At this, the other boys began to chant menacingly.

'White feathers! White feathers!'

The ringleader split open a pillow he had been carrying and a deluge of feathers flew about like a white storm.

Maggie advanced on them with the chamber pot her grandmother had just used and which she had been going to empty. She hurled the contents at the boys. They squealed in disgust and jumped back.

'Shove off, you little wasters!' Maggie yelled at them.

'You're a witch, a bloody witch!' the tall boy screamed.

'Aye, I am,' Maggie cried, 'and I've plenty more of that witch's brew you've just tasted!'

They turned and ran off down the hill in fear. Maggie laughed in relief, but later, when she recounted it to George, he seemed to take offence.

'I'm no coward,' he bristled.

'Of course you're not,' Maggie soothed 'I know that.'

'And I don't like the thought of you being up here on your own all day with your grandmother,' he fretted. 'I think we should move back into town.'

'I'm not afraid of a bunch o' silly bairns calling me names,' Maggie scoffed, 'and I don't want to leave here.' She searched his troubled face. 'What is it, Geordie?' she asked. 'Something else is on your mind, isn't it?'

'Aye,' George admitted at last. 'It's our Billy.'

'He's been sent to France?' Maggie guessed.

George looked at her unhappily. 'He's already back. Sent up the line the minute they arrived. Fought at Ypres. Poor buggers weren't there long enough to know the Germans from the French.'

'You've seen him?'

George nodded

'Is he... all right?'

George shrugged. 'He's still in one piece, but he's ill from that poison gas the Germans are using against our lads. He's - changed. Even Irene can't get more than two words out of him.'

After that, George grew more preoccupied and subdued and he and Jimmy would disappear for most of the evening to the rowing club. Wounded soldiers became an increasingly common sight in the town as they haunted the parks in their blue hospital uniforms and regimental bonnets, taken on picnics by worthy committees and photographed with munitions workers. On several occasions Maggie saw Alice Pearson's name in the newspapers, praised for her fund-raising efforts for the newly created local battalions, with no mention made of her one-time association with the suffragettes.

Sometimes Maggie wondered whether the past turbulent years of women's struggle had ever been, so little was there to show for it. The government were taking increasingly Draconian powers to stifle any dissent to the waging of war and George came home fuming one July day with news that strikes had been declared illegal.

'They've got us over a barrel,' he growled. 'Any push for better wages or conditions is being seen as unpatriotic or worse. We're working flat out and Pearson's are coining it in but we're told we're putting the country in jeopardy by asking for more pay.'

'You will be careful, won't you?' Maggie urged in concern. 'We need your job to pay for this place - I can't go out and leave Granny alone all day.'

George gave her a bewildered look. 'What's happened to the fighting suffragette?' he demanded scornfully. 'I thought you were on my side.'

'Of course I am,' Maggie answered irritably, 'it's just...'

'What?' George demanded.

Maggie shrugged in despair. She could not explain her feeling of foreboding at a future she could not see but could sense lay in wait like a predatory animal. Her biggest fear was that their tranquil life at the cottage would not last.

When she did not reply, George grunted, 'I'll tell you something queer. That Turvey's working down at the yard.'

'Richard?' Maggie asked in surprise. 'What's he doing there?'

"The devil knows. Some sort of clerking, I expect. Bobs up all over the place - even union meetings. Never struck me as the political type, but you never know who your friends are.'

'Or your enemies,' Maggie murmured and turned away, deeply troubled.

Then, quite suddenly, on a warm summer's morning, Granny Beaton called Maggie to her bedside. The urgency in the old woman's voice made Maggie drop the wet washing she was about to hang out and hurry over.

Her grandmother was trying to sit up, her eyes for once clear, her speech lucid.

'Maggie, don't trust him,' she warned.

'Granny, lie back,' Maggie coaxed 'Were you having a bad dream?'

But the ancient woman resisted with surprising strength. 'Not a dream, lassie,' she cried. 'He's a wicked man ... he betrayed you.'

'Who, Granny?' Maggie asked, perturbed.

'Thinks I'm mad but I knew what he was up to. That's why . . .' She clutched Maggie's arm, her eyes filled with sudden terror. 'Don't let me go back to that place!'

'I won't,' Maggie assured her, watching the old woman's mind recede back into chaos. She must have been thinking of the workhouse and her dreadful days of imprisonment there, Maggie thought. Agnes Beaton began to mumble and call her Peggi, until her eyes closed and she sank into unconsciousness, her breathing shallow and ragged.

Maggie sat by the bed for an age, holding on to the soft skeletal hand of the old woman, recalling her life. Her craggy, ancient face had at last lost its tense fretfulness and lay serene on the linen-covered bolster. Maggie was reminded of the vigorous, red-haired lady who had burst into their life on the death of her father with her fanciful tales and magical songs. She had protected and loved them, always a calming presence in the wake of the storms wreaked by her volatile mother.

Maggie tried to imagine the young Agnes Beaton who had grown up in the shadow of Sgurr Beag, delighting in the songs and tales of her people and singing them to her small boy, oblivious of the terrible hardships that lay ahead. Her grandmother had endured eviction and banishment from her beloved Highlands and had been forced to flee to the strange and terrifying city of Glasgow. She had told Maggie how she had to be taught to use a stove, for the young Agnes had only ever cooked on an open fire, but she had adapted and managed without complaint.

Maggie began to croon softly, an old lullaby that her grandmother had taught her. She stroked her wrinkled brow with affection, sensing that Granny Beaton was slipping away from her and taking with her the last contact with her childhood.

Sometime in the afternoon, old Agnes Beaton gave up the struggle and died.

Maggie sat in the stillness, aware only of a sense of peace. Finally she leaned over and kissed her grandmother tenderly on her brow, torn between relief for the old woman's release and deep sorrow at losing her dear relation. For they had been close companions, even during the last months of her grandmother's growing weakness and senility. Her whole daily routine had been set round caring for her and now she felt a huge cavernous emptiness opening up inside.

'Oh Granny!' she cried aloud, tears falling at last. 'What shall I do now?'

But in the days that followed, she felt strangely comforted, as if her dead grandmother was telling her to be strong and that she was never alone in her struggles.

Jimmy was sent out to alert the family to the funeral arrangements and the burial was held the following Saturday at the kirk in Elswick. It was the first time Maggie had seen Susan since their estrangement the year before over their grandmother.

Susan was well dressed in a navy dress with black trimmings and a black hat, but to Maggie's amazement she was obviously heavily pregnant once more. For a moment Maggie felt a stab of guilt that she had never tried to visit Susan or make a fuss over her firstborn, Alfred.

Walking away from the fresh grave, Maggie made an effort to be friendly.

'How are you, Susan?' she asked, regarding her sister's tearful, swollen face.

'Well enough,' Susan answered stiffly without meeting Maggie's gaze.

'And Alfred?' Maggie persisted.

The mention of the baby brought a smile to her sister's strained face and she looked at Maggie for the first time. 'He's grand,' she said with feeling. 'A real bonny bairn. Helen's minding him - she doesn't like funerals.'

Maggie had noticed her other sister's absence.

'Perhaps I could call and see the bairn sometime,' Maggie suggested.

Before Susan could answer, Richard was at her elbow and steering her away.

'Come on, Susan,' he ordered. 'This isn't the place to chatter.'

'You'll come back to the cottage for a cup of tea, won't you?' Maggie asked. 'I've done some baking.'

'My wife needs to rest,' Richard replied firmly. 'She couldn't possibly walk all that way in her condition.'

'Mr Heslop could give you a lift in his van,' Maggie said directly to Susan.

'No,' Richard said, his tone acid. 'We don't approve of the goings-on up there, if you want to know. My Susan's a respectable girl, so don't embarrass her by asking her round. We've done our duty.'

'Susan?' Maggie appealed to her sister, galled by the man's rudeness. But her sister stood mute, staring intently at the ground.

'I've told you no,' Richard said threateningly. 'And you're not welcome to call on us either, so don't try sneaking round when I'm out, 'cos Susan'll tell me.'

'Don't threaten me, Richard Turvey!' Maggie stood her ground. 'You'll not stop me seeing me own family if I want to.'

Richard gave her a look of contempt. 'Susan's not your family any more, she's mine. She's a Turvey and she does as I say.' He lowered his voice and leered into her face. 'Interfere again and I'll make sure your life isn't worth living. So keep away from us, you little slut!'

Without thinking Maggie raised her gloved hand and smacked him across the face. The small group of mourners from the kirk stared in astonished embarrassment. George quickly came to Maggie's side.

'She's upset,' he explained, trying to calm the situation. 'Come on, Maggie, don't let him provoke you.'

'She's the provoker!' Richard shouted. 'And I'll not forget this!'

'Please, Richard, come away,' Susan urged in a timid voice, touching his arm. He threw her off.

'Get yourself off home, woman,' he snapped 'I've already wasted enough time at the old hag's funeral.'

As he stormed off, Maggie felt George grip her aim. 'Let him go,' he said.

'Susan!' Maggie appealed to her sister, but Susan gave her a look she could not fathom and hurried after her husband.

Maggie stood looking after them, furious at the rebuff and upset to see her sister so meek and downtrodden.

Well, they could go to hell! Maggie railed inwardly. Why should she make an effort to see her sisters when they clearly thought so little of her?

Maggie was subdued for days afterwards. She grieved for her grandmother but realised she had lost even more, for her own sisters were now strangers and wanted nothing to do with her.

Of all her family, only Jimmy now acknowledged her and even he rarely came home more than once or twice a week. George remained her one true friend, yet it frightened Maggie how dependent on him she had become. What would she do if they ever introduced conscription and George was forced to join up?

They lay together in the wide bed that had been her grandmother's, physically close yet far apart in their thoughts. Maggie could tell that George was troubled by something, but she could not get him to talk about it. Whenever he visited his invalid brother, he returned belligerent and fulminating about the folly of the war and the stupidity of those who oversaw it.

That September brought heavy losses in Flanders, with gruelling battles at Artois and Loos which gained little ground from the Germans. The first flush of patriotism was waning as life grew more grim at home. Pub hours were curbed to tackle drunkenness and absence from the shipyards and armaments factories, and there was renewed pressure on single men to enlist or be assessed for active service.

As the fields were harvested around them, Maggie increasingly felt that their days of detachment on the farm were numbered. Then one evening, as darkness descended, George did not return home from work,

Maggie had heard the buzzers blow at the end of his shift, the ghostly sound carried uphill on the chill evening breeze. But George did not appear.

She sat alone by the dancing fire, waiting. She no longer expected Jimmy; he had wheedled his way into Aunt Violet's affections and was almost permanently living with her and his favoured Uncle Barny. Perhaps George had gone to a meeting that he had forgotten to mention, she tried to comfort herself. Tempted to go out and search for him, Maggie realised with alarm that she would not know where to begin. She had cut herself off from the town for too long, content to live a hermit's life on the farm.

Then just as she could stand the waiting no longer, she heard his footsteps on the path and the door banged open.

She could tell immediately that George had been drinking.

'What do you mean by staying out till all hours?' she ranted, sick with relief and anger at his appearance. 'I thought you'd gone under a tram! Do you ever stop to think what would happen to me if you weren't here? No! A few beers and any thought of me goes flying out the window!'

He stared at her across the room.

'What's the matter?' she demanded, suddenly alarmed at the sight of his haggard face.

'They've sacked me,' he said bleakly. 'The bastard bosses have sacked me.'

Maggie gawped in bewilderment. 'What on earth do you mean? They need you night and day at the yard!'

George shook his head violently. 'An agitator - they called me an agitator. Said I was trying to stir up trouble among the men.'

'But it's not true!' Maggie exclaimed, stepping towards him.

George brushed her off, weaving his way to the fireside. Staring into the dying flames, he spat viciously.

'Somebody took notes at the meetings, put words into me mouth. Someone doing Pearson's dirty work. Needed a scapegoat - said I was subversive - against the war.'

'It's not a crime to be against the war,' Maggie answered robustly. 'You've grafted as hard as any for Pearson's.'

He lifted his head to look at her and she thought she saw resentment cross his harrowed face.

'Well, they'll never have me back,' he answered coldly. 'Whoever betrayed me's made sure of that. Told the bosses I'm living with a known revolutionary, a suffragette who went to prison for trying to burn down Pearson's mansion. Well, as soon as they heard that they started talking about a conspiracy inspired by you. Pearson's will probably make sure I'm blacklisted anywhere on the Tyne.'

'But the union . . .' Maggie gulped, horrified by the implications of what he was saying.

George let out a harsh laugh. 'They won't rock the boat for me, not Pearson's boat or any other! This war's tied their hands tighter than any bosses' legislation's ever done. Pearson's said they wouldn't charge me or take it any further with the police if I went quietly, so the union told me to do just that. I divn't care what they do to me but I'd not see you go back to prison.'

He slumped into a chair and later slept by the fire rather than go to bed. Maggie lay alone, her mind in a turmoil. George had accepted defeat for her sake, to protect her from further trouble, but at the same time she knew he blamed her for being thrown out of work. She had seen the look on his face and it made her insides turn to ice.

Yet who was it who had really betrayed him? she wondered. Who could dislike him enough to arrange for his sacking and be vindictive enough to bring her past into it?

Her grandmother's words echoed in her mind again, warning her to beware of the wicked man who had betrayed her. At times, Maggie had wondered if the old woman could possibly have meant George, but had felt guilty for even entertaining the thought.

Then, in the middle of the night, it came to her. Richard Turvey had done this to them. George had mentioned that he was working at Pearson's. Richard had no interest in union politics except to spy on the activists. He was probably in Pearson's pay to seek out and name radicals who might be suspected of trying to incite unrest among the workforce. The bosses were jittery enough to employ *agents provocateurs*, Maggie thought grimly as she tossed in the empty bed.

And then her mind searched for clues about Richard. They had known nothing about him until his abrupt entry into their lives two and a half years ago. She had been the only one of the family to dislike and distrust him from the start, Maggie realised, and he had neither forgotten nor forgiven her disdain of him - he had shown that plainly at her grandmother's funeral. She knew he had lied about his job and his involvement in the brawl in the town, but he had wormed his way into the heart of her family anyhow.

So was it Richard Turvey who had betrayed her to the police? Maggie wondered bitterly. And by so doing had he been the cause of her mother's heart attack? Suddenly Maggie was sure of it. Her mother must have suspected him too and that was why she had gone to confront him at Aunt Violet's. He would have done it for spite or for money - or both, she thought angrily. That would explain how he always had money to squander on himself and Susan - and Helen, she thought with disgust. He might well have been in Pearson's pay that long ago and taken money for trying to subvert the Women's Movement. Anything was possible.

Maggie got up and paced outside to quell the waves of nausea that overwhelmed her at the thought of the harm Richard Turvey had done to her family and now to George. He had seeped into their lives like a poison, infiltrating every relationship until he was rid of the ones who stood in his selfish way or dominated the ones he could more easily exploit. She cursed her Aunt Violet for ever introducing her evil nephew into their family.

Shivering violently in the damp, chill night air, Maggie contemplated an angry confrontation with Richard where she would vent her fury and hatred of him and accuse him of his wickedness. But to what avail? she countered wearily. He would only deny it and throw her out - or bar her from entering in the first place. Did Susan and Helen know the extent of his deceit? she wondered. They could not be completely innocent, Maggie concluded, and yet they chose to stay with him. She felt betrayed by them all and achingly alone as she stood shaking uncontrollably in the fitful night wind.

But when she tried to speak to George the following day of her suspicions about Richard, he seemed irritable and uninterested in her theories. He disappeared for the whole of the day and returned without telling her where he had been.

George soon found that his suspicions about being blacklisted were right. He could not find employment with any of the naval yards on Tyneside or with any related industries that were owned by the men who did business with Pearson's. He was an outcast on Tyneside and the bitterness and frustration of his predicament ate into his being, so that he lashed out at the person closest to him - Maggie.

He took to staying away at his family's home in Benwell or sleeping in the loft, leaving Maggie alone and miserable and at a loss to know how to comfort him. As for herself, she had nowhere else to go. The Samuels had sold everything and bought a passage to America. She thought of approaching Rose for help, but they had not spoken for two years.

Once, she tried to suggest to George that they move away and start where no one knew them, as they had once joked of doing when she had been on the run from the police. But he seemed too far sunk in gloom to register what she had said.

'What's the use?' was his despondent reply as he gazed down at his idle hands.

When they had nothing left to pawn for the rent, Maggie went to Farmer Hibbs and asked him to take on George. For two weeks be got work lifting potatoes and his mood improved. But when the harvest was over, George took to his chair by the fire and hardly moved from the cottage.

Worried they would be evicted and no longer able to bear his sullenness or bouts of bad temper as Christmas approached once more, Maggie sallied down to her old workshop on the riverside. She was not surprised when her old boss, Mr Roberts, gave her a curt refusal and hurried her out of his office. But Eve Tindall made an excuse to leave her desk and came rushing after Maggie.

'Read about you in the papers,' Eve crowed, peering at Maggie over her spectacles. 'What a shock you gave us all! It's no wonder they'll not have you back here.'

'No,' Maggie smiled at her old colleague, 'I didn't really expect them to. I'm glad to see you again though. Eve.'

'Aye, pet,' the older woman nodded awkwardly. Then she blurted out, 'Did they treat you badly inside?'

Maggie's smile was strained as she quipped, "Not half as bad as me own kin have done.'

'Eeh, pet!' Eve gasped in sympathy.

'Don't worry about me,' Maggie assured her with a pat on her plump arm. 'Nowt keeps me down for long.'

'Listen,' Eve said, lowering her voice. 'I could have a word in Mr Tindal's ear - see what he can do. They're taking on women in the workshops now - short of men since the autumn.'

Maggie's face lit up with hope. 'That would be canny of you, Eve.'

A week later Maggie started in Number 16 workshop, packing munitions into wooden crates under the huge dusty arc of glass and metal that resounded with the bangings and hammerings of scores of aproned workers.

The tasks were monotonous, the atmosphere noisy, the discipline strict, yet Maggie revelled in the company of the other young women who had taken up the jobs of men now at the Front. Dressed in her anonymous overalls and cap, she felt relief at not being singled out for special attention or abuse as she had grown used to over the past years. To the others she was just Maggie, the girl with the quick tongue and a sharp joke when the foreman's back was turned. No one knew where she lived exactly or what she did after the buzzers blew, but everyone nodded and called in a friendly fashion on her return the following day.

And there was money for Christmas! Maggie came home laden with parcels and treats on Christmas Eve. She had stopped at the shops on Alison Terrace on her way home from work and bought a leg of pork from John Heslop and sausages and black pudding for George's breakfast. It was even more of a sacrifice and treat than usual because meat was becoming scarce - Heslop had secured the pork especially for her. Maggie had felt obliged to promise the butcher that she would attend chapel on Christmas Day.

She had found some second-hand books at the pawnshop for George's Christmas present and stopped to buy roast chestnuts at a brazier on the corner, unable to resist the sweet aroma of the grilled nuts.

A few days before, Maggie had decorated the cottage with holly and red ribbon and hung mistletoe above their bed in the hope of rekindling George's appetite for lovemaking. They had been abstinent for too long, Maggie reflected.

Returning up the hill, she could see the faint glimmer of firelight through the green blackout blinds, beckoning and welcoming her home out of the dark night. Behind her she could still hear the faint melody of a hurdy-gurdy churning out Christmas carols.

Entering the cottage, brimming with holiday spirit, Maggie was dashed to find it empty. The fire had been banked up but there was no sign of George anywhere. For weeks she had been urging him to go out and now she was vexed not to find him in.

Still determined to make it a happy Christmas, she unpacked and busied herself preparing the meat and vegetables for the next day's feast. Stoking up the fire, she boiled up a pease soup and baked bread and currant buns. She was just pulling these out of the oven when the door opened.

She turned to see George standing in the doorway with her brother. He had gone to fetch Jimmy to please her, Maggie thought with gratitude.

'Jimmy!' she cried in delight 'You've come for Christmas! Haway in and sit yourselves down. There's a pan of soup on the boil. I'm that pleased to see you both - thought I'd be seeing in Christmas Day on me own. I've been that busy at work, I've hardly set eyes on you for weeks, Tich.'

She saw him bristle and laughed apologetically. 'Sorry, Jimmy it is.'

George pushed the youth towards the fire and blew on his hands, holding them out to the flames. Maggie sent her brother out for more coal and then sat him down at the table.

'So what you been up to of late?' Maggie asked, her face glowing with the heat of baking.

'I've got summat to tell you, Maggie,' Jimmy said, his face animated as he sniffed the soup. 'You're the first to know - except for Geordie, of course.'

She threw George a quick look of enquiry, but saw him glance away and move nearer to the hearth.

'Well?' she smiled, intrigued.

'I've enlisted with the Fusiliers,' he grinned. 'We've been out celebrating!'

'Celebrating!' Maggie cried in dismay. 'But I thought they wouldn't have you.'

'I'm eighteen now,' Jimmy pulled back his scrawny shoulders proudly, 'and anyways, they've reduced the height for recruits - I'm not too small any more.'

She saw the look of triumph on her brother's lean, childish face and felt a pang of sympathy for him. All his life he had been constantly told he was too young or too puny to do the things he wished, but now he had achieved recognition as a raw recruit into Uncle Barny's old regiment - into the British Army that was guzzling up young men with a voraciousness never seen before.

Her sympathy for him turned at once to anxiety. She rounded on George in annoyance.

'Why didn't you try to stop him?' she accused. 'I thought you'd have better sense.'

"Stop me?' Jimmy laughed. 'It was Geordie gave me the courage to try again.'

'What?' Maggie shouted.

'Aye,' George turned and looked at her directly for the first time since entering. 'I've joined up too, Maggie.'

She stared at him in open-mouthed disbelief, her slim face flushed and framed by tousled dark curls of hair. His stomach lurched as he noticed for the first time in months how pretty she was, how much he wanted her. What a waste of fruitless months, he thought with regret, while he wallowed in depression about his unemployment, his worthlessness. He had been so angry with Maggie for being partly to blame for his sacking and then making him feel doubly inadequate by going out and supporting them with her wages. He was no use as a worker and no use to her either, he had told himself brutally.

So he had been left with no option but to join the war. No longer could he look at the maimed men in the street or even his own damaged brother without pangs of guilt at his safe, directionless life.

'There's talk of conscription coming in soon,' George tried to justify his decision to Maggie. 'I'd be one of the first to be called up anyway as a single unemployed man.'

He saw her flinch at his words and hated himself for inflicting the pain that showed in her grey eyes. But he could not go back on his decision. Joining up had given his battered pride a sudden lift; his life now had purpose again. He had convinced himself that he could best support his comrades by joining them in the trenches. But looking at Maggie's stricken face, George knew that she would never see it that way. The price he would have to pay for regaining his self-esteem might be losing the woman he loved more than anything in the world. They looked at each other helplessly, aware of the gulf that yawned between them.

Maggie felt too sick to speak. Without a word, she handed the soup ladle to Jimmy, then walked out into the night.

Chapter Twenty-Three

Looking back several months later, Maggie could remember little of that Christmas Day in 1915. Jimmy had gone by the time she had returned from pacing the town, body frozen and mind numbed. On Boxing Day, George went too.

'It's all I can do,' he said defiantly. Then, less sure, 'Will you stay here?'

'It's my home isn't it?' Maggie answered robustly. 'I'm earning enough to pay the rent and have a bit put by, so don't bother yourself about me.'

'I didn't want it to turn out like this, Maggie,' George insisted. 'I'll send back money.'

'I don't need your money, Geordie,' Maggie answered proudly. 'Send it to your Billy if you want to send it anywhere.'

And so he had gone, with a brief peck on her turned-away cheek and she had not seen him since.

It was spring now and Maggie had got through the past months by plunging herself into her work at the factory and returning exhausted to the cottage to sleep. New families had moved into temporary huts at the bottom of the hill, drawn to the riverside by the offers of work in the munitions sheds. But she heard their children being told to stay away from her cottage, suspicious of her solitary existence. In their games they called her a witch and threw stones down her chimney for dares.

Maggie ignored the jibes and stayed within the close surrounds of the cottage, working in the garden or reading by the hearth. Her one weekly trip to town was to the penny library on Alison Terrace. Increasingly, she avoided places and shops where she might encounter her family or past neighbours, for she had lost her appetite for sociability. She had grown accustomed to her own company, for at least that was reliable. What, she asked herself, was the point of allowing a new friendship to blossom when the people she loved were always taken from her?

Then her ordered, uneventful life was disturbed by a letter from George. He was writing from camp. His training was over and they were about to be sent to France. Could he see her before he went?

The letter arrived on the Thursday and the following day on her return from work, she found him digging in the black earth of the garden, beyond the spring daffodils. The sight of him in uniform filled her with nervous foreboding, so that her words of greeting lodged in her throat.

"Thought I'd do something useful while I waited,' he grinned at her, unsure.

'If you've dug up me spring vegetables, there'll be hell on!' Maggie replied, unpinning her hat and letting the wind ruffle her black hair. 'Come in and I'll make some tea.'

'I've made some,' George answered, pulling on his army jacket.

'Well, come in and drink it,' Maggie ordered.

They sat either side of the fire, awkward and tongue-tied.

'When do you leave?' Maggie asked.

'Catch the train from Central Station on Monday,' George told her. 'I'll stop at home if you don't want me here.'

Maggie cocked her head and replied thoughtfully, 'Funny how you still call your father's house your home. You haven't lived there in donkey's years.'

'I didn't mean—'

'I know what you mean,' Maggie cut him off and abruptly stood up. 'You'll stay for tea, won't you?'

George stood up too and rummaged in his knapsack. 'I've brought some sausage and sugar - a few other things. You'll not have time to stand in queues.'

Maggie moved around the kitchen, preparing the food.

'Do you see anything of Tich?' she asked.

'Once or twice,' George answered. 'We're in different companies. But he seemed in good fettle when I last saw him.'

'He seems so young,' Maggie sighed. Whereas she, at twenty-three, felt so old, as if she had lived ten years in the past two.

. 'The lad has a stout heart,' George commented. 'You lasses treated him like a bairn for too long, that's all.'

'And throwing him at the Hun will make a man of him, I suppose,' Maggie mocked. 'You lads are all the same, not happy unless you're scrapping.'

'You used to like a fight, remember?' George countered.

'Aye, well, not now,' Maggie replied, tossing the sausage into a heavy pan. 'I want a quiet life. I've done with protestin' and all that.'

'I doubt it,' George grunted.

After they had eaten and Maggie was about to clear the table, George caught her hand.

'Come and sit a while by the fire, Maggie,' he said quietly and led her to a chair.

They sat together while George talked of his months at camp and the men who had become his companions. Maggie watched his face grow animated and realised that he was enjoying his new life. She felt a stab of envy, recognising the heady pull of comradeship. She had experienced it herself among the suffragettes and the knowledge of it had fortified her flagging spirits in prison. Yet somewhere along the way, her ardour had been extinguished, Maggie thought with regret. Or maybe it merely lay untended but smouldering like the embers of a fire that refuses to die...

She looked at George and accepted for the first time that she should not condemn him for what he had chosen to do. The war was hateful, but he wanted to fight not just for his fellow comrades but for his own self-esteem, his own sense of justice. When Pearson's had sacked him they had robbed him of his work and his reason for being; now he had found it again among the Tyneside Scottish.

'Read to me,' Maggie suddenly requested, interrupting George's tales. 'Read to me like you used to - poetry, anything.'

George drew the blinds and picked a book from the mantelpiece and read. From time to time, he would pause to put coal on the fire and then continued his story. Maggie closed her eyes and listened to his strong familiar voice, recounting the words of Dickens.

Sometime in the night, he roused her from sleep on the chair and carried her to their bed in the corner. For the first time in months they made love and George whispered his longing for her, his regret at the wasted period of growing apart.

'I love you, Maggie Beaton!' he declared 'When I come back I'll wed you. You'll not put me off any more, do you hear?'

'I hear,' Maggie laughed and kissed him.

'We should've done it long ago. Why didn't you let me marry you, Maggie?'

Maggie sighed and put her head on his shoulder. 'I was happy as we were - our own little Utopia,' she answered. 'Besides, everywhere I looked, married women seemed imprisoned, unhappy, like our Susan. I didn't want that.'

'It wouldn't be like that with me, lass,' George insisted.

'No.'

'So you're agreed?' he persisted. 'When I come back, we'll get wed?'

Maggie shivered. 'Don't you mean *if* you come back, Geordie?'

George gripped her to him and kissed her hard, as if he could smother her doubts.

'Course I'll come back, Maggie, so you better wait for me!'

They stayed in the cottage for three brief days and nights, like creatures reluctant to give up hibernation. They ate and read and slept and made love and talked of plans for the future. All talk of the war was avoided, but it hung over them, like a storm cloud, intensifying their last bitter-sweet moments together.

On the final morning, George crept from their bed and put on his uniform as the pink dawn light nudged under the sleepy blinds. Maggie watched him dress in silence, clinging to the moment. Soon she would have to get up and answer the blare of the factory hooter. It would be a relief to have the mindless work to do; it was the return to the empty house that she dreaded, more than this parting.

'I'll send you one of them fancy French postcards, lass,' George promised.

'Just come back safe, Geordie,' Maggie implored. 'That's all I want.'

Then George kissed her quickly, urgently, and left. She watched him from the cottage door, fighting down the fear that she might never see him like this again - tall, broad-shouldered, smiling confidently beneath his thick moustache. A sick longing for him engulfed her and nearly made her rush after him. If it would have stopped him going, she would have done so, but Maggie knew that nothing could now keep George here, not even their love for each other.

George looked back and waved. Maggie stood barefoot in the doorway, her hair still tousled from sleep, wrapped in an overcoat. He felt a rush of guilt for leaving her there, alone and sad-faced in the early morning light. Then she raised her hand in farewell and smiled, the warm, confident smile that had won him to her years ago. He turned and marched down the hill with the picture of Maggie in his mind. She was a fighter and survivor, he assured himself, and would be there standing in the doorway to greet him on his return.

Maggie submerged herself in work once more, escaping to the farm to enjoy the lengthening spring days. Clouds of blossom appeared on the fruit trees and were shaken off by brisk west winds. The trees broke into new lush green and the smell of mown grass came once more to the surrounding fields.

She thought of George most in the twilight hours, when the half-light played games with the shadows of trees and walls. Once or twice she was sure she saw his figure approaching up the pathway and rushed out, only to see the shadow disappear as the light shifted and faded from the garden. Often she sat down to write to him but fell asleep exhausted before she had begun. It was easier to cope with living without him by pretending he was just out at a meeting or the pub and would soon be back. If she wrote to him in France, then his being there amid all the danger became frighteningly real. She would write to him soon, Maggie vowed half-heartedly.

It was about the time of the first haymaking that Maggie realised something was wrong. She had been working long hours and had felt an uncharacteristic lethargy. Increasingly, she had to drag her weary body back up the hill at the end of the day. At times she was so nauseous that she had to rush from the workshed without permission, to retch outside.

One day, one of the women followed her out and startled her with the question, 'Have you missed your time, hinny?'

'What do you mean?' Maggie spluttered, colouring hotly.

'Your monthly bleed, lass,' the woman said forthrightly.

Maggie thought, then nodded slowly.

The woman snorted. 'Better be gettin' your lad up the aisle sharpish, then!'

Maggie's mouth gaped open in bewilderment. The woman turned to go but Maggie gripped her arm: 'Do you mean … am I...?'

'Expectin'? Aye, looks like it to me, hinny.'

Maggie went pale and felt her legs go weak. 'My lad's in France,' she whispered.

The woman clucked in disapproval. 'Well you'll have family to help out, won't you?'

Maggie, too ashamed to admit how alone she was, simply nodded. 'But you'll not tell the bosses,' she begged. 'I need the work.'

'I'll not tell,' the woman agreed with a sympathetic look, 'but it'll show in time.'

Maggie toiled home that evening, sick and worried. She was carrying George's child. How could she possibly manage alone, up here, once she could no longer work? At first she cursed him for the seed implanted inside her that now threatened her livelihood. He had always been careful to avoid making her pregnant. But on his last visit they had not been careful, Maggie admitted, they had been reckless in their lovemaking, silently afraid it might be the last time.

Then the disgrace of what she had done overwhelmed her. She was carrying an illegitimate child, a child with no name and probably no home. What would her mother and grandmother have thought of such foolishness? As for her sisters and Aunt Violet, Maggie could well imagine their horror and disgust at the shame it would bring to the family. She knew without asking that they would never take her back now. Even if Susan were to take pity on her, Richard Turvey would never allow her to seek refuge under his roof.

George was the only person she could tell, Maggie realised. She sat down and attempted to write him a letter, breaking the news. But as she wrote the stark words, panic filled her and she crumpled it up and threw it on the fire. Why had she waited so long to write to him?

Maggie looked at his photograph on the mantelpiece and reread the three elaborately decorated postcards that had arrived from France in the last month telling her how much he missed her. Maggie felt encouraged and wrote again. She asked him to send her money so that she could continue to pay the rent on the cottage once she could no longer work. Somehow she would manage until he returned, Maggie assured herself, her optimism growing as she sealed the envelope.

The next day, Maggie posted the letter and willed herself to be patient for a reply.

After a week of attacking exercises, George's brigade was moved eastwards by train and billeted among the ruined houses of Albert. They left the pretty, undulating countryside of neat farms and flowering gardens for a land of stunted woods and muddy farm buildings. They marched past stagnant ponds choked with tins and broken crockery, with only a solitary chateau on the outskirts of the village to relieve the dismal landscape of the Somme valley.

At Albert, the bombed cathedral stood like a stark skeleton among the fields; there was one remaining cafe miraculously serving meals. Everywhere was a maze of telegraph wires. They were draped along hedges and drooped from trees like abandoned washing lines, needing continuous repair after shelling.

For a month they prepared for an offensive. George sweated under the June sun, digging support trenches at the Front and beavering underground, building galleries for the laying of mines. There was constant strafing from the enemy trenches, some of which stood only fifty yards away across the cratered ground, impenetrable fortifications protected by strong barbed wire and deep ditches planted with sharp spikes.

But George volunteered for raids on these trenches on windy dark nights when the wind was blowing from the German lines to theirs. With blackened hands and faces they went on short ten-minute raids to cut wires, damage a communication trench or raid a supply trench and then retreated quickly, with turned-up collars showing white linings so they would not be mistaken for German raiders.

Better to join in such raids than endure the waiting, smelling the fear of impending battle, George thought. Every day there were casualties from machine-gun fire or mortar attacks as they dug, or accidents from gas canisters being transported up to the Front. George had learned to dread the urgent ring of gongs, which meant reaching at once for his gas mask as the breeze brought the poison gas from the enemy trenches. He had caught whiffs of it from attacks on other units and shuddered at the deathly smell that had sent his brother mad.

The wounded would disappear, whisked from dressing station to field hospital, never to be heard of again until weeks later when word might filter back that they were home or deployed in a different battalion - or dead.

A week ago, George had come across Jimmy in Albert on a few days' rest from the front line.

'Champion!' was Jimmy's bright reply when George asked how he was faring. He was a runner between communication trenches.

'Have you heard from Maggie?' George asked diffidently.

'Aye,' Jimmy grinned. 'She sent me some black bullets and a bag of lemon drops. Knew me sweet tooth would be missing them!'

'That's grand,' George tried to smile, though it pained him that she had found the time to write to her brother but not to him.

He thought about her constantly in the dragging hours of inactivity, when the men sat around playing cards or writing long letters home in their cramped quarters. Did she miss him with the same intensity as he missed her? George wondered. Or did her silence mean she had put him from her mind, convinced that he would not return? What if she had found someone else?

George tortured himself with the thought, then chided himself for doubting her love, recalling that last sight of a sorrowing Maggie putting on a brave face at his going.

She loved him, he rebuked himself, but was working too hard to have time to write him letters. After all, Maggie was always better at spouting words than writing them, he thought ruefully. He would hear from her in good time.

'Take care of yourself, lad,' George told Jimmy with a clap on the shoulder.

'Aye.' Jimmy's eyes shone with excitement 'There's summat big on, isn't there?'

George nodded. 'Seems so.'

'Bloody great!' the boy cried.

Yes, bloody it will be, George thought grimly, but said nothing more, not wanting to dampen the boy's enthusiasm. To Jimmy it seemed a huge adventure, a game more thrilling and daring than anything he had played at home with Tommy Smith and his old street friends. What tales he would have to tell!

George could see Jimmy thinking.

'I'll be in the newspapers back home, an' all,' Jimmy said, brimming with pride.

George snorted. 'And how's that, young'un?'

'Lord Pearson's daughter - she took me picture yesterday with the other lads.'

'Alice Pearson's out here?' George asked incredulously.

'Aye. Said she was official like, taking photographs for the army. Just wait till that yellow-bellied Turvey sees me all over *The Journal*. He'll not be calling me names no more!'

The next day George went back up the line. It started to rain heavily, huge thunderous deluges that filled the trenches like baths and turned them to quagmires. It made the daily job of trying to mend walls after shelling even more hazardous and some trenches were so waterlogged they could hardly be reached.

Then in the early hours of 25 June the artillery bombardment they had been waiting for began in earnest. The mortar teams fired and reloaded and fired on the trenches opposite and the Germans answered in kind. But the British assault was incessant and unlike anything George had ever witnessed. After that, it became impossible to repair the trenches and George and his comrades took cover and waited for 'Zero Hour' - their signal to go over the top.

For three days the British bombardment of the enemy continued. The world outside had turned into an inferno of flashing, bursting shells and dense clouds of smoke and dust. George, looking across at the German lines, thought he was seeing the mouth of hell. Everything smouldered angrily while the earth shook with the pounding from heavy guns, the air acrid with the stench of explosives.

'No buggers can survive a drubbin' like that!' said one of the Tyneside Scots. 'Not even Fritz.'

They were ready, every nerve strained by the deafening assault of the past few days. Then word came that 'Zero Hour' had been inexplicably postponed for another two days.

In frustration, George retreated to write to Maggie.

He wrote her a poem, teasing but tender, knowing he would probably never send it.

I long for the lass with the raven hair, with dancing eyes and face so fair.
I long for a drink of Newcastle ale, with its earthy body and froth so pale.
I long for a dance on a Friday night, to hold a lass in my arms so tight.
I yearn for a northern sky that's fine, and a canny row along the Tyne.
I wish for a soak in a hot tin bath, and to hear my brother Billy laugh.
But most of all I long for the girl with the dancing eyes and the raven curl.
I would give up the rest without a care, for my bonny lass with the raven hair.

When someone tried to look at it, George blushed and shoved the damp piece of paper self-consciously into the D.H. Lawrence novel he had borrowed from the subaltern and laid his head down in an attempt to rest. The following afternoon, the battalion colonel paid a final visit to the men. Their mood was confident, for surely the enemy would be completely demoralised by the pounding of the last week.

That night, ladders and bridges to span trenches were brought up to the reserve lines in wagons. George was among those who went out in the dark to cut the final wires for their advance.

The men slept fitfully. At six the next morning, they were given a good breakfast. George looked up at the pale July sky and thought of Maggie awaking in the cottage and stoking up the fire to boil the kettle. She would be going about the mundane routine of getting ready for work, humming to herself and lifting the blinds to blink sleepily at the same summer sky...

He felt a searing pain in his stomach at the thought of her, then beyond the woods came a massive explosion that shook the ground beneath him. Another mine went off on the other side of the front line, and the Battle for the Somme began.

It had been weeks now since Maggie had sent the letter and she had heard nothing. Surely George must have received it by now, she fretted. Was it possible that he was considering his reply, thinking of some way out of his responsibility for their unborn child? Perhaps he, too, would be ashamed of its illegitimate status. Maggie's worry mounted as July wore on and no word came.

Her sickness was passing, but her trim body was beginning to thicken noticeably around the waist. She was thankful for the voluminous overalls at work that helped her to hide her shameful condition.

Then rumours began to filter through of the battles that had been raging in Flanders. There had been fierce fighting and some gains, some stout defending, went the official reports. But the full horror and scale of losses became increasingly apparent as lists of dead and wounded came through at last. Many women at work went home to be faced with the dreaded telegram telling of their husband's or son's death. Black armbands seemed to appear on every other person in the factory and in the street.

Tens of thousands of men had perished. Whole battalions had been wiped out in a single day. Maggie was seized by a new fear for George and her brother Jimmy, who had not written to her for weeks either. She scanned the newspapers for confirmation that they were not among the casualties.

One afternoon on her return from work she glimpsed the postman toiling up the hill. Her heart began to bang painfully in her chest and her stomach turned as the grim-faced man approached. She waited by the gate, outwardly composed but inwardly sick at heart, dreading his missive.

He handed her a small square envelope with a gruff, 'Miss Beaton?'

She nodded, speechless.

'Letter for you. Glad it's not a telegram. I've delivered too many o' them lately.'

Maggie nearly fainted with relief. She took the letter with trembling hands, recognising George's stiffly slanting script.

'Ta very much!' she croaked and fled into the house to read it.

Collapsing into a chair by the hearth, she prised the envelope open with a kitchen knife. Inside was a hasty scrawl from George and a short poem. Maggie read the tender words about her raven hair and laughed and wept over the silly, affectionate verse. She read and reread it.

Pressing it to her lips, she cried aloud, 'Oh, Geordie, I love you, you daft man! Thank God you're safe!'

Later as she was drawing the blinds and settling for the evening, she heard the gate creak open and footsteps approach up the pathway. These days she was more nervous of strangers calling, especially so late in the day. Someone knocked.

Maggie opened the door a crack and peered out 'Who's there?' she demanded.

'Irene,' said a flat voice. 'Irene Gordon.'

Maggie was taken aback by the sudden appearance of George's sister but not

191

altogether displeased at the young woman's approach. They would after all be family soon.

'Come in,' Maggie beckoned, holding wide the door and noting how Irene had George's strong-featured face.

'I'll not stop,' Irene said, glancing in at the cottage warily. 'Me da didn't want me to come but I thought you should know.'

'Know what?' Maggie asked

'We got a telegram last week - about George.'

'What are you saying?' Maggie gulped, numbness creeping into her chest.

'They said he was missing in action,' she answered dully.

'George? Missing? He can't - I got a letter from him today...'

Irene gave her a pained look. She shook her head 'It must've been written before ... You see, he's dead. They sent back his things.'

Maggie just stood rooted in the doorway, gripping the wall for support. 'He can't be dead,' she wailed. 'He can't be!'

Irene pulled a crumpled envelope from her jacket pocket and thrust it quickly at Maggie.

'This came back,' she said shortly. 'Here, tak' it!'

Maggie, taking the letter, saw at once that it was the one she had sent George weeks ago telling him of their baby. It was unopened.

She closed her eyes tight and crumpled it in her hand ' Oh, my God! How can I bear it?'

Irene sniffed at her, embarrassed by her show of grief. 'You would think you were his wife the way you're carrying on. Just think what it's like for me and his da and his brothers - we're his family.'

Maggie was wounded by the woman's insensitive words.

'I was closer to Geordie than family,' she answered defiantly, her eyes blazing with hurt. 'We were going to wed when he came home.'

Irene laughed scornfully. 'George never said any such thing to me. If he'd half cared for you he'd have married you long before.'

'He wanted to,' Maggie insisted. 'It was me who put him off.'

Irene gave her a look of pure dislike. 'Well, if you kept my brother waiting, you've only yourself to blame if you're on your own now. I always told him he was far too good for you. Never did see why he kept going back to you when he could've had any respectable lass he wanted.'

'Get away from here, Irene!' Maggie shouted, trembling with rage and distress. 'I'll not listen to any more of your spiteful tongue!'

'And I'll not stop a minute longer in this wicked place,' Irene retorted. 'I'm glad you never became family - you were a bad influence on our George. You, with your radical ideas. At least you can't touch him now, God rest his soul.'

Maggie's knuckles went white as she clung to the doorpost, determined to keep her composure as Irene hurried away down the path. When she was through the gate, Maggie closed the door and sank against it, letting out a racking sob.

She was unsure how long she cried, crumpled on the stone flags, but when she finally levered herself up and dried her eyes, the sky outside was a dusky indigo. She lit a candle and curled in George's chair by the fire to reread his poem. It was the only thing she had left to give her comfort and reassure her that Irene's terrible doubting words were untrue.

Then, quite suddenly, Maggie felt a strange fluttering in her belly. At first she thought it was caused by her upset, a spasm after so much weeping. Then she felt again the rippling across her stomach and placed her hands gently on the small swelling. Sitting in the pale candlelight, Maggie instinctively knew that she had felt the baby stir in her womb for the first time.

Chapter Twenty-Four

Outside in the frosty courtyard, the workhouse children were singing carols for the Master and his family. They stood huddled in their drab serge suits and pinafores on the steps of the Master's house, warbling about shepherds and the baby Jesus, their breath ascending in frozen clouds.

Maggie could see them as she passed along the open corridor between the infirmary and the dining hall. She was stiff from bending and ached all over from scrubbing the floors of the ward, but she still paused in the cold to watch the determined group of carollers waiting for some small treat for their efforts. Were they all orphans? she wondered. Or were they separated from their parents, locked away in their own wards and schools while their widowed mothers or pauper fathers worked as scrubbers and gardeners, kitchen maids and bricklayers for the workhouse?

Maggie had been inside St Chad's for barely a month, yet it felt like an age since she had done anything else but wash floors in the hospital alongside the drunks and the mad. At first she had been horrified that all patients were thrown together - he consumptives and the mentally sick, the elderly infirm and those with venereal disease - and all looked after by a handful of probationer nurses who were largely pauper girls raised in the workhouse. And then there were the unmarried mothers like herself; young and homeless, spurned by their families or without any relations at all. They were looked upon by Matron and the Master as the most sinful and inferior of them all. This was as near to the children as the staff allowed Maggie and the other pregnant inmates, lest their wickedness contaminate the innocent.

'Idleness breeds sinfulness!' Matron would cry as she set them the backbreaking tasks of cleaning or doing laundry in the hospital, right up until the birth. And there was no luxury of confinement afterwards as there was for married mothers, Maggie thought bitterly. She had seen a girl return to work on the wards the day after giving birth, her baby whisked away without her even knowing if it was a girl or a boy.

Maggie put protective hands over her swollen belly where her unborn baby turned restlessly.

She could hardly recall the summer, after the news of George's death. She had gone around like a pale ghost sunk in mourning for her lover. She had continued working, mechanically, like one of the automated pistons at the factory, acting without thought. Then after weeks of this half-living, she had pulled herself together and walled up her grief for George, forbidding herself to think of him. It was the way she had coped with her father's death as a child.

During all this time John Heslop had been her only visitor. He came to share his sorrow at hearing the news of George's death and asked awkwardly if she needed any help. It had not been obvious then that she was pregnant and Maggie had been far too embarrassed to tell him and so she had sent him away, telling him she could manage quite well on her own. Heslop had not called again.

Once, Maggie had been to try and see Susan, but Richard had been there and refused to let her in and all Maggie caught was a glimpse of her cowering sister surrounded by squalling infants. She had shuddered at the sight of messy motherhood and retreated quickly.

It had not been until November that her pregnancy had really begun to show and then the foreman had told her she was no use to them in such a condition and would have to go. There were plenty of other eager girls who would snatch at her job to pack shells into boxes, he told her bluntly.

First the furniture was pawned and then George's books and the silver frames from Alice Pearson to pay the rent and eat and keep warm during the dark, chilly November days. Then she could pay the rent no longer and Hibbs told her she would have to leave, there was a family from Cumbria desperate for lodgings who were working at the yards. She saw the relief on the farmer's face that he would be rid of her at last, the strange, lonely woman who the children thought was a witch and who he knew had been a troublemaker before the war. Besides, she had lived like a trollop with George Gordon and was now obviously carrying his child and Mrs Hibbs had been badgering him to evict her for months.

Maggie had gone in the only clothes that now fitted her and carrying a bag of precious belongings - a book of poems, the photograph of her and George and the one of Emily Davison, George's postcards and letter, a Bible that had been her grandmother's and her suffragette sash. Looking around the bare cottage that had been home to her and George, she gulped back the tears and lifted her chin defiantly at the children from the huts who had crept up the hill to see her go.

'Witch!' they shouted at her as she laboured down the pathway.

'Whore!' shouted one of the older boys she had once drenched in urine.

Maggie stopped by him, her eyes ablaze. 'I'm a suffragette!' she roared at him and marched on with as much dignity as a woman eight months pregnant could muster.

She knew of no one who might take her in. The Samuels had sold up and sailed to America at the beginning of the war and none of her family would have her under their roofs. In desperation she thought of her former friend Rose who might just take pity on her until she had the baby, even though Rose had not spoken to her since the arson attack on Hebron House and her cohabiting with George.

She went to the house in Elswick but found it occupied by a young family.

'They moved away,' the new tenant revealed. 'We've been in nearly two year.'

'Where did they go?' Maggie asked, her hope fading.

'Seaside somewhere, for the old mother's health - or so the neighbours told me. Don't know where.'

Maggie had wanted to faint on the pavement as it suddenly struck her how alone in the world she was, how estranged from everyone by the life she had chosen to lead. For a moment she thought of Heslop but could not bring herself to go begging to the preacher. He was a chapel man and in his eyes she would be a fallen woman bearing a bastard child. She could not bring such disgrace to his doorstep. Besides, his cleaner Mary Smith would soon tell everyone in Gun Street of the depths to which she had fallen.

No, it was best if no one from her old neighbourhood knew, Maggie determined; she would go quietly into the workhouse, have her baby and return to the outside world with few the wiser. She had heard whispers of such scandals before, where foolish, luckless girls had disappeared for a few months and returned without fuss as if nothing had happened, the illegitimate babies adopted or disposed of in orphanages.

So Maggie had gone to the Poor Law Guardians and thrown herself on their mercy. The next day she had been admitted to St Chad's and given a bed in a dormitory among other female paupers.

Her first surprise was to find the old prostitute, Millie Dobson, among them, wheezing and with a face like parchment. She let forth a string of abuse on seeing Maggie, blaming her for the state of her daughter Annie who was wasting away in the infirmary, her delicate health ruined by her stint in prison for suffragism.

'And I'm too old to make a living on the streets,' Millie had snarled.

Too drunk, you mean! ' another woman scoffed.

Millie swore foully at the other inmate and Maggie had to intervene to prevent them fighting there on the dormitory floor.

'I'm very sorry about Annie,' she said simply. 'I didn't mean her to get involved in my campaign.'

'Aye, well, where's all your high ideals got us now, eh? In the bloody workhouse, that's where!' Millie spat. 'And look at the state of you.' She pointed at Maggie's belly. 'Whose is it?'

'George Gordon's,' Maggie said, flushing.

Millie snorted. 'Men! They're the source of all trouble. Not owning up to it, is he?'

Maggie winced 'He never knew. George died in France before 1 could tell him,' she told Millie quietly.

The haggard woman was silenced. She put a hand on Maggie's arm and squeezed it, then turned away and said no more.

But after that, she and Maggie had helped each other, sharing their chores and any extra food or warm clothing they could scavenge. Over the past month, the old, foul-mouthed prostitute had become her closest friend, Maggie thought ruefully, and with the friendship had returned a deep determination to carry on striving for something better. After all, any life would be better than the one she was living now, Maggie told herself as she stopped to listen to the carol singing. Unaccustomed tears stung her eyes as she heard their young voices singing the Christmas hymns of hope and she thought how each one of them had been brought into the world in the same way as her baby would be, struggling and pushing from the womb. Maggie was filled with a strange mixture of fear and expectancy.

Millie appeared beside her.

'Got a piece of bread for you,' she hissed. 'Annie couldn't manage it at tea.'

'You have it,' Maggie answered.

'You need it more than me, hinny,' Millie insisted, patting Maggie's stomach.

Suddenly the baby within gave an answering kick, so lively that Millie felt it too.

'Eeh, it's wantin' out!' the older woman cackled.

Maggie laughed and put her hands over the moving baby. It kicked again as if it were playing a game with her. If only George were with them to enjoy the moment, Maggie thought. Then, all at once, tears were streaming freely down her cheeks and she was sobbing uncontrollably.

'Eeh, hinny, whatever's the matter?' Millie asked, putting a concerned arm about her thin shoulders. 'Get yourself inside this minute, you're shakin' with the cold!'

'I can't do it!' Maggie cried to her in distress, weeping into her shoulder.

'There's nowt to be afraid of,' Millie assured her. 'Just a bit of pain and shoving and then it's all over.'

Maggie looked up at her, still weeping, and shook her head. 'It's not the birth I'm frightened of,' she sobbed.

'What then?' Millie asked.

'It's having them take me baby away!' Maggie admitted at last.

It had come to her with such force as she stood watching the children sing, that the only thing she really cared about was the baby - George's child, her child. She had denied her feelings for the baby for so long, desperate not to grow attached to it, knowing she was to lose it. Yet this unborn child was all she had left to remind her of George and it was the only reason she wanted to go on living. Only this baby made sense of her shattered life.

'You'll get over it,' Millie tried to comfort. 'You're just a young lass, you can gan out in the world again and find a new life. The workhouse's just for the likes of me and Annie at the end of the road. It's no place for a lass like you who can make summat of herself.'

. But Maggie shook her head violently. 'No! I'll never get over losing George and I can't bear the thought of losing the bairn too - it'd break me heart.'

'There's nowt you can do about it, hinny,' Millie replied with a fatalistic shrug.

'Aye, there is, Millie.' Maggie looked at her defiantly and vowed, 'I'm going to keep it!'

Maggie went into labour on Christmas Day. She thought it was indigestion from the luxury of having a scrap of meat for dinner with a heap of turnip and stuffing and potato. The annual treat of beer had been dispensed to the men and somehow a couple of jugs had been smuggled to the women's tables and Millie Dobson was supping determinedly. The staff seemed content to let them have their way this once and were turning a blind eye to the drinking.

'I think I've eaten too much.' Maggie nudged Millie and clutched her stomach as a spasm of pain seized her again.

'Have a sip o' beer to settle your digestion,' Millie cackled and pushed her cup at Maggie's lips.

Maggie gave a groan of pain and turned her head away. Millie put a hand on Maggie's swollen womb and said, 'It's not the food, hinny, the bairn's startin'. Could it not have waited till after our dinner!'

With a large belch, Millie hauled herself to her feet and helped Maggie to hers. Alerting one of the attendants, they left the dining hall and mounted the stairs to the labour ward above the infirmary. Along the icy corridor, Maggie gripped her friend by the arm.

'I'm that scared!' she whispered.

Millie patted her hand and told her to be quiet.

Two rows of cells made up the ward; the woman on duty who did as a midwife led Maggie past these to a room with a plunge bath.

Take your clothes off in here and wash yourself down,' she ordered. 'I'll get the bed ready. You,' she turned to Millie, 'can go now.'

'Please, I want her to stay,' Maggie said in panic.

'She's been drinking,' the midwife said with distaste.

'I can still help,' Millie protested. 'I've had one of me own and helped plenty other lasses down the quayside.'

'She's me auntie, please let her stay,' Maggie begged.

The woman nodded reluctantly and left them alone.

After a tepid bath, Maggie was dressed in a coarse, loose gown and led by her friend into a tiny cell where brown paper had been laid out on the thin mattress. A towel was tied round the iron bed frame.

'What's that for?' Maggie asked in trepidation.

'To hang on to, hinny,' Millie told her. 'Pull it when you feel the pains come.'

Maggie's courage nearly failed her, then she felt another spasm and lurched for the bed, doubling up in pain.

'Haway, let's get you on the bed,' Millie ordered.

'I'd rather walk around,' Maggie protested restlessly, eyeing the hard bed with its paper bedding in alarm.

'We can't have this bairn of yours born in the corridor!' Millie was sharp. She helped lever Maggie up. 'Be quick before the Kaiser comes back.'

Maggie grinned weakly at Millie's irreverence and set her teeth determinedly as she felt another contraction coming on. Millie covered her in a thin blanket and rubbed her back to ease the pain. From far away the sound of singing and the wheeze of a harmonium drifted up to them.

'"God Rest Ye Merry Gentlemen",' Millie snorted. 'Aye, well, make the most of it, hinnies, 'cos it'll be gruel the morra!' she shouted "Cept for the Master and his missus. They'll be supping into the New Year, that pair.

Maggie was torn between laughing at Millie's commentary and crying out at the mounting pain. The purgatory seemed never-ending as she twisted and moaned and shifted position and tried to get comfortable. It grew dark outside and an attendant came in to light the gas lamp.

Later in the evening, Millie began to sing in her raucous, tuneless voice.

The midwife appeared and reprimanded them for making a noise.

'The other patients are trying to sleep! You'll have to leave if you can't keep quiet.'

'What time is it?' Maggie asked, already exhausted.

'It's nearly midnight,' the nurse replied sternly and shut the door firmly behind her, leaving them in a sallow pool of light from the gas lamp.

'I've been here hours!' Maggie cried in dismay. 'How long does it take?'

'Could be all night, hinny,' Millie sighed. 'Don't worry about the old cow, the Kaiser. We'll make a din if we want to and there's nowt she can do but twist her face.'

Maggie lay, alternately shivering and sweating, trying to fight the spasms that gripped her whole body and left her weeping with weakness. She was terrified by what was happening to her and baffled as to how the baby would force its way out of her. No one had told her exactly how a baby was born and she had been too young to witness the birth of either Helen or Jimmy. Yet she was past caring, only wanting the ordeal to be over and the pain to stop.

Suddenly, in the middle of the night, she felt a gush of liquid between her legs and thought her insides were spilling onto the bed.

'What's happening?' Maggie screamed. 'Am I dying?'

Millie was roused from a groggy half-sleep and investigated.

'Your waters have broken,' she announced. 'It'll not be long now.'

Maggie sank back on the bed in fear and confusion.

The night crept on endlessly and it seemed to Maggie that she had lain there an eternity and still the baby did not come. Yet the contractions that convulsed her body became increasingly severe and more frequent and she shuddered and cried out and tried to follow Millie's urgings.

'Take deep breaths, hinny! Don't fight against the pain.'

'It's killing me!' Maggie screamed.

'Pull on the bloody towel!' Millie shouted.

Maggie did so and felt something hard pushing down between her legs. It felt as if her whole body was trying to empty itself.

'What's that, Millie man?' she cried, terrified.

'The bairn's on its way. Don't push yet!'

'What do I do?' Maggie wailed.

'Sing!' Millie shouted

'Sing?' Maggie gasped in disbelief. 'What the hell am I supposed to sing?'

'Anything. Just don't push till you feel another spasm!'

Maggie began a breathless rendition of *The Women's Marseillaise*. Millie joined in and they sang in the eerie silence of the night: 'To Freedom's cause till death, We swear our fealty. March on! March on! Face to the Dawn, The dawn of Liberty!'

This brought the furious midwife to the cell.

'Shut up!' she ordered. 'At once!'

Maggie cried out in pain and the woman moved quickly to the bedside and slapped her across the face.

'There's no need to make such a fuss!'

'Leave the lass alone, her baby's coming,' Millie protested. 'You should be helping.'

The angry attendant turned on her. 'And you can shut up or get out, do you hear? Don't you go telling me my business.'

Millie scowled and Maggie thought she might start a fight there and then.

'Please!' she begged. 'Help me!'

The midwife turned to her and began issuing abrupt instructions. Millie returned to rubbing Maggie's back.

'Support her,' the midwife ordered. 'When you feel the contractions again, this time push as hard as you can.'

'Push what?' Maggie asked, bewildered.

'Down below, you idiot lass,' the woman snapped.

A moment later, the tightening began and grew into a searing pain that enveloped her stomach and pressed on her back. The midwife stuffed a piece of rolled-up rag into Maggie's mouth and told her to bite on it.

'Now push!'

Maggie pushed and bit on her gag, her dark eyes wild with terror. She sank back into Millie's arms, but almost immediately felt the pangs of labour claim her exhausted body once more.

'Push, girl!' the nurse ordered.

Amid the waves of nausea, Maggie could now feel the presence of her struggling baby between her legs, but try as she could, the infant would not dislodge itself from its position.

The midwife peered closer in the poor light.

'It's breech.'

Millie went to inspect too. 'Fetch the doctor then.'

'We can manage,' the woman answered testily.

'Maggie can't!' Millie protested 'She's all done in.'

'She's not trying hard enough,' the midwife complained.

Millie advanced on her with hands clenched. 'She'll die and lose the bairn too unless she gets help. That may not matter to you, but by heck it does to me! Now send for the doctor before I put this fist in your gob!'

The woman fled from the cell and Maggie lay back whimpering, faint from the effort. All she was aware of was Millie holding her hand and stroking the damp hair from her face, murmuring encouragement.

Finally a young doctor appeared, dishevelled from sleep and smelling of stale wine. He rummaged around in his bag and pulled out a fearsome instrument.

Maggie was galvanised from her stupor. 'What are you ganin' to do with that?' she yelled.

'I'll have to deliver the baby with forceps,' he said curtly. Maggie could see his hands shaking as he waved the metal pincers towards her.

'No,' she whispered, then screamed in fear, 'No! Don't touch me with that!'
The midwife moved swiftly to hold her down. 'Shut up, you little slut,' she hissed. 'Nobody speaks to the doctor like that.'

'Have you ever used these before?' Millie demanded The doctor gave her a dismissive look and carried on. 'You never have, have you?' Millie accused.

'Out of my way, woman,' the doctor snapped and shouldered her aside.
The next moment, Maggie was aware of red-hot pain between her legs as the young physician came at her with his implement and skin tore under the pressure from the forceps and that of the wedged baby. The agony engulfing her whole body was worse than anything she could remember of her torture in prison. She did not know if she would die first from the pain the doctor inflicted upon her or from suffocation from the nurse who pressed the gag in her mouth to muffle her screams.

She wanted to cry out to Millie but could not. All she could see was her friend's horrified expression as she watched the delivery, powerless to help. Maggie closed her eyes and sobbed in agony and terror as she felt her insides rip.

Perhaps she passed out in the end, she could not remember. The assault seemed to last for ever and then the baby was out between her legs, lying in a bloodied heap. Maggie summoned the last of her energy to raise her head and look at it. The doctor was already washing his hands in the bowl of water in the corner.

'Look at the bloody mess you've made of her!' Millie screeched at him in fury.

Maggie's head pounded and her whole body throbbed. But she spat out the gag as the midwife set about cutting the sticky cord that bound her to her baby.

'Is it a girl or a boy?' Maggie asked weakly, trying to make sense of the pink scrap of life lying on the soiled paper, still slimy with blood.

The woman did not answer. She mopped up the baby and wrapped it in a piece of torn sheet.

'Let me see it,' Maggie begged, panic beginning to seize her. The hateful woman was going to remove her baby without even telling her what it was and she was too weak to do anything to stop her. 'I want to hold my baby!' Maggie cried.

Galvanised by her cries, Millie waded in and grabbed the infant. It wailed for the first time as she plucked it from the attendant's grasp and bundled it into Maggie's waiting arms. Millie fended off the midwife with her bulk while Maggie explored her new baby. The doctor took one look at the truculent women and left quickly without another word.

Maggie gazed at the tiny wrinkled face that trembled and bleated at her like a protesting lamb. Unwrapping the sheet she touched the delicate limbs and body, so soft under her rough fingers, so perfectly formed.

'It's a lass,' Millie commented.

Maggie nodded, quite speechless with triumph and pride, for her daughter was beautiful despite the marks left by the doctor's violent forceps.

'What you going to call her?' Millie asked.

Maggie's mind was a blank. She had been sure of having a son to replace George and he would have borne his father's name. But here in her arms lay a girl and Maggie was filled with an unexpected delight.

At that moment, the baby opened its eyes wide, dark pools that fixed on her, trusting, expectant, demanding, as if this tiny newborn infant awaited the answer.

'Well, it's Christmas,' Millie pointed out, 'so give the bairn a Christmas name - Mary or Christina.'

Maggie gazed into the solemn eyes and knew at once that her daughter was strong and resilient and must have a name that would match her own unique character.

'Christabel,' Maggie said, her mind made up, 'like Mrs Pankhurst's daughter.'

Millie cackled with delight. 'Another wee fighter, eh, bonny lass?'

'She'll need to be,' Maggie smiled sadly, leaning forward and kissing Christabel lovingly on her head of matted dark hair. The baby stopped her quavering cry and began to make small smacking sounds with her tiny lips.

Suddenly Maggie felt her body seized by convulsions again. 'Please God, no!' she whimpered.

Millie was at her side at once, gripping her shoulder.

'It's just the afterbirth, hinny. Nowt to worry over,' she reassured her.

'I must take the baby away now,' the midwife said abruptly, shaking off her discomfort at the intimate scene she had just witnessed.

Maggie cuddled her daughter tightly to her in fear.

'Leave them be the night!' Millie rounded on the woman and took Christabel protectively while the afterbirth was ejected from Maggie's womb.

The attendant, weary of battling with the defiant pair, bundled up the waste in the soggy brown paper and took it with her to be burned.

'I'll be back before Matron comes round,' she warned as she left.

Millie returned Christabel to her mother.

'Here, why don't you try and feed her - she's clammin' for a bit feed.'

'Show me,' Maggie urged, pulling her gown free.

Millie saw her friend was too weak to sit up, so she guided her onto her side and snuggled the baby in beside her. She helped the baby onto Maggie's small round breast, gently prising open the searching mouth. Within seconds the hungry infant had latched onto Maggie and begun an instinctive sucking.

Maggie watched in wonder, weak but elated. She stroked her daughter's cheek and felt an answering enthusiasm in her sucking. She had never imagined that such overwhelming happiness could spring from the simple, mundane act of feeding. Maggie gazed at her baby and felt love for her flooding every inch of her battered being. Never before had she loved so unconditionally or completely, Maggie thought, trembling at the realisation.

In that dismal, badly lit cell, still smelling of the stench of childbirth, Maggie wept with exhaustion and joy and love and trepidation. She looked at the sweet contented face at her breast and cuddled her closer still.

'My Christabel,' she whispered in wonder, kissing her again.

Millie sniffed and Maggie glanced up to see her friend was crying.

'We'll change the world together, me and Christabel,' Maggie smiled. 'She's already changed mine, anyways.'

She saw Millie wipe her nose vigorously on her sleeve and then Maggie closed her eyes, weary beyond words, but content, fulfilled. She fell asleep still feeling the rhythmic trusting tug of her daughter's suckling.

It was daylight when she woke. Grey light seeped in at the high barred window above her bed. Every inch of her ached and Maggie thought for a moment she was back in prison.

Then she remembered.

She turned on her side to find the space beside her empty and cold. She could still smell her, but Christabel was gone. Maggie tried to move, seized by panic, but the pain that shot down her back and between her legs was paralysing. She could see blood seeping into the blanket - her blood.

The room was empty. I'm dying, Maggie thought numbly. They have left me to die. Then a far worse pain gripped her and caused her to cry out in agony.

'Christabel!' she screamed. 'Millie! They've taken my baby!'

Chapter Twenty-Five

Maggie lay for weeks in a dingy dormitory recovering from the birth, hardly aware of the bleak empty winter days. The ward was filled with old women who babbled to themselves and wet the floor in their confusion, while Maggie lay on a corner bed with her face to the wall and gave in to her deep despair. She had nothing left to live for. Relentlessly fate had taken everything from her - her father, her mother, Granny Beaton, her beloved George; even her suffragist cause was dead. And finally they had taken from her the only precious thing that she had to call her own, her sweet daughter Christabel. Her physical pain was nothing compared to her mental torment and she seemed content to waste away in that cold, stinking, disinfected ward for abandoned old and insane paupers.

Her grip on life would have loosened faster if it had not been for the interference of the old whore Millie Dobson. From time to time Maggie was aware of Millie snatching moments at her bedside while under orders to scrub down the floor. Her craggy, bulbous face would peer over her in concern and speak softly. Maggie remembered little of what she said, only that the tone was gentle compared to the sharp barks from Matron or the disinterested grunts from the pauper nurses.

'You must get your strength back, hinny,' Millie encouraged. 'You lost a lot of blood after the birth and they had to stitch you up like a burst pillow. That doctor should swing for what he done to you, hinny. I could tell he hadn't the first idea what to do. Should've left it to us women.' Millie held her hand. 'It's no surprise you cannot walk. But don't let them bully you, hinny, you'll be back on your feet when that poor body of yours is fully rested. I'll bring you summat extra to eat the night.'

Maggie lay half listening, her eyes staring out at the blank pale green wall, not caring if she never walked again. She had grown used to the excruciating ache in her back that throbbed whichever way she lay and the searing pain between her legs when she tried to urinate.

Perhaps the Matron was right, Maggie thought listlessly, and her suffering was her own fault, brought on by her wickedness. In the workhouse they called her proud and sinful and told her that God was punishing her for her past selfish life. When she had screamed for her daughter, they had slapped her and told her she would never be allowed near the child, for fear the girl would turn out the same.

'As it is, there'll be badness running through that child!' Matron had prophesied 'Her only hope is to be brought up strict by godly folk - aye, and kept away from the likes of you.'

'What's left for me?' Maggie had whispered in desolation.

'You?' Matron had snorted. 'You're beyond saving.'

Maggie had felt her spirit shrivel at the woman's cold judgment and began to wonder if what she said was true. Had she really been too proud and stubborn in her life, too sinful? Had her persistence and defiance in the name of suffragism been a monstrous show of arrogance and ungodliness? The Master and Matron of St Chad's firmly believed so and the spawning of a bastard child was merely confirmation of her deep wickedness. They held out no hope for her and swiftly Maggie had sunk into a blackness that surpassed even what she had experienced in prison.

A worried Millie came and stood over her as she lay motionless and gaunt on the narrow bed and did not cry for her stolen baby. She was frightened that Maggie had lost the will to live and she fretted as to what to do for her friend. For Millie had grown fond of the strident, humorous, spirited girl who had befriended her in this grim fortress when others had shunned her. Now, more than ever, she needed Maggie; this past month she had gained much comfort from being near her and she was determined she would not lose Maggie.

One early spring day at the end of February, Millie sneaked into the workhouse garden and plucked a small bunch of crocuses. She found Maggie curled up on her bed, her cropped black hair limp against her papery skin, her eyes huge and hollowed. Millie realised with shock that Maggie was quite deliberately starving herself to death, this time not for any great cause but because she had lost all her causes.

'Look,' Millie said, thrusting the small delicate flowers under Maggie's pinched nose. 'Spring's here.'

Maggie closed her eyes.

'Thought you'd like 'em - being your colours, hinny.'

Maggie's eyes opened again, but her look was vacant.

'Purple and white, with green stems,' Millie persisted. 'You know, suffragette colours.'

Maggie stared at them for a long while as if trying to remember something. Millie was not sure, but she thought she detected a glistening in the young woman's eyes. Maggie's lips opened and mouthed a silent thank you, but she did not attempt to take the flowers and her grey eyes retreated behind hooded lids.

Millie shook her gently. 'Listen, hinny, it's time you stopped your grieving and started to take a bit more interest in things. You're nowt but skin and bone. You've got to get your strength back, hinny.'

Maggie opened her eyes. 'Why?' she whispered. 'I've nowt to live for.'

Millie was suddenly very afraid. She was losing Maggie and the truth made her angry. Millie seized her friend's bony shoulders and shook her so that the iron bedstead squealed.

'How can you say that?' Millie demanded. 'Your daughter is alive somewhere and being looked after, even if it's not by you.'

Maggie looked startled by the sudden violence in her voice. She raised her head from the pillow. 'She might as well be dead,' she answered bleakly, 'for I'll never see her again.'

'You don't know that,' Millie cried. 'You said you were going to fight for her. Well, where's the fight in you now, 'cos I can't see it?'

Maggie tried to turn her head away. 'Just leave me alone, won't you? Go and bother someone else.'

Millie leaned over and spoke inches from her face. 'I don't have anyone else,' she hissed. 'Annie died a month ago and now you're the only family I've got! Don't you die on me as well, you little bugger!'

Maggie's face went tense with shock. 'Annie?' she gasped. 'Dead?'

Millie nodded, unwanted tears pricking her eyes. She was breathing hard and could not trust herself to speak again.

Suddenly Maggie's face crumpled like a small child's as it dawned on her that Millie had lost her only daughter too, finally, irrevocably lost her. She had been far too deep in her own grief even to think about asking after Annie and now it was too late.

Wordlessly, Maggie reached up and put her arms about the desolate woman in an attempt to comfort her and felt the sturdy arms grip her with an answering warmth. In that bleak dormitory they clung to each other and wept their pent-up tears until the noise brought shouts from the other patients and a stern reprimand from the attendant in charge.

'Hoy, you!' the woman shouted. 'Get away from her.'

'I'm that sorry,' Maggie sniffed as Millie pulled away. Millie nodded.

Maggie looked down and saw the crocuses had been crushed. She picked them up and kissed them. The two women looked at each other in silent understanding.

'You'll not give up the fight, will you?' Millie whispered as the nurse marched up the ward to remove her. 'For little Christabel - for all us lasses?'

'"Freedom's cause till death!"' Maggie croaked a snatch of the suffragette march with a weak smile.

Millie was hauled away, leaving Maggie shaking and tearful on the bed. But as Millie glanced back at the door, she saw with triumph that Maggie had swung her feeble legs over the side of the bed and was contemplating trying to stand.

It was many weeks before Maggie walked and months before she was fit enough to carry out menial tasks around the workhouse. Yet that day in February, when Millie's robust kindness had penetrated her blackness, had been a turning point. Maggie pulled back from the abyss and determined to carry on living.

At twenty-four she had the creaking body of a much older woman and the limp she had acquired as a result of the brutal birth appeared permanent. But by the end of the year she was able to work in the kitchens, peeling vegetables and scrubbing tables and sneaking out scraps of food to Millie. The two were inseparable, sharing their meals and jokes among the simple and senile, trying to keep up their spirits in their imprisonment.

Their meals had become increasingly meagre as the effects of rationing and hardship from years of war took their toll. Inside the workhouse it was possible to live from day to day as if there was no war in France, so narrow was their existence. Yet Maggie noticed the changes - the decrease in the number of men catered for in the kitchens, the drop in numbers of vagrants seeking a night's shelter, the shortage of trained staff and the number of women inmates working the gardens. Most obvious was the deterioration in rations - the absence of any meat, the tasteless bread, the thinness of the porridge and the scarcity of sugar.

On New Year's Eve 1917, Millie became maudlin on the bottle of beer Maggie had smuggled out of the kitchen to celebrate the new Reform Bill, giving the vote to women over thirty.

'Votes for women at last!' Maggie toasted the news.

'You still can't vote, mind,' Millie reminded her. 'You're too young.'

'Aye, but it's a step forward,' Maggie insisted 'We're being listened to at last.' She took a triumphant swig and passed the bottle back to her friend.

'Nineteen eighteen,' Millie sighed. 'What'll it bring? An end to the Kaiser's war and bad food?'

'Maybes revolution, like in Russia,' Maggie speculated. 'People can only take so much of butchery and hard labour and going without. They see their men being killed off and their bairns dying of lack of food and the bosses have still got it all their own way. Folk won't put up with that for ever.'

'Hush!' Millie ordered. 'Don't let the Kaisers round here catch you talking of revolution.'

Maggie pulled a face and .took another sip from Millie's bottle. 'George would have been celebratin' the workers' overthrow in Russia, so why shouldn't

I?'

Suddenly Millie put an arm about her. 'You still miss that lad of yours?'

Maggie set her face grimly. 'I don't think about him any more, he's in the past. Mind, I still worry for me brother Jimmy.' All she knew was that he had survived the summer battles on the Somme, for a postcard had arrived the day she was evicted from Hibbs' Farm. But that was an age ago and all she could do was pray for his safety. 'No, the only thing I want out of nineteen eighteen is to have me bairn back, and I don't even know where they've taken her.'

'Why don't you leave and find yourself work in the factories or summat?' Millie suggested.

'I'll not leave without you, Millie, you're me family now,' Maggie answered.

'Eeh, hinny, I couldn't gan back to the streets at my age. I'm better off in here, for all it's a prison.'

'Then I'll stay with you,' Maggie declared. 'I've been licking Matron's boots to get a job clerking in the office - they're short since that lad was called up and I've got the skills.'

'But you could do that outside,' Millie said, baffled as to why Maggie should want to stay now she had recovered.

'But if I work in the office I'll find out where they've taken Christabel,' Maggie said with urgency, her grey eyes lighting with determination.

Millie shook her head and drank the dregs. 'So that's your plan?' she grunted.

'Aye,' Maggie nodded. 'To think me bairn is already one year old. I sometimes try and imagine what she looks like, Millie. She must be dark-haired like me and George, but does she have his dark eyes? Or perhaps she's like our Susan and me dad with fair hair and blue eyes.' She turned suddenly to Millie, the tears springing to her eyes. 'It's terrible not knowing,' she whispered.

Millie hugged her tightly. 'I know, hinny, I know.'

By the spring, Maggie had wheedled her way into the office and set about organising the files and books that had been left in a shambles by a series of temporary clerks and untrained attendants. The Master was ageing and no longer took an interest in the running of the workhouse; he was almost a recluse in his house across the courtyard, confined by gout and lethargy. Maggie worked for the Senior Relieving Officer who kept short hours and drank from a bottle of whisky he kept locked in his desk. He seemed surprised by Maggie's efficiency and diligence and was soon content to let her work alone while he became increasingly absent.

In March, Maggie heard rumours of dissatisfaction among the Board of Guardians that the workhouse was being badly run. She overheard an argument between the Master and Matron about the lack of trained staff and the shoddiness of equipment.

'I've got inmates sleeping on the floors with only two nurses to control nearly three hundred women on the night shift,' Matron complained. 'It's Bedlam!'

'Then take some of the older girls from the children's wing as probationers,' the Master replied. 'I don't want to be bothered with your problems, woman, I'm a sick man.'

Matron had stormed off and Maggie had buried her head in her work in case anyone suggested she should turn nurse.

Disappointingly, she had found no reference to Christabel in the dusty registers and it occurred to her that the place was so lax they may not have recorded her birth or her subsequent removal. All she had to go on was a curt remark from the midwife who had been there at the delivery, saying that her baby had been taken from the workhouse soon after birth but she did not know where. Still, Maggie determined to go on looking.

Then in April a storm blew up around her when it was discovered that funds had gone missing. Matron warned her that she was under suspicion and that the Board of Guardians would be interviewing her the following day. Until then she was suspended from working in the office. Maggie waited, furious at the accusations and ready to give any fat Guardian who pointed a finger at her a piece of her mind.

She was ushered into a stark room in the Master's house where three of the Board awaited her.

'Margaret Beaton,' Matron introduced her and left, banging the door.

Maggie stared boldly at the men before her. Then suddenly the man on the end raised his head and Maggie gawped.

'Mr Heslop?' she gasped and coloured in confusion at seeing the butcher.

'Maggie!' Heslop spluttered. 'What in God's name are you doing here?'

'You know this inmate?' the middle Guardian asked sharply.

'Yes indeed,' Heslop said, standing up. 'Please, Maggie, come and sit down.'

The others muttered their disapproval but the butcher ignored them.

Maggie found herself shaking, all her resolve to be insolent gone. She answered their questions quietly and at the end John Heslop asked to question her alone for a few minutes. He led her out into the Master's garden and sat her down on a wrought- iron bench surrounded by fading daffodils.

'Tell me what happened to you, Maggie,' Heslop asked gently, his whiskered face full of concern.

Maggie told him of her struggle to stay outside the workhouse and then how she had given in for the sake of the baby.

'Why didn't you come to me for help?' he chided.

Maggie could not look at him. 'I was too ashamed,' she admitted. 'I thought you would have despised me. Like the rest of my family.'

Heslop tutted. 'I could have done something for you,' he insisted. 'It would have been better than this.' He waved at their surroundings. 'St Chad's is a godless place. That's why I agreed to come on the Board two months ago, to try and change things. If only I'd known.'

They sat in silence for a moment while two thin pigeons swooped about looking for food.

'I'll have this business about the money cleared up,' the preacher continued. 'The Relieving Officer is under suspicion but the authorities here would have preferred to blame an inmate. Then we must get you out of here.'

Maggie looked at him directly. 'I don't want to go. Not until I've discovered what's happened to Christabel.'

He briefly covered her hand with his own. 'They won't let you keep her. The child may very well have been adopted by now.'

Maggie drew her hand away and glared 'They've no right to keep her from me! I want to bring Christabel up as my daughter so she knows where she comes from, who her father was, to know that she's loved.'

She saw Heslop flush at her directness.

He gripped the back of the bench. 'Let me find you a position outside the workhouse,' he pleaded. 'Since inheriting my uncle's house in Sandyford, I'm in need of a housekeeper myself. I've delayed moving into it because domestic help is so difficult to find these days.'

Maggie was touched by his offer. 'You're a kind man, Mr Heslop, but all I ask of you is help in finding Christabel.'

The butcher sighed and shook his greying head. 'Come and keep house for me, Maggie, and I'll do what I can to discover your daughter's whereabouts.'

Maggie smiled for the first time and touched his hand fleetingly. 'Thank you, Mr Heslop.' As he stood up, she added, 'There's just one other thing you should know.'

Heslop looked at her.

'I promised Millie Dobson I would take her with me when I left.'

'Millie's here too?' he exclaimed. 'And Annie?'

Maggie shook her head. 'Annie died over a year ago. Millie's on her own, apart from me.'

Heslop answered without hesitation. "Then she must come and live in Sandyford too. I seem to remember she could cook soup after a fashion.'

'Between the two of us we can manage,' Maggie smiled. Walking back with the lanky butcher, feeling the spring sun on her shoulders, Maggie felt a tug of optimism. She no longer believed Matron's pronouncements that God was punishing her for her wickedness, for such a God would not have allowed Millie to be there to comfort her in her blackest hours. And it could just be possible that this benign God had sent Heslop to rescue her from the workhouse and set her on the road to finding Christabel...

Chapter Twenty-Six

'Why don't you go and see her, Maggie?' John Heslop suggested.

They were sitting having tea in the drawing room of the house in Sandyford, the August sunshine spilling in through the lace curtains of the bay window. Maggie had still not grown accustomed to living in such a beautiful house, with its view onto the ornate railings and pocket gardens of the terraced row opposite. She inhabited the attic rooms with Millie but John Heslop insisted that they share their meals and that the women should have the use of the drawing room in the afternoons and evenings.

Increasingly, while Millie went out at night to find company in the town pubs, pretending to Heslop she went to visit a cousin, Maggie would spend her free time reading - newspapers, books, pamphlets - whatever she could lay her hands on. It was as if she had been starved of words for two years and now could not devour enough of them.

She looked up from the newspaper which had been telling her of the new offensive by the Allies on the German front line.

'She'd not want me to,' Maggie countered 'Not after all this time.'

'I think she would. You wouldn't have to explain about anything, Susan knows you're working for me.'

Maggie looked across at the gaunt-faced man in the winged brocade chair by the unlit fire and marvelled at how he tried to solve everyone's problems. Often in the past she had thought of him as interfering, trying to order people's lives when they did not want it, trying to save them from what he saw as their mistakes. But there was a deeper quality to John Heslop that Maggie had discovered while living under his roof. He cared nothing for the wagging tongues at chapel who disapproved of his taking in the women from the workhouse; he just went ahead and did what he saw to be right and just.

A week ago he had come home from the shop in the west of Newcastle to genteel Sandyford fulminating about Richard Turvey's treatment of Susan. The feckless Londoner had finally run off with Helen, having pawned most of Susan's possessions and left his wife with three young infants to care for alone. Maggie could well imagine the fear and humiliation that her husband's going had brought Susan. It would be the final shattering blow to all her unattainable dreams of respectability and prosperity. Yet Maggie dreaded returning to her old neighbourhood, for fear of stirring up past ghosts. It suited her to live quietly and industriously in distant Sandyford where she was known only as the housekeeper at number 28, biding her time until she found Christabel.

This was now her most important mission and she was growing impatient with John Heslop's half-hearted attempts to find her. All he could discover was that the baby had been removed shortly after birth from St Chad's to some other institution; indeed many of the infants had been scattered to different homes when the nursery wing had been requisitioned for war wounded. Heslop told her to be patient and that tracing the child would be easier once the war was ended. Until then, Maggie wished to live a life cocooned from the pains of the past, suspended in limbo until that time when her daughter would need her.

To go and comfort Susan now, to see again the places she associated with her divided family, her growth to womanhood and suffragism, her life with George, would only bring the painful past back to haunt her. Not for one moment did she allow herself to reflect on what might have been had George survived the Somme. Such thoughts only came to her in sleep, tearing at her new-found peace and waking her sweating and weeping in the night.

'Susan would think I had just come to lord it over her,' Maggie said, shaking her newspaper irritably. 'And I couldn't face going back to Gun Street anyway, not without Mam and Granny Beaton there.'

'You wouldn't have to. Susan and the children are living with your Aunt Violet,' John told her.

'Aunt Violet's taken them in?' Maggie exclaimed.

'She's been a lonely woman since your Uncle Barny died last year,' Heslop replied .'I think it gave her the excuse to make her peace with Susan.'

Maggie snorted. 'Aye, and make Susan feel beholden to her forever.'

Heslop said nothing but the look he gave her showed Maggie he thought she was being unfair. Her annoyance grew.

'Well, she would never have taken me in when I was carrying George's baby,' she said, and saw the pink spots of anger or embarrassment flood John's cheeks as they did whenever she mentioned her dead lover.

'You'll never know because you were too proud to go to anyone for help,' he replied sharply. 'Besides, she'd probably view Susan's predicament differently.'

Maggie sprang up, allowing the newspaper to cascade to the floor. 'Meaning what?' she demanded 'That my baby was worth nothing because she had no legitimate father?' She glared at the preacher's aghast face. 'Tell me, was it better to be married to a creature like Turvey who flaunted his adultery with Helen under Susan's nose and made her life a hell or to reject the sham of marriage like I did and live with a man because I loved him and he loved me?'

' 'm not going to judge you,' John replied tersely.

'Why not? Everyone else has!' Maggie cried. 'George would never have been shunned and condemned for spawning an illegitimate child like I was. But an unmarried mother is the lowest of the low in our hypocritical society. Men can do as they please while women are dependent on their charity or cast beyond the pale!'

'That's nonsense,' John blustered, standing up and clasping his hands in front of the empty grate as if a fire burned there. 'You talk as if women have no power at all and yet they are running our factories in the war effort, they run the home, our churches. . .' His voice trailed off at the sight of Maggie's contemptuous face.

'Aye, on behalf of men,' she replied with scorn. 'The power is still all yours even if some of us do have the vote. We might fight for a hundred years but nothing will change because men don't want it to and women like Susan and Helen just allow men to carry on having it their own way. They lie down and let lads trample all over them because they think they're inferior and don't expect any better, because society tells them they're capable of doing nowt beyond the bed and the kitchen stove!'

John flushed puce at her outspokenness. 'Maggie, you're so full of anger,' he fretted, 'but we're not all Richard Turveys, believe me. I admire the capability of women and I encourage where I can. Didn't I help you in your suffragism, trying to keep you from prison?'

Maggie saw his distress and tried to control her temper. 'You did help me and I was grateful that you hid me at the mission. But you only did that out of friendship for my mother, out of common kindness, not because of any great conviction for the women's cause. You made it plain you were unhappy with my involvement as I grew more militant. Remember the time you came to me at Arthur's Hill and told me to renounce my beliefs?' Maggie reminded him.

She knew he remembered well the time he had burst into her home with

George and urged her to give herself up. Until now she had never alluded to the painful episode. Now the memory of it seemed to hang between them like poisoned air.

Maggie gripped the back of her chair and challenged him with her look. 'Unless you fight against the inequality between us, you condone it and therefore support it. You're kind and considerate and I would never insult you by comparing you to the Turveys of this world. But the powerlessness we feel is just as strong here for me and Millie, we're still dependent on your charity for a roof over our heads. We know if we don't both behave ourselves - improve ourselves - we'll be back in St Chad's.'

He stepped towards her and she saw anger in his face for the first time. 'Is that what you think? That I only took you in out of charity? That all I want to do is improve you like some sanctimonious reformer?'

'Aye! Why else would you take in an old whore and a fallen woman with a criminal record to boot? So you can reform our wayward characters, of course, save our souls. Aye, and score some extra points with the boss in heaven, isn't that it?'

John reached out and grabbed her from behind the chair, seeming incensed by her words, and Maggie felt a flicker of fear. He pulled her towards him and she froze as his bony hands pinned her arms. She almost screamed, but he began to speak in a low urgent voice.

'It may have been charity in Millie's case, but not in yours,' he growled. 'I care for you, Maggie Beaton, care for you deeply. Surely you're aware of that by now?' His brown eyes seemed to burn with a desperation that she should believe him. 'I want to marry you, Maggie!'

Maggie gawped at the man before her. He was still the gaunt-faced, middle-aged butcher she had known all her life and yet he was different, his expression that of a younger man, full of eagerness and uncertainty and fear of being repulsed.

Maggie gulped back her astonishment. 'Please let go of me.'

He dropped his hold at once, but his eyes still beseeched her.

'I know there are many years between us but we share interests in common. It would be no form of slavery, I promise, more a chance of freedom - to follow your own causes or to help me in mine. All I want to do is cherish you, Maggie, and you would never have to fear a return to the workhouse or poverty again. These past months with you here - well, they've been the happiest I can remember. I'd find it very hard to return to the loneliness of my past life. I'm asking you, Maggie, to consider becoming my wife.'

All Maggie could do was to stare, for once quite lost for words. John's quiet plea had diffused her anger but left her deeply shocked. Never once had she guessed his feelings for her. To her, he had never been more than a family friend - of her mother's generation - who had been kind to them all and helpful to her in particular. This declaration of love, for that was what it was, dumbfounded her. How long had John Heslop loved her? Maggie wondered faintly. Just these past months? Or much longer - since her suffragette days? Had he loved her all the time she had lived with George and suffered to see her with another man? Was that why he flinched every time she mentioned George's name and seemed reluctant to find George's child?

Maggie felt sudden revulsion at such thoughts. She did not love John Heslop! How could she love a man as old as her father would have been, who according to Susan had almost married their mother? His proposal was monstrous!

Maggie backed away from him. 'No, I couldn't. . . don't ask me. I don't love

211

you!'

She stumbled towards the door and wrenched at its shiny brass doorknob. Without looking to see John Heslop's expression, Maggie escaped from the sunlit room and rushed out of the house, not even stopping to put on a coat or hat. She ran three streets before she could stop shaking, then she slowed and forced herself to breathe more easily.

As she calmed down she realised she had been wrong to vent her anger and frustration at the world on the well-meaning butcher. It was not with men like Heslop that she quarrelled but with the Pearsons and the Turveys and the masters of workhouses and the uncaring landlords and bosses who misused their power and held women in such low regard. But it had stirred up something deep in John Heslop and prompted him to declare himself to her. Now she had a stark choice: marry a man she did not love or leave his employment, for they could not carry on as they were as if nothing had been said.

Maggie felt anger again that he should have spoiled their easy relationship and her new-found tranquillity, for she, too, had enjoyed the past months of companionship and quiet industry.

Twenty minutes later she found herself jumping a tram heading towards the west of the city, down towards the forest of cranes and grey glinting sheds. She had no idea what she would say to her estranged sister, but Maggie suddenly needed to see her. Susan was the closest member of her family left and Maggie recalled the childlike feeling of going to Susan when things went wrong. Her elder sister had always been the one to fuss and scold and comfort the younger ones and at that moment she yearned for the comfort and familiarity of her sister's mild scolding - anything to blank out John's disturbing proposal.

To her relief, Aunt Violet was out at the park with Susan's two older children, enjoying the late summer sunshine. Susan came to the door, balancing a large baby on her hip. She looked years older, the pink bloom quite gone from her pasty face, her hair carelessly piled on the back of her head.

Susan stared at her in silence for a long moment, as if she had seen a ghost.

'Haway, man Susan, and let us in, I'm not the tickman,' Maggie teased.

At once, her elder sister burst into tears. Maggie bustled her inside and closed the door on prying neighbours. She steered her into Violet's kitchen and pushed her into a seat, lifting the baby up to inspect it.

'Who's this then?'

'Bella,' Susan sniffed in reply. 'She's fifteen months.'

Maggie gave the infant a swift kiss, but she wriggled from her hold and staggered across the kitchen floor, whining at her mother. Susan reached for a bottle of milk that was keeping warm on the stove and flicked a few drops onto her wrist to ensure it was not too hot. Bella grabbed it greedily from her hand and began to suck, leaning back into the crook of her mother's arm.

Maggie watched, trying not to imagine Christabel in just such a homely scene. She would be older than that now, walking properly, perhaps in her first pair of shoes … The thought tugged painfully at her insides.

'I hear you're over at Heslop's,' Susan broke into her thoughts.

Maggie flushed as she thought of her recent flight from his presence. 'Aye, he gave me a job a few months back.'

Susan stared at her with puffy eyes.' Where did you disappear to? I tried to find you up at Hibbs' Farm but they told me you'd left long ago. Course I'd heard about George but I thought you'd still be around somewhere. Have you been away?'

'Aye, to hell and back,' Maggie joked to hide her discomfort. 'Why were you looking for me?'

Susan bowed her head.

'Susan?' Maggie asked, moving closer. 'Are you all right?'

Susan's shoulders shook as she sobbed and the baby spluttered on her milk and began to protest.

'Oh, be quiet, you little pest!' Susan shouted at the whingeing child.

'Here, let me,' Maggie said, pulling the girl and her bottle off Susan's lap and plonking them on her knee in the opposite chair. Bella looked at her wide-eyed and uncertain. 'I'm your Auntie Maggie, hinny, but don't believe any tales your mam or Aunt Violet tell you.' Bella gave her one more assessing look, then settled to drink her milk.

Susan spoke tearfully, her body crumpled and round-shouldered with defeat. 'I was that desperate,' she whispered. 'Richard pawned everything - *everything!* When I complained, he started to beat me, not just once or twice but regular like and in front of the bairns.'

Maggie was horrified. 'That terrible man! I thought the least he was doing was providing for you. What about that job of his he was always bragging about?'

Susan looked bitter. 'He got the sack. Pretended he hadn't, but word soon got back to me that he was spending all his time in the pub or betting on street corners. It was then I took over the second-hand clothes from Helen - I'd been too busy with the babies before. She'd run Mam's business down to nothing, always in the boozer drinking with Richard. So I started doing the rounds again, collecting, then selling clothes round the quayside. I'd take the bairns and be out all day.' Susan gave a shuddering sob. 'One day I came back and actually caught them at it - Helen and Richard.' She looked at Maggie with haunted eyes. 'In my bed!' she hissed. 'In Mam and Dad's old bed!' Susan began to sob again. 'They were too drunk to crawl out of it. So I got the bairns and brought them up here.'

Maggie cringed at her sister's words, furious at her selfish sister Helen for causing so much distress but even angrier at the hateful Turvey who had all but destroyed their family.

'I never want to see him again,' Susan sniffed. 'Her neither. And to think how I did everything for that selfish lass, stood between Mam and her that many times! I must've done something wrong somewhere along the line ...'

'Don't say that!' Maggie reproved. 'You weren't to blame for any of this. Helen was always one. for taking what belonged to others, she was never satisfied just being herself. But Turvey 'll just dump her when he's used her and she'll realise her family weren't so bad after all.'

Susan wiped away tears with the back of her hand and sat up straighter.

'You know, Aunt Violet thinks now that he's not even her nephew. She never did hear from his mam after the wedding. Thinks he might have met the real Richard Turvey somewhere and just taken on his name - sponged off his relations.' Susan gave a harsh laugh. 'To think I was married to a hoaxer and you were right about him all along.'

Maggie vowed silently that she would never voice her suspicions that Turvey had caused her arrest and brought on their mother's death, or got George blacklisted on Tyneside, for she did not want Susan to carry the burden of that guilt too. It was time for them to forget Turvey for good.

'If I ever set eyes on that bastard,' Maggie fumed, 'I'll string him up by his bollocks from the High Level Bridge!'

Susan glanced up in shock. Her face was taut with disapproval, then unexpectedly she started to laugh. 'Eeh, Maggie, I can see you haven't changed!

I hate to admit it, but I've missed your quick tongue around the place. The number of times I've backed off from Richard for fear of being hit and told myself that you would never have put up with such carry-on. I used to wish I'd been born you.'

Maggie looked at her sister in amazement. 'You shouldn't wish that,' she answered gently. 'Besides, it's not a life many would choose.'

She glanced down at Bella's soft brown curls and her snub nose, breathing noisily as she sucked the last of the milk, and felt an overwhelming sense of loss for her own daughter. It felt so natural and right to be holding a child in her arms and she knew instinctively that when she had to hand Bella back, her arms would ache with emptiness. She had experienced the feeling so many times over the past eighteen months; rather than growing less with time, her desire for Christabel increased.

'I don't know how long Aunt Violet will put up with me and the bairns,' Susan said, her face creased in worry again. 'And to think I was that stubborn about wanting to move back to Sarah Crescent. How I'd be thankful for anywhere to call me own.'

'Why should Violet want rid of you? You're company for her and she needs someone to nag since Uncle Barny passed on,' Maggie smiled encouragingly. But she saw her sister's worried look and knew how she must fear her insecurity.

'Aunt Violet's been good to me,' Susan defended her. 'But I'm that frightened for the bairns if anything should happen. I couldn't go into the workhouse, Maggie,' she whispered, her eyes wide with terror.

And Maggie thought suddenly that Susan would probably never survive in a place like St Chad's, separated from her children. She would die a slow death from the degradation and daily humiliations. Maggie shuddered as she remembered.

It was then she realised she had it within her power to do something positive for her sister. She could help her financially and practically - if she accepted John Heslop's offer of marriage. Maggie's heart sank at the prospect and she knew that she would be marrying the butcher for hard-headed reasons, but once she had entertained the thought, it became easier to contemplate. She had sworn to harden her heart and never love anyone again after George died and they took Christabel from her. But she did not love Heslop and so when she lost him as she would - he being so much older - there would be no pain.

And one other exciting thought spurred on her decision. Once respectably married to the butcher, she would be able to apply to adopt Christabel. They might never allow her near her daughter while still a disgraced unmarried mother, but how could the authorities object to adoption by a respected businessman who was also a Methodist lay preacher and a Guardian of the Poor Law? Marrying John Heslop was her best chance of finding and securing Christabel, Maggie realised.

'I can help you, Susan,' she offered.

'How?' Susan asked, her face hopeful.

'Well, to start with I could help you with the clothes business,' Maggie suggested. 'Or you could leave the bairns for me and Millie to look after while you go round the houses. You'd look less like a pack of gypsies if you didn't have them tagging on.'

Susan gawped. 'Is that you speaking, Maggie? You never used to be bothered with bairns.'

Maggie flushed. She kissed the top of Bella's head. 'I'd put up with your devils - if you'd trust me not to turn them into little suffragettes and revolutionaries by the time they gan to school.'

'I wouldn't trust you at all!' Susan laughed. 'Still, it's good of you, Maggie, and it would be a grand help to me. But wouldn't Mr Heslop mind you filling his house with bairns?'

Maggie cleared her throat and looked away. Now was not the time to share her news with Susan. 'He's a good man, I'm sure he won't mind me helping out,' she answered.

Susan grew animated for the first time, showing a glimpse of her old bustling self.

'If I can just manage till the end of this war, then Tich'll be home and able to help bring in some money.'

Maggie's heart lurched. 'Do you hear from Jimmy?' she asked excitedly.

'Aye, once in a blue moon, but he has written. They're optimistic that this time they're going to push the Boches back to Germany.'

'Did he ever mention about George?' Maggie asked hoarsely.

Susan glanced away. 'Just that he'd seen him shortly before the Somme. He said there were that many of them killed they never found all the bodies, just buried them in mass graves. Likely that's what happened to George.'

Maggie shuddered and got up, handing Bella quickly back to Susan.

'I'm sorry,' Susan said, 'but you did ask.'

'Aye,' Maggie nodded. 'I wish I could put it all from me mind but sometimes he comes back to me that strongly.' Maggie stopped herself. She must finally forget George if she was to have peace of mind in a future with John Heslop. She was thankful to have known love with a man and not abuse and fear like Susan, but now it was time to stop grieving for George Gordon and to look ahead.

Susan stood looking warily at Maggie, with Bella straddling her hip once more.

'I'm sorry I wasn't nicer to George,' Susan apologised quietly.

'Aye, well,' Maggie sighed, 'we'd all do things differently if we had our time again, no doubt. Anyways,' she smiled, 'you bring the bairns over to Sandyford the next time you're collecting clothes and leave them with me.'

'Ta, Maggie,' Susan smiled back. 'Maybe I'll see you at chapel one of these days,' she suggested with a touch of her old brusqueness.

Maggie laughed at the veiled reproof. 'Maybes you will,' she answered and left smiling. There had been too much heartache among her family for too long and she was glad that she had made her peace with Susan. They at least could try to make amends for their past quarrels.

As Maggie walked back through the streets of Elswick, she realised that it was John Heslop who had urged her to go and see Susan. He was a perceptive man, Maggie admitted with a blush. She began to feel uneasy about returning to the house at Sandyford. Recalling the way she had fled from the house, crying that she did not love him, she doubted whether John would have her back, let alone agree to marry her.

Arriving in trepidation, she found the house empty. She prepared a cold supper for them in the kitchen and then sat, waiting for John or Millie to return.

It was nearly dark by the time she heard the front door open and close. John's footsteps went first to the drawing room, then the dining room and then approached the kitchen. Maggie stood to meet him.

The blinds were drawn, but Maggie had not lit the lamp, and the only light was from the flickering fire.

'Where have you been?' John asked, his voice curt, his face hidden in shadow.

'To see Susan,' Maggie answered quietly. 'I said I'd try and help her.'

'I see,' he replied. 'So what will you do? Go and live with your sister?'

Maggie raised her chin. 'I would like to accept your proposal of marriage,' she said, 'if it still stands after the way I ran off this afternoon like a deserter.'

John heard the self-mockery in her voice and smiled in relief.

'Of course it still stands,' he said and walked eagerly towards her. 'Maggie, I'm so happy—'

'There's just one thing,' Maggie said, stopping his advance. 'I've always been one for plain speaking, so I might as well say it now.'

'What is it?' John asked anxiously.

'The doctor at St Chad's,' Maggie explained, her throat drying as she spoke. 'He said I couldn't - I wouldn't be able to have another baby. I'm too damaged, you see.' Maggie found her eyes swelling with tears as she admitted aloud the bitter truth. 'He blamed it on my times in prison, said the force-feeding had weakened me and it was all my fault. It was nothing to do with the way he butchered me with his instruments, of course!' Suddenly Maggie was convulsed in sobs, her whole fragile body shaking with the disappointment. She had never repeated any of this to anyone, not even to Millie, for she had wanted to deny it.

Immediately, John had his arms round her and was pulling her towards him. His old-fashioned jacket smelt comfortingly of mothballs.

'It doesn't matter,' he insisted. 'I wouldn't put you through childbirth again. I couldn't risk losing you. If you want you can have your own bedroom.'

Maggie peered up at him in the wavering firelight.

'Why are you so understanding?' she said, almost accusingly. 'Don't you want a child of your own?'

She felt him tense, then he spoke very low.

'Twenty years ago, before I moved to Benwell, I was married. My wife was dark and spirited like you, but she wasn't strong in body. She died giving birth.' His voice broke as the long buried pain resurfaced. 'The baby died too. I lost them both.'

'Oh, John,' she spoke his Christian name for the first time. 'I'm that sorry. I never knew.'

'That's why I moved - sold my old business in Howdon and came to West Newcastle. I - never liked to talk about it. It's the first time I've spoken of them for years. I felt such a sense of failure, you see, of being responsible.'

'You poor man,' Maggie said softly and reached up to touch his face. 'Was it a girl or a boy?'

'A girl. I named her Emily after her mother.'

Their eyes met in deep understanding and Maggie felt closer to him than she could ever have imagined.

'I know you don't love me, Maggie, and I can only guess why you're marrying me,' he said quietly. 'But for me, it's different. God is giving me a second chance of happiness. Emily was taken away so soon, but now I've been given the gift of caring for you, at an age when other men are thinking of retirement. You don't know how young that makes me feel! And perhaps in time you'll grow a little fonder of me.'

Maggie's eyes pricked at his hopeful words and she felt a stab of guilt at her self-seeking reasons for becoming his wife. Yet he knew how she felt and still wanted her and had confided in her his great and painful secret about his dead wife and child. How heavy had been his burden of guilt all these years for being the cause of his wife's pregnancy and death, Maggie thought in pity. The least she could do was comfort him.

'You'll not lose me so easily,' she promised him gently and reached up to brush his cheek with a kiss.

It was only then that she felt the wetness of tears that had spilled down his face in the dark.

John's arms went round her more tightly in a hug of gratitude and they stood holding each other comfortingly, until they heard Millie stamping down the basement steps and bang in at the back door.

Chapter Twenty-Seven

Maggie and John were married in a quiet ceremony at the chapel on Alison Terrace at the end of September. Susan and her children and Aunt Violet attended, along with their old neighbour Mary Smith who still cleaned the butcher's shop. Millie had bought a flamboyant hat covered in mock birds for the occasion, which to Maggie's amusement gave her Aunt Violet something to criticise.

Apart from a handful of chapel members who came to watch - those who did not disapprove of the match between the lay preacher and his young bride - no one else attended.

Maggie, with Susan's help, had altered a purple dress from the clothes stall and embellished it with white beaded lace at the collar and cuffs.

'It's the colour of mourning,' Susan complained with disapproval when Maggie rejected the pink satin dress that she had wanted her to wear.

'I've never worn pink,' Maggie protested. 'Purple's my colour.'

'I thought all that suffragette carry-on was over now women have got the vote,' Susan huffed.

'Only women over thirty,' Maggie had reminded her. 'We still can't vote. Besides, there're plenty other causes need taking up. Women can't stand for Parliament yet, and there's so much inequality in the workplace, barring married women from good occupations. And women like you should have more rights for yourself and your bairns, like child allowances—'

'Oh, for goodness sake, stop your speeches!' Susan groaned. 'It's two preachers we'll have in the family, not one!'

But Maggie knew that Susan approved of her marriage to John, for she had always respected the lay preacher. Her sister had been unable to hide her astonishment at John Heslop's wish to many Maggie but she had welcomed the idea with enthusiasm. It was a contrast to the disapproval that Susan had shown on hearing of Maggie's illegitimate child. She had told Maggie she should forget about the search for George's child and be thankful that John Heslop was prepared to take care of her. Maggie had been hurt that Susan did not understand her yearning for Christabel, but she was not going to let their differences come between them this time. Susan, after all, had suffered enough herself.

As she pinned on the lace, ordering Maggie to stop fidgeting, Susan said, 'I'm not surprised at you marrying a much older man.'

'Oh?' Maggie queried. 'It surprised me.'

'No,' Susan shook her head and took another pin from the padded cushion on the floor. 'You've never had much time for younger lads. I remember you once saying that lads were all like spoilt bairns who never grew up.'

'Well, aren't they?' Maggie answered with a grin.

'Aye, maybes,' Susan laughed.

There was a silence while Susan finished, then she looked at her sister reflectively. 'I know you loved George Gordon but you never married him. It's as if you've been waiting for a man you could respect. A man like ...' Susan broke off and looked away.

'Like who?' Maggie demanded

'No one.' Susan began to bustle about, clearing the discarded clothes. 'It was just a daft thought.'

'Tell me,' Maggie insisted. 'Haway, Susan, it's not every day of the week you get philosophical.'

'A man like our dad,' Susan said quietly.

They stared at each other, Susan adding hoarsely, 'After he died, you never seemed to care much for men. You've never really got over his dying, have you?'

Maggie felt her heart stop at the suggestion, shocked to hear the truth spoken by her sister whom she had always regarded as too unimaginative to guess how she had felt all those years ago.

Quite overwhelmed, Maggie rushed from Violet's parlour and out into the back yard. In the back lane she stopped, her chest heaving for breath as if she had run a mile.

Was Susan right? Maggie wondered, her eyes smarting. Had she bottled up her grief for her father all these years, denying her sense of betrayal at being left behind to fend in a cold unjust world? It was true that all her childhood memories were bathed in a distant sunlight that never seemed to return after his abrupt death. As a ten-year-old, she had been hurt, bewildered and angry at his sudden desertion. Had she turned this anger against the world around her, a world she saw as dominated and ruled by men? Maggie searched for the truth.

Well, if that was so, she thought, then it had been put to good cause in the fight for justice for women. Brushing back the tears that brimmed in her eyes, Maggie determined there and then that whether Susan was right or not, she would carry on fighting the injustice that she saw, believing that her father would have approved. After all, he had been made homeless as a child in the Highlands and was brought up by the strong-minded Agnes Beaton to care about his people. And Alec Beaton had passed on to her, Maggie realised, a deep feeling for fairness and justice.

And although she did not love John Heslop, could never love any man as she had loved George Gordon, Maggie realised that she was content to be marrying him. He offered her companionship, intellectually and emotionally, and he would tolerate her causes. And once they were married, she felt sure he would redouble his efforts to find Christabel.

At the marriage ceremony Maggie promised herself to John Heslop without regret and would have been almost joyous in mood had she not caught sight of Irene Gordon standing in the street afterwards, watching. There was a pack of small children waiting around the door, greeting them with shouts of, 'Hoy oot your silver, mister!'

While John good-naturedly obliged by scattering a shower of coins into the road for the children to scramble after, Maggie stared at the dark woman across the street. She found the brutal reminder that George would never be the man at her side upsetting. She cursed the wretched Irene for turning up to spoil her wedding day, just as she had come to blight her life with the news of George's death all that time ago.

Maggie determined to push the incident from her mind and enjoy the rest of the day and it was a small but jovial party who returned to the house in Sandyford. Though rationing reduced the fare to potted meat sandwiches, John had commissioned a wedding cake at great cost, decorated with silver horseshoes, which was eagerly consumed with the tea.

Mary Smith talked nonstop about her son Tommy in the Royal Navy and her hopes that he would soon be home. There was an air of optimism about the war. There had been no airship attacks on London for weeks and Tyneside no longer experienced the scream of the Zeppelins upriver or the vibrations from anti-aircraft guns. Bulgaria was suing for peace with the Allies and it seemed only a matter of time before the Kaiser would do the same.

For their honeymoon John had arranged a visit to a farmhouse up the Tyne valley for a few days, as it was difficult to travel far. The farmer was a fellow lay preacher and his wife had agreed to take them as guests. Rationing, it appeared, was not as severe as in the towns, and Maggie relished the freedom to walk the hills and fill her lungs with fresh country air. Her progress was slow as her limp still gave her trouble, but John seemed content to walk at her halting pace.

One day they borrowed a horse and trap from the farmer and went on an expedition further up the valley. Stopping to devour their picnic of cheese and pickles and homemade bread that tasted like real bread, Maggie spotted a large mansion hidden in a dense spread of trees and bushes below their viewpoint on the moor.

'That's a canny-sized house,' she commented.

'It's Oxford Hall,' John told her. 'The Pearsons' country retreat.'

Maggie felt the food in her mouth turn sour and found she could eat no more. 'How do you know?' she asked.

'I've been on walking holidays out here many a time - tramped all these hills. I can remember the hall being built. There were scores of men working on it.' John stopped munching as he saw Maggie's hostile expression.

'Must you go on hating them for ever?' he asked gently. 'You'll have no peace of mind until you stop.'

Maggie was stung by the reproof. 'I don't need you to preach at me. Pearson's treated us like scum after me dad died and if they hadn't blacklisted George he would never have gone to France and ...' She saw the flicker of hurt in John's eyes, but ploughed on. 'And they did all they could to stop women's emancipation. Did you know Herbert Pearson was one of the twenty-three MPs who tried to stop the bill going through? And as for Alice Pearson, well, she was the biggest betrayer of them all.'

John was quick to challenge her. 'She befriended you once. Perhaps it was your arson attack on her home that turned her against the cause. Has that ever occurred to you?'

Maggie flushed and glared at him hotly. 'Her heart was never in it. She just enjoyed lording it over the others in Newcastle society.'

'Perhaps she did,' John acknowledged, 'but nevertheless she did you a great personal service.'

'You mean arranging me escape from the nursing home, I suppose,' Maggie said begrudgingly.

'Yes, that - and paying for you to recuperate there in the first place.'

Maggie stared at him in surprise.

He nodded. 'It was thanks to Alice Pearson that you were able to recover after your first imprisonment. What do you think your chances of regaining your health would have been if you'd had to return to the likes of Gun Street?'

Maggie was dumbfounded. She had never known of Alice Pearson's intervention, assuming the Movement had paid for her nursing. Her mouth dried and she could not speak as the truth hit her - the stark realisation that the Pearson woman had probably saved her life, for she had entered the home desperately weak and deeply depressed after the weeks of force-feeding. In return she had agreed to burn the woman's home because the Pearson men were implacably opposed to women gaining the vote. Was it any wonder that Alice Pearson had become disenchanted with the local militants, Maggie thought, and by all accounts pleased to see her go to prison for arson?

Maggie stood up, her small figure seeming lost in the vast landscape of browning bracken and purple bell heather.

'I wish I had known,' she sighed deeply.

'She didn't want you to know. She only told me in confidence during one of her visits to the mission,' John explained. 'She said she didn't want you to think she was trying to buy your trust or friendship, she wanted to earn it. It struck me she was a very lonely woman, isolated within her own class. I probably shouldn't be telling you all this now, but you're still so bitter, Maggie, it might help you see things differently.'

Maggie looked away into the distance, to the house of the family she had grown to hate with a passion. She had no idea what had happened to Alice Pearson except that she had gone to France to photograph the troops and Hebron House had been turned over to the military while the MP and his family moved up here to their country mansion.

'Miss Alice gave funds quietly to the mission too,' John continued. 'She was never one for grand gestures.'

Maggie gave him a reproachful look. 'Like me, you mean?'

John shook his head. 'Perhaps she never had the courage to do the things you've done - few of us have,' he smiled. 'But there are other ways of fighting for what's right, Maggie, and you shouldn't judge the rest of us so harshly.'

Suddenly Maggie reached out to him and John stood and went to hold her.

'I'm sorry,' she whispered as she put her arms about his neck. 'I've never meant to criticise what you've done. I've always admired your work at the mission, the way you treat people all the same, no matter where they come from or what they've done. It's what I like about you most, John.'

He held her more tightly and kissed her hair.

'Come, let's forget the Pearsons and go home,' he urged.

That autumn, Maggie accepted a part-time position at the offices of the Women's Co-operative Guild to occupy her time, while Millie took on the role of housekeeper and a new cook was appointed. On Saturdays, Maggie helped Susan down on the quayside with the second-hand clothes and used her new-found status among the middle-class of Sandyford to procure clothing for the business. But the task that occupied her most was the search for Christabel. She thought of little else all day and her sleep at night was filled with dreams of finding her daughter and plagued by nightmares of losing her.

Sometimes she would wake to find John had come into her room to discover why she cried out in her sleep. He would stroke her forehead and stay by her side until she fell asleep once more, but he was always gone when she awoke in the morning.

He spent hours at St Chad's, trawling the records and interviewing the staff in the children's wing, but the matron and the midwife who had assisted at the birth had both left without trace and the records were a mess of inaccurate and missing entries. The Relieving Officer who had disappeared with Poor Law funds seemed to have taken registers with him, or disposed of them to cover up a web of embezzlement.

They visited orphanages and grim asylums for the feebleminded, but no one had any information on a Christabel Beaton, born on 26 December 1916.

'It's as if she never existed!' Maggie howled after a forlorn visit to an institution in Gateshead.

She had scanned the peaky faces of the children in the nursery for any family resemblance or likeness to George or herself, but had seen none. They gazed at her from blank, sad eyes, penned into iron cots or sitting on the linoleum floor playing with pieces of rag, skinny and uninterested. She had never seen such subdued infants; none of them appeared capable of speaking when she asked them their names. Maggie left swiftly, their dismal whimpering echoing down the dingy, urine-smelling corridors.

There were times when she caught a look in her husband's eyes, as if he had begun to doubt whether the child had ever existed. If it had not been for Millie's forceful confirmation that she had held the baby in her own arms, Maggie suspected John might have persuaded her to give up the fruitless search.

Then one day in early November, he came home with some news. Maggie was sitting at the roll-top desk in the corner of the sitting room, bathed in a pool of light from the gas lamp on the wall bracket above her. As soon as he strode into the room, she knew something had happened.

'I've found Lily Smart, the midwife who was there at the birth!' he told her.

'Where?' Maggie said, springing out of her seat.

'She's living in lodgings on Pandon Bank. A woman who comes into the mission lodges in the same tenement. Lily Smart is still helping out at lie-ins, by all accounts.'

Maggie shuddered to think of the heartless woman bullying other young mothers through their labours.

'I imagine she has to, to make ends meet,' John said, seeing Maggie's look of distaste.

'Well, let's go to her now!'

'Dearest, it's late in the day,' John protested, 'and the streets are dark—'

'I'm not afraid of the dark, John,' Maggie answered impatiently, already making for the door.

He sighed. 'You won't build up your hopes too much, will you, Maggie?'

She turned and gave him a direct look with her grey eyes. 'I'm full of hope,' she answered simply. 'I can't be any other way.'

John insisted they took a cab through the town. They alighted on the steep bank that plunged down to the quayside, its tall slum dwellings clinging together as if they might topple over at any moment.

John took Maggie's hand firmly and led her up a narrow, covered lane with stinking water dripping from its slimy walls. Children were playing war games around the steps and Maggie had to dodge their crudely fashioned wooden guns.

They were directed to Lily Smart's room by the woman from the mission. Maggie hardly recognised the grey-haired woman who answered their knocking with a wheezing shout. Lily Smart had aged dramatically in the past two years of wartime deprivation, dismissed from St Chad's in the shake-up of staff.

At first she was reluctant to speak, but John produced a sovereign and she came out onto the landing.

'Aye, I remember the bairn,' Lily grunted. 'But she never stayed more than a month or two at St Chad's. Matron wanted her out of harm's way.'

'Meaning me, I suppose,' Maggie said tersely.

'Aye,' Lily said, eyeing her with resentment. 'She could tell you were one of them troublemakers.'

'But the child,' John intercepted quickly. 'Where did they take her?'

'Sent her to a cottage home - up Tynedale.'

'Which one?' John questioned.

'Can't remember the name. Small place, paid for by the Pearsons.'

Maggie thought of their futile search of Tyneside. 'So we've been looking in the wrong place all the time!' she cried.

'But why send the child all that way?' John puzzled.

Lily snorted. 'Matron was on to some fiddle. She picked out the pretty bairns.'

'Why?' Maggie asked, her heart pounding painfully.

'Well, it was a model home, see. And rich folk could have their picking of me orphans - you know, the ones what couldn't have their own, or didn't want to risk childbirth. That's what was rumoured, anyways.'

Maggie could not speak. She was paralysed by the thought of Christabel being chosen like some pretty ornament to adorn some rich person's nursery.

'Thank you for your help, Mrs Smart,' John said politely, steering Maggie towards the stairs.

'Oh, there's one other thing I remember,' the craggy-faced midwife called to them on the dark stairwell. They looked back. 'The bairn - the Matron changed her name to Martha, said it was a plain, dutiful name and wouldn't give the lass ideas above herself like her mother had. Maybes that's why you couldn't find her.'

All the way home, Maggie could not stop shaking.

'Where is this place?' she demanded. 'John, we must go there tomorrow.'

'I have the shop to run, my dear,' John reminded her. 'I can't just go tearing off to search Tynedale. Besides, we need to discover the name of the home first.'

'Daniel can manage the shop quite well without you,' Maggie answered bluntly. 'You should be giving the lad more responsibility anyways at your age.'

John flushed. 'I can't go before Saturday,' he insisted.

"That's nearly a week!' Maggie protested.

Her desperation made him relent. 'Just give me time to make enquiries about this cottage home first, then we'll go,' he promised.

Maggie could settle to nothing for the rest of the week. She tried to immerse herself in her work at the Guild's office but could not concentrate. She trailed around town with Susan while Millie watched the children, but she was tense and preoccupied.

Her mood unnerved Susan and made her impatient.

'What if she's not there?' she dared to ask. 'You've got to face the fact that with all the upheaval of the war, she may not be. Will you give up looking for her?'

'Never!' Maggie cried.' How could you think such a thing?'

'But is John not tiring of it all?' Susan demanded. 'It might be kinder on him if you were to put it all behind you and settle to the life he's given you. Why can't you just make the best of what you've got, Maggie? You're always hankering after what's just around the corner.'

Maggie spun round and glared at Susan. 'You're a mother. Could you imagine a life without Alfred or Beattie or Bella?' she challenged.

'No, of course not,' Susan admitted, 'but...'

'So why is it any different for me?' Maggie demanded. 'I carried my bairn for nine months and brought her into this world with as much pain and effort as any other woman. You may think I'm hard but I've just as much feeling inside as the next lass.' Maggie put a hand on her sister's arm, willing her to understand 'I held that bonny baby in me arms, Susan. She sucked at me breast. I was a mother for those brief moments and it felt grand! I was lying, half bleeding to death in that hellhole, yet I felt so at peace...' Maggie struggled to explain. 'When John talks of the love of God, I think of that time in that dark cell with

Christabel lying beside me.' Her eyes glistened as she dropped her voice to a whisper. 'It was the most comforting feeling you could ever imagine. I knew that Christabel was mine and that I'd always be bound to her whatever happened.' Maggie looked pleadingly at Susan, then her voice hardened in determination. 'Christabel doesn't belong in an orphanage, Susan, or to anyone else. She belongs to *me*.'

Susan stared at her sister in awe. She had heard Maggie rant about politics and rights but she had never heard her speak before about something so personal. It surprised and touched her.

'Of course the bairn belongs to you,' she said, squeezing Maggie's hand. 'I just hope you find her.'

By Friday, John had discovered that the most likely orphanage was the Hebron Children's Home, named after the Pearsons' Newcastle mansion and situated outside a small village in the upper Tyne valley. They travelled by train up the valley and then walked the steep dirt track that wound its way up the valley side to the moortop institute. Maggie drank in every detail of the sturdy stone building, hidden among a spinney of wind-blown trees. It must have been an old vicarage or gentleman farmer's house which had been taken over for the orphans, for its windows were large and unbarred and its aspect in the summer must have been pleasant. It was early November now though and the wind battered the ivy-clad facade with a squall of icy rain and whipped around their chilled faces. Even so, Maggie could hear the shouts of children playing in a field at the side of the house, half hidden by a thicket of hawthorn. She was pleased and surprised that they were given such freedom and quickened her step.

Two young boys ran up the steps ahead of them, their faces rosy and well nourished, to alert the staff. A pleasant-faced nurse showed them into a large schoolroom and went off to find the housemother. Maggie looked around her in astonishment. There were bright maps and pictures adorning the walls and one corner had been given over to a play area with dolls and toys like a children's nursery.

Maggie lowered herself carefully into one of the miniature benches attached to the infant desks and breathed in the smell of ink and chalk and children. For a moment she was transported back to her own classroom where Rose Johnstone had nurtured her passion for learning and she remembered that she had once yearned to be a teacher. Where was Rose now? Maggie sighed to herself and thought how differently her life had turned out.

'I like the feel of this place, John,' she murmured, listening to the clatter of feet on a staircase beyond the door. 'It's so different from St Chad's.'

'I quite agree,' her husband nodded, picking up an exercise book and flicking through its pages. 'It has the atmosphere of a happily run home.'

Maggie felt her spirits lighten at the thought that her daughter might have been here for most of her two years of life, breathing in the fresh country air and cared for by kind people.

When the smiling housemother appeared, Maggie's optimism increased further. The woman was about Rose Johnstone's age, neatly dressed in a suit rather than a uniform and with a concerned and interested demeanour.

She stretched out her hand in greeting. 'I'm Lucinda Cooper, the housemother here. What a way you've come! If you had given me some warning I could have made arrangements for you to stay in the village.'

'We didn't have time,' Maggie answered, returning her smile.

'I apologise for the abruptness of our arrival,' John intervened, 'but we've come on a matter of some urgency.'

'You'll take tea with me then?' Miss Cooper suggested. 'While we discuss the matter.'

She ushered them into a small sitting room across the hall. As they followed her, a stream of small children came hurrying in from outside, their pink faces muffled in scarves and hats. They squealed and chattered as they took refuge from the sleety rain, cajoled and fussed over by an older woman in a brown cape.

Maggie's heart lurched as she scanned the faces of the small girls, wondering ... But they appeared older than Christabel, already fluent in speech. They disappeared in a giggling band while their nurse tried to curb their noisy exuberance.

Inside the cosy sitting room, a coal fire blazed and teacups and teapot were already laid out on a gate-legged table. The furniture was ill matched and a touch shabby, but the walls were lined with pictures and bookcases, denoting the interests of Miss Cooper.

As she poured tea, she chatted to them about the running of the home to put them at their ease. Then she turned to Maggie and fixed her with a direct look.

'But perhaps your interest doesn't lie in the management of the home,' she said. 'You have some particular concern?'

'Yes,' Maggie blurted out. 'We're trying to find my daughter, Christabel.'

Lucinda Cooper's eyebrows rose in surprise.

'Your daughter? Christabel you say?' She shook her head. 'I'm sorry, we have no child named Christabel Heslop.'

John interjected quickly, 'No, the child is not mine.' He stopped suddenly, aware of Maggie's discomfort, and wished he had not been so quick to disown the girl.

'She carries my maiden name, Beaton,' Maggie explained bashfully. 'We believe her name was changed from Christabel to Martha when she arrived from St Chad's. She'll be nearly two now.'

'Ah,' Miss Cooper exclaimed in understanding, 'the child came from the orphanage at St Chad's.'

Maggie nodded eagerly. 'Is she here, then? Do you know my Christabel?'

The woman's brow furrowed. 'There was a Martha Brown who came to us from St Chad's a little less than two years ago, a sweet baby. It's very possible that the surname was changed as well as the Christian name.'

'Can we see her?' Maggie questioned eagerly. 'Please!'

Miss Cooper looked at her with sad compassion. She took a deep breath. 'I'm sorry, but little Martha - Christabel - was adopted over a year ago.'

Maggie felt her mouth and throat go dry.

'Are you quite sure about this?' John demanded, reaching to hold Maggie's hand.

Lucinda Cooper nodded. 'Quite sure.'

'But she can't be,' Maggie gasped, closing her eyes. 'She's mine!'

'We had no idea the natural mother had any interest in Martha,' Miss Cooper answered quietly but firmly. 'In fact we did not know of your existence, Mrs Heslop.'

'Who adopted her?' John asked forlornly.

'I'm sorry, I can't tell you that.' The housemother was adamant.

Maggie opened her eyes and looked at the other woman with such desolation that she flinched.

'Please,' Maggie whispered, 'I have to know. I need to know that my

225

Christabel is in good hands - caring hands.'

Miss Cooper hesitated, then shook her head again. 'I really can't give away their identity. All I can say is that your daughter will want for nothing in her new life. I can show you a photograph of her if you wish.'

Maggie could not speak, merely nodding her head vigorously.

Lucinda Cooper crossed over to a filing cabinet and pulled out one of the drawers. She rummaged for a minute and returned with a binder. From it she drew a photograph and handed it to Maggie.

She stared down at the small child in the picture. She was wearing a tailor-made outdoor coat and hat and buttoned-up boots beneath flounces of petticoats. But it was not the expensive clothes that interested Maggie, it was the enquiring look on the little girl's face. She was not smiling at the camera but gazing at it in curiosity with round dark eyes, her petite face framed by dark ringlets. In that moment, Maggie had no doubt that this was Christabel; it was as if she already knew this inquisitive infant. The eyes seemed to look at her directly, accusingly, as if to ask why she had not been there to claim her.

Maggie's eyes brimmed with tears and she broke down in front of the concerned housemother.

John took her to him and tried to comfort her, but she was overwhelmed by her grief. Lucinda Cooper withdrew to give them time alone together to come to terms with the bad news, carefully locking away the file while leaving the photograph of Christabel on the table.

Maggie made a supreme effort to pull herself together, blowing hard into John's cotton handkerchief.

'Look at her, John,' she insisted. 'Look at her before we leave and know that she exists.'

Reluctantly John picked up the picture and glanced at the stubborn-faced child that challenged him. He was struck immediately by how like Maggie she was, the same oval eyes and determined mouth. It was a sudden relief to him that Christabel held no resemblance to George Gordon and he thought sadly how he could have cared for this child, even grown to love her...

Maggie heard his small involuntary gasp. 'What is it?' she asked.

'No, it's nothing,' he stammered. 'I just thought…'

'What, John?' Maggie persisted. 'Tell me, please.'

John took a deep breath and pointed to something in the background of the photograph. Maggie peered at the out-of-focus building behind Christabel. She had been far too absorbed in the girl to notice anything else.

'Does it remind you of anywhere?' he asked, almost in a whisper. 'Look at the domes - cupolas they call them.'

Maggie knew at once what he was thinking. She froze at his side.

'Oxford Hall?' she whispered.

John nodded 'I'm sure of it.'

'The Pearsons?' Maggie gasped. 'Please God, no!'

But as she stared again at the well-dressed child in front of the hazy mansion, she was afraid John was right. Suddenly she thought of Alice Pearson and her love of photography and wondered if her adversary had been the one to capture Christabel's puzzled gaze ...

Chapter Twenty-Eight

The Armistice was declared on 11 November, and just before eleven o'clock the noise of clanging and hammering in the shipyards stopped. Trams halted, horses were held and children in the playgrounds stood still; the world seemed to hold its breath as the bugles sounded out the end to the war. Maggie had been crossing town on her way back from seeing Susan when the hour struck.

With the traffic and bustle of the city calmed, she could hear clearly the chirp of birds. The moment was unexpectedly poignant as everyone around her became lost in their own private world of remembrance. She thought sadly of George, though the pain of grief for him had lessened since her fondness for John had grown, and her new agony over losing Christabel to the Pearsons overshadowed all other emotions.

After their depressing trip to Hebron Children's Home, Maggie had scoured the local press for any mention of another child in the Pearson household. She could find no announcements about a daughter but she found a picture of the MP, Herbert Pearson, shaking hands with Red Cross workers with his family arrayed behind him. There stood his thin wife and a boy of about eight or nine dressed in a fashionable sailor's suit. Beside him was a small girl with dark ringlets under a fur hat. The photograph in the newspaper was blurred, but Maggie was convinced the girl was Christabel.

For a week she had rowed with John about confronting the Pearsons and asking for her daughter back, but he had been firmly against any action. There was no law to protect orphans or to give her the right to claim Christabel, he pointed out endlessly. Maggie had grown so desperate she thought of posing as a nursemaid and snatching Christabel, but she knew such action would be futile. It was her helplessness and rage that kept her pounding the streets of Newcastle, unable to settle to her work at the Co-operative Guild or return home to her husband.

But for these few brief moments, she was forced to be still. The quietness wrapped itself round her like healing bandages and she realised she was so tired of fighting. Her desire to see Christabel gnawed at her like toothache but for the first time she doubted her own strength to carry on the battle. There seemed to be too much opposition ranged against her, she thought bleakly.

As the traffic moved again, Maggie turned for home, thinking suddenly of her brother Jimmy. As far as she knew, Tich had survived the carnage in Flanders and for that at least she was thankful. Maggie felt a faint lifting of her mood to think she might see her brother again soon.

That night the sky was lit with bonfires burning all night on the slag heaps around the edge of the town and people took down the dark green blinds from their windows so that the whole street shone with cheery light.

Later in the week a 'Victory Tea' was held in the street, with tables dragged out onto the cobbles and Union Jacks strung along the railings. Somehow the women managed to produce a feast of cakes and fruit and ham sandwiches for the children to enjoy, and talked to them excitedly of their fathers coming home. Maggie would have preferred to hide indoors but Millie and John persuaded her to join in the street party.

Maggie watched numbly until one small girl from the house across the street, who often chose her doorstep on which to play her games of 'house', climbed onto her knee. Suddenly, to Maggie's consternation, Sally burst into tears.

'What's wrong, pet?' Maggie asked, cuddling the girl to her.

'It's that man,' the girl sobbed.

'Which man. Sally?'

'There's a strange man coming - I've seen his picture and Mam says he's going to live with us in the same house and I've got to sit on his knee and give him a kiss!' The child howled once more.

Maggie rocked her comfortingly in the raw November air and kissed her cold cheek. 'Don't be frightened, hinny,' she crooned. 'It's your da, not a strange man. You'll soon get to love him.'

'No I won't!' cried the girl.

Maggie felt unexpectedly distressed by the girl's fear. Was this how Christabel would have felt about George returning to them? She forced herself to smile at the confused girl.

'Bet he'll bring you summat back from France.'

Sally stopped sniffing. 'Do you think so?' she asked, suddenly interested.

'Aye,' Maggie nodded.

'But I've got nothing for him,' Sally worried.

'Yes you have, bonny lass,' Maggie assured her. 'You've got yourself and your mam and that's all he'll be wanting.' Suddenly she was overwhelmed by everyone else's joy and laughter and felt an unbearable stab of loss.

John saw at once that Maggie was distressed and swiftly handed Sally over to Millie, steering Maggie indoors. He pulled her into the dining room at the back of the house, away from the excited noise of the party. He tried to hold her close but she struggled to be free of him.

'Why me?' she raged, tears streaming down her face. 'What have I done to your God to be suffering like this? Will I never be able to stop thinking of George and Christabel and what should have been?'

John stood stem-faced but hung on to her hands. 'You have to give it time,' he told her.

Time?' she spat.

'Yes, time!' he answered. 'You're not the only one in this world to suffer, you know. I know what it's like to lose those closest to me too. Don't you ever think how I've suffered?' he shouted.

Maggie was taken aback by his anger. It was true, she often forgot how his first wife and baby had died, for he never mentioned them. But her own personal agony was too all-consuming to be able to think of his.

'But I'm in so much pain!' Maggie rasped. 'Why do we have to suffer? What's the point of it all? All this death and misery? Why?'

John was shaken to the core by her hurt and lack of belief. It was like watching her drowning before his very eyes and he fought to throw her a lifeline, knowing if he said the wrong thing now he would lose her for ever.

'I don't know,' he answered in a low, intense voice, his grip digging into Maggie's bony hands. 'All I know is that there must be a purpose to pain - you have to make it matter!'

She looked at him in bewilderment.

'You have a choice, Maggie,' he spoke urgently. 'To give in to the pain and give up on life, or to use your pain to learn from it and become a fuller person. There are some people - like the Pearsons perhaps - who sail through life undisturbed, never being challenged like you have, never exposed to real suffering. But such people are inward-looking, cocooned in their cosy lives, content to drift through life, never having the chance to change. They are the ones to be pitied, Maggie, for at the end of their comfortable, empty lives, what do they have to show for it?'

Maggie searched his lean face, trying to comprehend whether this stern man before her held the answer to her doubts and despair. She saw a face lined with experience and suffering, yet the brown eyes shone with compassion and love. While she sank deeper into the depths of her unhappiness, she was aware that John Heslop might be the only person who could pull her back out of the blackness.

She reached out and held on to him, not knowing if she loved him or not, only aware that he seemed to be offering a dim light in the darkness, with his caring eyes and his strange words about suffering.

They clung to each other and Maggie sobbed out her heart as the wintry light faded from beyond the velvet curtains and the sound of a brass band thumped the chilly air in the street outside.

It was John's idea to take Maggie to London for a holiday.

'Treat ourselves to a proper honeymoon,' he joked shyly. 'Daniel can manage the shop. Like you said, I should be giving the lad more responsibility.'

'We'll be there for polling day,' Maggie said with a stirring of interest. 'I'd like to see all those women turning up to vote for the first time.'

John laughed, pleased to see his wife taking an interest in the outside world after the past bleak fortnight when she had refused to leave the house. Lloyd George had called an election now the war was over and a bill had been rushed through the Commons allowing women to stand as parliamentary candidates.

'We could go and hear Miss Christabel Pankhurst speak, or Mrs Despard, or Mrs Pethick-Lawrence. They're all contesting seats, according to the papers.'

'Yes,' Maggie's eyes lit with enthusiasm, 'that would be grand!'

In early December, they stayed at a boarding house run by Methodists and spent the days exploring London's famous sights. Maggie dragged John along to countless political meetings to listen to former suffragettes speaking from the hustings. Now they represented different parties and concerns, but Maggie experienced again the thrill of the public meeting with its lively speeches, its hecklers and jostling crowds. London seemed full of servicemen in uniform waiting impatiently to be demobbed.

It had been so long since she had felt any fervour for politics and protest that she was quite taken by surprise by the enthusiasm which gripped her now. It lit inside her like a small fire, fanning quickly as she listened to speaker after speaker.

'It's so grand to see these women in the flesh after all this time,' Maggie enthused, 'really see them - and hear their voices!'

'That could be you, Maggie,' John said, slipping his arm through hers as they left an open-air platform of vying politicians.

Maggie laughed. 'Who would come and listen to me?' she scoffed.

'I remember a young woman who used to stand on street corners accosting decent folk with suffragette newspapers every Saturday afternoon before the war,' he teased. 'Plenty folk listened to you then.'

'How do you know?' Maggie asked in astonishment.

'I was sometimes one of them,' John confessed with a bashful smile.

Maggie laughed, then added reflectively, 'That was different, I had a prize to fight for then. And I was that impatient for change.'

'There're plenty more prizes out there,' John insisted, 'and plenty that needs changing.'

She stopped and smiled up at him. 'John Heslop, you're growing more radical the older you get!' she laughed.

He squeezed her arm. 'It's having a wife of twenty-six that does it. I feel I'm growing younger by the day.'

On 14 December, election day, they roamed around London, watching the voters arrive at polling stations in Chelsea and Battersea, Richmond and Chiswick where women candidates were standing. Maggie, wearing her frayed suffragette sash, stood and clapped the women voters as they marched proudly into the polling booths. There were no scenes or demonstrations, just a proud exercising of their right to vote. Their quiet dignity caught at Maggie's throat.

By mid-afternoon it was almost dark and Maggie noticed that John was chilled through.

'I'm sorry, we've been out too long. Let's go to a tearoom to warm up,' she suggested. 'I've seen enough.'

They entered the first cafe that they came to, its windows steamed up and its door decorated with festive holly. As they were ushered to a table by a waitress, Maggie glanced across the room and her heart stopped.

'Look, John,' she gasped. 'It's Miss Alice!'

Alice Pearson looked up at the same moment and at first did not recognise the neatly dressed, pale-faced woman staring at her. It was John Heslop that she placed and then she realised who his companion was.

Maggie saw the look of discomfort on the older woman's face but knew that she could not ignore them. Maggie approached her table and held out a hand.

'Miss Pearson,' Maggie said stiffly, 'this is a great day for us women, don't you agree?'

Alice hesitated, thankful that she had slipped into the cafe on her own and did not have to explain her relationship with this lower-class woman to anyone. The cafe was only a minute's walk from her Chelsea studio and she often came in for afternoon tea.

Then Alice fought with her prejudice, instilled over countless years, telling herself that she no longer acknowledged such differences. She took Maggie's proffered hand.

'Maggie, Mr Heslop - this is a surprise. How are you both? Please, will you join me?' she said as graciously as her conflicting emotions would allow.

Here was the girl who had caused her family so much strife and made her so angry, Alice thought, suddenly disturbing her contented world again. For she was contented, living in London and advancing her career as a photographer. She had had a successful war, Alice thought wryly, for it had given her the opportunity to break out of the stifling provinciality of her home life and travel into the dangers of the Western Front, capturing the war on film. It had changed her from a self-opinionated snob, she admitted candidly to herself, to someone who thought more deeply about the world - more highly of the common people whose bravery she had witnessed time and time again.

But Alice was forced to admit that if it had not been for Maggie Beaton she would have experienced none of it. She had been furious at the desecration of her beloved Hebron House, and after the arson attack she had never felt the same about her home, as if it were somehow sullied. Looking back, she wondered why. After all, it was only a summerhouse, a symbol - as Maggie's arson had pointed out - of the stranglehold of privilege that her father and brother exercised over her and other women.

Disenchanted by Herbert's new regime there, Alice had taken her camera and set off aimlessly for London in 1916. A chance meeting with a Fleet Street editor had sent her off to France and from there to the trenches in Flanders.

Looking at Maggie now, Alice faced up to the truth, that this stormy, unrefined young woman with the passionate eyes and voice, who came from the obscurity of Newcastle's slums, had given her the courage to cast aside her security and plunge into the unknown. She had told herself that if a working-class girl like Maggie Beaton could risk everything, then so could she.

Often, in France, Alice had thought of Maggie in prison and wondered what had become of the tragic, tempestuous girl. She had been plagued by guilt that she had turned her back on Maggie and the Movement when they needed her support most, merely to advance the interests of her own family, a family with whom contact was increasingly rare. Now she was about to find out.

Maggie gave her a cautious look, surprised by the woman's civility, then sat down. For a few minutes they talked about the election and the end of the war and Alice told them about her studio and her war photography. Tea came. John told her proudly about his marriage to Maggie in the late summer and his continuing work at the mission. Alice managed to hide her surprise that such an unlikely pair had ended up as husband and wife but was struck by how at ease they were in each other's company, so unlike the petty warring between her brother Herbert and her unhappy sister-in-law Felicity.

Suddenly Maggie leaned across the table and blurted out, 'I need your help, Miss Alice.'

'Maggie,' John tried to stop her. 'You mustn't—'

'Please, John,' Maggie pleaded. 'This might be my only chance of seeing Christabel.'

Alice looked at them in confusion. 'I'll help if I can. But who is Christabel?'

'She's my daughter,' Maggie told her bluntly, her grey eyes fiercely proud, 'my illegitimate daughter.'

Alice was flabbergasted. She just sat and stared, not knowing what to say. Yet she was less scandalised than she would have been five years ago. The old Alice would have recoiled in disgust and seen Maggie's behaviour as confirmation of the lower classes' loose morals. But the war had opened her eyes to many things, not least the fact that ordinary people's lives had been thrown into turmoil by separation, fear of death and the struggle for survival. She knew nothing of the reasons for Maggie's predicament and would not condemn her as she once would have done.

John intervened. 'Maggie's child was taken into a children's home endowed by your family - Hebron Children's Home.'

Alice nodded. 'I know it. I was on the interview board for the appointment of the housemother in nineteen fifteen. It was the last task I did before leaving the north, as a matter of fact.'

'We went there to find Christabel last month,' John continued, 'but she'd already been adopted.'

'So how can I help?' Alice asked, baffled.

'We think Herbert Pearson adopted her,' Maggie replied. 'It is true your brother has a young daughter of about two, isn't it?'

Alice gawped at her. 'Yes, Georgina, but...'

That would explain all the secrecy surrounding her niece, Georgina, she suddenly thought. Herbert and Felicity were trying to pass the girl off as their own, Felicity having kept a reclusive life at Oxford Hall since Zeppelins had flown up the Tyne and made Hebron House too risky to live in. But Alice had been almost certain that the girl had been adopted in an attempt to present her brother as an upright family man. Herbert had once told her in a fit of self-pity that Felicity had not allowed him into her bed for years. Was it possible, Alice wondered, that the wilful Georgina who appeared to be ignored by her parents as much as Henry was could really be Maggie's daughter? Was she their attempt to stitch together a marriage that was coming apart at the seams?

If it were true, Alice thought, she felt deeply sorry for Maggie but was reluctant to become involved in a battle with her brother over the girl. Since Herbert had become an MP, Alice had grown steadily apart from him, disillusioned by his broken promises of allowing her more involvement in the family business. After her father had died her visits north had become short and infrequent - a token few days to see her ailing mother whose memory was shrivelling as fast as her once beautiful face and figure.

'It seems rather farfetched, Maggie,' Alice blustered. 'Have you any proof that my niece Georgina is your daughter?'

'A photograph - from the home,' Maggie said eagerly, reaching into an inner coat pocket. 'The housemother let me keep it though she gave away no confidences. But John and I recognised Oxford Hall behind her.'

She handed the photograph of Christabel to Alice and saw the look of recognition on the older woman's face.

'You took that picture, didn't you, Miss Alice?' she asked quietly. 'Is it the girl you know as Georgina?'

Alice nodded slowly.

Maggie felt her throat water. 'Please, help me to see her,' she pleaded.

Alice looked at her drawn, vulnerable face and saw how she suffered. For a moment she wondered who the father was, but knew she would not ask.

She sighed I'll be visiting my mother at Christmas. Perhaps I could arrange to take the children out for the day.'

'Aye!' Maggie responded quickly. 'That would be a grand idea. You could bring them to our house for dinner.'

Alice cleared her throat uncomfortably. 'I think it might draw less comment if I was to bring them to Hebron House and you could come over and meet them. I could pretend you were ...' Alice floundered for an explanation.

'An old colleague from the suffrage movement,' Maggie said swiftly. She was not going to be passed off as some former nurserymaid or servant.

'Yes, very well,' Alice agreed. She finished her tea.

'That's very good of you, Miss Alice,' John thanked her and pulled out a visiting card with their Sandyford address. 'Perhaps you could send us a note with the arrangements.'

Alice took the card and prepared to leave.

'Would it be possible to visit your studio while we're in London?' Maggie asked unexpectedly.

Alice was surprised but pleased at her interest in her work. 'Of course,' she agreed and told them the address.

They arranged to call a couple of days later, before taking the train north again.

Maggie's spirits were quite lifted by the encounter and she simmered with energy and optimism. John was delighted to see her more like her old self but feared that her expectations were too high.

'If this meeting with Christabel takes place,' he warned her, 'you will be cautious, won't you? You can't go telling the child you're her mother or any such wildness.'

'I know that,' Maggie answered impatiently. 'I just want to see her.'

John kissed her head in a gesture of affection that told her he knew how she felt. These past two weeks with Maggie in London had been the happiest he could recall. He had revelled in having her to himself, sharing experiences and conversations that they normally had no time for in their busy lives at home. And to crown it all, not only had they shared the same room at the boarding house but also the same bed.

Alter a week of lying together, Maggie had reached for him one night in the darkness and asked for intimacy. They had been shy and fumblingly inexperienced with each other at first, but finally they had managed a gentle, tentative lovemaking and held each other for a long time afterwards. John had felt the dampness of Maggie's tears on his nightshirt and wondered what thoughts were going through her head, but he had not dared ask in case she was full of longing for George Gordon.

Still, they had made love the following night and the night after that, so that he began to hope that Maggie's affection for him might be growing. Yet she said nothing, as if these intimate episodes in the night never took place, and John was left feeling fearful and full of doubt.

Now, their visit to London almost at an end, they made their way to Alice Pearson's Chelsea studio.

It was down in a basement yet her workroom was surprisingly light, with French windows at the far end opening onto a small garden and electric lighting at different points around the room. The walls were lined with photographs - stark landscapes of bomb-blasted fields and scorched trees, groups of soldiers preparing for action or resting behind the trenches.

Maggie walked around slowly, gazing at the faces. They captured the very spirit of the people, she thought, as if, were she to stretch out and touch them, she would feel warm flesh. The faces seemed so young, anxious and furrowed before battle, relaxed and grinning over a game of cards when off duty. There was one of a Red Cross nurse pushing an amputee in a wheelchair, the expressions on both faces resigned, enigmatic. The photographs brought the war so vividly alive that Maggie could only pass from one to the next in a state of awe at what these people had suffered and sacrificed. No newspaper reports or lists of the dead had come close to making her realise the scale of the tragedy. Each soldier here had been loved and worried over by family and friends and neighbours, just as each loss had been felt as keenly as her own by countless others.

'This will interest you,' Alice said, breaking into her absorption. 'I quite forgot about it the other day, with my mind being taken up with Georgina - Christabel, I mean.' She searched in a folder.

Maggie turned. 'Your work is so powerful,' she said 'You deserve your success, Miss Alice.'

Alice smiled and went on rummaging. 'You remember that friend of yours - I used to meet him at the mission.'

Maggie exchanged looks with John.

'Gordon, I think his name was.'

Maggie felt her heart stop. 'George Gordon?' she asked, her throat tight.

'Yes, that's the man,' Alice said, pulling out a photograph.

Maggie stared at her, "You have a picture of George?' she gasped.

'Here.' Alice held it out to her.

Maggie took it with trembling hands. She looked. Three men sat smoking on a bench, while a fourth stood leaning against the wall behind. She recognised none of them. Then staring harder at the aloof one, she began to see a resemblance to George in the dark ringed eyes, the set of the mouth. Yet this man was gaunt, his hair cropped and upper lip shaven. He was a shadow of the broad-shouldered, square-faced George she had last seen alive.

'Are you sure it's him?' Maggie asked. 'Perhaps the memory plays tricks, but he can't have changed that much in the short time between leaving for France and being killed at the Somme.'

John moved towards her. 'Let me see,' he said quietly.

Alice seemed puzzled. 'The Somme?' she queried. Then her jaw dropped open as realisation dawned. 'Oh no, my dear, it's you who must be mistaken. I took that photograph a month ago - they're prisoners released from behind the German lines. These men were used on the land.'

Maggie met John's incredulous look. 'Prisoners?' she whispered.

John turned to Alice. 'Are you saying that George Gordon has been a prisoner all this time?'

'Yes.' Alice was definite. 'He recognised me and made himself known when I asked if I could photograph them. He seemed rather dazed by his release, but it was Gordon all right.'

Maggie felt her knees buckling from the shock. 'George is alive,' she croaked. She flopped into a chair and leant forward to ward off a surging faintness. Covering her face with her hands, she dissolved into tears.

John hesitated, then went to put his arms about her shaking shoulders.

Alice stared at them in bewilderment 'But I thought it would be good news.'

John regarded her with pained, sad eyes. 'George Gordon is Christabel's father,' he explained simply. 'Everyone thought he'd died over two years ago. That's the reason Maggie agreed to marry me.'

Alice looked at the wretched couple and cursed herself for producing the photograph, for she trembled to think what unhappiness she had just unleashed.

Chapter Twenty-Nine

The journey back to Newcastle was subdued and tense. Both Maggie and John were thankful that their carriage was full and they did not have to speak of what lay ahead. Platforms seemed to swarm with men in khaki and John was aware of Maggie scanning their faces while she sat mutely with hands gripped in her lap.

Reaching their home in Sandyford at last, John gave Millie a curt account of what they had learned and left swiftly for the shop. But there his worst fears were confirmed, for all the gossip was of how the miner's son George Gordon had come back from the dead, to the joy of his brothers and sister and elderly father.

'Arrived home while you were away, Mr Heslop,' Daniel told him. 'Caused quite a stir around Benwell, They had a street party for him. Mind, he looks like he could do with feeding up - nowt but a skeleton he is.'

After closing the shop, John decided on impulse to go and see Susan. He found her busy at her aunt's house preparing tea, while a young man sprawled on the floor playing with her children.

'It's young Jimmy, isn't it?' John gasped in delight 'You're back!'

Susan's brother leapt up and greeted his new brother-in-law with a bashful shake of the hand. He had filled out and grown a thin moustache.

'I'm glad you're safely home,' John smiled. 'Maggie will be so pleased to see you.' Then he stopped, remembering his reason for coming. But Susan had already guessed.

'Aye,' she said with a sympathetic look, 'likely you've heard of George Gordon's return. Jimmy's been up to see him. George already knew about Maggie getting wed to you - his sister Irene was quick to tell him.'

John looked at Jimmy.

'Aye,' Jimmy confirmed. 'He's taken it badly. I think - well, that thinking of Maggie kept him going, like.'

John shuddered. 'Yes, it would,' he murmured.

'Well, he'll just have to accept the situation, Mr Heslop,' Susan said brusquely. 'She's married to you now and that's an end to it.'

John wished silently that it could be that simple, but knew that George's return might mean the break-up of his marriage. How Maggie must resent being his wife! he thought bleakly. Only he stood in the way of her finding happiness at last with the only man she had ever truly loved. If he was honest with himself he wished that Gordon had died at the Somme and he despised himself for such thoughts.

He stayed for a cup of tea and listened to Jimmy's breathless accounts of life in the trenches, marvelling at how the immature and irresponsible boy that he remembered had coped with such experiences. If old Mabel Beaton could hear her son now, John thought ruefully, she would no longer be calling him the runt of the family. Here was a son she could have been proud of at last.

Susan saw him to the door. John lowered his voice and briefly described their encounters with Alice Pearson and asked if she would come and see Maggie. 'She's in turmoil,' he said. 'I know she's frightened and nervous at the thought of meeting Christabel after all this time. And now with this news about George Gordon - it seems to have paralysed her. I'm really at a loss as to what to do. She won't speak to me about anything. You will come and spend Christmas with us, won't you? Jimmy and your aunt as well.'

Susan put a reassuring hand on his arm, touched by his concern. 'That would be canny,' she smiled. 'And I'll do all I can to make Maggie realise where her loyalties lie.'

'No,' John answered swiftly, 'you mustn't be hard on Maggie. I'll not have her forced to do anything. I just want you to be there - to support her.'

Susan sighed. 'Whatever you think's for the best. I haven't told Jimmy about Maggie's daughter yet, or George being the father. No one else knows.'

'Good. Keep it that way, Susan,' John replied. 'I want her protected from any harmful scandal.'

Maggie tried to occupy her waking hours with preparations for Christmas. She paced the house being critical of Millie and interfering in the kitchen, upsetting the new cook. Millie finally banished her to the parlour and told her, 'Mind you stay at that desk of yours, or I'll hoy you oot to the park. But don't you go telling the rest of us what to do!'

Maggie seized her coat and hat and escaped to Jesmond Dene. She walked restlessly along the Ouseburn, gazing into its sluggish brown water, its banks blackened with piles of dead wet leaves.

She was so confused. Her first thought on hearing that George was alive was relief - a strangled, choking relief. All the way home from London she had been itchy with impatience to see him, to hear his teasing voice again, to *hold* him and know beyond all doubt that he was real. She would explain to him about everything, how she had written to tell him of their baby, how she had misguidedly married John because she had thought he was dead and believed it the only way of gaining their beloved daughter back again ... The speeches had spun in her head to the sound of the clanking train on the railway line. Yet, once home, she had done nothing. She had deliberately kept away from the west of Newcastle, fearful of seeing George, as if by not seeing him she could pretend that life was as it was before his reappearance. What did she want? she demanded of herself savagely. Her indecision, her cowardly unwillingness to face up to his return made her angry with herself.

So it was with some relief that on her return from her walk she heard the sound of Alfred and Beattie playing on the stairs and found Susan waiting for her.

'There's someone with her an' all,' Millie winked as she took Maggie's coat and pushed her towards the drawing room.

A figure loomed round the door as she entered.

Tich!' she screamed as her brother swept her off the floor and twirled her around. 'By, they must feed you well in the army - look at the size of you!'

He plonked her down again. Bella toddled up and grabbed Maggie's skirt possessively. Maggie ruffled her niece's hair affectionately and heaved her into her arms.

'Aye,' Jimmy grinned, 'it was a canny bit better than eating me sisters' scraps, I can tell you!'

'Eeh, and you're growing hair on your face,' Maggie gazed at him in delight. 'You'll be courtin' next!' She gave him a playful push with Bella.

'Jimmy's already been offered a job at Milligan's,' Susan told her proudly.

'The laundry?' Maggie asked in surprise, putting Bella onto the sofa beside her.

'Aye, well,' Jimmy blushed, 'it's not in the laundry, it's in charge of the deliveries. It's a start, but.'

'A canny start,' Maggie encouraged.

'We're going to look around to rent somewhere bigger,' Susan went on, her eyes shining with excitement. 'Aunt Violet will come with us, of course.'

'Aye,' Jimmy grinned. 'And when I'm in partnership with Milligan, we'll have ourselves a place on Sarah Crescent, eh, Susan?'

Susan giggled like a girl.

'And then your mam will think she's died and gone to heaven,' Maggie told Bella with a teasing look at Susan.

Bella clapped, not understanding what they were talking about but aware of the warm atmosphere between her mother and special aunt.

No one mentioned George but his unspoken presence hung in the air and Maggie could not resist asking Jimmy about him as he left.

'You'd get a shock to see him,' her brother warned, 'he's that thin. His sister Irene is trying to feed him up a bit and his brother Joshua drags him out for a pint but he says he's lost the taste. Spends his time wandering about like a stray dog. Says he can't get used to being allowed to go where he likes.'

Maggie gulped. 'How did they make the mistake of thinking he was dead?' she asked angrily. 'They sent his things back. They should be shot for making such a mistake!'

Jimmy put an awkward hand on her thin shoulder. 'Thousands of men died on the Somme, Maggie. Whole battalions were wiped out. It was impossible for them to find and identify everyone. It seems they found his jacket later on a dead German, so they thought he must've been killed and robbed. The word was the Hun weren't taking prisoners, so no one suspected he'd been captured and kept alive.'

Maggie groaned at the chain of misfortune. 'Then they should've listed him as still missing in action if they didn't find his body. They shouldn't have said he was *dead*.'

'Aye, I know,' Jimmy said sadly, dropping his hand, 'But they probably thought it kinder to let the family get on with their grieving than wait for years not knowing.'

Maggie hung her head. All she knew was that if they had held out the slightest hope that George might still be alive she would never have gone into St Chad's. If she'd had to beg or steal or go on the streets she would have kept her daughter with her and waited for his return. And she would never have entertained the idea of marrying John Heslop.

Christmas came and Maggie determined to put on a brave face, keeping her spirits up with the thought that she would soon see Christabel. To her surprise she found herself enjoying the family party, making a fuss over Susan's children and gathering round John's piano while he played carols. Later, emboldened by the sherry, Millie took to the piano and played more raucous songs with Jimmy joining in enthusiastically. Even strait-laced Aunt Violet, mellowed by the feeling of good will, added her voice to a rendering of 'The Blaydon Races'.

That night, after her family had left and Millie had retired to the attic with the remains of the sherry, Maggie slipped into John's bedroom.

'Hold me, please,' she whispered, shivering on the bare floorboards. He reached for her and pulled her in beside him, exultant that she had chosen to lie with him again. They made love, buried deep below the blankets for warmth, and afterwards Maggie fell asleep, undisturbed by nightmares for the first time since returning from London.

When John woke in the early morning, Maggie had gone. If he had not smelt the scent of her on his sheets, he would have doubted she had ever been there, for at breakfast she seemed as remote and preoccupied as before.

Alice's message came later that day - Christabel's second birthday, Maggie thought with emotion. The plan had been changed. Alice would now bring the children to see her in Sandyford, Maggie read with relief, and suspected Alice was doing so to put her more at her ease.

Maggie ordered a special tea to be laid on, with cake and jelly and scones and jam and biscuits and fruit. She asked John to be present when they arrived and to be prepared to play the piano for them. She brought out the train set that they kept for Alfred and Beattie, along with two balls, a spinning top and a doll that was Bella's favourite.

She lay sleepless and tossing the night before the visit and got up early. John found her in the drawing room laying the fire.

'You shouldn't be doing that,' he protested.

'I have to do something,' she said, carrying on with the task. 'It reminds me of the times I used to go and lay fires for the Samuels on their Sabbath. I often wonder if they settled in America.'

It made John nervous when she harped back to the times she lived with Gordon and the friends they had shared.

'You don't have to do menial tasks any more,' John reminded her sharply.

'I'm not ashamed of getting me hands dirty,' Maggie snapped. 'Christabel will have to take me as I am.' She bit her lip and looked up at her husband. 'I'm sorry, it's just I'm so nervous.' She looked at him doubtfully. 'What if she doesn't like me?'

John crouched down beside her. 'Just be yourself, Maggie. She has no reason not to like you; she's just an infant of two.'

'Aye,' Maggie sighed, 'but she's being raised as a Pearson. What scares me most is that she might just look straight through me as if I was a piece of muck, the way the Pearsons do.'

'Miss Alice doesn't any more,' John commented. 'Don't judge the poor child before you've even met her.'

Maggie watched from the bay window for an hour before Alice arrived, her heart pounding relentlessly. By the time the gleaming car drew up outside the house and the passengers disembarked, she was shaking with more nerves than before any of her suffragette exploits. Neighbours came out to stare at the noisy motorcar and the well-pressed visitors outside the butcher's house and speculated as to who they might be. Millie greeted them with an elaborate show of deference, enjoying the gawps and gasps of the onlookers. Taking the children's coats and hats and fussing around them like an old hen, she showed them into the parlour.

Seeing that Maggie was quite tongue-tied, John greeted them and made the introductions. Henry shook hands politely, but the small, dark-eyed Georgina clung to Alice's hand in mute suspicion of the strangers.

Alice told them to sit on the sofa while she exchanged trivial conversation with Maggie, trying to put the young woman at ease. All Maggie could do was gaze at her daughter who was now inspecting the room with inquisitive eyes. Soon the small girl slipped from her seat and went to investigate the miniature painted figures around the manger displayed in the bay window.

'Georgina!' Alice admonished her. 'Don't touch them.'

'That's all right,' Maggie intervened swiftly and went to the child's side. 'Look, there's the baby Jesus, Georgina.'

'Baby. Baby!' the girl repeated and began to finger the statues.

Maggie picked up a shepherd and handed it over. Her insides fluttered as she touched the girl's small warm hand. This is my Christabel, she thought, savouring the bitter-sweet moment and resisting the impulse to crush her to her breast. She was only too aware that the girl was quite oblivious of how she felt. To Christabel she was a stranger, a friend of her aunt's and nothing more, Maggie thought, full of regret.

John watched his wife closely, guessing at her feelings, and thought to distract the boy.

'Henry,' he said jovially, 'do you like trains?'

'Yes, Mr Heslop,' he replied earnestly.

'Well, come and help me assemble the train set,' he suggested. 'We could lay it out on the dining-room floor. Would you like that?'

'Yes, sir,' Henry answered, his plump face solemnly polite.

They left the room and Maggie held her breath to see if Georgina would rush after her brother in a panic, but she did not. She had begun to rearrange the figures on the sofa, adding a china ornament and a small glass bowl that stood on a side table. Jesus was plonked in the bowl with the shepherd and his lamb, while Joseph was placed head first in the china vase.

Tiring of her game, Georgina began to roam around the room and found the rag doll that Bella played with when she visited. She eyed it critically, then deciding she liked it, clutched it in a fierce hug.

'That doll's called Bella,' Maggie explained. 'It belongs to a little girl I know with the same name. Perhaps you'd like to come and play with her one day.' Maggie looked at Alice questioningly.

'I suppose that could be arranged,' she said tentatively. 'The children are staying with me until after New Year. Their parents - Henry's parents,' Alice corrected quietly, 'are having houseguests and are glad to have the children occupied elsewhere.'

'Bella!' Georgina suddenly cried, hugging the doll again and kissing its worn face.

Then it happened. The small girl looked across the room at Maggie and ran towards her, holding up her arms to be taken onto her knee. Maggie grabbed her gratefully and cuddled her on her lap, thrilled at the feeling of having Christabel in her arms once more. For, although she forced herself to use her daughter's adopted name, she would always be Christabel in her mind.

She looked across at Alice in silent gratitude, tears stinging her eyes, then bent her head close to the girl's dark ringlets and talked to her about Bella the doll and Bella her niece. Once she had started, Maggie found she could not stop talking, telling her daughter stories that came rushing into her head while they dressed and undressed the doll and made her visit the Nativity scene.

Probably Christabel understood little of what she said, Maggie thought, but the girl seemed content to sit on her knee and play and repeat words. She was a solemn child who did not appear to smile or laugh easily like Bella did and Maggie wondered what sort of lonely childhood she endured at Oxford Hall. Yet Maggie was convinced a bond was strengthening between them; the close, inexplicable bond of love and possessiveness that is there between a mother and child before birth. It had always been there and Maggie rejoiced at the chance of experiencing it again. But as they sat there in companionship, she knew it would never be enough; she would want to go on seeing more and more of Christabel like an addict dependent on morphine.

Millie called them through for tea in the dining room where John was crouched on the floor playing enthusiastically with Henry. They broke reluctantly to join the others, but the boy was soon tucking into the food before him, encouraged by a vocal Millie who stayed to have tea with them. Henry gazed at the brashly dressed woman and marvelled at her words, trying to understand her broad dialect.

'Gan on, hinny, have your fill,' Millie said, piling more food on his plate. 'I divn't want it for breakfast.'

The children seemed particularly keen on bread and jam, to Maggie's surprise, rather than the special cake that Cook had made from their precious supply of flour and sugar.

'I'm glad we came here, Aunt Alice,' Henry said at the end. 'It's such a jolly house.'

Alice smiled. 'Would you like the Heslops to visit us at Hebron House in a day or two?' she asked.

Henry's face puckered and Maggie thought disappointedly that the boy was going to refuse.

'I'd rather come here again,' he answered bashfully. 'It's so small - like coming into a doll's house. Couldn't we come here instead, Aunt Alice?'

'Of course you can, Henry,' Maggie answered before Alice had time to refuse. 'We like having company. And we could invite some children for you to play with an' all. Would you like that?'

'Yes, please!' Henry cried.

The next visit was arranged for 2 January. Maggie lifted Christabel up to say goodbye and could not resist a kiss on her cheek. The girl giggled and wiped her cheek, then grabbed her brother's hand as he went out of the door.

Alice murmured, 'I warn you, they're not used to playing with other children. They might prove a bit of a handful next time.'

'I don't mind,' Maggie grinned, 'just bring them.'

The start of 1919 could not come quickly enough for Maggie and she set about organising games for the children to play on their next visit.

'We'll have "Pin the tail on the donkey" and "Blind Man's Buff",' she told John excitedly.

'Don't you think they're a little bit young for that?' he dared to suggest.

'Well, Henry's not,' she answered briskly, 'and Alfred'll soon cotton on.'

So they held a party for them, but as Alice had predicted, the second visit was not so easy. Quite unused to sharing, Henry argued with Alfred over the train set, calling the boy 'common', and stormed off to sit on the stairs in a huff. Bella was furious at the attention Georgina received from her favourite Aunt Maggie and hurled the rag doll behind the piano so no one could play with it.

The afternoon was saved by John gathering them round the piano and playing nursery rhymes. Soon they were all joining in, their rivalries forgotten, and after tea they attempted a chaotic 'Blind Man's Buff' that reduced them all to a giggling, struggling heap on the floor.

Susan glowed with pride to think of her children playing with young Pearsons and to Maggie's amusement attempted an affected accent when speaking to Alice. Not long ago, Maggie thought wryly, she would have bristled at her sister's behaviour, but she recognised what a special day it was for the careworn Susan as well as for herself.

Finally the children left, still wearing the paper hats that Maggie had made and shouting farewells to each other. Maggie returned to the empty parlour, suddenly deflated.

'It went well in the end, my dear,' John said, kissing her on the head.

Maggie sighed 'Aye, but it'll not be long before they're old enough to know there's a class gulf as wide as the Tyne between them. Young Henry knows it already - he was cruel to our Alfred. I saw the Pearson in him for the first time.'

'He would have been jealous of any boy that hogged the train set,' John pointed out. 'He's a lonely boy, craving friendship. Thanks to you, Henry's discovered that there are grown-ups who want his company - even if we do live in a doll's house!'

Maggie turned and regarded him. 'No, it's thanks to you, John,' she replied quietly. 'You're the one he responds to. But I fear for Christabel. She's a bright lass. How long before she's full of airs and graces and won't want to come visiting common people like me?'

John stroked her cheek gently. 'If she's allowed to keep coming here,' he answered, 'and seeing you, she'll not grow up with any fancy airs and graces. She'll be a girl of principle and passion like her mother.'

Maggie bent her head, embarrassed by his adoration. She felt guilty that she had leant on him so much for support in the past few days and yet had constantly been thinking of George and how he should have been there to see his own daughter. What would he think of his child being brought up by the Pearsons? Maggie shuddered. She knew that soon she would have to go and see him and relive the painful past in order for him to understand. She suspected that John thought of George too; he loomed between them like a spectre, neither daring to mention him. They could not continue in such uncertainty for much longer, Maggie knew, it was not fair on John. Sooner or later she must make some painful choices.

'Thank you for your help, John,' she said, turning from him. 'I mustn't keep you from the mission any longer.'

'Maggie—'

'We'll talk later,' she cut him off and hurried from the room.

A week into the New Year, Maggie left her work at the office early and made her way west across town. She realised she had never visited the Gordons' home before and was not sure which of the squat miners' cottages it was in the high part of Benwell around the pit. She searched the rows nervously and finally asked directions at a tiny shop carved out of the front room of someone's house. The shopkeeper directed her up the dirt lane to the end house in the next row.

Outside Maggie saw a muddy vegetable plot where three scrawny chickens scavenged in the raw air. Behind loomed the pithead, like a giant watchtower planted at the end of the terraced streets, keeping a whirring eye on its workers.

Feeling faint from nervous anticipation at seeing George again after so long, Maggie forced herself up the cobbled lane and in at the battered gate of the Gordons' cottage. At first no one answered her knocking, then a face peered out of the kitchen window and a moment later Irene came to the door. She stood in a voluminous apron, coal smuts on her face, and glowered at her neatly dressed visitor.

'You'll wake our Joshua with all that banging,' Irene complained. 'He's trying to sleep before the night shift.'

'I'm sorry,' Maggie apologised, feeling at a disadvantage being kept on the muddy doorstep, aware that George's sister had no intention of letting her inside. 'I've come to see George.'

She gave a harsh laugh. 'You've got a nerve, Mrs Heslop! Does your husband know you're round here sniffing after my brother?"

Maggie's anger lit. 'I've better things to do with me time than shivering on your filthy doorstep and listening to your foul tongue, Irene Gordon. Is he in or isn't he?'

Irene's face coloured in indignation. 'No he's not, but you wouldn't get past the door even if he was!' She smiled maliciously. 'He doesn't want to see you, not now, not ever! He sees now you're not worth bothering about, so don't go pestering him.'

Maggie was shocked by the vehemence of the rebuff. Was it true that George could be so bitter towards her for marrying John?

'I don't believe you,' she answered angrily. 'Where will I find him?'

Irene folded her arms and stared at her tight-lipped.

'Tell me this, Irene,' Maggie glared at the hostile woman. 'Did you tell your brother that I'd written to him when he was in France, but that me letter was returned - that you returned it to me?'

'What difference would that have made?' Irene said disdainfully.

'It would have shown George that I cared for him, that I'd been thinking of him,' Maggie answered with emotion, 'that...' She stopped herself blurting out that she had been carrying George's child. She was not going to give Irene the satisfaction of gloating over her disgrace or misfortune.

And as Maggie thought of it, she was not even sure if she should tell George of their child, for he could do nothing now to change the situation. He would only suffer the more, torturing himself about what might have been, as she had done these past years, Maggie thought.

If he really despised her now for abandoning his memory so soon and marrying another man, then perhaps it was better for him not to know about Christabel. She could do nothing to alleviate his bitterness or unhappiness, so maybe it was better if he hated her and got over her than be burdened with the knowledge of what she had suffered - still suffered!

'Just tell him I came - to say sorry,' Maggie said in a tight voice.

Irene stood silent and stony-faced in the doorway and Maggie doubted George would ever hear of her visit. She turned and hurried from the mean cottage and the blackened street, the hissing and clanking of the pit chasing her away. No wonder George had chosen to leave home so young, Maggie thought as she fled, hardly able to breathe in the dank, grimy air.

She caught a tram on Alison Terrace that took her swiftly uptown, determining never to visit the Gordons again. If George had decided to blame her for all his ills, then let him, Maggie thought defiantly. She would forget him and make the most of the life she had.

Chapter Thirty

Spring returned and Maggie recovered some of her old energy. Since being rescued from the workhouse her health had steadily improved and her limp grew less troublesome as her limbs strengthened with all the walking she did into town and back. She enjoyed her work at the Co-operative Guild, but by summer increasingly felt the need for something more. Susan, with Jimmy's regular wages coming in, had opened up a secondhand clothes shop on the Scotswood Road while a mellowing Aunt Violet and their old neighbour, Mary Smith, looked after the children. Although Susan said nothing directly, Maggie felt her sister now wished to manage without her help or John's money and so she began to keep out of Susan's way, apart from Sunday teatime visits at Sandyford.

What gave Maggie her greatest pleasure were the occasional visits from Alice Pearson and the children. She delighted in seeing Christabel develop, marvelling at each new word and accomplishment that she revealed. The warm weather arrived and they went for picnics in Jesmond Dene and once Alice drove them down to the seaside where they paddled and ate sandwiches on the sand and bought ice creams from an open stall.

'I've never done this before,' Alice admitted candidly. 'Fancy not discovering the delights of the seaside until my age!'

'You're never too old to gan plodging in the sea,' Maggie replied, holding Christabel's hand as they walked along the promenade.

'What's plodging?' Henry asked. 'It sounds a stupid word to me.' He had had a term at boarding school and was more distant, affecting an air of maturity and bored tolerance of the childish enthusiasm of the adults.

'Plodging?' Maggie echoed. 'Plodging's plodging - getting your feet wet in the sea.'

'Papa and Mama are in the south of France and Mama wrote and said the beaches are much better there than in England. I bet they don't plodge in France,' he said with a superior look.

'Well, maybes you'll go there one day and find out,' Maggie laughed.

'Oh, I will,' Henry said earnestly. 'Papa promised he'd take me one day - when I'm older.'

Maggie and Alice exchanged brief looks, each aware of the boy's yearning to be noticed by his father. Then Christabel tugged on Maggie's hand.

'Auntie Maggie, look! Look!' the small girl cried in wonder as she pointed to a troupe of players performing in the open air.

'That's Pierrot,' Maggie told her, 'and the lass is Columbine. Her partner's the one with the fancy costume - Harlequin.'

'Me see!' Christabel shouted excitedly.

'Course you can, pet,' Maggie smiled and lifted the girl into her arms with a kiss. It was a source of wonder to Maggie that she could feel so attached to this child. It had always been Susan who had been credited with the maternal feelings, while she had been called the hard one, showing impatience with everything except politics, so her mother and sisters had declared. But loving Christabel had shown her that it was possible to do both and Maggie hoped she had grown more aware of the feelings of others, more tolerant. She often wondered about Alice, a seemingly solitary woman, hiding behind her camera. Yet here she was enjoying this seaside trip like an excited child. Did she love

Christabel too?

It became increasingly hard saying goodbye to her daughter at the end of the visits and there were long periods while Alice was away in London when she did not see Christabel at all. It was towards the end of the summer that Maggie's restlessness and her dissatisfaction with her quiet, orderly life grew intolerable.

John noticed her impatience and short temper with alarm. He had been so relieved to see her regain her old enthusiasm for life and work after the trauma of discovering George Gordon was still alive. Maggie had never told him what had happened after her visit to Benwell, but he knew she had been because one of his customers mentioned it soon afterwards. He did not pry; he was just thankful that she appeared to be over him and that they had resumed their intimacy in the marital bed

But this new broodiness made him anxious once more, for he saw the boredom on her face, the frustration after visits from Christabel. His worst fear was that she would tire of living with a man twice her age, turn to Gordon and run off with him.

'You need a new cause, Maggie,' he told her one September afternoon while they strolled aimlessly through the Dene and watched children playing by the side of the burn. 'Why don't you come and help more at the mission?'

Maggie stopped and gazed at two boys who were jumping in and out of a rock pool. She did not reply.

'You have so much experience of the knocks life can give,' John continued, 'that you seem wasted in what you're doing. You're a campaigner, Maggie, you could be using your gifts to better the lives of others.'

Maggie felt stung by his gentle rebuke that she was choosing a safe, quiet life, content to snatch at the small precious moments with her daughter that were granted her. But then she was no longer content. It echoed her own feeling that she should not be settling for a half-life of middle-class comforts and these fleeting moments with a daughter who still thought of her as a kindly friend of her aunt's. She would never be fully responsible for Christabel as a mother should be, she told herself brutally, and she could not go through the rest of her life waiting for those brief, unreal times together when she played a game of make-believe, pretending that the child was legally hers.

Maggie turned pained eyes on her husband. 'You're right, John,' she answered heavily. 'I'm wasting my time waiting for the day Christabel will become mine again. It's never going to happen, is it? In a year or two she'll have a governess to tell her how to behave and probably won't be allowed to visit me any more. Or she'll be sent off to boarding school like Henry and will soon learn to be too embarrassed to visit the likes of us.'

John moved close. 'We don't know that. Ideas have changed since the war, people aren't prepared to put up with so much class restriction.'

'It hasn't changed so you'd notice,' Maggie replied scornfully.

'Well, put your energies into changing things then,' he challenged her. 'You women won a great victory with the vote last year, but there're plenty more injustices to right. Where's your suffragette spirit gone to, Maggie?'

Angered, she retorted, 'It's gone nowhere. I still feel strongly about improving things for women. But I'm not as pig-headed.' She glanced at him, flushing. 'I admit now I used to think everything was either black or white and that everything I did was right. And perhaps I didn't always do the best thing but I always believed I did, so I'm not afraid of being judged for it.'

Her look was defiant, but her voice was more controlled as she went on, 'But I now see that society's problems are more tangled. It's not just a matter of changing the law and everything will be champion. Nothing will change unless what goes on in people's heads change. I remember thinking so in St Chad's when I saw the look of contempt on the bosses' faces. I thought, they're not seeing me, they're looking at me crime - if crime it was to bear that beautiful lass. We've got so many small battles to fight to make things better for women, it's not just the big campaigns that matter.'

John regarded her. 'So what are you going to do about it? Tear down St Chad's? It may be a dismal place but it's somewhere for the very poor to go to.'

Maggie returned his steady look. Now was the time to speak of what had been occupying her mind for months. 'To lead by example rather than tell people how to lead their lives. Isn't that what you're always preaching is the Christian way?'

John nodded.

'Aye, well that's what I want to do.'

'Go on.' John observed her closely. Maggie took a deep breath.

'I want to improve things for lasses like me - the ones who find themselves at the bottom of the heap, unmarried and penniless and carrying someone's bastard child.' Her eyes blazed at him in defiance as she expressed her ideas. John kept quiet, willing her to go on.

'If I had the money, I'd set up a home for lasses to live in, a decent place, a safe place, where they wouldn't be treated like the very devil and made to scrub floors until their babies dropped. They'd be allowed visitors - family, fathers of their bairns - not just locked away out of sight until it's all over.' Maggie started to walk as her ideas took shape. 'But it wouldn't end there with the birth of the baby,' she continued. 'The bairns wouldn't be just whipped away and never seen again. Their mams would be allowed to keep them while they had a decent confinement, recovered from the birth.' She looked at her husband for encouragement.

John pursed his lips, unsettled by the idea. 'It sounds all very humane, Maggie,' he frowned, 'but if it's all made so easy, won't it just encourage immorality among young women?'

Maggie bristled at the suggestion. 'Why do men assume it's always the women who are immoral?' she demanded in annoyance. 'To my mind it's society that's immoral treating lasses with such cruelty while the men take no responsibility. The hypocrisy makes me stomach turn. It may offend your sense of propriety, John, but there will always be vulnerable lasses who find themselves in such a state. What they need is somewhere they'll be cared for and not judged and condemned for the rest of their lives. Lasses like us may not get to heaven, but at least we can ask for a brief haven from a hostile world.'

John regarded her warily. 'And afterwards, when the baby is born? What then?'

Maggie stopped and spoke more calmly. 'I would actively seek employment for them, jobs where they could keep their bairns with them, or help them find lodgings and get started in the world again with a bit support and money. Reconcile them with their families if they've got them. When I think what a difference a bit help would've done me at the right time ...'

Maggie stopped herself, not meaning any criticism of John, for had she known the depths of his compassion she would have gone to him in her need rather than turning to the workhouse. But she had been too proud, too full of guilt and grief for the loss of her lover to do anything but run and hide her shame in St Chad's until it was all over.

'And how will you fund such a home?' John pressed her.

Maggie let out a long breath as she thought it through. 'In Utopia,' she said with a twitch of a smile, 'it would be funded by the state, for all lasses, no matter what their class. But barring a revolution, I need to find a wealthy patron, I suppose.'

They looked at each other in understanding.

'Have you spoken of this to Miss Alice yet?' John asked.

Maggie shook her head 'Not yet, but I will. She's never exactly said so, but I think she's still trying to pay a debt to the suffrage movement. She once told me that she felt responsible for encouraging her old friend Emily Davison to go to Epsom. I think it's still on her mind.'

John gave Maggie a questioning smile. 'The Emily Davison Memorial Home then?"

Maggie was swift to follow up her plan and called on Alice Pearson at Hebron House in early October when she heard she was back from London. It felt very strange entering through the high iron gates and passing the summerhouse she had once burnt down. Yet it was here also that her passion for suffragism had been fuelled, sitting in Alice's vast, elegant drawing room listening to the inspiring voice of Emily Davison all those years ago.

She was surprised at how shabby the house looked now, then remembered that for part of the war it had been taken over by the army. Only a section of the grand old house appeared to be used, with a whole flank of windows shuttered against the wind and Maggie caught a glimpse of white dustsheets covering furniture in a downstairs room.

She took tea with Alice in a small, cosy sitting room where she felt at ease spelling out her ideas.

'I'm interested,' the older woman nodded reflectively, 'but I think it would be important to gather other subscribers to such a scheme. I myself don't have any great personal wealth, despite what you see around you.'

'Perhaps Mr Herbert might lend us some money?'

Alice pulled a face. 'I doubt it is something he would have much enthusiasm for. Besides, Pearson's is contracting now that the war is over and the demand for arms and ships has dropped. Herbert can no longer afford to be the kind of patron that my father was.'

'You'll consider it, though?' Maggie pressed her.

'Indeed,' Alice nodded vigorously. 'No matter what my brother thinks, I will help with what I have.'

Maggie drank her tea in triumph and their talk turned to Christabel and when she could next visit.

By December Alice had found a likely house for the experiment in the west of Newcastle and was contacting sympathetic individuals and charitable bodies for funds. She used her Pearson name for all it was worth, but this soon drew the disapproving interest of her brother. He demanded to know more about the scheme and who was involved.

Annoyed by his sister's evasiveness, he had her followed and soon discovered her involvement with Maggie Heslop. It was not long before he learned that she was none other than the infamous Beaton woman who had so damaged his family's interests in the days before the war.

Herbert came storming down from Oxford Hall just before Christmas and tore into Alice.

'I suppose this is the woman Henry and Georgina talk about so much,' he fumed. 'I'm horrified to think you've been allowing them to mix with such a woman. Worse, *encouraging* them to see her. But then you've always been such an appalling judge of character. Well, it's not going to continue. I forbid you to take them to that woman's house or I'll never let you have them here to stay again. Do you understand, Alice?'

Alice swallowed her indignation and tried to reason with her brother. 'Maggie Heslop is a friend of mine and respectably married to a Methodist preacher and prosperous businessman. All that suffragette business is long over. And the children enjoy going to see the Heslops. Why spoil their fun, Herbert? Besides, the Heslops are holding a party for them after Christmas, it's all arranged.'

'Fun?' Herbert thundered. 'With a suffragette and one of those radical preachers! Imagine what Felicity would say if she knew the children were consorting with such riffraff! No, it must stop.'

Alice would probably have bowed to her brother's will, as she had so often in the past, if he had not added with such contempt, 'And as for this nonsense about a home for fallen women, you'll not have it in my constituency. We don't want to be seen encouraging immoral behaviour. I'm baffled by why you should want to sully the Pearson name by involving yourself in such a farce.' He poured himself a large brandy and laughed mirthlessly. 'You're much too old still to be trying to shock me with your petty posturing. I'll not indulge you like Papa did. Stick to your depressing photography if you must, but leave the politics to me.'

Alice sat stunned for a moment, quite wounded by his patronising contempt. Did her brother really hold her in such little regard? Then something within her finally gave way, some inner wall of restraint came tumbling down, breached by years of frustration and hurt at the way her brother treated her. In that instant, she saw how futile had been her attempts to win his approval as she had tried to do with her father, in order to feel wanted and of worth within the great Pearson dynasty. But it was plain he had never viewed her as anything more than an eccentric, recalcitrant female who had refused to be married off to further the family fortunes and was therefore valueless. She looked at Herbert's disdainful, bloated features and realised he cared nothing for her, in his eyes she was merely a nuisance that had to be controlled. How had she allowed him to use and manipulate her for so long?

She stood up and faced him, ignited by her new-found rage.

'Don't you scold me like some wayward hunting dog of yours!' she cried. 'Whatever my interests in the past, or the reasons behind them, I'm quite serious about this home for unmarried mothers and I'll set it up without your help - and in your precious constituency. You'll not stop me this time, Herbert, so don't cross me!'

He slugged his brandy and laughed in disbelief. 'Tut-tut, Alice, aren't you a little old for throwing tantrums? And what could you possibly threaten me with, eh?'

Alice glared at him. 'I could go to the newspapers with an interesting story,' she said menacingly. 'About how Herbert Pearson MP paid for a baby girl to try and salvage his rotten marriage. A sweet creature called Georgina whom her so-called parents show absolutely no interest in.'

Herbert, his brandy glass halfway to his lips, froze in surprise.

Alice ploughed on before he could deny it. 'But the irony is she's really called Christabel after the famous suffragette, so named by her real mother who was also a well-known suffragette on Tyneside. Have you any idea whose child you're nurturing, Herbert? It would really be very funny if it wasn't so tragic. Georgina was born to one of those fallen women you so despise.'

He was gawping at her open-mouthed, stunned by her attack. 'You're making this whole preposterous story up,' he spluttered. 'You're a vindictive bitch, Alice, just because you can't have your own way for once. Little Georgie is our child.'

'Don't be so ridiculous! Georgina isn't your daughter, Herbert. No one really believes Felicity bore you a second child. You've slept apart for years and we both know who Tish would rather be sleeping with, don't we?'

She saw Herbert turn puce at the allusion to Felicity's affair with Poppy Beresford. He advanced on Alice with the brandy glass raised menacingly as if he would dash it into her face.

'Shut up! Shut up!' he bawled.

But Alice could not stop now as the frustration and anger of years came pouring out of her. She wanted to hurt him, wanted to see him reduced to tears as he had so often reduced her.

Standing her ground, she cried, 'Can't you guess whose bastard child you're rearing, Herbert? Do you know whose little girl is being brought up as a respectable Pearson? Georgina - *Christabel* - is the illegitimate child of Maggie Beaton and that so-called agitator George Gordon. You probably don't remember how he was blacklisted from Pearson's at the beginning of the war - just another casualty of petty Pearson vindictiveness. Now wouldn't that make a fascinating story for the papers?'

'You're lying!' Herbert was apoplectic. 'Georgina's real name was Martha Brown, not Christabel. She was orphaned. She's nothing to do with that evil Beaton woman!'

Alice shook her head in triumph. 'No orphan, Herbert. Just look at her - she's the double of Maggie, with those startling eyes and the dark ringlets. She reminds me of her mother every time I look at her!'

Herbert let out a strangled sound like a trapped animal and hurled the brandy glass over her head, smashing it against a lacquered tallboy. The look that blazed in his eyes was pure hatred and Alice flinched from him, fearing he would seize and throttle her.

But he turned without another word and rushed blindly from the room, banging into furniture in his haste to get away from her. For minutes afterwards, Alice stood breathing fast, her heart racing painfully. Her elation at having for once defeated her brother gave way to foreboding at what she had done.

She walked to the window and peered down at the sweep of frosted drive, watching Herbert roar away in the family Bentley that he liked to drive himself. What had she done? Alice trembled. And what would she tell Maggie now that she had certainly ended any possibility of her ever seeing Christabel again?

Chapter Thirty-One

Maggie read the Christmas letter that had arrived that morning with delight. Millie was lighting the lamps and there was a warm smell of orange and ginger punch filling the room, spiced with cloves and cinnamon. The Christmas decorations sparkled around the mantelpiece and doorway and the Nativity scene was laid out in anticipation of Christabel and Bella wanting to play with the figures. She and John had just returned from the mission where he had been taking a Christmas Eve carol service.

'It's from Rose - Rose Johnstone!' she told John and Millie. 'I can't believe she's written to me after all this time.'

'That's canny. What does she say?' Millie asked immediately.

'She's back in the area, teaching. Her mother died earlier in the year.' Maggie scanned the letter. 'She heard about our marriage, John,' Maggie smiled at her husband.

'Is that why she's written?' Millie snorted. 'Cos now you're respectable?'

'No,' Maggie laughed. 'She's heard about the appeal for the home and wants to help. It says here that her uncle left her a small legacy, so she's got a bit extra put by.'

"That's very generous of her, Maggie,' John commented.

'Isn't it,' Maggie agreed. 'Eeh, it'd be grand to see Rose again after all these years. I thought that much of her when I was younger - she had a great influence on me, John. It was wrong of me to let things come between us like they did ...'

She fell silent, thinking back to her militant days when she had set up home with George. It was the breach of morals that had most offended and upset her friend, and Rose's condemnation had hurt Maggie deeply. But that was all in the past and she was thankful that she was to be allowed the opportunity of being reconciled with her former teacher.

They were pouring out a celebratory drink of the mild fragrant punch when there was an urgent knocking on the front door.

Maggie's delight at seeing Alice appear on Christmas Eve evaporated as she quickly took in the woman's agitated gestures and distraught face. Alice came swiftly to the point and told Maggie of the awful confrontation with her brother and his refusal to allow Maggie to see Christabel again.

'I'm afraid I was so angry at his threats to jeopardise the home and stop the children from seeing me that I told him everything about Christabel,' Alice admitted. 'I really thought he was going to hit me, he was so outraged.'

Maggie sat down stunned. 'He knows I'm Christabel's mother?' she gasped.

Alice looked at her helplessly and nodded. 'And that George is the father,' Alice added hoarsely.

Maggie looked at John's pained face and said in a hard, dull voice, 'Then he'll never allow me to see her again. After all this struggle, I'll never see Christabel again, will I?'

No one contradicted her. There was a heavy silence in the cosy room.

'I'm so very sorry, Maggie. I've ruined everything for you,' Alice said in agitation.

'At least you stood up to your brother over the home for unmarried mothers,' John said, trying to salvage some hope from the devastating news. 'That is something to strive for, isn't it, my dear?' He looked pleadingly at Maggie but knew that at that moment it was no comfort to his wife. Her figure seemed to have shrunk under the weight of the news, her face was desolate. It frightened him to think that the main joy in Maggie's life, to see her daughter, had been stolen from her.

Maggie felt a creeping cold numbness in her stomach. 'I can't think about the home just now,' she said in a colourless voice. 'I can't think of anything.' She stood and walked swiftly from the room, unable to bear their helpless pity.

John went out after her. 'I'm sorry, Maggie,' he began.

'No, don't touch me!' Maggie shrank from his reach. 'Nothing you can say can make me feel any better, so don't try. I just want to be left alone.'

Pulling her shawl over her head, she rushed from the house and ran blindly through the ill-lit icy streets.

At times she slipped and fell, but she just picked herself up and kept on walking, nowhere in particular just away, as if she could escape the horrible truth that the Pearsons had finally denied her the one happiness that gave her life meaning. How cruel, to have her daughter snatched away just as she was getting to know her properly and as the girl was growing to love her in return.

Maggie found herself in the centre of town, the large bulk of the cathedral looming before her in the dark. The bells rang joyously. For a moment she was tempted to go in and seek refuge, but the thought of weakening made her angry.

'Where are you?' she cried, looking up at the crowned dome of the church. 'Why do you allow such things to happen?'

She stumbled on as people stopped to stare at her ranting. The streets were full of revellers going between the pubs or returning home. Their cheery, flushed faces and jocular calls made her feel all the more alone and miserable. Tears streamed down her face as she walked aimlessly towards the quayside.

Suddenly, her arm was grabbed by a passer-by. Maggie tried to shake off the man's hold, but he clung on. 'Maggie?' he demanded. 'Is it you, Maggie?'

She would never have recognised the becapped, thin-faced man who accosted her, but she knew his voice at once.

'George?' she queried.

'Aye, it's me. What the hell are you doing down here on your own the night?'

When she did not answer, he peered closer and saw her pinched, tear-stained face and noticed that her frail body was shaking. Seeing her so close, he could see how she had aged around her dark eyes. Were they lines of laughter or pain? he wondered suddenly and the anger that had been welling up inside him at the sight of his former lover dissolved at once. He held on to her arm and steered her off the street and into the snug of a nearby pub.

It was fuggy with smoke and the smell of warm bodies, but Maggie did not protest as George pushed her gently into a corner seat, ordering a rum and ginger from the barmaid. An elderly man smoking a clay pipe and belching contentedly nearby reminded her of her Uncle Barny, but she noticed no one else, so panic-stricken was she by the abrupt meeting with George. They did not speak until the drink arrived.

'Gel that down you,' he ordered gruffly.

She sipped at the strong-tasting drink, feeling it burn its way down her throat and warm her numbed body. She stared at him, taking in the gaunt face and the prematurely greying hair and the lines of suffering around his mouth and eyes. He looked so much older, yet the warm brown eyes were those of the man she had loved and the sound of his familiar voice sent warm shivers through her.

He sat and watched her, waiting for her to explain.

There was so much to say, Maggie thought desperately, how could she possibly begin? 'I came to see you months ago,' she croaked at last, 'but your sister wouldn't tell me where you were.'

'I've been away, looking for work, wandering about,' George answered. 'I don't stop in the same place for long - can't stop.' He looked at her with a mixture of desire and impatience. 'God, Maggie, I've hated you this past year. When I heard you'd got wed to that preacher . . . Why couldn't you have waited?'

'I thought you were dead, George!' Maggie replied in agitation. 'Dead! Do you know what I've been through since I've heard you were alive? The guilt, the longing ...' Maggie broke off, bowing her head, unable to meet his accusing look.

'I could never have looked at another woman after you, Maggie,' George said harshly, 'but you can't have grieved for long. And Heslop of all men! You, Maggie - the one who called marriage being in chains. Look at you now, living like the ladies you once despised in your grand house on the other side of town, doing charity work. Oh, I've walked along your street, just to catch a glimpse of you in your posh clothes with your posh house with servants and the like. I tried to call, just the once, but that daft Millie Dobson wouldn't let me over the doorstep.'

'Millie never said anything,' Maggie gasped, wondering if she would have acted any differently this past year if she had known.

'No, she wouldn't,' George growled. 'Said I was to leave you be, that you were happily married. Are you happily married, *Mrs* Heslop?'

Maggie winced at his savage tone, but she knew that it disguised a deep pain. 'I've had times of happiness - well, contentment, at least,' she replied awkwardly.

'Contentment!' George scoffed. 'By! I never thought you could've changed so much from the fighting lass I used to love. What happened to all those principles?'

Maggie drank her rum and glared at him in sudden fury. 'Don't you preach at me in your high and mighty way, George Gordon. You know nothing of what I've been through these past years - what I've been through because of you! You weren't the only prisoner of war. There are different ways of being in hell and captivity and, by heck, I've been there too!'

'You didn't have to marry Heslop,' George was scathing. 'You chose to.'

'I'm not talking about me marriage! I'm talking about being pregnant with your bairn and destitute and having to gan into St Chad's and being treated like scum and having the bairn taken off us. That's the hell I'm talking about, Geordie!' Maggie was shaking violently. She saw George's stunned look, as if he could not grasp what she was telling him. 'Aye, George, a bairn! That's why I married John Heslop,' she said, breathing fast, 'because I thought I'd stand a better chance of getting our daughter Christabel back if I was respectably married. That's what happened to me principles. When it came down to it I wanted that bairn more than anything in the world. *Anything.*'

George's look was harrowed. 'A daughter? We've a lass, Maggie?' As she nodded she thought he was going to cry.

'I wrote to tell you but the letter came back with your things when they thought you'd been killed. It was unopened, so I burned it.'

'Why did no one tell me?' George rasped.

'None of your family knew, I was that ashamed. So you can't blame them. No one knew - except Millie Dobson in the workhouse. She helped bring the bairn into this world. And then I told John when he rescued me from St Chad's.' Maggie coloured. 'He knew why I married him, yet he was prepared to have me

251

even though I didn't love him.'

'Didn't?' George questioned.

Maggie met his searching eyes and answered with difficulty. 'He's a good man, Geordie. I couldn't have got through the past years without him. I can't deny I've grown fond of John.'

George flinched and gripped the table top: 'What of the bairn?' he demanded.

'Christabel? She was taken to an orphanage.' Maggie felt her eyes sting as she relived that terrible visit to Hebron Children's Home. 'But by the time we'd discovered where she was, she'd been adopted by - by another family.' Something prevented Maggie from telling George that it was Herbert Pearson who had charge of their child. She saw how he suffered from the shock of discovering he had a daughter, yet how much worse it would be for him to discover she belonged to the hated Pearsons.

Maggie stretched out her hand and touched his. 'But I've seen her several times. She's a bonny lass, Geordie, and trying to talk nineteen to the dozen. She's that interested in the world around her.'

George's eyes filled up with tears. 'Can I see her too, do you think? Just see her for a minute?'

Maggie swallowed and shook her head. 'That's why I was in such a state when you found me in the street. Miss— a friend came and told me I wouldn't be allowed to see the lass again. Her new parents don't want me interfering. She doesn't live in the town.'

For a moment they gazed at each other, aware of the other's deep hurt. Then they reached out and Maggie felt his arms go about her, seeking and giving comfort. She clung to him and wept into his shoulder and felt the wetness of his tears on her hair. If people stared at them in curiosity they did not notice or care. All that mattered was that they had each other, nothing else in the world counted. Maggie had waited so long to feel his warm embrace, fearing never to see or touch him again. Yet here he was, alive and forgiving in her arms as if the past terrible years of separation had never been.

She needed little persuasion to follow George back to his lodgings on the quayside where he picked up odd labouring jobs. He rented a room in a squalid tenement, yet he had managed to make it almost homely with a fire in the small grate and candles on the mantelpiece whose flickering light showed that the bare room was strewn with books and newspapers as their past homes had been. Maggie found herself in tears once more at the thought of what they had missed.

George steered her into the solitary chair by the fire and encouraged her to talk. He held her hand as they quietly recounted their stories of separation, of the years apart. She learned something of the horrors George had witnessed, of the times he had been on burial duty, digging pits for mass graves, of finding trenches with human remains buried into their walls from previous battles.

'Those fields in Flanders are thick with the bones of Europe's dead,' he told her bleakly. 'They sent so many over the top, you can't imagine how many. Will there ever be a time when we're in charge of our own destiny, Maggie? Ordinary folk like you and me?'

Maggie shivered. 'We can strive for it,' she answered. 'We can hope and pray for it.'

'Pray?' George echoed suspiciously. 'Don't tell me Heslop's converted you into a little missionary, lass?'

'I'm no Bible-thumper, but there've been times when I've prayed as if me life depended on it - those times in prison, in the workhouse, in labour.'

George put his arms round her. 'Maggie,' he whispered, 'I'm that sorry. If

252

only I'd been there to help you, I can't bear to think what you've gone through for me.'

'I've missed you so much, Geordie,' Maggie cried. 'I was that hurt when you wanted nothing to do with me. I so wanted to explain.'

George stroked her hair and kissed her brow gently. 'I was sick when I came home, lass,' he murmured. 'Sick in me mind as well as me body. I'd lost so many friends. Bob Stanners and half the rowing club are dead... Hearing you were wed - well, it finished me. I went off on me wanders. I was so angry I couldn't stop still because everywhere reminded me of you. But I couldn't settle anywhere either. I kept coming back hoping I'd hear that Heslop had died and you were free again. I know it's a terrible thing to say, but I wished him dead.'

Maggie pulled away at the mention of her husband. He would be worrying about her and here she was with George as if she had no responsibility to anyone else. Her guilt made her answer sharply.

'Don't say that, George!' Yet had she not entertained the very same thoughts? she accused herself. 'I ought to go,' she said restlessly and stood up.

George gripped her shoulders and made her look at him. 'I need you more than he does, Maggie. I love you more than he does. Stay with me. Leave Heslop. You said you only married him to get our lass back but that hasn't worked. It feels right you being here with me again. You can't go back to him now, Maggie.'

Maggie looked at him, experiencing both fear and excitement at his words. 'You mean leave John, for good?'

'Aye,' George urged. 'You were mine long before you married him. You know I would have wed you years ago, Maggie, if you'd wanted. We could go away together and start somewhere new like we used to plan when you were a suffragette in hiding.'

Maggie thought again of the intimate times they had spent in their small rooms in Arthur's Hill, ridiculously happy with just each other's company, sharing their dreams of escape.

'Where would we go?' she asked, daring to let herself think the impossible.

'I've been thinking of going abroad for some time,' George told her eagerly, taking her hands in his. To Canada.'

'Canada!' Maggie exclaimed.

'I met this Canadian near the end of the war - another prisoner. He never stopped talking about the rich farmlands and the forests,' George enthused. 'His family emigrated from Scotland when he was a bairn. It's a new country, Maggie, where ordinary people graft for themselves and not for a pittance. No more bosses telling us what to do. Imagine it. Ever since I was a nipper playing around Hibbs' Farm, I've always wanted to work the land, Maggie.'

Maggie began to feel carried away with his vision. Was this really what her life had been leading up to? she wondered headily. Had all the pain and striving and hardship been to bring her here, to this new future with the man she loved, bringing energy and hope and justice into a new world?

'And the rivers, Maggie, they're all crystal clear and full of fish. Not like the filthy Tyne, killed off with the badness from the factories and the yards.'

The River Tyne, Maggie thought, her mind jerking back to the present at its mention. That dirty, powerful river was the only one she had ever known. She had lived by its banks all her life, she thought with a shiver.

'But what about here? What about England?' she pressed him. 'You always wanted to change things here.'

George snorted. 'A land fit for heroes? That's a load of bollocks! England's never going to change. The bosses will always be promising us something better around the comer while working us into the ground for fewer wages and longer hours. They're laying men off at the yards and pits already. It's nearly nineteen twenty, Maggie, and they've already forgotten what they promised the lads who won the war for them. Who gives a toss about the poor beggars ganin' round the doors wearing their medals trying to sell stuff no one has the money to buy? Pearson's will never employ me again, Maggie, and I'll not spend the rest of me life humping cargo on and off boats on the quayside.'

Maggie sighed, sharing George's disillusionment with their post-war world. There had been so much expectation at the end of the Kaiser's war that things would be better, yet had anything really changed?

'I must go,' she said quietly, 'before they call the police out for me.'

'I'll walk you back across town,' George insisted, seeing that she would stay no longer.

They walked together through the wintry streets as the last of the revellers wove their way out of the closing pubs. 'You will think on what I've said, Maggie?' George urged. 'I want you with me - always.'

Maggie felt a desperate thrill at his words but quite torn as to what to do. 'And what if I decide to stay?' she murmured from within the folds of her shawl.

George stopped and pulled her round to face him. His look was determined. 'Then I'll go anyway, even if you won't come with me. I'll not stay in this town and watch you live with another man - a man twice your age.' Then he bent and kissed her with a desperate passion, as if he could will her to choose him.

The taste of his kisses was still on Maggie's lips when she entered the house in Sandyford. John and Millie were waiting up for her anxiously.

'Where've you been, you little bugger?' Millie exploded. 'We've been worried sick. And you without a coat in this cold. We thought you'd be found frozen to death. Mr Heslop's been out looking for you all evening.'

Maggie could not look at them. 'I'm sorry to make you worry,' she mumbled like a scolded child limping towards the fireside to warm herself. 'I'm very tired and I'd rather not talk about it.'

'Well, listen to the cheek of it!' Millie exclaimed.

'Thank you, Millie,' John said swiftly. 'You get yourself to bed.' His look silenced any further protestations. Maggie tried to follow her, but John stood in her way.

'Maggie, where did you go?' he asked once the old woman had gone. 'Have you been to Susan and Jimmy's?'

She looked directly into his concerned eyes but could not tell him. It had been a pure accident running into George as she had, but he would not see it like that. Then she began to wonder if it had been an accident. Perhaps something inside her had led her to him, a part of her that had been searching for him all along and would have gone on looking for him until she had found him.

John saw the brightness in her eyes and felt a leaden weight in his stomach.

'You've seen Gordon, haven't you?' he whispered in horror, his hands clenched. 'Have you, Maggie?'

She nodded, hating herself for inflicting this pain on him, but unable to lie. 'He wants me to go away with him.'

'Away?' John echoed incredulously.

'Abroad.'

She expected him to protest and denounce the idea, accuse her of being wicked and ungrateful. But he did not. His shoulders sagged and in that moment

254

he looked his age, old and grey-faced and bent with years of hard work.

'But you're married to me, Maggie. Doesn't that count for anything any more?' he asked wearily.

Maggie gulped. 'I know I'm married to you!' she burst out. 'Why else would I have come back?'

The look he gave her was more than she could bear. She ran from the room and bolted upstairs to the refuge of her room, giving way to searing tears. Whatever she did, Maggie realised in desperation, she was going to hurt one of them. Unresolved in her own mind as to what to do, she fell into an exhausted sleep.

The tense atmosphere spoiled Christmas and John spent his time down at the mission, out of her way. Susan brought the children over on Boxing Day, but it only served as a painful reminder of how Christabel was missing and would never visit Sandyford again. Maggie felt as if she had been bereaved once more, yet her sorrow was compounded by frustration in knowing that Christabel lived, close by but for ever out of reach.

She confided in her sister about her encounter with George.

Susan clucked and shook her head, but to Maggie's surprise she did not tell her what to do.

'Well, after the mess I made of my marriage, I'm not going to lecture you about yours. I can understand you being upset now that you can't see your bairn, but Mr Heslop's been that good to you, Maggie, to all of us.'

'I know,' Maggie said, seeing no way out of her dilemma, 'but it's George I love!'

'Well,' Susan said, putting a comforting hand on Maggie's shoulder, 'it's only you can decide. But you should make your mind up quickly and be done with it.'

The New Year came and went and the dark, dreary days of January crept by. Maggie sent a message to George that she was uncertain what to do, but in the meantime she would not embarrass John by visiting him. A letter came back, full of tenderness, saying he would wait for her and continue to lay his plans for emigration.

Maggie tried to occupy herself once more with plans for the home and she resumed a working friendship with Alice, though both were too upset to mention Christabel. The hollow emptiness Maggie felt at the loss of her daughter grew more unbearable as the weeks passed. She could not stop herself imagining what Christabel was doing and even thoughts of starting a new life with George could not prevent her dwelling on the girl. She would gaze endlessly at a photograph that Alice had taken of Christabel at the seaside, as if staring hard enough would bring the image to life in her hands. Christabel was watching enthralled as a troupe of players performed on the promenade, her small elfin face full of wonder and delight...

John saw how his wife tortured herself but he seemed unable to comfort her as he had once done. Their affectionate, intimate friendship had been blighted by the loss of Christabel and the threat of Gordon's emigration and John saw no way of winning Maggie back. So he stayed out of her way, throwing himself into his work as a salve for his hurt feelings, spending long hours at the shop and then at the mission.

Finding herself alone in the evenings, Maggie turned to her old friend Rose Johnstone and found a measure of consolation. The two women slipped easily into their old friendship. Increasingly, Rose came round to visit Maggie or she would call at Rose's neat flat in Heaton to read and talk together as they had in the past. They argued only once, when Rose told her she would be a fool to give up everything for George Gordon.

At once Maggie was defensive. 'You've never liked him, so why should I listen to you?'

'Because you've got so much to stay for - a comfortable home, your work, a kind husband—'

'Christabel was my only reason for staying,' Maggie cut in. 'What is the point of anything here without her?'

Rebuffed, Rose never spoke of Maggie's future again.

By early spring the home was almost ready to open. Staff were appointed and Maggie spent most of her time attending to last-minute details. The first residents were to be admitted in mid-March. As the date neared, Maggie felt a strange premonition that something momentous was about to happen, though she could not tell if it was good or bad. Since the time as a child when she had foreseen her father's death, she had smothered these insights into the future, dismissing them as fey nonsense instilled in her as a child by her dear grandmother. But she found herself pacing the house anxiously, increasing the tension between John and herself beyond endurance.

'Perhaps I should move out of the house,' she offered. 'I can see how unhappy I'm making you. I could stay at Rose's until …'

But John was swift to protest. 'Please, Maggie, don't do that. You know I don't want you to go anywhere. I just wish Gordon would go and leave us in peace.'

She saw his anxiety but it only served to irritate her. 'Why do you still want me here when I've brought you nothing but heartache?' she asked impatiently. 'Can't you just let me go, John?'

He looked at her in misery. 'I love you, Maggie, it's as simple as that. But I won't beg you to stay.'

He left abruptly and for the next two days they did not exchange a word.

Then it came. A message from George: his passage was booked in a fortnight, when the spring voyages began. He would earn his passage by loading and unloading cargo at the various ports.

Maggie went to find him, unable to stay away any longer.

Chapter Thirty-Two

George was triumphant at seeing Maggie as he came off his shift at the quayside, but she refused to go back to his gloomy lodgings.

'I'd like to see Hibbs' Hill again with you,' Maggie said on impulse, hoping that visiting their old home might help her see things more clearly and come to the right decision. They caught a tram across town and from Scotswood climbed up towards the farm. Much of the mediocre, semi-derelict land on the fringe of the countryside had been turned to cultivation during the war; a patchwork of small vegetable plots divided by battered fences and advertising hoardings.

Finally they reached the steep slope up to their old cottage. Maggie was out of breath and her back was throbbing by the time George pulled her up the path. They stopped outside the gateway and peered at their former home.

It was shabby and dilapidated, with boarding at one window where the glass had never been replaced. The garden they had tended so lovingly was overgrown with thistles and weeds and the ground was a mulch of last year's leaves and rotten, unpicked fruit. At first sight, Maggie thought the cottage must be uninhabited, but then the front door swung open and a small, barefoot child emerged in a ragged dress, her hair matted and face filthy. She was probably about three or four, Maggie thought, Christabel's age. She had a sudden chilling thought, that this was how her daughter might have looked had she managed to struggle on alone at the cottage, emaciated and dull-eyed by extreme poverty.

George saw her look of horror and steered her quickly away. They walked along the edge of a ploughed field, the trees still bare under a steel-grey sky.

'I've never had the courage to come up here before,' George admitted.

'Neither have I,' Maggie answered, shivering in the chill air.

George put a warming arm round her. 'It's not the same here any more, Maggie. Coming here's brought that home even more strongly. It's no good searching for the past, 'cos it's gone. We should be looking to the future, lass, a fresh start in a new country - together.'

Maggie smiled at him wistfully but said nothing. She gazed back over the distant town with its packed streets and thought of its teeming humanity going about their everyday chores, trying to survive as best they could. Below lay the silver-grey ribbon of the Tyne, cranes stooped over its waterfronts like huge birds of prey. She felt attached to the view before her. How could she ever describe to George that she was bound to its river and its low-lying hills and its rows of brick houses by strong cords of familiarity that stretched deep into her childhood? Over there lived Susan and Jimmy and the children, and Rose Johnstone and John and Alice Pearson, and all the other people with whom she shared this common bond of belonging beside the Tyne.

And it came to Maggie with a force like a westerly wind that whenever she looked at the scene before her, she would think of Christabel, living her life close by, up the Tyne valley.

'I can't go with you, George,' she whispered. 'I'm sorry.'

He turned to scrutinise her face and saw his own sorrow mirrored there.

'Why not?' he demanded. 'Don't lose your courage now, Maggie!'

She shook her head. 'Oh, Geordie, I need courage to stay. It's the hardest thing in the world to let you go again.' Her grey eyes were full of tenderness as she spoke in a quiet but clear voice. 'I belong here, among these streets, beside that dirty river. And there are so many things here need putting right that I feel I can help with, like the mothers' home. I can't just turn me back on them all.'

She tried to laugh through her tears. 'Look at me, Geordie! Worn out by prison and the workhouse. I'd be no good in Canada, I'm not made for the countryside like you are. I've a gammy leg and a puny body; they'd probably hoy me overboard as scrap for the birds before the voyage ended. I'd just hold you back.'

'No, you wouldn't.' George tried to fight her resolve. He looked at her in despair. 'Is it Heslop? Are you staying just for him, a worn-out old man who probably won't live another five years?'

'He's my husband,' Maggie sighed, 'and I would feel guilty leaving him. But it's not just that.' She put a hand up to his unshaven face. 'It's you I love, Geordie, far more than I could ever love John. There will never be anyone else in me life to make me feel like this - ever.'

'Then why can't you come with me?' George cried in exasperation.

Maggie took a deep breath. 'It's Christabel. She will always keep me here.'

'But you can't have her, Maggie, you told me!'

'No, but I can never give up hoping. At least while I live here there's hope. If I gan to Canada then I give up that hope of seeing her for ever.'

George gripped her shoulders. 'But we could have other bairns.'

Maggie shook her head as her eyes flooded with tears. 'I can't have any more bairns, Geordie,' she whispered. 'They saw to that at St Chad's - ripped me apart so much, I'm barren now. Christabel's the only lass I'll ever have.'

George pulled her to him and held her tightly, while they both wept for what they had lost and what was never to be in the future.

'Oh, Maggie,' George said hoarsely, 'it would've been easier for us both if I'd never come back. This separation's worse than death.'

'I know!' Maggie said, clinging to him.

They kissed tenderly, desperately, then Maggie pulled away.

'Don't ever doubt how much I love you, George Gordon,' she said, her voice breaking.

'Lass, I'll miss you!' George replied, and turned abruptly away, ashamed to show his tears.

They hurried down the hill without speaking again and when the first tram appeared, George pushed her on.

'It's better if I walk,' he told her, trying to smile.

'Let me know where you go,' Maggie urged as the tram jolted away. She strained to see him through the grimy window, a tall, solitary figure watching the departing tram, until it rounded a corner and he disappeared from view.

The following day she went down with a heavy cold and took to bed, unable to speak to anyone, thankful to take refuge in her room like a wounded animal. On the day that George's ship sailed, she sat by her bedroom window and looked towards the river, imagining him going aboard with what few possessions he had - a bundle of books, the photograph of them both that Maggie had given him, taken by Alice before the war, and his army coat.

Did he gaze at the quayside while the boat slipped its moorings, she wondered, still expecting her to come at the final hour? It took all her willpower not to dress hurriedly and rush off to join him, and it was almost a relief when the terrible day came to an end and the chance of going with him was finally gone.

A couple of days passed and Maggie rallied her spirits, emerged from her room and went off to the home to help in the office. Alice was away in London until the end of the month but Maggie busied herself getting to know the staff and wandering around the house introducing herself to the young pregnant women who had just arrived. It was comforting to speak to these ordinary women and carry out mundane tasks such as making cups of tea. She told them that while they stayed there they would be able to learn new skills such as typing and bookkeeping and cookery and gardening to equip them for when they left. Looking at their swelling bellies, she renewed her commitment to give them the care that had been denied her.

From that evening, she began to take meals with John and Millie again, though her conversation was confined to what was going on at the home. She avoided being alone with her husband or allowing herself to be comforted by his presence. Her feelings for him seemed to have been cauterised by the events of the past weeks, leaving her numb to his needs.

Then one day in April, John came bursting into the sitting room where she was writing letters at her desk. He was holding a copy of the morning paper.

'Read this,' he said, waving it at her. He had a strange look on his face and Maggie could not tell if the news was good or bad.

'What is it?' she asked anxiously.

'Here.' He pointed at an inside page.

Maggie read the brief announcement: 'Lady Felicity Pearson, wife of Sir Herbert, MP, tragically passed away two days ago while staying with friends in the south. It is believed she was a victim of the Spanish flu that raged to epidemic proportions last year. The body of the deceased is to be brought north for burial on Saturday.'

Maggie looked up at John. 'What does this mean for the children?' she gasped.

'I don't know, my dear,' he answered gravely. 'We can only wait and see.'

They did not have to wait long before Alice made contact. She raced back from London for the funeral and came to visit the following day.

'Herbert is quite devastated,' she told them. 'They fought like cat and dog all their married life, and she was continually unfaithful, but he doted on her all the same.'

'But what of the children?' Maggie asked impatiently. 'What will happen to them?'

Alice shrugged. 'At the moment, Herbert has little thought for them. But I'm going to stay up at Oxford Hall until everything is a little clearer and arrangements can be made.'

'Will - will I be able to see Christabel now?' Maggie dared to ask. 'You could bring her—'

'I can't promise anything at this stage,' Alice silenced her abruptly. 'It's all happened so suddenly. For all I know, Herbert may decide to take the children to London where he spends most of his time nowadays. I never mentioned this before so as not to upset you, but there's been talk of selling Oxford Hall.'

'To London?' Maggie echoed in dismay.

'Maggie, we'll just have to be patient,' John insisted gently.

April passed in a frenzy of frustration and uncertainty for Maggie. Then, quite suddenly, after weeks of hearing nothing from Alice, she appeared at the home and sought her out.

'Walk with me in the garden,' she ordered, her strong-featured face alive with news she was eager to share.

Around them the small sheltered garden was a riot of bright spring flowers and pale scattered blossom. Alice walked her away from two women who were sitting in the summerhouse, sewing, with rugs tucked round their knees.

'Tell me!' Maggie demanded, bursting with curiosity.

'It's Herbert,' Alice announced. 'He's come to a decision.'

'And?' Maggie gripped her friend's arm.

'He's taking Henry to London with him - his boarding school is nearer London than here anyway. Typically, Herbert only seems concerned with his son's education.'

'But Christabel? What's to happen to Christabel?'

'He doesn't want her with him,' Alice said awkwardly. 'Ever since he learned that she was your daughter, he hasn't been able to bear her near him.'

Maggie flushed indignantly. 'Poor lass!'

'It was Felicity who chose her in the first place, apparently. Herbert was never very keen on the idea of a daughter, he would have adopted another boy, but Felicity was insistent. All my brother is concerned about is Henry. It's likely that Pearson's will be taken over soon by a larger armaments firm - it's really in a bad way since the end of the war - and Herbert's keen to advance his political career in London. So,' Alice sighed, 'he's given responsibility for Christabel to me - washed his hands of her.'

Maggie gave a whoop of joy. 'Then I can start seeing her again?'

Alice smiled broadly. 'Of course. But there's something else.'

'What?' Maggie asked, a shadow falling on her happiness.

'I don't really wish to stay in Newcastle either. I've been thinking of selling Hebron House and moving to London full time too, to further the studio.'

Maggie's insides went cold.

Alice faced her squarely. 'Christabel's had such a grim childhood so far, with only me paying her the slightest bit of attention. The only times I've seen her acting like a normal, boisterous child is when she's been to your home. I can't give her what she needs here and I'm not very good with children at the best of times.'

'So you think she'd be happier in London?' Maggie said dully.

Alice looked at her in astonishment 'No, that's not my idea at all! I'm sorry, I'm not making myself plain. It depends on Christabel herself, of course, but if she's happy with the idea, I'd like you to take her back.'

'Me?' Maggie gasped, quite dumbfounded.

'Well, it's what you want, surely,' Alice said briskly, afraid Maggie was going to cry and make a scene. 'Herbert doesn't care; he'll sign anything to be rid of the responsibility.'

'Of course I want her back!' Maggie cried vehemently. And she threw her arms round the startled older woman and hugged her.

It was arranged that Christabel would be brought on a visit and stay for a few days to see how she adapted. Maggie rushed home to tell John the good news. But when she got home there was no sign of him and she was about to set off for the mission when Millie appeared on the stairs. Her face was harrowed.

'It's Mr Heslop,' she said. 'Doctor's with him.'

Maggie sprang up the stairs. 'What's happened?'

'He collapsed this morning at the shop. Doctor thinks he's had a stroke.'

Maggie gulped in fear. She went barging into John's bedroom where the doctor was just collecting up his belongings. He saw her stricken face and tried to be reassuring.

'He's had a stroke,' the doctor said quietly. 'It's affecting his speech at the moment and you'll have to help feed him. He must rest in bed, of course, and I'll call tomorrow.'

'Will it happen again?' Maggie asked in concern.

The physician shrugged 'It's possible. He must have been under stress from work or worry of some kind, so you must keep him quiet and make him rest.'

Maggie went to her husband's side at once, riven with guilt for the strain he must have been enduring in silence for months. She took his hand and kissed it. For so long she had thought of nothing else except herself and Christabel and George that she had had no room to think about her quiet, gentle John. How he must have been suffering at the thought of her running off with her former lover. She had thought she felt nothing for him any more, but seeing him lying there so gaunt and grey-faced, she experienced an overwhelming concern, a fear of losing him.

'I deserved a kick up the rear end,' she grinned at him, 'but there's no need to frighten me like this!'

He tried to smile back and say something. 'Don't talk.' She put a finger to his lips. 'I've got some news that'll make you better,' and she recounted everything that Alice had said in the garden.

John attempted to raise his head. 'I - I'm - so - happy!' he managed to say.

She saw the tears in his eyes and leant over and kissed him softly, affectionately.

'So you get yourself on the mend,' she ordered, 'then you can play to her on the piano, do you hear?'

Maggie sent word to Alice to delay Christabel's visit until John had recovered. She spent long hours at the house, nursing him herself and encouraging him back on his feet, realising that she cared for him greatly and that the fondness and regard she had for him was akin to love.

So it was not until late May that the visit was arranged. By then John was back on his feet and although some paralysis remained down one leg, his speech had returned to normal. Maggie had finally persuaded him to give up the shop and hand over the running of the mission to others at the chapel.

'I want you around a canny bit longer, John Heslop,' she told him, 'if we're going to raise this child of ours.'

John spun round and she saw that his eyes were glistening with tears.

'You said our child, Maggie,' he gasped.

She went to him and took his hands. 'I know I did,' she answered gently. 'And I meant it. If it hadn't been for your support, I would never have found Christabel again. I know you love her too, more than her real father ever will because he's never known her like you have.'

John put his arms round his wife and hugged her. 'Thank you, Maggie. It's the greatest gift you could give me,' he whispered.

The day came and Maggie was suddenly gripped by doubt that Christabel would want to give up her grand life and come to stay with them.

'It's been eight months since she saw us last,' she fretted to John. 'She's probably forgotten who we are.'

'Give the girl time,' John replied, kissing his nervous wife on the lips.

Maggie watched from the bay window in the sitting room, flooded in sunlight. The room was full of the smell of polish and warm houseplants and the time ticked noisily on the grandfather clock in the corner. Maggie felt as if her life was suspended in that room, as if the past twenty-eight years had all been building towards this moment and that soon she was to be put to the test as she had never been before. If she was found wanting, Maggie thought in dread, then the rest of her life would have no purpose at all...

Alice Pearson's car chugged up the street, nosing round the children with their balls and hoops, who stopped to stare. They will be playmates for Christabel, Maggie thought in sudden hope, and the excitement of the moment made her rush out to greet her visitors.

Christabel was shy and clung to her Aunt Alice.

'Come in, pet,' Maggie encouraged. 'Do you remember me and Uncle John?' The girl nodded solemnly and looked around the hallway while Millie took her coat. Maggie and John stood hovering nervously, so Millie took the girl by the hand and led her into the sitting room.

'I've made jam sandwiches, 'cos I know you like them best, hinny,' she chatted. 'And Auntie Maggie's bought you a new doll to play with.'

Christabel picked up the doll dressed like a ballerina with dots of red painted on its pale cheeks. She put it down in disappointment. "Where's Bella?" she asked with an accusing look at the adults around her.

Maggie stepped forward. 'The rag doll?'

The girl nodded.

Maggie hesitated, then held out a hand. 'You come with me, Georgina, and we'll look for Bella. I think she's hiding upstairs.'

'The girl's large dark eyes looked unsure. Maggie held her breath. Then the three-year-old put out a tentative hand and reached towards Maggie's. Maggie gave it a gentle squeeze and the girl gave a quiver of a smile.

They went upstairs and Maggie took her into the small sunny bedroom at the front of the house where she had spread a patchwork quilt over the bed and arranged the Christmas figures on top of a blanket chest for Christabel to play with. At the head of the bed sat the bartered doll, Bella. Christabel ran towards it and grabbed it to her, covering it in kisses. To Maggie's amazement, she immediately began to talk to the doll as if it were a long lost friend. She spoke to the doll about her mother dying and her brother going off to live in a place called London.

'But I 'm coming here to live with you,' the girl said brightly. 'Aunt Alice said I could.'

Maggie felt her throat constrict as emotion swelled inside. She went over swiftly to her daughter and lifted her into her arms.

'You don't mind if Auntie Maggie gives you a little cuddle, do you?' she asked with a tearful laugh.

She felt Christabel's soft head of dark curls lean against her cheek in a trusting reply of acceptance. Maggie kissed the small head gratefully. It was a tiny, tentative beginning and she was sure there would be clashes and difficulties along the way, but for now they were together, Christabel content to be held in her arms in the warm sunshine of the modest bedroom.

Maggie closed her eyes and gave swift, exultant thanks. Given time, the girl might allow her to call her Christabel and come to accept the truth that this woman she knew as her aunt's friend was really her own mother. Given time, Maggie dreamed...

'You must kiss Bella too, Auntie Maggie,' Christabel insisted, thrusting the doll in her face. Maggie kissed the doll and then kissed the child again.

'Shall we go down and see Uncle John and the others now?' she asked, smiling and thinking of how full of joy her husband would be to see her return with Christabel happily clutched to her side.

Christabel nodded. 'Then can we go to the seaside and see the dancers with the funny faces?' she asked suddenly.

Maggie looked at her in astonishment. 'Columbine and Pierrot? You remember that from last summer?'

'Course I do,' Christabel giggled. 'It was my best day I ever had.'

Maggie hugged her close. 'Oh, mine too, you bonny bairn,' she whispered tearfully. 'And we're going to have plenty more from now on, I promise you!'

Lightning Source UK Ltd.
Milton Keynes UK

175547UK00002B/4/P